About

When Maria V. Snyder was younger, she aspired to be a storm chaser in the American Midwest so she attended Pennsylvania State University and earned a Bachelor of Science degree in Meteorology. Much to her chagrin, forecasting the weather wasn't in her skill set so she spent a number of years as an environmental meteorologist, which is not exciting ... at all. Bored at work and needing a creative outlet, she started writing fantasy and science fiction stories. Over a dozen novels and numerous short stories later, Maria's learned a thing or three about writing. She's been on the *New York Times* bestseller list, won a half-dozen awards, and has earned her Masters of Arts degree in Writing from Seton Hill University, where she is now a faculty member.

Her favorite color is red. She loves dogs, but is allergic, instead she has a big black tom cat named … Kitty (apparently naming cats isn't in her skill set either). Maria also has a husband and two children who are an inspiration for her writing when they aren't being a distraction. Note that she mentions her cat before her family. When she's not writing she's either playing volleyball, traveling, or taking pictures. Being a writer, though, is a ton of fun. Where else can you take fencing lessons, learn how to ride a horse, study martial arts, learn how to pick a lock, take glass blowing classes and attend Astronomy Camp and call it research? Maria will be the first one to tell you it's not working as a meteorologist. Readers are welcome to check out her website for book excerpts, free short stories, maps, blog, and her schedule at MariaVSnyder.com.

Also by Maria V. Snyder

Sentinels of the Galaxy series

Navigating the Stars

Study series

Poison Study
Magic Study
Fire Study
Shadow Study
Night Study
Dawn Study
Ice Study (available as an ebook)

Glass series

Storm Glass
Sea Glass
Spy Glass

Healer series

Touch of Power
Scent of Magic
Taste of Darkness

Inside series

Inside Out
Outside In
(collected as *Inside*)

THE EYES OF TAMBURAH

MARIA V. SNYDER

First Published 2019
First Australian Paperback Edition 2019
ISBN 9781489252807

Published by
HQ Young Adult
An imprint of Harlequin Enterprises (Australia) Pty Limited (ABN 47 001 180 918), a subsidiary of HarperCollins Publishers Australia Pty Limited (ABN 36 009 913 517)
Level 13, 201 Elizabeth St
SYDNEY NSW 2000
AUSTRALIA

A catalogue record for this book is available from the National Library of Australia www.librariesaustralia.nla.gov.au

Printed and bound in Australia by McPherson's Printing Group

To Natalie Bejin, my Chief Evil Minion,
for being a wonderful friend, a spreadsheet maestro,
a beta reader virtuoso, and the best evil minion
an author can have.

CHAPTER

1

The heat thickened the air in Shyla's room to an uncomfortable level. Sweat slicked her skin and dampened her sleeveless tunic. She adjusted the mirrors to better capture the thin ray of sunlight streaming through a single mirror pipe extruding from her ceiling. Moving another reflective panel until it illuminated the ancient map spread over her table, she resumed her work. The faded ink was barely discernable as it crossed the velbloud skin.

The temperature rose another few degrees, warning her that she needed to retreat to the deeper levels before the sun reached angle eighty. Despite being three levels underground, it still wasn't safe to be this high. All of her neighbors had descended angles ago. But excitement zipped along her spine—she was *so* close.

Shyla continued to translate the archaic symbols. Nothing but sunlight would reveal the location of the Gorgain crypt and the meeting with her client was scheduled for angle two-ten. The historian had paid her in advance for the information, which was proving to be more difficult to find than she'd expected.

A damp strand of her long pale-yellow hair slipped free of the tie, but she didn't have time to fix it. According to the map's legend, the blue line represented the tunnel the grave diggers had used. She traced it with a fingertip, honing in on—

An impatient pounding on her door broke her concentration. She glared at the thick slab of rough sand-coated glass that guarded her room. It vibrated with each knock. There wasn't time for interruptions, but if it was a client—

"It's an emergency," called Banqui.

She sighed. Everything was an emergency with Banqui. As the Water Prince's chief archeologist, he believed *his* projects should be *her* top priority. But the man had referred her services to his colleagues, helping her establish her business. After a forlorn glance at the map, she unlocked the door and slid it aside, allowing Banqui to enter.

He hustled into her room and stopped dead. "Scorching hells, Shyla. It's a thousand degrees in here."

Banqui also tended to exaggerate.

"Hello to you too."

Ignoring her, he said, "I've been looking all over for you in the lower levels. The sun is almost at angle seventy. What are you still doing up here?"

She gestured to the map on her table. "Researching."

"You need to leave right away."

"There's plenty of time before I'm cooked. Before I was interrupted, I was just about to finish up." She gave him a pointed look.

But instead of apologizing for barging in on her and leaving, he just stared at her in shock. "Shyla, haven't you heard?"

She studied her best client and perhaps friend. His short black hair stuck up at various angles—probably from running his fingers through it in agitation. He was frequently anxious and stressed by the Water Prince's demands. But this time fear lurked in his dark brown eyes and his tan tunic and pants, normally impeccable—he had plenty of diggers conscripted by the prince to do his dirty work—were torn and stained with… blood?

"Heard what?" she asked as unease stirred in her chest.

He paced around the table. Tall and lean with lanky legs, it didn't take him long to make a circuit. Her room was small and filled with the basics—a table, sitting cushions, a couple shelves filled with her trinkets and clothes, a water jug, her sleeping cushion mounded with a fur, and the mirrors.

Banqui made another loop. She stepped into his path, stopping him. "Tell me before you wear a groove in my floor."

Lines of sweat streaked down the sides of his face, darkening his brown skin. His gaze settled on the map. "How long have you been working?"

"Two or three sun jumps."

"And you get immersed in your research," he muttered then drew in a deep breath. "I found The Eyes of Tamburah. They were in the temple's hidden vault just like you predicted."

Excitement warred with confusion. "That's wonderful. Right?"

"It was glorious. They were exquisite. Crafted from diamonds, emeralds, onyx, and the purest white topaz I've ever seen." His voice held an almost fanatical reverence. "They were magnificent, Shyla. My greatest find in my *entire* career."

Considering he'd been uncovering ancient ruins and artifacts for over seven thousand sun jumps—roughly twenty circuits—they must have been impressive. "And then the Water Prince claimed them. You knew that would happen. He finances your digs."

"It's worse than that."

What could be worse? "You *lost* them?"

"No! They were stolen!" Unable to remain still, Banqui resumed his pacing.

Treasure hunters were always a problem. Despite the Water Prince's proclamation that all historical items found within Zirdai's official boundaries became the property of the crown, the richer citizens collected antiquities through a thriving black market—the rarer the find, the more lucrative. And The Eyes of Tamburah were legendary. Rumored to give their owner magical powers, the gemstones had a long and bloody history. No wonder they were stolen by some greedy hunter. They would fetch a staggering sum in any city in Koraha, assuming the thief lived long enough to leave Zirdai.

"Sorry to hear that," Shyla said. "The Water Prince must be—"

"No words can describe his anger." Banqui clutched her shoulders. "Which is why you must hide."

She jerked from his grasp in surprise. "Me? Why?"

"He thinks you are the thief."

It took her a moment to sort through his words. Did he really say… "Why would he believe that?" Fear coiled around her heart and squeezed.

Banqui's broad face creased with anguish, flaring the nostrils of his flat nose. "Because I told him you were the only other person in all of Zirdai who knew where The Eyes were located."

Scorching hells. Shyla stepped back. Perhaps calling him a friend was being rather generous. "But your diggers—"

"None of them were part of the extraction. Only me. I trusted no one with the information."

But someone had to know. Unless… "Surely you don't think that I—"

"Of course not, Shyla! You could have kept the location to yourself and retrieved them without anyone the wiser, which is what I *tried* to explain to the prince, but he wouldn't listen. I suspect a spy in my crew, but I need time to figure it out and I don't wish you harmed."

How nice, but she didn't voice her sarcastic response. Instead her mind whirled with the possibilities. The heat in the room baked the sweat off her skin, another warning that they needed to go below. "I can go talk to him. Explain—"

"No. He will not listen. You'll be tortured until he's satisfied you've told the truth and then, if you're lucky, you'll be locked in the black cells. And if you're not, you'll be staked to the sand and cooked."

Gee, what a prince. The fear tightened.

"You need to hide until I can find the culprit. Perhaps the monks will hide you?"

"No," she said.

"But they raised you."

"Doesn't matter. I will not run and hide, Banqui." She had lived in the monastery for eighteen circuits and refused to run back to them at the first sign of trouble.

"But—"

"I'm going to help you."

He shook his head sadly. "You don't have any contacts among the people." Banqui gestured to the piles around them. "Your expertise is with translating these historical tablets, sifting the facts from the fables."

True, but she did have other clients. "What about the spy? Do you know who he or she is working for? I can talk to the other archeologists." And treasure hunters, but Banqui didn't need to know she'd worked for them as well. His lecture would last an entire sun jump.

His full lips thinned into a scowl. "At first I suspected the Heliacal Priestess."

She grunted. "If that's the case, you'll never get them back."

The sun neared the kill zone. The mirror pipe blazed with light as the air in her room seared their throats, creeping toward sixty degrees Celsius. Time to go. Shyla grabbed her pack and without a word, they exited to the empty tunnel—everyone else had abandoned this level angles ago. Sliding the door in place, she locked it and they bolted for the closest stairway. It spiraled down into the gloom.

Druk lanterns hanging on the sandstone walls glowed with a warm yellow light. As they descended, the air cooled fifteen degrees for each level. By the time they reached the safe zone at level six, it was thirty degrees.

At level eight, Banqui grabbed one of the lanterns. "This way." He headed down a side tunnel.

The temperature on this level reached ten degrees. Shyla shivered and pulled her wrap from her pack. At least it wouldn't get any cooler unless they traveled past level eighty where the dry air turned damp.

In Zirdai, the popular routes were all well marked with lanterns and symbols etched into the sandstone walls—the others were left in darkness. Druk lanterns were cheap to produce and plentiful. People frequently carried them and left them at various places for others to use. At least one or two druks lit every room.

The special substance inside the druk changed its tint with depth. At the very bottom of their world—level ninety-seven—it shone with a violet hue. The distinctive colors came in handy for those who were easily lost, unlike Shyla, who'd been exploring the underground city since the monks kicked her out about two circuits ago. Actually it had been exactly eight hundred and twenty-five sun jumps ago—there were three hundred and sixty sun jumps in one circuit. Not that she was counting.

A thin layer of grit crunched under their boots as they walked. The dry air held a salty scent mixed with the faint gingery anise odor of the desert.

"Where are we going?" she asked him.

"Since you won't go to the monks, you need a place to stay."

She waited, but he failed to continue. "And that would be..."

"My upper-level work rooms."

"They will be the second place the prince's soldiers will look after checking my room," she said.

"They already searched them. You can hide—"

"I'm not hiding, Banqui," she snapped, which wasn't helping. Shyla considered the problem, viewing it the same way she researched lost artifacts. "After you found The Eyes, what happened next?"

He sighed. "I wrapped the marble container with layers of silk and put it into my satchel. I headed back to the entrance and someone jumped me from behind." Banqui rubbed the side of his head as anger flared in his eyes. "When I woke, my bag was gone. And before you ask, I didn't see or hear anyone in the temple before or after the attack."

She mulled over the information. "What about the guards? Don't you always station them at a dig site?"

"I do. According to them, no one had entered or left since I'd gone in." He held his free hand up. "They're loyal to the Water Prince and they've already been *questioned*."

"Is that code for tortured?"

"Shyla, this isn't a joke."

She gave him a flat look. "The Water Prince thinks *I'm* a thief so I'm well aware of the seriousness of the situation."

"Er…right…sorry."

"How long ago did the theft happen?"

"Two sun jumps."

"Do you still have the map of the temple?"

"There's no other entrance. I checked."

She waited.

"Yes, I still have it," he said with annoyed exasperation.

"Good. I'll take another look. And when the sun is lower, we'll visit the temple."

Banqui swallowed his protest. Instead, he asked why.

"To find clues, of course."

Various emotions flicked over his face before he settled on a tired acceptance. "All right. And who knows, maybe you'll find something. Despite your youth, your attention to detail is unparalleled."

Shyla huffed in amusement. "Really? Normally you're irritated by that trait." And she didn't think twenty circuits and one hundred and five sun jumps that young, but compared to Banqui's forty-two circuits or so, she conceded his point.

"This isn't a normal situation. Besides, I'm starting to suspect the Heliacal Priestess does not have The Eyes."

"Why not?"

"Because she would have taken control of the water supply and proclaimed her right to rule Zirdai by now."

"Banqui, the rumors that The Eyes have magical power are just that, rumors. I've found nothing that provides proof." This was an old argument between them.

"But you only have access to the monk's First Room of Knowledge. There could be plenty of evidence in the Second Room of Knowledge or the Third or the Fourth."

Shyla swallowed the sudden knot in her throat. When she'd reached eighteen circuits old, the monks offered her a choice. Stay and take the oath, becoming a monk—with full access to the four Rooms of Knowledge—or go. From what she had managed to piece together, staying meant keeping the knowledge to herself and never seeing the great underground cities of Koraha, their world. Leaving meant loneliness and being viewed as an outcast. Her pale blond hair, eyebrows, eyelashes and even the fine hairs on her arms and legs, which all stood out starkly against her dark skin, all marked her as sun-kissed. Sun-kissed babies were considered the Sun Goddess's children and they were abandoned in the desert to die so they could return to their proper mother.

The Monks of Parzival didn't believe in this barbaric sacrifice. They had found her a couple kilometers from Zirdai and raised her. When she chose to leave the monastery, they gave her a pouch of coins and one boon, continued access to the First Room of Knowledge, but she no longer had access to their hearts.

Shaking her head at her maudlin—childish—thoughts, Shyla concentrated on keeping track of the turns and twists as Banqui led her down another five levels to his "upper-level" work rooms. They were all well lit with costly trol lanterns—the now orangey glow from the druk weak in comparison to the bright white of the trol. The Water Prince spared no expense for his personnel.

Banqui's equipment normally occupied the first of the three large caverns, but since he had an active dig site, all that remained were broken shovels, frayed ropes, and worn pulleys. The second cavern housed his diggers. The rows of sleeping cushions were empty.

"They're working on uncovering the lower levels of the Shem burial grounds," Banqui explained. "Deep enough to be safe." He guided her into the last room, which was his office and occasional sleeping quarters. "You can stay here until the sun reaches angle one-fifty-seven, then we'll go topside." Rummaging through the piles on his desk, he pulled out a roll of velbloud skin. "Here's the map of Tamburah's temple. I'll be back later."

The thought of being alone scared her. A surprise, considering she preferred to be alone. "Where are you going?"

"To check with the black market dealers, see if they heard anything." He left, taking the druk lantern with him.

Right. Finding The Eyes needed to be their sole focus. She glanced at the sand clock. The grains poured through the narrow glass at the same rate the sun jumped across the sky. The clock read angle ninety, which meant the ball of fire that baked their world was at its zenith.

Shyla spread the map on the floor and weighed down the edges with the lanterns. Tamburah's temple was located about three kilometers from Zirdai. The place had been built about fourteen hundred circuits ago in the classic hexagonal shape of that time period with one level above ground and twelve below. She bent over the velbloud skin and examined every centimeter of each line, shape, and smudge for all twelve underground stories. Many times hidden entrances or rooms were marked with an almost invisible symbol.

When nothing caught her attention, she searched for a magnifying glass and found one under a pile of broken pottery. How could Banqui get any work done in this mess? Returning to the map, she peered through the glass, repeating her scrutiny. Other than the slight flourish indicating the hidden vault where The Eyes had been, nothing else stood out. She sat back on her heels. Guess she'd have to wait and inspect the walls inside the temple. Shyla circled the areas she wanted to inspect with a piece of chalk.

Her stomach growled. When had she last eaten? Last darkness? She tended to lose track of time when working. Too bad she couldn't visit one of the dining caverns. No doubt the Water Prince's soldiers waited in all the common areas, hoping she'd appear.

A feather of fear brushed her ribs. All the rumors about the prince painted him as corrupt, power-hungry, and cruel. She didn't trust rumors, but Banqui's constant apprehension over upsetting the man gave them some weight. Yet the prince ensured every citizen of Zirdai had access to water. His soldiers built the aqueducts, maintained the air shafts, protected the city, and collected the taxes. If a citizen couldn't afford to pay, they could join the Water Prince's guards or, if too old or infirm, they could enter into the service of the Heliacal Priestess. No one died of thirst. Food was provided by the Heliacal Priestess and her deacons—they cared for the velbloud flocks and gamelu herds, and tended the vegetation caverns. Not wishing to draw unwanted attention from either group, Shyla paid the required stipend to them both each circuit.

Of course others tried to circumvent the tariffs. Refusing to pay or be indentured, they found their own water and grew their own food. Rumors of illicit water sources flew through the population like a grain of sand carried by high winds. All illegal activities were quickly stopped by either the deacons or the soldiers. The laws were spelled out quite clearly to all citizens, even a sun-kissed like her. Shyla didn't know what became of those unfortunates once arrested, nor did she care. Her focus centered on her own survival—her income just enough to keep her independent.

Banqui returned and interrupted her morose thoughts. Shyla didn't think it was possible, but he appeared even more disheveled and vexed than earlier.

"No luck." She guessed.

He cursed and insulted the dealers' mothers and grandmothers as he slammed the lamp on his desk.

When he calmed somewhat, she said, "You really didn't expect them to tell you where they are. Did you?"

"None of them can sell The Eyes. Not without getting caught. If the Water Prince even suspects they have any knowledge…" Banqui cast about for a proper descriptor.

"What if they sell them to someone in another city?" Travel between cities required a great deal of funds. Most people remained in the city they were born in. But the treasure hunters were likely to have the means. "If it was me, I'd be long gone by now."

He grabbed two fistfuls of his hair. "The Water Prince is going to kill me when I have nothing to report!"

She stood. "Calm down. If he kills you, he has no hope of finding The Eyes."

"Not helping."

"All right. Do you have any food or water here?"

That snapped him from his panic. "Oh. Of course. Here." He strode over to a stone cooler and lifted the lid. Pulling out a jar of water and two thick rolls of velbloud jerky, he handed one to her while he searched for a couple of glasses. "Sorry, it's all I have. My diggers live on this stuff when on site."

"That's fine." Too hungry to care, Shyla gnawed on the end. The spicy ginger flavor of the dried meat filled her mouth. She washed it down with the water.

When they finished eating, Banqui donned a sun cloak. Woven from the hair of the velbloud, it provided protection from the sun's rays. It also helped keep a person cool when traveling topside in the sun and provided warmth when the sun dropped from sight—an essential garment. Of course when the sun reached the killing zone, nothing worked. She exchanged her wrap for her sun cloak, smoothing out the wrinkles from being folded for so long in her pack.

"You'll also need dillo leather boots." Banqui strode into the diggers' quarters. "Velbloud leather melts."

She chased after him. "I already have them."

He stopped short and turned. "Really?"

Shyla waggled a booted foot at him. "The monks and acolytes walk the sands every sun jump."

"Oh, right. Good." Banqui shouldered a pack and then peered at the clock. "Almost angle one-fifty. If we hurry we can return before full dark."

She followed him through the tunnels. The air warmed as they ascended. The hot gingery anise scent of the desert dominated as the corridors brightened with sunlight. Since Shyla lived close to the surface and Banqui worked in the desert, neither of them had any trouble adjusting to the brilliance. Their skin color was also similar. It naturally darkened when exposed to the sunlight—the longer the exposure, the darker the skin. A survival mechanism that had evolved as their sun grew hotter and hotter.

The skin tones of the citizens of Zirdai ranged from the darkest brown all the way to a tawny color. Many of those so-called "ghosts" who lived in Zirdai had never exposed their skin to the sun and had no desire to either. It was a hard concept for Shyla to fathom.

Living with the monks, she was considered an acolyte and had been required to be topside at least a few angles of every sun jump. Plus the fact that there were historical ruins, cities, and other amazing discoveries buried by the sands and just waiting for them to discover sent shivers along her skin. Not only ancient temples, but tombs, forests, oceans, and long extinct animal bones had all been slowly buried by the sand the last hundred thousand circuits, forcing the people to dig underground to survive as their world's water level dipped deeper and deeper. And, after learning about all the wonders in the cities of Koraha, she longed to visit them all.

Banqui motioned for her to stop and wait when they neared one of Zirdai's many exits. He peeked around the corner and cursed, withdrawing. "Cleaning crew. All right, pull your hood down low, stick close to me and follow my lead."

Unease bubbled, but she tugged the material over her head and down to her nose, keeping her gaze on his boots. The crew, while not trained soldiers, were part of the Water Prince's guard.

Striding out as if on a mission, Banqui called a greeting to the men and women shoveling and sweeping the vermillion-colored sand from the entrance. Another vital service. If left to its own devices, the tiny grains would eventually bury the entire city, blocking all the entrances and air shafts.

They reached topside. The heat pressed against Shyla's sun cloak. Drawing the hot air into her lungs required effort. She squinted in the harsh light. The distant stubby vegetation and dunes appeared as if undulating in a breeze—an optical illusion caused by the waves of heat rising from the surface of Koraha. The light pink sky a pale reflection of the reddish-orange sand.

Banqui kept walking, taking one of the popular paths that snaked away from the city and was easy to travel on since the sand had been compressed down by many pairs of boots. Shyla peered over her shoulder, but no one followed them. The only things behind them were the groups of one-story structures made of brightly colored sand and stained glass—Zirdai's top level. The colors were a defiant gesture against the desert's unchanging landscape. Each cluster marked an entrance into the city below. They also served as a brilliant landmark for travelers.

An image of a desiccated corpse half-buried in the sand rose unbidden in her mind. When she was a little over five circuits old, the monks had shown Shyla what happened when a person was topside during the sun's killing angles. Was that her fate if they didn't find The Eyes? Would she feel her blood boiling in her veins, or would she be unconscious by then? Shyla concentrated on remembering the series of paths Banqui traveled in order to banish the fear simmering in her chest.

Banqui turned off the road and shuffled through the soft sand. He counted under his breath. Stopping when he reached twenty, he crouched down and swept the grains away from a round flat stone. An iron ring rested on top. Banqui yanked on the ring, sliding the slab to the side and exposing a dark hole.

Shyla glanced around, but no other structures marred the desert landscape. "The temple?"

He waved a hand, indicating a big mound in the distance. "We uncovered the top story a kilometer from here, but I always have my diggers make an escape tunnel just in case of a collapse."

Oh. "Then this must be how your thief was able to enter undetected."

He frowned at her. "It was the first place I checked. It was undisturbed. And unless the thief can float above the sands like a velbloud, he or she would have left tracks."

And Banqui was well qualified to determine if the sand had been disturbed. The man was rumored to see buried buildings when others saw nothing but dunes.

He sat on the edge, then lowered his body into the darkness. "Watch. There's a bit of a drop."

Shyla's chest squeezed and her hands itched to hold a map. Too bad a map that predicted the future and showed her what she might encounter below had not been invented. Dropping down into the unknown wasn't high on her "to-be-accomplished" list. However the sun neared the end of its jump so she smoothed her cloak and gathered her courage.

Grabbing the edge of the hole, she hung from her hands, but her feet didn't touch the ground. She let go. After a second of weightlessness, she hit the floor. Hard. The impact sent a pulse of pain up her calves and into her knees.

"That was more than a bit of a drop," she said, wiping her hands.

"Not for me." Banqui hunched over in the narrow tunnel. He held a druk lantern. It glowed white, illuminating the vermillion sand arcing over them.

She gestured to the rounded walls that appeared a bit…soft. "How do you know it won't collapse?"

He smiled. "Because my crew dug it and they are very serious about their safety."

Good to know. Shyla stayed close as Banqui navigated the tight corridor. It didn't take long until the sand walls were replaced with smooth stone.

"This is the third level of Tamburah's temple," Banqui said. His voice bounced off the hard surfaces. When he turned down another hallway, small clouds of dust succeeded each of his steps.

As her eyes adjusted to the semi-darkness, shapes appeared. Faces had been carved into the walls. Gruesome expressions of pain, terror, and desperation contorted the visages of the men and women. Looking closer, she pulled away in revulsion. They were all eyeless. Some faces had gaping holes, others had tattered skin and mutilated sockets. A shiver crawled up her spine and she attempted to shake off the unease that, even without their eyes, they stared at her with accusation.

Sensing her interest, Banqui stopped and illuminated the carvings. The faces woke with the light's touch, mouthing their suffering in a silent wail of anguish.

"Horrible yet so finely wrought," Banqui said. "Tamburah's temple has many hallways of the dead." He moved ahead and led her down three more levels into a spacious room.

The round chamber had six entrances that disappeared into shadows. Rows of benches made a semicircle pattern, facing an altar. Another face had been carved into the wall behind the altar. But this one was different. It filled the entire wall, and when Banqui drew closer, the light revealed a detailed pattern of blue and purple sand coloring the face.

"And here is the big man himself. King Tamburah overlooking his followers, making judgments. Unfortunately for his people he rarely ruled in their favor," Banqui said.

The king's expression was smug despite the deeply carved and empty eye sockets. Red sand lined the sockets and red sand tears dripped down the cheeks.

"According to the legends, Tamburah would gaze into a prisoner's eyes, reading his or her soul with his magic," he said. "If he detected guilt of any crime, the accused was secured to the altar where Tamburah removed the criminal's eyes. The royal artist would engrave the poor soul's new likeness on the wall before the prisoner was taken outside to await the sun's punishment. We uncovered a deep pit full of bones next to the temple."

Swallowing down a nervous cough, she said, "Legends are not historical facts, Banqui. No doubt he was ruthless, cruel, and evil. There are records that thousands of people died during his reign, but there is nothing to support he used magic."

Undaunted, Banqui continued, "His temple corroborates what was written on the tablets. It contains twelve underground levels. The two lower levels were his living quarters. They're complicated mazes of hidden rooms and corridors littered with some interesting traps."

Only Banqui thought traps were interesting. Many archeologists died by inadvertently setting them off.

"Was the vault booby trapped?" she asked.

"Of course. Good thing the bones of a treasure hunter tipped me off." He huffed with amusement. "First time one of those blasted hunters did something useful."

Tamburah's vault was located on level twelve. Banqui led her down a spiral staircase. By the time they reached the bottom, the druk lantern shone with an orange light.

"Stay close," he said. "Touch nothing."

She remained one step behind him as they wove through rooms and hallways. Other than the sand crunching under their boots, the place was silent. A musty stale odor scented the thin air.

"Banqui, did you clear all the ventilation holes?"

"In the upper floors. I didn't want anyone deeper than level nine."

"What—"

"The air is fine. Besides, we won't be here long."

He halted and hung the lantern on a nearby hook. The light revealed a rectangular shape that had been carved into the stone. Banqui pulled a knife and dug into it with the point of his blade. A horrendous scraping echoed in the room as Banqui opened a thick door. He gestured her inside. The space was just big enough to fit three, maybe four people.

He pointed to a shelf on the back wall. "The container with The Eyes was the only item in the vault. The gemstones had been removed from Tamburah's mural to keep them safe from treasure hunters."

She stepped closer. "May I?"

Banqui handed her the lantern. "Go ahead." He waited in the threshold.

Shyla shone the light on the walls, examining them. An involuntary yelp sprang from her lips when she found the skeleton of a hunter slumped against the left corner.

"Don't worry," Banqui called. "I've disabled the trap. Those slits on the walls are for the sword blades. Trigger the trap and they'd shoot out, impaling the would-be thief." He chuckled. Banqui hated treasure hunters.

After peering at every centimeter, she inspected the stone shelf. A line of tiny symbols had been etched across the edge. "Did you see these?"

"Yes. Probably a warning about the booby trap."

Focusing on the script, she transcribed the symbols. "It also includes a warning that The Eyes are cursed."

"That's standard." Banqui didn't sound worried.

Nor should he. Curses and magic—both nonexistent. Shyla continued her examination, running her hand over the shelf. Smooth except for a rough patch in the middle. Rising up to her tiptoes, she shone the light on an unknown graphic. Odd. Tracing it with a fingertip, she realized it'd been carved recently. "Banqui, I've found something."

He joined her.

She pointed. "Was this here when you found The Eyes?"

"No." Banqui studied the glyph. "Scorching hells," he whispered.

Her pulse skittered. "What does it mean?"

He straightened. "We need to get out of here."

"Not until you tell me what it means."

"I'll tell you on the way." He took the lantern from her and retraced their route at a quick trot.

When they reached the stairwell, she tugged on his arm. "Banqui."

"Come on." He mounted the steps, taking two at a time. At the top, he stopped to catch his breath. Then he said, "That's the symbol for the Invisible Sword. I think they have The Eyes."

"Who are they?" she asked.

"They formed back in Tamburah's time. A secret organization that was credited with assassinating Tamburah. The group is rumored to still be in existence."

"I've never heard of them. Sounds like a bedtime story."

"You don't know everything, Shyla," Banqui said in angry exasperation.

Stung, she shot back, "I did a great deal of research on Tamburah in order to find the location of his temple and vault for *you*. Don't you think I would have read about this Invisible Sword?"

"The whole point of a secret organization is to keep it secret."

"Then how do *you* know about them?"

"I—" He jerked his head up. "Did you hear that?"

"No."

"Probably sand rats." Banqui grasped her wrist. "Let's get out of here. We can argue about this later."

They entered Tamburah's judgment room. When they were halfway across, a yell echoed. They both froze as figures poured from the other doors. Banqui's grip tightened. "They found us."

CHAPTER 2

As the figures drew closer, Shyla broke Banqui's grip on her wrist. They wore turbans with veils, disguising their features, but short swords hung from their belts, which meant they worked for the Water Prince. She slid into a fighting stance without thought. And without any real hope. Fear swept through her. They were outnumbered. And soon to be surrounded.

But the Monks of Parzival had taken their duty as her guardians seriously. They trained her body in the Ways of the Yarin. Pushing the distracting emotions aside, she blocked the first set of hands reaching for her, ducked a fist, spun, kicked another attacker, and stepped in to deliver an uppercut to a chin. They responded with punches and grasps, but not with their weapons. A good sign they didn't wish to harm or kill them.

Banqui was yanked from her side. He grunted with pain as the druk lantern crashed to the floor, spilling its glowing innards. "Do you know who—oof."

The bodies closed in tighter, grabbing her arms, pulling them behind her. The hot ginger and anise scent of the desert clung to their black tunics and pants. She stomped on booted feet and kicked shins. Curses, hisses of pain, and groans were her reward for her efforts.

"Shyla stop, you're going to get hurt," Banqui called.

She froze. The hands gripping her relaxed just enough for her to yank her wrists free and break loose. For a heartbeat. Arms wrapped around her legs, pitching her forward. Her right temple connected with the edge of a stone bench. Then nothing.

* * *

The sound poured through her, teasing and inviting. A musical hum unlike anything she'd heard. It called to her on a primal level. Unable to resist the summons, she opened her eyes. And squeezed them shut. Bright, expensive trol lanterns seared her vision and woke a sharp throbbing in her right temple.

Her thoughts moved as if trudging through soft sand. What happened? Where was she? With her eyes closed, she determined a few facts. One, she reclined on a soft surface. Two, no boots on her feet, but she wore clothes. Three, the temperature of the room was perfect—dry and warm. Four, the air smelled fresh with a crisp clean scent mixed with the buttery odor from the lanterns. So far so good.

Through the slit in her eyelids, she figured out another clue. She was in an opulent room with silk tapestries on the walls and rugs covering the stone floor. The owner of the room had to be rich. And not well-off rich, but deep-level wealthy. Maybe even past level eighty. Not good. Not at all.

When she spotted the source of the hum, Shyla gawked at it despite the brilliant light. A single ribbon of water flowed from a spout jutting from the wall. It arced into a basin of glistening rocks arranged in a circle on the ground. Tiles covered the wall behind the fountain. The colored pieces had been artfully arranged in a mosaic of blues, starting with the darker hues at the base to a pale wash at the ceiling. Green tiles ringed the basin and a pattern of yellow circles dotted the floor.

An oasis? A mirage? The afterlife? It didn't matter. Wishing to touch the decadent abundance of water, she struggled to a sitting position. A knife of pain stabbed her temple. Spots swirled in front of her as nausea climbed her throat. Lying back down to keep from passing out, she closed her eyes, breathing in deep.

"My physician says you need to keep still," said a male voice.

Shyla jerked with surprise, opening her eyes. Focused on the water, she hadn't finished scanning the room. A young man approached. He'd probably been sitting over by the desk. Another colorful mosaic—this one orange and yellow—decorated the wall behind it.

Crouching next to her, he said, “Here.” He pressed a cool wet cloth to the right side of her face. “At least the cut stopped bleeding.”

She stared at him. His black hair was a striking contrast to his light tawny face. Shyla suspected his skin had never been exposed to the sun. But those eyes. Emerald green with flecks of silver. And, damn. The man was attractive. He wore what appeared to be a black training uniform similar to those the monks donned when they practiced the Ways of the Yarin.

He cocked his head in concern when she continued to stare. “You had quite the blow to your head. How are you feeling?”

“Confused and sick to my stomach.”

“Ah. That’s to be expected. This will help.” He handed her a glass.

Shyla pushed up on one elbow and sipped the drink. The ginger-flavored water eased her nausea. The man settled on a nearby cushion. She puzzled over his identity. Long eyelashes and strong jaw, he appeared to be around twenty-five circuits old. The tight-fitting uniform outlined his athletic build. He wore no jewelry or insignia.

The pain in her head dulled to a bearable level. Her mind cleared. “Where am I?”

“What do you remember?”

Good question. She'd been studying a map, searching for…something, and—

Her memories returned in a rush. The Eyes. The temple. Attackers. She sat up. "Banqui! I need to—"

"Relax. He's fine."

She sagged in relief. "Where is he?"

The man gave her a tight smile. "He's *my* guest."

Her stomach churned. And this time it wasn't due to nausea. Scanning the room, her gaze snagged on the water fountain and the clues clicked together. Scorching hells. She was cooked.

"Figured it out?" he asked with amusement.

"You're…" All moisture fled her mouth, causing the words to stick.

"Yes?"

"Younger than I thought," she blurted. To be fair, she'd only seen the Water Prince twice in her life and both times at a distance.

He laughed. The resonant sound did nothing to ease her growing panic. Banqui said she'd be tortured if caught. Shyla glanced at the door, thinking she'd make a break for it.

"Go ahead, Sun-kissed." Anger laced his words as he gestured. "You won't get far and then we'll continue this conversation in one of my *special* rooms."

She had a feeling that his definition of special didn't match hers. If she wished to survive this encounter she needed to be smart. "I'm sorry."

He shook his head. "No, I'm sorry." He settled into a more comfortable position next to her. "I thought you wouldn't be scared of me."

"Why not? Everyone's scared of you." Why did she just say that? So much for being smart.

"Because you're sun-kissed. A survivor." He shrugged. "Because Banqui told me you're not influenced by rumors and speculation, preferring facts to make a decision. My reputation is due to exaggeration and misinformation. Not that I mind, it keeps others from thinking big dangerous thoughts. I fought hard to become the Water Prince and I don't plan on giving it up."

Only the deep-level wealthy and the Heliacal Priestess had the resources to challenge him. The King of Koraha didn't care who ruled the cities as long as he received his taxes on time. Whoever controlled the water governed the city as the Water Prince or Princess. It was as simple as that.

"What else did Banqui tell you?" she asked, surprised by her sudden boldness.

"That you are the best at finding lost artifacts." His tone remained neutral, but he tensed.

"I *locate* them," she corrected.

"There's a difference?"

"Yes. I'm hired to research, study maps, transcribe ancient tablets in order to find the location of a lost temple or structure. Then I give the information to my client. I don't go into the desert and dig."

"I see." He studied her. "If you're the best, then why are you living on level three? Even the poorest Zirdai citizen can afford to live deeper."

In other words, what was she doing with her income. It was none of his business, but she wasn't going to anger him further. "Sunlight. I need it for my work."

"And I'm sure it's quieter up there. No neighbors to bother you."

"Exactly." She kept her expression dispassionate. Although she wanted to punch him. He'd no idea what her life was like. As a sun-kissed, she hadn't expected to be welcomed with open arms. After all, the monks had warned her. But the lengths people went to ignore her was quite the shock. She'd been lucky to get a room at all.

"And you haven't been tempted to retrieve these artifacts for yourself?"

Ah, finally—the real reason for this little chat. "No."

"I find that hard to believe."

"If I was tempted, then why would I have clients? I could easily do the research for myself."

"But not the labor to clear a site. You needed Banqui for that and once he found The Eyes, all you had to do was jump him and steal them."

The conversation had just taken a turn for the worse. The Water Prince made an excellent point. Shyla laced her hands together to keep them from shaking. She needed to choose her words with care. "Let's say that's what happened. Then why am I still in Zirdai? Why am I helping Banqui to recover them?"

"The Eyes will give you the power to overthrow me."

Unable to stop herself, she laughed. Shocked, he stared at her and she rushed to control the nervous giggles before he recovered and sent her to one of his special rooms. "I'm sorry. It's just The Eyes do not have magical powers. There is no evidence."

"What about King Tamburah? His accomplishments are well documented. He was a poor velbloud shearer and he became king."

"He also was a charismatic speaker and very intelligent. He used fear, intimidation, and the claim of having magic to keep his people loyal and obedient. In his later years, he killed without mercy or reason—a sign of his insanity." Remembering the faces carved into the walls, she shuddered. "Look, I've no desire to rule Zirdai. I'm happy to pay my taxes and be left alone." Nor did she care what happened to the people in the city—they'd rejected her after all. "If I wanted power, I could have stayed with the monks and risen through the ranks. I didn't steal The Eyes. I don't know where they are."

The Water Prince appeared to consider her comments. "Let's say you are telling the truth. Then that leaves Banqui."

"He didn't steal them either."

"How do you know?"

"He's upset and has been frantically searching for them. One of his people must have figured it out and sold the information to a treasure hunter. Banqui is loyal to you."

"That could be an act. Does Banqui believe The Eyes have magical powers?"

Not liking where this was going, she squirmed. "Yes, but—"

"Banqui is my fourth archeologist because the three before him eventually turned greedy and decided to keep the treasures for themselves, which resulted in their immediate…removal. It was just a matter of time and the right prize to turn Banqui as well."

Shyla shook her head. "No. I don't believe that."

"You're rather loyal. Are you that way for all your clients or are you friends?"

Another uncomfortable question. She'd been truthful so far, and lying well wasn't a skill she possessed—at least that was what the monks had said. "*I* consider Banqui a friend. I don't know how he views our relationship."

"So you're biased."

"No. Like he told you, I'm skeptical. It's the same with people. I collect…er…facts when I'm with a person and form an opinion based on those instead of sentiment. Banqui's proven to be trustworthy."

"Fair enough. You don't know me, right?"

"Yes."

"Yet as soon as you figured out who I was, you panicked. Why? You had no *facts* about me."

Clever. "Banqui is scared of you, and I trust him."

"And I threatened you."

True. She couldn't resist asking, "Is Banqui in one of your special rooms?"

"Not yet." His gaze sharpened. "That will depend on you."

"Me?" Did her voice just squeak? Yes, it did.

"Yes. Despite my reputation, I'm a reasonable man. I apologized for my bit of temper earlier and we've been having a nice conversation ever since—there's a fact in my favor." His smile made the trol light seem dim in comparison.

Her heart flipped in her chest and it had nothing to do with fear.

"Banqui says you're the best so I'm hiring you to find The Eyes for me."

Not good. She had no idea how to go about it. "But that's—"

"In exchange for recovering The Eyes, I will release Banqui."

Swallowing the dread lumped in her throat, she asked, "What if I can't find them?"

His expression turned cold. "Then Banqui will meet the same fate as his predecessors."

So much for being a reasonable man. In desperation, she appealed to his intelligence. "I don't have the contacts in Zirdai needed for this job. Not many people will talk to me. I can't pay for information. Banqui thinks I'm the best, but he's the only one. The clients who haven't been referred by Banqui only hire me when they're desperate."

The Water Prince gazed at her with an amused half-smile. "Since my soldiers have found nothing, I guess you could say I am desperate. And not to worry, as your client, I will provide the funds and I will give you my sigil. If anyone refuses to cooperate, show it to them. If they still refuse, I will ensure they change their minds."

He countered every one of her arguments with ease. Shyla had no other choice. She was as trapped as if she'd just stepped onto a patch of sluff sand. The more she struggled the faster she would sink. Best to remain still and hope for rescue. Except it was Banqui's life at risk and not her own. That made it worse.

"All right, I will do my best to find The Eyes."

"I expect nothing less." He held out his hand.

Shyla grasped it. His hand was warm and calloused, which was a surprise. He had a firm handshake. She met his intense gaze.

"You have the most unusual eye color—it's like liquid gold. Do all sun-kissed have the same color?"

"No." There were about a dozen sun-kisseds at the monastery, but only two had eyes close to her color. One older monk's eyes matched the sun's golden red hue exactly.

"May I touch your hair?" he asked.

"Uh…" Kinda creepy.

"Pardon my curiosity, but I've never met a sun-kissed before."

At least he hadn't fondled her while she was passed out on his cushion. "Sure."

The Water Prince stroked the pale yellow hair on the uninjured side of her head. His fingers combed through the long strands—her tie was long gone so it flowed to the middle of her back. A shiver raced over her skin, leaving goose bumps in its wake.

"It feels like silk. I'd thought the sun would have dried it out like a velbloud's coarse hair. Thank you."

Silk? He was being kind. Considering that she'd sweated, crawled through tunnels, and fallen to the ground, she thought velbloud hair a more accurate description. She suppressed the urge to run her hands through it.

A light knock broke the awkward silence.

"Come," he called.

The door slid open and a stout man wearing a long white tunic and black pants entered. He carried a tray.

"I see the patient is awake," the man said.

"This is my physician," the prince said to her. "He'll see to your recovery." He stood. "Timin, let me know when she's healthy."

"Yes, sire."

She stifled a gasp. Not once had she shown the proper respect. The Water Prince kept his expression neutral, but amusement shone in his eyes. "Then I'll leave her in your care." He strode to the door.

Springing to her feet, she opened her mouth to protest—she needed to start her search for The Eyes, but black and white dots swarmed her vision. Her legs turned to jelly. She sank back onto the cushion.

Timin set his tray down and tsked over her. "You need food, water, and sleep. And your cut will need to be stitched and bandaged." He handed her the glass of water that she'd left on the floor. "First, finish this, and then we'll proceed."

The physician treated her wound with a numbing paste. When he stitched the gash, Shyla focused on the hum of the water nearby instead of the tug and pull of the needle. After he finished, he applied a bandage, then handed her a bowl of snake-meat stew with a pepper broth. Timin waited until she emptied the bowl before ordering her to sleep. He jabbed a finger at the cushion underneath her.

"But isn't this the Water Prince's room?" she asked.

He chuckled. "It is but one of many. The entire ninety-seventh level is his domain." When he saw her surprise, he added, "Granted, this level isn't as wide as the upper levels. Zirdai is funnel-shaped."

Still, it had to be at least a couple kilometers. Timin stood with his arms crossed until Shyla lay down.

He turned the lanterns low and said, "I'll check on you at angle zero."

She couldn't resist asking, "How do you know when the sun starts its jump?" There wasn't a sand clock in the room.

"We have moisture clocks. Why do you think it's nice and dry down here?"

Pushing up to an elbow, she said, "I wondered about that."

"The deep levels that have access to water are always damp. We import a special silica that absorbs the moisture in the air. The substance changes colors as it reaches saturation and it takes a full sun jump to reach that point. We mark the passage of time by the color change. The best part of this clock is it transforms the moisture into usable water. Now get some sleep." He strode to the door. "There are guards just outside should you need anything."

An interesting way to tell her she couldn't run away, but that wasn't Timin's fault. She touched the bandage. "Thank you."

Timin made a short bow and left.

She counted to ten and then scrambled to her feet. If she failed to find The Eyes, she might share Banqui's fate. So she finally gave in to the temptation that had been humming in her ears since she woke, and thrust her hands into the water fountain.

Cold! Not as cold as the air topside during darkness, but her skin tingled and her bones ached with it. Cupping the water, she drank. Pure, fresh, and satisfying. No wonder people waged war to control the source. However, she'd just be happy to find The Eyes, free Banqui, return to her normal life, and never be this deep again. Except she doubted it would work out that way. The facts didn't look good.

CHAPTER

3

Comfortable, warm, and with only a slight headache, Shyla should have been sound asleep on the luxurious cushion. Yet the constant splash of the water and her swirling worries kept her awake. How could she possibly find The Eyes when Banqui had failed? Small and priceless, they could be anywhere in Zirdai or halfway to Catronia by now.

Regardless, she had to track them down or Banqui would die. Instead of focusing on her lack of qualifications, she made a mental list of tasks. She'd check with her clients—oh scorching sand demons! She'd missed her meeting with the historian. Even though she had a good excuse, the client had probably complained about it to her colleagues. Shyla's already shaky reputation would crumble and the only people willing to hire her would be the treasure hunters. A group she'd only worked for to pay the bills. She had hoped eventually she wouldn't need their business.

At least she could ask them about The Eyes. Banqui said he didn't have any luck with the black-market merchants, but the treasure hunters might know something. Perhaps the thief was holding on to them until the ruckus over their disappearance died down. Except it wouldn't. Not until they were found—an impossible task.

She pulled the fur over her head, quieting the music of the water but not her pessimistic thoughts. In order to settle them, she drew in deep breaths and focused on the meditation techniques of the Yarin. Envisioning fingers of sand blowing over the dunes, listening to the soft hiss of the grains as they kissed the surface, she calmed. A billowing curtain of fabric accompanied the light clear notes of the monks' chimes as the twilight breeze entered the monastery through unshuttered windows. She drank in the wind, savoring the scents of the desert as the air cooled. Soon after, sleep claimed her.

* * *

A muffled, but clearly angry voice woke her. Shyla kept still and listened.

"…possible…idiots…find her."

The fur was yanked away in one harsh motion. She blinked in the sudden light. The Water Prince stood with the fur clutched in his hands. All the lanterns in the room blazed.

He gazed at her for a moment as if stunned. Did he think she'd escaped?

"Uh, how does your head feel?" he finally asked.

She sat up and fingered the bandage on her temple. Pain answered her touch, but the deeper throb had disappeared. "Better."

"Good." He dropped the fur and strode to the door.

Two guards straightened at his approach, and he said something to them that was too low for Shyla to understand. The Water Prince wore a form-fitting green silk tunic tucked into black trousers. His dusty black ankle boots appeared to be crafted from a soft leather. The two times she'd seen him, from a distance, he'd worn formal silk robes and a golden crown.

He returned and pointed to a door on the other side of the fountain. "Feel free to use the water closet to freshen up."

A closet full of water? Confused, she glanced at the door.

He chuckled. "Sorry, I forgot there are no water closets above level eighty. Come."

She followed him. He entered the small room and twisted a knob on the equally small lantern fixed to the wall next to a mirror. It flared to life.

"Turn the faucet on to let the water flow." He demonstrated, creating a small fountain. The water splashed into a bowl and disappeared. "When you're done, turn it the opposite way to shut it off." He noticed her amazed expression. "There are metal pipes throughout the deep levels. We've plenty of water down here." Then he swept an arm out, indicating the two seats along the opposite wall. "I assume you know what to do there. Liquids on the left. What do they call them in the upper levels?"

Heat rushed through her. "Collection stations."

"Ah, yes. No need to be embarrassed, they're very important for our survival." He left.

True. The wastes from the citizens of Zirdai were collected each sun jump and used to fertilize and "water" the crops. The plants grew in spacious caverns on level six and were tended by the deacons. Mirror pipes brought in the sunlight. Technically people could survive on velbloud, snake, and gamelu meat alone, but it wasn't ideal.

Shyla "freshened up" and then washed her hands and face using the cleanser provided. When it didn't dry soon after, she realized she had to rinse it from her skin with water, which explained the mini fountain and basin. While vegetables and fruit were important to their world, this water was vital. And to just let it pour through her fingers was such decadence! She hoped it was collected, cleaned, and reused—like almost everything in Zirdai.

When she exited the water closet, the Water Prince gestured for her to join him at a low marble table. Two plates of scrambled velbloud eggs had been set out along with two cups of steaming mint tea. Shyla settled on the cushion opposite him.

"Go on, eat. You must be starving." He dug into his pile with gusto.

She picked at her food.

He paused. "What's wrong?"

The words burst from her before she could stop them. "I'm having first meal with the Water Prince!"

"And I'm eating with a sun-kissed." He pressed a hand to his chest in mock horror. "Don't tell the wealthy elites." Then he sobered. "Look, I usually eat alone because of the…awkwardness from everyone. I'd hoped you'd be more relaxed." He leaned forward. "How about this? Let's pretend we're ordinary citizens having first meal together. We'll make small talk, discuss the tasks we have planned for this sun jump. Can you do that, Shyla?"

It was the first time he hadn't called her sun-kissed. She sipped her tea to settle her nerves. Nothing wrong with small talk. "Yes. Er…what do you have planned for this sun jump?"

"I've a history lesson scheduled with the visiting professor from Catronia University." He spooned a large heap of eggs into his mouth.

"I didn't know you still attended lessons."

He flashed her that brilliant smile. The sun had nothing on him. Nothing at all.

"I'm taking advantage of Professor Emeline's visit. I believe that you should never stop learning. Those that do are making a big mistake. While history isn't my favorite subject and she can be rather dull, I still might learn something."

"I agree with you. I almost stayed at the monastery just to have access to all those Rooms of Knowledge."

"Why didn't you?"

The question seemed innocent, but he had accused her of stealing The Eyes in an attempt to overthrow him. She chose her words with care. "I wanted to explore our world and visit the grand cities of Koraha. Plus I'm helping Banqui and others find lost temples and palaces. We're unearthing our history and learning new things. Unlike the monks who are isolated in their monasteries. What good is all that knowledge if you can't *do* anything with it?"

"I agree. I think they should do more, and the Heliacal Priestess would love to be admitted into those rooms. But they're protected by the King and the Sun Goddess. And no one is crazy enough to upset either one."

Despite being raised by the monks, Shyla wasn't convinced of the Sun Goddess's existence. The monks prayed and prayed, but as far as Shyla could tell, none of their prayers were answered. But she wouldn't say that aloud. The Heliacal Priestess was equally as powerful as the Water Prince, and her deacons kept a close eye on her flock. Shyla paid her tithe and attended services without fail to avoid being accused of lacking the proper devotion.

The prince's physician entered as they finished their meals. He changed the bandage over Shyla's cut.

"Keep it clean and dry," he said, handing her a couple extra bandages and some adhesive. "After three sun jumps you can stop covering it. And in another four sun jumps, have a healer remove the stitches. Understand?"

"Yes."

"Good."

Soon after he left one of the Water Prince's guards entered. If his role was to be intimidating and formidable, he aced it by barely fitting through the entrance. The guard wore all black, including his well-stocked weapons belt, scabbard, and the hilt of his short sword—long blades didn't do well in small spaces. Although she doubted the big brute's wide shoulders allowed him access to some of those narrow areas. With his dark mahogany skin, Shyla thought he blended in well with the shadows. Perhaps that was why the prince chose him. Shyla suspected the rumors about the Water Prince being smart might just be true.

"Did you bring it?" he asked the guard.

"Yes, sire." The man pulled a gold metal bracelet from his pocket.

"Shyla, hold out your left arm," he ordered.

Uneasy, but unable to refuse, she did as instructed. The guard snapped the bracelet around her wrist. The touch of its cold metal sent a shiver up her arm. He fiddled with something and it tightened. Alarmed, she tried to pull away.

"Stop moving or it'll pinch your skin," the guard growled with a deep commanding voice.

She stilled. He finished and stepped back. Shyla fingered the band of gold. While tight, it didn't hurt, but it didn't budge either. It was about two centimeters wide. A silver crown symbol decorated the top.

"My sigil," the prince said. "Show that to anyone who refuses to render you aid. It should change his or her mind."

"And if it doesn't?" she asked.

His tight smile didn't reach his emerald-silver eyes. "Show it to my guards and explain the situation. They'll assist you in *extracting* the needed information."

No doubt by beating the poor fellow. She decided that would be a desperate last measure. Tugging on the band, she asked, "How do I take it off?"

"You don't."

Surprised, she met his gaze. "I—"

"This ensures you won't lose it or lend it or sell it. When you complete your mission, Captain Rendor will be happy to unlock it."

The words were reasonable, but a threat rumbled through his tone. She rubbed her bare arms, wondering what had happened to her pack and sun cloak. She'd have to hide the sigil. The treasure hunters would be way too interested in it and she didn't trust them not to cut off her hand to claim it.

The Water Prince strode to the desk and returned with a small pouch that jingled. Handing it to her, he said, "This should be enough to help you with your initial inquires. If you need more, let my guards know. They'll get a message to me and Rendor will be happy to deliver it to you. In fact, he'll be checking up on your progress from time to time."

The big brute bared his teeth in what he probably thought was a smile. It wasn't. No emotion shone from his almond-shaped eyes. His long black eyelashes curled slightly at the ends, seeming out of place—a softness against the harsh lines of his face. If he wasn't so dangerous, she'd think he was attractive.

"And when you find The Eyes, get them to my guards right away. They can protect you both," the prince said.

Not if, but when. Such confidence. "All right."

"Do you need anything else?"

Her cue to leave. "Where is my sun cloak and pack?" The high levels would be cool this early in the sun's jump. Plus the cloak would hide the sigil.

"The cloak was stained with blood and ripped. When my people are finished cleaning and repairing it, I will have it delivered to you. One of the guards has your pack."

She sensed his impatience, but she had to ask, "How do I get back to my room?"

"Rendor will escort you. I'm sure you're anxious to get started. And Banqui will be quite relieved once you've recovered The Eyes."

Nothing like a reminder of what was at stake. As if she could forget the consequences of failure. But she played nice and followed Rendor.

"Good hunting, Shyla," the Water Prince called as she left.

* * *

Rendor took a trol lantern and led her out into the hallway. Another guard stood waiting—she was so still and rigid, Shyla thought she might be a statue. But Shyla's pack rested in her arms and the guard handed it over.

"Thanks," Shyla said, grateful to have it back.

Then the captain escorted her to a small room where two very muscular men stood next to ropes made from velbloud tethers. The four ropes disappeared up through holes in the ceiling and down through ones in the floor. Panic simmered in her chest. Was this one of the Water Prince's special rooms? Had he tricked her?

"Level twenty," Rendor said to the men as he slid the door closed.

They each grabbed a rope and pulled. The room jerked upward. Shyla gasped as the room shifted up each time the men yanked down more rope. A rolling rumble vibrated the walls with each movement.

"It's called a lift, Sun-kissed," Rendor said. "One of the wonders of Zirdai that you shouldn't be privy to, but the Water Prince has shown you great favor. So when you disappoint him, I'll ensure the sun finishes the job."

After all the insinuations from the Water Prince, it was nice to have a direct threat. "I think you mean *if* I disappoint him like you did."

He stiffened and his oversized hands curled into fists. When his glower focused on her, it was almost a physical force. She locked her knees to keep them from folding under her. But she stared back at him, answering his challenge. If she showed her fear, she'd always appear weak in his eyes. Instead she asked him where they had searched for The Eyes.

After another attempt to intimidate her with his searing glare, he said, "We recently completed a level by level investigation. They are not in Zirdai."

To imply that they had done a poor job would be suicide at this point. But The Eyes were small and easily concealed. Plus a complete map of Zirdai didn't exist. Many tunnels, caverns, and even levels remained hidden from various officials, including the city's map makers. In fact, she suspected no one in Zirdai knew the true boundaries of the underground city. Her explorations had only covered a fraction of the levels. And it was obvious that she lacked knowledge about wonders like water closets and lifts. What else didn't she know?

Except for the grunts of the men, the rest of the trip passed in silence. Shyla removed her wrap and another hair tie from her pack before slinging it over her neck. The strap crossed her body and the rectangular velbloud leather satchel rested on her left hip. To avoid drawing attention, she pulled her hair into a knot and arranged the colorful striped material to cover her head and shoulders. Anyone who came near enough to see her face would recognize her as sun-kissed, but most people didn't bother to look that close. And if she kept her left hand tucked up underneath her satchel, she'd be able to keep the sigil hidden as well.

Rendor watched her without comment. At level twenty, he slid the door open. "This is as high as this lift goes. I'll be seeing you around, Sun-kissed."

"Not if I see you first." Yes, it was childish, but she couldn't stop the words. She stepped out before he could counter and strolled down the dark tunnel as if she knew exactly where she was going. She didn't.

Once out of sight, she stopped to allow her eyes to adjust to the semi-darkness, which meant a light source was nearby. Shyla tracked the faint orange glow to a corridor. Following the line of druk lanterns, she traversed level twenty until she reached an area she recognized—the crafters' tiers.

It spanned at least ten levels and housed all the various specialty workers in one location. Instead of each level being separated by steps and piled one on top of the other like a tower, the tiers were giant ramps that just circled down to the bottom, each one smaller than the previous. Looking down from the top tier, it resembled a bunch of circles nestled inside each other.

A few people walked past the workshops, while others hurried as if on a mission. Groups chatted. Everyone wore the colorful tunics and flared pants woven from gamelu wool. The material was warm enough for the constant temperature, although some people also wore wraps and shawls. Shyla tended to wear colors that matched the tunnel and caverns' walls—dark browns and tans to avoid being noticed.

Just like the city's population of cats. She watched a black cat dash under a table full of jugs. With their dark-colored fur, they disappeared in the shadows and kept the sand rat population to a manageable level. Some even allowed themselves to become pets.

Having no desire to be spotted by the shoppers and workers, Shyla skirted the tier at a fast pace. She climbed to level three without encountering anyone.

Weak sunlight illuminated her room, which appeared to be undisturbed. The ancient map remained spread over her table. She needed to finish the job, but there wasn't enough light yet. After changing into a long-sleeved tunic, she left.

The treasure hunters tended to live between levels ten and twenty—deep enough to be safe from the sun, but still able to have convenient access to the surface.

At this time of the jump, she guessed most remained in the dining cavern that spanned levels eighteen and nineteen—one kitchen served ten levels.

Unlike most people, the hunters noticed Shyla as soon as she entered. First meal was served between angle three-fifty and angle twenty, but they tended to hang around, remaining at the tables sipping tea. She counted about six men and four women, and, while they didn't stop their conversations as she approached, their postures transformed from relaxed to alert.

Normally, she didn't seek them out. When one had a job for her, he or she visited her room. About half of them she knew by name.

"Excuse me," she said to the group. "Do you know where I can find Fadey?" He was their unofficial leader.

"Why do you want to see him?" Aphra asked. Her long brown hair had been pulled up into a complex knot.

"I need to speak with him."

"We heard you *located* a sweet," Dekel said. "Don't bother going to Fadey to sell it, he won't touch it. No one will. You're wasting your time."

"Is that so?" She scanned their faces, wondering if he was alluding to The Eyes. A few avoided her gaze. If they thought she had them, then many of the hunters were now plotting a way to steal them from her. Just what she needed—more danger. "Shouldn't Fadey be the one to decide if he wants the sweet?"

"That's not a sweet, that's a curse," Aphra said.

That just confirmed they were referring to The Eyes. Seven hells.

"And we're just saving you time," Dekel said. "In fact, why are you still in Zirdai? If the Water Prince's goons catch you, you're cooked."

"I don't have The Eyes. But I still need to talk to Fadey."

Aphra shrugged. "I'll show you where he is…for a price."

Shyla agreed. A prickling feeling flared between her shoulder blades as she followed Aphra from the dining cavern. She resisted the urge to turn around. They navigated through a number of well-traveled tunnels and climbed to level seventeen. When others passed them, Shyla kept her gaze on the ground. Walking with another person helped her remain unremarkable as not many people would want to be seen with a sun-kissed.

"I thought you were smarter than that," Aphra said when they were alone. "You realize that you just made yourself a target, don't you?"

"But I told them—"

"No one believed you. You've a lot to learn." A pause. "Gotta respect your daring, though."

"I really don't have them. And I'm guessing that you and your friends don't know where they are either."

"Like Dekel said, possessing them is suicide." She slowed. "If you really don't have them, then why do you want to find them?"

"I've been hired to."

Aphra gave a low whistle. "Banqui must be desperate."

Shyla's emotions wavered between insulted that Aphra thought Banqui only hired her when he had no other options, and intrigued that the treasure hunter believed Banqui didn't have The Eyes. "Why do you think it's Banqui?"

"Oh no, this information isn't free."

Shyla removed two coins from her pants pocket. Zirdai's currency was a two-centimeter-wide disk made from osmium—a rare bluish-silver metal that wouldn't melt even if left out during the sun's apex. The King of Koraha's visage graced one side and the city's seal the other. Most people bartered and traded goods and services, but when you didn't have anything to offer, then osmiums worked fine.

Aphra moved to snatch them, but Shyla closed her fist. "Not so fast. This will pay for more information."

"Banqui was talking to the black-market dealers. He's never done that before." Aphra noticed her expression. "The man's too honest. Either that or he's too terrified of the Water Prince. Or..." She drummed her fingers on her thigh. "He's been bidding his time, collecting items over the sun jumps until he has enough to cover the cost of a trip to Catronia. In fact, the university there will pay large sums for ancient artifacts."

She doubted Banqui would risk upsetting the Water Prince. But there was that visiting professor. "Is this a rumor?"

Aphra crossed her arms and her jaw tightened. Then she huffed. "No. I've sold them a couple of sweets, but keep that to yourself. I don't want a bunch of hunters horning in on my lucrative market." She brightened. "I'd be happy to act as middleman if you discover a sweet or two you'd like to sell. Provided you live through the next couple of sun jumps."

Wonderful. "Thanks for your offer, but I've enough trouble right now."

"I'd say. But if you change your mind, let me know." She gave Shyla an appraising glance. "Unlike the others, I don't mind doing business with a sun-kissed."

Not sure how to reply to that comment—should she thank her?—Shyla remained quiet.

When they reached Fadey's rooms, she handed Aphra the osees. "Can you try to convince the rest of the hunters that I don't have The Eyes, but if they have any *legitimate* information about The Eyes, my client is willing to pay."

"I'll try and who knows? Maybe your request for info will help. Good luck." Aphra waved goodbye.

Shyla set her shoulders and drew in a breath. Then she knocked on the thick colored glass door—a sign of modest wealth despite the level.

One of Fadey's minions peered at her through a slit. "What do you want?"

Normally, she would have played the game. Instead, she flashed a couple of coins and they gained her an immediate invite inside. Shyla had to admit it was fun spending the Water Prince's money. Her meager pile of savings wouldn't have enticed anyone to talk to her. But it was hers and eventually, she'd have enough to leave.

The minion led her to a sitting room while he fetched his boss. Oversized cushions of various colors littered the floor. She settled on a red one. A hand-woven rug with a dune pattern covered most of the stone. Druk lanterns hung from the walls. On a low stone table sat a pitcher of water next to a teapot. And was that—lava stones! A luxury item. Put them together and they generated enough heat to boil water. Shyla suspected this room was Fadey's showcase—a place to impress visitors. He'd succeeded.

When she'd first arrived in Zirdai, Fadey had sought her out. He'd guessed she'd spent time walking the sands with the monks and might know the location of some hidden temples. She'd helped him find a few sweets, but had insisted that her help would be temporary. He'd scoffed at her desire to be a legitimate researcher, but, in the end, he'd put in a good word for her to Banqui.

After a few angles, Fadey arrived with two of his minions. They circled around to the back of the room, taking up positions on either side of the table. Did Fadey think she'd steal his treasures?

But Fadey spread his arms as wide as his smile, greeting her. "Shyla, this is an unexpected surprise."

She stood and endured the embrace. At one hundred and eighty centimeters he was about ten centimeters taller than she was, and his long curly black beard tickled her neck. "Thanks for seeing me on such short notice."

He stepped back and laughed. "Well, you showed the magic key." Snapping his fingers at his minions, he ordered them to make tea. Fadey gestured to the cushions. "Sit, sit. Tell me what brings you here."

By the glint in his golden eyes, Shyla guessed he already knew. "The Eyes."

"What? No small talk?" He rubbed a hand over his short curly hair. It sprang right back into place. "Do you even know how this is supposed to work?"

"You're assuming I have The Eyes and wish to sell them to you. I don't have them. I've come to purchase information about their whereabouts."

He tugged on his beard, which, when straightened, reached his portly stomach. Combine that with the opulence in the room, it meant he probably hired others to dig for his treasures.

"That is unfortunate," he finally said. "But if you don't have them, then, for a price, I can tell you who must."

"It's not Banqui either."

"Nonsense. He disappeared."

"He's a guest of the Water Prince."

"Oh." Fadey gripped the bottom of his tunic. "How unfortunate."

The minions handed them each a cup of tea. Shyla sipped hers—it had an earthy paprika flavor.

Fadey downed his in two gulps. "I'm afraid The Eyes must be gone. The thief cannot be in Zirdai, my hunters would have heard something."

Not good. "Are you sure? They were stolen only a couple sun jumps ago."

"Yes. It's just too big a find to keep quiet."

She mulled it over. If the thief was gone, then perhaps someone else had been reported missing. "Are all your hunters accounted for?"

"Ah. Yes, but there are other groups besides mine."

"How many?"

He laughed. "More than I'd like." Leaning forward, he peered at her. "I can have my people ask around. For—"

"A price?"

"You catch on quick."

The monks had said the same thing about her. No. Not thinking about them. "Do we haggle now or is it time for small talk?"

He spread his hands. "I'm a reasonable man. How about if you work exclusively for me?"

Now it was her turn to laugh. "That's reasonable?"

"You know I can keep you employed. Face it, you haven't had many jobs since you turned legitimate. You'll make enough to move down to a safer level. And I can protect you."

Was that genuine concern? She doubted it. "I have clients."

"Banqui was your biggest patron. Without him…"

"He's not dead."

"Yet."

"I'm not going to work exclusively for you. How about four osees? Two now and two if you find any information."

"That's an insult!"

Almost. Shyla suppressed a sigh. This negotiation was going to use up many angles to complete and she needed to find that hidden tunnel for the historian or she just might have to work for Fadey.

In the end, he was way too pleased with the outcome. At least they weren't her coins. She hurried from his rooms and raced up to level three, ascending into the dry heat. She checked the public sun clock. Angle fifty—just enough time. She reached her room and skidded to a stop. A crack zigzagged through her door as if someone had forced it open.

CHAPTER 4

Fear pulsed along her spine as Shyla crept to the door. The crack hadn't gone all the way through the cheap translucent glass, but the lock was broken. Due to the mirror pipe in her ceiling, it was brighter inside than out in the corridor. She watched for any moving shadows on the other side. After a couple angles, nothing moved. Still didn't mean someone wasn't crouched by the entrance waiting to pounce on her.

Should she fetch one of the guards? Or she could set up her own ambush. The killing heat would eventually drive an intruder to the lower levels. There were perks of living so high. But it irked her to waste the sunlight.

Making a bold—stupid?—decision, Shyla took off her wrap, slid the door wide and set her feet into a fighting stance. Her heart tapped a fast rhythm, but nothing else happened. Poking her head in, she scanned the interior. Empty of attackers—the good news. The place had been wrecked—the bad.

Stuffing from her slashed cushions coated the floor. The water jug, mirrors, and shelves lay in pieces. Sand spilled from her clock. Her ripped clothes were strewn about. Her sleeping fur slashed to ribbons. Shyla picked through her ruined possessions in a numb daze, wondering who had caused this mess while obviously searching for The Eyes. As if she would hide them here if she had them. In fact, this room did not contain any of her meager valuables. Not trusting her neighbors—or anyone in Zirdai for that matter—had proven to be a smart move.

Nausea churned in her stomach as she swept debris aside and dug through the drifts of stuffing. Her legs trembled with relief when she found the map of the Gorgain crypt intact.

Shyla righted her table and smoothed the crinkled chart over its surface. The heat increased as the light brightened. No need for a clock at this point. With roughly twenty angles left before the sun hit the danger zone, she needed to move fast. Finding the pieces of mirror, Shyla arranged them to redirect the rays emanating from the mirror pipe to the table's top. With uneven sharp edges and many small shards to position, it took her ten precious angles to finish the job. By then, sweat soaked her tunic and the skin underneath the Water

Prince's sigil itched, reminding her of her *other* client. She shoved that thought down.

Ensuring her shadow was behind her, she peered at the map. She found the tunnel the grave diggers used to escape the crypt. Tracing it to its origin, Shyla pin-pointed Gorgain's final resting place. Yes! She circled the tiny spot with a piece of broken—of course—chalk. Hopefully this would make Utina, her client, happy.

A blast of hot dry air pressed against her skin in warning. Shyla rolled the chart, grabbed her pack, picked up her wrap, and retreated to the lower levels. Typically, she remained in the safe levels from angle seventy to angle one-ten—ten angles before and after the danger zone which was from angle eighty to angle one-hundred. As she tucked her hair under her wrap, Shyla debated her next move.

Utina, a historian, worked on level forty-three, but, by the time she reached her, Utina might be at second meal, which was served from angle ninety to angle one-twenty. The historian's dining cavern was on level forty-nine, providing food to the residents on levels forty through forty-nine. The best thing to do was to wait until after second meal. Her stomach rumbled in agreement.

Meals were not her favorite time of a sun jump. Too many people. Most ignored her or pretended she didn't exist by staring right through her. At least the workers tended to be…well, not nicer, but they tolerated her more. They filled her plate and she could always fill her water skin when needed.

And then there were the deacons at the entrance to her dining cavern on level nine. They scowled at her when she stated her name, which started a charade on their part. One they insisted on doing three times a sun jump.

"Are you sure you paid your tithe?" the deacon-on-the-left asked.

This too, was part of the song and dance. "Yes. Please check again."

A dozen heartbeats later. "Oh, lookie. Here it is." A fake smile from deacon-on-the-right. "Huh, didn't think a sun-kissed could afford to pay. How long do you think she'll last before Zirdai rejects her again?" he asked his partner.

"I'd give it another three, four sun jumps, tops."

Same question. Same answer.

They checked her name off and she entered the large dining cavern. The space extended over two levels. Colorful tile mosaics decorated the sweeping expanse between the floor and ceiling. Druk lanterns hung every couple of meters and sat on tables, but the yellow glow couldn't banish all the shadows that lurked at the edges and obscured the roof. The spicy scent of roasted gamelu meat teased her nose. Her stomach snarled in response.

As she waited in line, she glanced at the various family groups who already occupied half the tables. The children squealed and ran around as their parents made weak attempts to get them to sit and eat. The little girls had their long brown hair in braids while the boys kept theirs short. Most had dark skin and sand dust covered most of them as well. The reason became obvious when two boys wrestled on the ground, kicking up a thin cloud.

In the roughly two circuits since she'd left the monastery, she hadn't encountered another sun-kissed. Growing up, she imagined that a few parents had refused to sacrifice their babies to the Sun Goddess. That there had to be a couple sun-kissed living happy lives with loving families in Zirdai. But the monks had warned her. The sun-kissed they rescued all took the oath, having no desire to return to a place that had rejected them. But she guessed she really hadn't believed it. It was one thing to be told something and quite another to experience it for herself.

With a plate full of gamelu meat and potatoes in one hand and a glass of water in the other, Shyla navigated around the tables, avoided the cats seeking dropped food, and found an empty table tucked into a dark corner. Thirsty, she gulped the tepid water and almost spat it out. It tasted like dirt and left a gritty residue on her teeth and tongue. She had never minded it before, but now that she had sampled the Water Prince's clean cold water, she noticed the significant difference. She sighed.

After she finished eating, Shyla took out a small piece of velbloud skin, her bottle of ink and a stylus. While she didn't believe Banqui about the so-called Invisible Sword, she didn't want to forget what the symbol looked like. Someone had carved that into the ledge so it must be important. See, she wasn't being selfish, she was working on *both* her jobs. She sketched the sigil onto the skin. It resembled two swords crossed about a quarter way down from the tips. Where the metal guards above the hilt would be, there was a curved line that swooped through both swords, bowing away from the top. Another curved line arced between the two swords, bowing opposite the bottom one.

When the ink dried, she put the skin into her pack along with her supplies. Then she walked through level nine to the outer edges of the city, where tunnels suddenly ended, druk lanterns were few and far between, and there was no guarantee that the steps or ramp or ladder you encountered would actually go anywhere. But it had its charms. The quirks and twists made navigation a challenge. One that appealed to her since she loved maps. And the others who frequented these unpopular routes tended to mind their own business. Those who couldn't afford the taxes tended to keep to the edges, acquiring their food and water from other…vendors.

Instead of taking a druk, she stood in the semi-darkness, letting her eyes adjust. Carrying a lantern limited her sight distance to that small bubble of light.

While the chance of an attack remained low, it never hurt to be prepared.

Once ready, she set off. Familiar with the route, she kept a quick pace for the first twelve levels, but then slowed when she reached unfamiliar levels. She'd been drawing her own maps of Zirdai one level at a time. The sheets of velbloud skins were tucked safely away with her valuable possessions along with a basic overall map of Zirdai that she'd purchased when she first arrived. Not that they were doing her any good at this point.

However, according to the Monks of Parzival, she'd been blessed with a good memory. After a few wrong turns and a couple dead ends, she attained level twenty-five. On level twenty-six, she stumbled into a ventilation tunnel.

The dry warm air pressed on her back and she fought to stay on her feet. Her pant legs flapped. She clutched her wrap to keep it from flying off. The strong gingery anise scent of the desert mixed with cooking smells and a variety of sour odors. This must be one of the main air conduits. Coughing, she quickly exited the tunnel.

Shyla admitted defeat at level thirty and abandoned the edges for a more popular route. She readjusted her wrap, ensuring the material covered her hair and cast a shadow over her face. By the time she reached level forty-three, it was angle one-thirty-five. At this depth, the druk lanterns glowed with a greenish tint. Utina shouldn't be at second meal, and Shyla hoped the historian wasn't teaching a class.

The Zirdai University was considered the smallest university of Koraha. Shyla found it hard to believe when the maze of its lecture rooms, offices, and dormitories was five levels deep and two kilometers wide. She'd only been to Utina's office once when Banqui introduced them.

A nervous twinge of guilt flared in her chest. This had nothing to do with finding The Eyes and freeing Banqui. But it had everything to do with her future. Unless she failed to find them and no longer had a future. No. Not going to think bad thoughts. She would focus all her efforts on recovering The Eyes as soon as she delivered the Gorgain crypt map to Utina.

Shyla waited until a group of students passed her before she pulled her wrap back to expose more of her face. Then she knocked on Utina's half-opened door. The bright white light of a trol lantern spilled into the hallway.

"Come in," Utina called.

Pushing the door wider, she paused. A man sat in front of Utina's desk. Both he and Utina stared at her in shock.

"Am I interrupting something?" Shyla asked.

The man jumped to his feet. "No. No, we…uh… were just finishing." He exchanged a glance with Utina before bolting from the room.

Utina pointed at the empty cushion. "Have a seat." Her hard voice matched her stony expression. And her black hair had been pulled into a severe bun.

"I'm sorry I missed our meeting." Shyla perched on the edge. Touching the bandage on her temple, she said, "I fell and—"

"Save your excuses," Utina said. "I didn't want to hire you. But Banqui insisted I give you a chance."

This wasn't going as she expected. "I found the location of Gorgain's crypt." Shyla took the map from her pack and spread it over Utina's desk, tapping a finger on the spot she'd circled. "And I discovered a tunnel that the grave diggers used. You can reach the crypt without going through the main building, avoiding any traps."

Instead of looking happy, Utina crossed her arms. "Am I supposed to believe that Gorgain's diamond and gold crown and ruby torque are still buried with him?"

Shyla said slowly, "They should be."

"Oh, so you'll wait until I dig them up and then steal them from me?"

Ah, scorching hells.

Utina leaned forward. "And then what? You'll kill me and I'll disappear? Like you did to Banqui."

Son of a sand demon. "I didn't—"

The man returned with four guards right behind him. "That's her! The sun-kissed who stole The Eyes and killed the Water Prince's archeologist."

As the guards rushed her, Shyla held up her hands. The sleeves of her tunic fell down, revealing the sigil. All four halted a meter from her.

Puzzled, the lead guard grabbed her arm to inspect the bracelet. He grunted. "It's legit."

"Don't be an idiot," Utina snapped. "She must have stolen it."

"Impossible," the lead guard said without hesitation. "Do you need any assistance?" he asked Shyla in a respectful tone.

Her emotions flipped from outrage about being falsely accused of murder and theft to amusement over the sudden change in the guards' demeanors.

"Yes. Please escort this man from the room and ensure we are not disturbed."

They did as requested. Shyla had to clasp her hands together to keep from dancing around with glee. Instead, she turned to Utina. The woman gaped at her. Pulling the map from Utina's desk, she rolled it and tucked it back into her pack.

"I'm sorry, but I was unable to find the location of Gorgain's crypt." Shyla dug five coins from her pouch and tossed them onto the desk. They clattered. "Here's your refund."

"Wait," Utina said as Shyla turned to leave. "You can't sell that map to the treasure hunters. Those artifacts are historically significant and belong to Zirdai's people."

"If I *had* such a map, then I would give it to an honorable person. One who doesn't jump to conclusions and doesn't judge another based on the color of her hair. Someone like Banqui. Who is very much alive." Shyla left.

Anger fueled her steps. Well away from Utina's office, alarm grew when she realized that a steady crunching of boots had been right behind her for a while. Two people.

Ready to attack, she rounded on them and stopped. A pair of the guards had followed her. "What do you want?" she demanded.

"To see if you need anything else," the man said.

Oh. Shyla considered as she calmed down. It was obvious that Utina knew nothing about the location of The Eyes. Which meant the same could be said for Shyla's other legitimate clients—they tended to congregate and share knowledge and gossip. Shyla could ask them about the so-called Invisible Sword, but was hoping her reputation hadn't been completely destroyed. Asking about a secret organization would probably ruin any credibility she had left. No. She'd research on her own. Good thing she was already in the university.

"Yes, I do," she said to the waiting guard. "Can you accompany me while I visit the library?"

The man gestured to her defensive stance. "Are you worried about being attacked?"

She relaxed her posture. "No. About being accused of—"

"Being a murdering thief?" he asked. His dark features remained neutral.

They paid attention. "Yes."

"And how do we know you're not?" his partner asked as she rested her hand on the hilt of her sword.

"Shouldn't that be clear?" Shyla waved her left arm.

When they didn't answer, she added, "Because the Water Prince gave me his sigil."

He laughed. "That's not an affirmation of your good character. In fact, we wouldn't be surprised if you were indeed a murdering thief who is now working for the Water Prince."

Interesting and scary at the very same time. "Then you'll just have to trust me. Or not. You can return to wherever you've been assigned. Just don't get mad at me when you're called to arrest me again."

"While that would be the highlight of our sun jump, we'd rather just stick with you." He shrugged. "Who knows, we might see some murdering thieving in action." Humor glinted in his light brown eyes and it accented his high cheekbones and straight nose.

"No promises," she said.

Another laugh. "I'm Nuru, this is my partner, Vallie."

The woman nodded.

"Shyla. Thanks for the help." And for not treating her like she had a disease. Except, that was probably due to the Water Prince's sigil. Shyla needed to remember that. As soon as she found The Eyes and freed Banqui, everything would go back to normal.

The library's entrance was located on level forty-two, but it spanned all five levels of the university. Shyla had spent quite a bit of time there, researching for her various clients. While the monks had granted her access to the First Room, she hadn't had to use it. Yet. Dread always filled her when she thought about returning to the monastery.

Ennic, the head librarian, barely tolerated Shyla's presence in *his* library, but he had no recourse to outright ban her, so he settled for scorn, snide comments, and nasty glances. However, when he spotted the two guards following her, his expression turned from disapproval to almost glee.

"Finally," he huffed. "She should have been arrested circuits ago. How can I help you officers? Do you need me to vouch for her *character*? There's been a few thefts we can pin on her."

Wow. Shyla stared at Ennic. She'd known he disliked her, but to… Wow.

Nuru and Vallie gave Ennic a long silent stare. The librarian fidgeted under the scrutiny. When it was well past awkward, Nuru said, "You can assist this woman in finding the information she needs."

Ennic started to protest, but clamped his lips together when both guards gave him the just-try-it countenance.

Instead he turned to Shyla and asked in a somewhat civil tone, "What are you looking for?"

She showed him the Invisible Sword symbol. "Do you recognize this?"

He studied the rough drawing for a while. "No, but there's thousands of symbols used throughout our history." Ennic tapped a long finger on his chin. "It reminds me of the style of writing during the reign of Wequain the Horrible. The tablets and scrolls about him are located near the ones on Tamburah on level forty-four. I believe he ruled about three hundred circuits before him."

That was surprisingly helpful. Shyla thanked Ennic, who frowned in response. Then she descended to level forty-four and spent the next thirty angles learning that there was a person in their history who was more evil than Tamburah. No symbol, though, and because the symbol looked familiar, she reviewed all the information on Tamburah again just in case she'd missed it.

No luck. Also nothing when she searched for the symbol on tablets and scrolls that were created during that same time period. Would she have to go through all the documents in the library dated between Wequain and Tamburah? No. That symbol had to be related to Tamburah in some way. She read through the historical accounts on the next ruler—Queen Malin. It made sense that if the Invisible Sword helped overthrow

Tamburah, the next person would be very grateful and supportive. Nothing.

During all that time, the guards remained with her so no one accused her of anything. Best of all, everyone left her alone. However, Nuru and Vallie didn't witness any action—unless you called growling in frustration entertaining. When she finished, she thanked them and headed back to her room.

By the time she trudged up the thirty-nine levels, the sun neared angle one-eighty. Cool air breezed through the corridors, sweeping the heat away. Once the sun finished its jump, there would be a hundred and eighty angles of darkness while the sun jumped around the other side of their desert world. During that time, the temperatures on the surface would drop well past zero degrees and the three upper levels would hover at zero.

Her fur kept her quite warm at night. Too bad it had been turned to rags. She sorted through the wreckage, picking up a few needed items that hadn't been broken and putting them into her pack. Until the lock on her door was fixed, her cushions restuffed, and she purchased a new fur, she couldn't sleep in her room. Instead, she headed toward the dining cavern for third meal.

The deacons started their routine—did they really think their censure would make her leave Zirdai when it hadn't worked in over two circuits? She waited.

"...I wonder how a sun-kissed could afford to pay the tithe. Perhaps we should—"

The deacons clamped their mouths shut as their gazes slid past her shoulder.

Shyla shifted to the side. Rendor loomed behind her. Scorching sands, the big man hadn't made any noise.

"Are they giving you a hard time?" Rendor asked her. Her sun cloak was draped over his arm.

All color leaked from the deacons' faces. While they didn't report to the captain of the guards, Rendor was one scary man with his own reputation.

"Uh, no. They're just double-checking the list," she said. No sense giving them another reason to hate her.

He grunted. "Has this woman ever not paid her tithe?" he asked deacon-on-the-right.

She'd gone from *sun-kissed* to *this woman*. Not sure if that was an improvement or not.

"No, sir."

"Then perhaps you can find her name the first time. Or is that too difficult a task for you?"

"No, sir. Not too difficult at all, sir," deacon-on-the-left said in a rush.

"Good." He turned his full attention on Shyla. "Walk with me?"

It sounded more like an order than a request. "All right."

Rendor strode down the main corridor until they reached another tunnel. This one wasn't as bright or as crowded. He kept going until they were alone. Then he rounded on her. "Who tossed your room?"

It took her a moment to understand the question. "I don't know."

"Any guesses?"

"Treasure hunters and thieves probably looking for The Eyes."

His scowl rivaled the searing heat from the sun. "That's not helpful."

"Why does it matter? The Eyes were never there. They didn't take anything. Hells, it could have been someone who wants to drive the evil sun-kissed back to the desert."

She didn't think it possible, but his expression darkened further. Which confused her because he'd made his feelings about her quite clear. "Why would that upset you? You said so yourself that—"

"Here." Rendor thrust her cloak into her hands. "It's been cleaned and repaired. Any progress on finding The Eyes?"

"None so far."

"Any leads?"

"Not yet."

He drew in a deep breath. She braced for a lecture or a threat. Most likely she'd get both.

"Time is critical. The longer they're gone the harder they will be to find."

"I understand."

He stared at her as if he was reading her very soul. There were flecks of gold in his umber-colored eyes. A strange, uncomfortable heat flowed through her. It had been a long time since anyone had peered at her as a person and not as a sun-kissed.

"Let me know if you need anything," he said.

"Will do."

Nodding, he walked away. She leaned on the wall. The hard stone reassured her that her world hadn't just flipped upside down. Folding her cloak into a small bundle, she tucked it into her pack.

Shyla returned to the dining cavern. After she ate, she considered her next move. First she needed a place to sleep. There were rooms available for short-term leases—mostly for visitors, but they were down in the thirties. Too far. Her legs ached from her trip to level forty-three and back. And the cut on her temple throbbed, making it difficult for her to think straight.

If she had friends—Banqui! She could sleep in his rooms on level thirteen. Considering that getting enough sleep would help her think clearer, she figured he wouldn't mind.

Four levels didn't seem far until she started walking. Then her legs turned to stone, dragging on the rest of her body. Each step an effort. Dozens of angles passed before she arrived. Well...probably not dozens.

She was so focused on the door to Banqui's rooms, she failed to notice the four people waiting in the shadows until they stepped into the weak druk light. Instantly on guard, Shyla brought her hands up to protect her face. But the four didn't move closer. They waited with their hands tucked into the sleeves of their green robes. Hoods drawn over their heads kept their faces in shadow.

Deacons. She cursed under her breath and relaxed. "If you're looking for Banqui, he's a guest of the Water Prince."

"The Heliacal Priestess would like to speak with you, Shyla Sun-kissed," the deacon on the right said with a man's voice.

Bad news for so many reasons. The fact that the Heliacal Priestess knew she existed was the biggest concern. "When?"

"Now."

"But it's—"

"Now."

No one refused the Heliacal Priestess. And she wasn't going to be the first, so Shyla agreed to go with them. Two led while the others followed behind her. As they descended through the levels, the ache in her legs turned into sharp shooting pains. Her calves stung. At one point in the thirties, she asked about a lift. No response. By level sixty, her hip bones and lower back burned. Shyla imagined by the time they reached the Heliacal Priestess on level ninety-six, her legs would be worn down to nubs. Soon the trip turned into an endless blur of misery.

Drier air was the first indication that they'd passed level eighty. Trol lanterns replaced the indigo light from the druks. Rugs covered the wider corridors. Stained glass doors and mosaic tiles decorated the throughways. All evidence of the very wealthy residents who lived here. Extra guards also patrolled the wide tunnels. The soldiers studied them, but didn't question the deacons. The two factions avoided interacting if possible. Each had its own demesne. The prince provided water to the priestess and her holy army, while she supplied him and his guards with food. It was an almost perfect balance of power. Water was more vital, but eventually people needed to eat. There had been coups in other cities of Koraha, and, as long as it had been quick, the king had allowed it, but when it expanded into all-out war, he'd arrived with his battalions to stop it.

Deacons guarded the entrance to level ninety-six. It appeared that the Heliacal Priestess occupied the entire level—one level above the Water Prince's. Shyla wondered if that annoyed the woman as much as the fact that the Water Prince refused to attend worship services.

Shyla was led into an austere waiting room. The lack of wealth seemed to be calculated rather than a personal preference. She doubted the rest of the rooms were so plain. Deacons stood to either side of the door both inside and out—a clear signal of the nature of this visit.

Hobbling over to one of the cushions, she sank into it with a grateful groan. As she rubbed her legs, Shyla avoided thinking about the return trip—or the possibility there wouldn't be one. Rumors of the Heliacal Priestess's temper and stories of those who failed to be properly pious spun through the city like sand devils. While she didn't believe these anecdotes, she knew they all had a root of truth. The trick was finding that one true tendril among all the others. Normally, that would be an interesting challenge, but Shyla was far from her normal life at this point.

Without a sand clock, she lost track of time. Despite her nerves, the silence and warm dry air lulled Shyla into a light doze. When the Heliacal Priestess appeared, Shyla snapped awake. The woman wore a green robe styled similarly to the deacons'. While theirs were plain and woven from gamelu wool, hers was silk. The material pooled around her bare feet and orbs had been embroidered into the fabric with a bright gold thread. Bald and beautiful, with dark sapphire-colored eyes and angular features, her skin was almost black from all those angles she spent worshipping the Sun Goddess every sun jump. She wore only a single piece of jewelry, a platinum torque that ringed her neck.

The woman scowled as Shyla continued to stare. Finally remembering her manners, Shyla struggled to her feet. Her leg and back muscles screamed in protest, but she managed to stand. No need to anger the most powerful woman in Zirdai. She bowed in respect and waited.

"As you were," the Heliacal Priestess said with such a smooth melodious voice that Shyla wondered if the woman sang.

Shyla straightened and met her gaze. Censure and derision greeted her. Not good.

"Where are The Eyes?" she demanded.

So much for small talk. At least the prince had eased into the accusation. "I don't know."

"You're lying." She gestured to her deacons. "Take her to the well of sinners and drown her."

CHAPTER

5

Drown? Whatever that was, it didn't sound good. The Heliacal Priestess's deacons rushed her, grabbing her arms. Shyla clamped down on her instincts to break their hold—that would be the action of the guilty. Instead, she pulled her left arm forward enough to expose the Water Prince's sigil. However it didn't have the desired effect. The deacons failed to let go of her.

The Heliacal Priestess stared at the bracelet. "I see you managed to fool that young whelp. Not that it's hard to do." She crossed her arms. "Still, I can't risk upsetting him." Gesturing to the deacons, she said, "Release her. Pela, fetch our guest a glass of holy water."

The deacons obeyed and one—Pela presumably—left the room. Shyla smoothed her sleeves.

Settling on a cushion, the Heliacal Priestess pointed to the one across from her. "Have a seat…Shyla, is it?"

"Yes." Interesting that she didn't call her sun-kissed.

"What has the Water Prince offered you in exchange for The Eyes?"

The woman was certainly direct. "I don't have them."

She waved away Shyla's protest. "He must believe you can locate them. You're working with Banqui, you must know where they are. Did the prince offer you riches? Power?" She leaned closer. "Or did he seduce you?"

"No!"

The Heliacal Priestess settled back with a smirk. "He is handsome and charming when he wants something."

Shyla remained quiet. There was no way to win this conversation. At this point, all she wanted to do was survive it.

Pela returned. She held a silver tray laden with two glasses of water and slices of melon. Setting it down between them, Pela returned to standing by the door.

She handed Shyla a glass and took the other. "Help yourself, the fruit is fresh."

As she picked up a slice, Shyla marveled over the fact that she had eaten first meal with the Water Prince and was now having a refreshment with the Heliacal Priestess. Surreal. She bit into the melon. Its sweet juice filled her mouth and she almost moaned out loud. Instead, she finished it and then downed the cool clean water. The liquid held a hint of a citrus taste. If she had The

Eyes, she might be tempted to exchange them for an endless supply of this water.

A heavy languidness flowed through Shyla's limbs. The room swayed and everything softened. Her fear lifted as calm washed through her.

The Heliacal Priestess set her still full glass on the tray. "Where are The Eyes?"

"I don't know."

The woman turned to Pela. "Did you bring the holy water?"

"Yes, Blessed One."

"Shyla, why did the Water Prince give you his sigil?"

"To help me find The Eyes." The words poured from her lips. Unstoppable.

"Can you find them?"

"I have to try. I have to."

"That's not what I asked."

"No. Probably not. They're gone, gone, gone." Alarmed Shyla clamped a hand over her mouth.

"There's no use fighting the holy water," she said. "If you did find The Eyes, what do you plan to do with them?"

"Give them to the Water Prince in exchange for Banqui's life."

"Ah." The woman considered. "What if I told you I can save Banqui?"

Shyla straightened. The walls spun. "Then I would be very happy."

"Happy enough to give me The Eyes instead?"

"Of course. I will exchange them for Banqui—whoever has him. But the Water Prince would be mad and send Rendor after me." She slumped deep into the cushion, wishing she'd never heard of Tamburah and his troublesome eyes.

"Once I have The Eyes, there will be no need to fear the Water Prince and I will have the power to save Banqui."

Shaking her head, Shyla said, "The Eyes of Tamburah don't have magical powers."

"Why do you believe that?"

"I've found no evidence that magic exists or ever existed."

"And where did you look for this evidence?"

"The First Room of Knowledge." Even though she knew this was a sensitive subject, Shyla just couldn't stop talking.

The woman tucked her hands into the sleeves of her robe as the muscles on her neck tightened. "The monks let a sun-cursed whelp like you into the Rooms of Knowledge?"

"Only the first one." Then a beat later. "Sun-cursed?"

"When you were born, you were marked as a sacrifice to the Sun Goddess."

This wasn't new.

"You were kissed by the Sun Goddess while you were in your mother's womb. Babies born with yellow hair are left on the sand to be returned to her divine arms. It's an honor. But I'm not surprised the monks failed to explain how much of an honor it is. By saving you, they went against the direct wishes of the Sun Goddess, making you sun-cursed for the rest of your unnatural life."

An honor? This woman had spent too much time in the sun—it had fried her brain. Anger struggled against the calming effects of the holy water.

The Heliacal Priestess misinterpreted her concern. "You can redeem your soul by sacrificing yourself to the Sun Goddess. Once you find The Eyes, I can perform the ceremony myself. A high accolade."

Conflicting emotions swirled in Shyla's chest. Her confidence over Shyla's ability to locate The Eyes warred with the fear that the woman would force her to commit suicide…or would that be considered murder? Did it matter? No one would dare arrest the Heliacal Priestess.

She pulled in her scattered thoughts. "Why does everyone call me sun-kissed, then?"

"Not many citizens realize the monks are stealing the babies. Most figure you were either hidden by selfish parents or you came from another city that is ruled by a lazy priestess or lax priest who does not enforce the Sun Goddess's wishes as they should. Calling you sun-kissed is reminding you of your duty to the Sun Goddess."

That actually made sense to Shyla's drug-addled brain.

"I've prayed to the Sun Goddess about you, asking her if I should allow you to live in Zirdai or cast you out once again. However, you've been keeping a low profile, paying your tithe, and attending services since you arrived, and I took that as a sign from the Sun Goddess to leave you in peace." The Heliacal Priestess touched Shyla's hair, letting the yellow strands slip through her fingers. "Seems she has a plan for you after all."

Shyla shuddered.

"Have you told anyone that the monks rescued you?" she asked. "It's not common knowledge."

"Only Banqui."

For the first time since she entered the room, the woman's expression softened. "You care for him, don't you?"

"He's my friend."

"Then I will free him first when I have woken the power of The Eyes." She stood in one smooth motion. "Bring me The Eyes, Shyla Sun-kissed. If you fail, you'll be returned to the Sun Goddess, and I will *ensure* that no more sun-kissed babies are rescued by the monks."

Shyla stared at her, dumbfounded.

The priestess turned to her deacons. "Escort her to the exit." Then she left.

Shyla wished she could be that graceful. When she tried to stand, her aching legs buckled under her and she flopped back on the cushion with a whomp. It didn't help that the room still swayed.

The deacons hooked their arms under hers and heaved her to her feet. They half-supported and half-carried her back to the stairs they had descended many many angles ago. They dumped her at the base. She crumpled in a heap.

"Start climbing, Sun-kissed," Pela said. "You don't want to be here when the Blessed One makes her pilgrimage to the surface at angle zero."

Their laughter echoed off the stone walls as they returned to their mistress. With her legs, back, and hips on fire, Shyla had no strength to climb one level let alone…eighty-something. Her fuzzy thoughts couldn't do the math. Plus the spikes of pain in her temple matched tempo with her pulsing blurry vision.

Unable to go up, Shyla decided to go down instead. Well, not all the way to level ninety-seven, but to the first landing. There she wouldn't be spotted by the deacons and, if the Water Prince's guards bothered her, she'd flash the sigil and tell them to get lost.

At least that was the plan. Half sliding and half crawling, she reached the landing, removed her sun cloak and used it as a pillow. Her muscles objected to the hard surface, but it didn't take long before she passed out.

Voices woke her…later. Someone nudged her shoulder. Shyla waved the sigil and ordered them away. All was blessedly quiet. She drifted back to sleep. Her peace didn't last. Another voice—this one familiar—insisted on her attention. She opened her eyes.

Rendor peered at her in concern. "What happened?"

"Holy water and too many levels."

He scowled and muttered a curse. "Can you stand?"

"Can't you just leave me here?"

"No."

"But I have the Water Prince's sigil."

"That doesn't work on me."

Now she uttered a curse. Gathering her energy, Shyla pushed up to her elbows, but the lower half of her body refused to cooperate. "Then the answer is no, I can't stand."

Rendor crouched beside her and then scooped her up as if she weighed nothing. She squawked in protest, but the big man straightened, and carried her the rest of the way down to level ninety-seven. Nearby was the main entrance into the prince's domain. The six guards immediately parted and opened the double doors for him. Then he traversed a number of tunnels, passing other guards, servants, and officials. They kept their gazes focused straight ahead, but Shyla suspected they found this all very amusing. At least this time she was conscious.

He took her to the same room she'd woken in—only a sun jump ago!—and laid her on the sleeping cushion.

"Rest, I will fetch Timin."

"But—"

And he was gone. How could a big man like that move so fast and quiet? She sighed. Nothing she could do, so she squirmed into a comfortable position. Instead of lulling her back to sleep, the musical splash of the fountain made her aware of the bad taste in her very dry mouth.

As she debated her ability to drag her body over to the water, the door opened and Timin appeared. He brought his supplies and a surprise. The Water Prince strode in right after him. Her heart kicked hard. Seeing him again was not part of the plan.

The prince's black hair was sleep tousled and he wore a thin black short-sleeved shirt that clung to his muscles and a pair of loose gray pants. His feet were bare.

"Where does it hurt?" Timin asked her, drawing her attention away from the prince.

She explained about her muscles and throbbing temple. Timin mixed a powder into a glass of water, turning it light orange. He handed it to her. Although she was thirsty, she hesitated.

"It will help with the pain. Go on, drink it."

Might as well. After all, what else could happen? The cool liquid tasted divine.

"It will also help clear your head," Timin said. "But it may take a while for all the effects of the Heliacal Priestess's drug to wear off."

"She called it holy water," Shyla said.

The prince huffed. "There's nothing holy about it."

Timin straightened and turned to the prince. "She should rest."

"And she will *after* I talk to her."

"Yes, sire." Timin gave a small bow and hurried from the room.

The air filled with an awkward tension as the Water Prince studied her.

"If you wanted to see me again, you only needed to let one of my guards know," he said with a teasing grin. "Camping out near my door in hopes of catching a glimpse of me is sweet, but unnecessary."

"Let's just say I was knocked out by your charming personality."

"Ohhh, good one." He dragged another cushion close to hers and sat down. The humorous glint in his eyes died. "At least you've confirmed the Heliacal Priestess does not have The Eyes."

Confused, she said, "I thought we knew that before."

"We guessed. However, if she had The Eyes, then the smart thing for her to do would be to wait, pretending she didn't have them so she could spend that time planning her takeover of Zirdai. Then she would strike with a surprise attack."

And Shyla thought her head hurt before.

"But now we know she is desperate to get them. What did she promise you in exchange?"

The effects of the holy water no longer controlled her tongue. She debated what to tell him. "She offered to absolve me of my sins so I may have a blessed afterlife."

"In other words, forced suicide. Nice of her. You didn't believe her...did you?" His hopeful tone sounded almost too...practiced.

"I am sun-cursed."

"That's ridiculous." Unable to sit still, the prince stood. He paced. "It's an ancient prejudice over people born with yellow hair and has nothing to do with a so-called Sun Goddess. It's barbaric and something I've been wanting to stop in *my* city. Except the Heliacal Priestess—" he spat her name out "—encourages such thoughts and sacrifices. She rewards the pious for murdering their own children."

Shyla shrank back, glad that his fury was not directed at her.

"I don't have enough power to stop her. Not yet." He stared at Shyla. "If I had The Eyes, then that would be the first thing I'd change."

"Why can't you stop them now?" she asked.

"I've tried." Sighing, he settled back on the cushion. "But the parents contact the deacons right away. They take the baby to the surface, leaving the child exposed to the sun. My people never hear about it in time—it's always too late."

"The monks—"

"Will rescue some babies, but many die before they can be found." He swept a tendril of her hair from her face. "That's why I called you a survivor. You fought for your life."

She considered his words and remembered the priestess's threat. "Why does the Heliacal Priestess allow the monks to rescue the sun-kissed?"

"She doesn't. In fact, she hates that they do, but she can't stop them. Her deacons are no match for the monks and I refuse to help her. But I guarantee that if she gets Tamburah's Eyes, one of her first acts will be to overpower the monks. That would give her access to the Rooms of Knowledge, and she will sacrifice all the sun-kissed she finds living there."

While Shyla didn't believe The Eyes would tip the balance of power, she also couldn't risk her family getting hurt by the Heliacal Priestess. She told him about the woman's claim that she would free Banqui first.

He stilled. "You lied to me."

The Water Prince's warning tone sent fear skittering along her spine. "No," she rushed to explain. "She did offer to absolve me of my sins."

The muscles along his jaw tightened.

Suddenly exhausted, Shyla cradled her head in her hands. "Sorry. I don't know what to think anymore."

"What did you tell her about The Eyes?" he asked in a soft voice.

She lifted her head and met his gaze. "She assumed I would hand The Eyes to her so I didn't have to promise anything."

"Good. Have you made any progress?"

"I've discovered who doesn't have The Eyes."

"In other words, not much. What's next?"

"Would it be possible for me to talk to Banqui?" she asked, taking a risk. The prince had never offered proof that Banqui was his prisoner nor had she asked. The archeologist could be dead for all Shyla knew.

Once again he stilled. "Why do you need to talk to him?"

She chose her words with the utmost care. "I've some ideas, but I don't want to pursue them if Banqui already ruled them out."

"And you wish to ensure I do have him and he's alive."

That, too. She braced for his outburst.

"I was surprised you didn't make this request earlier," he said in a reasonable tone.

"Earlier I wouldn't have known what I needed to ask him." It was the truth.

"All right. I'll have Rendor escort you once you've rested."

"Thank you." She sank back into the cushion in relief. No doubt Rendor would be ordered to listen in on the conversation as well, but she could work around that.

He draped a light fur over her, turned down the lanterns, and left. Shyla marveled over the complex man. One angle he was a scary and powerful ruler, who held the city's life in his hands. And the next angle he was a teasing ordinary guy, who tucked her in and ensured she rested. If she believed Banqui, the prince would never be so nice, he'd force her to get to work, find The Eyes now and rest later if she was successful or be killed if she wasn't.

Banqui. While happy she would see him, she hoped he was well. To see him otherwise would confuse her more.

* * *

The scent of steaming noodles and sweet gamelu meat woke her. Timin carried a tray, but he wouldn't let her eat until he examined her. Although stiff and sore, her leg and back muscles no longer screamed in pain when she moved. Able to walk without too much difficulty, she demonstrated her range of motion for the physician. Once satisfied, he allowed her to eat.

"What time is it?" she asked between mouthfuls.

"Angle fifty-three."

Choking on her food, she almost spit it out.

"What did you expect?" Timin asked, but he didn't wait for an answer. "Healing takes time." Muttering under his breath, he left.

When she finished scraping every piece into her mouth, Rendor arrived. After using the water closet, she followed him through the corridors. Without the holy water blurring her vision and clouding her mind, she glanced around the level with the sharp clarity she used when reading a map. Expensive trol chandeliers hung at every major intersection. Rugs carpeted the entire floor. Large open caverns appeared almost at random and served no particular function other than to create a sense of openness. Tiles colored the walls and decorated the floors of these spaces and a few held statues of people—probably past rulers.

A rhythmic splashing echoed long before they entered one grand grotto. Shyla slowed. Rings of colored tile from the deepest purple to the brightest yellow surrounded a massive fountain, where a column of water as thick as Rendor shot into the air. The water hit a mesh of some sort high above and then cascaded down on all sides. The water disappeared into drains, but a fine mist coated everything, including the hard stone benches along the walls.

"This is the prince's favorite spot," Rendor said.

"I'm not surprised." She would have liked to linger, but Rendor continued through the cavern as if immune to such marvels.

Whenever they passed an open doorway, she stole a peek inside the rooms. Tile mosaics and sand paintings adorned the walls. Marble tables and cushioned seats were arranged in a pleasing manner.

The expanse of grottos and rooms eventually ended and they entered an area that was similar to the upper levels. Druk lanterns shone with a violet tint on the plain stone walls and floor.

Rendor noticed her expression. "This is where the prince's guards are housed. You didn't think we lived in luxury did you?"

Actually, she hadn't thought about it at all. "Guess I won't be signing up then."

He laughed. Shyla just about tripped over her feet at the surprisingly deep rumble. The man knew how to laugh. Wonders never ceased. And the change in his demeanor enhanced his features, turning him from an attractive man to…damn fine.

They walked for more angles than she'd anticipated. Then they reached a set of stairs, going down.

Shyla paused. "I thought we were on the lowest level in Zirdai."

"The lowest *residential* level," Rendor said. "Below are the black cells where we house criminals, political prisoners, and people who've angered the Water Prince."

"Oh." Her throat suddenly dry, she swallowed. "What's below that level?"

"Pipes for the water, then nothing but stone. Our city grows wider, not deeper."

He descended into the darkness and she followed close behind him. The musty air turned cold and damp. A greenish mold clung to the walls.

At the first landing, he stopped and turned to her. "Prepare yourself. This will be unlike anything you've seen before."

Nice of him to warn her, but her stomach still tightened with apprehension. She almost trod on his heels as they resumed their journey.

By the second landing, a bright purple haze emanated from below. The staircase ended in a large room.

Dozens of druk lanterns hung from the walls. A bunch of guards occupied the space, many of them sitting at the rough stone tables or standing by the metal doors blocking all the other entrances…or were they exits? She counted five women, eight men, and six doors.

When they noticed Rendor, they stood or straightened to attention.

"At ease," Rendor said.

They relaxed.

One leered at Shyla. "Did you bring us a new toy?" he asked.

Instinctively, Shyla stepped toward Rendor. The captain stared at the man without saying a word.

The man blanched. "Sorry, sir. How can we help you sir?"

"I need to see the archeologist," Rendor said in a deep growl.

The guard scurried to comply, unlocking the third entrance on the left. Rendor grabbed a druk and indicated Shyla should do the same. When they entered the dark tunnel, she kept an eye on the man with the big mouth, but he remained in the guard room. The metal door swung closed behind them with a clang. And she almost ran into Rendor when the lock snapped shut. If it hadn't been for their druks, they would have been in complete darkness. Now she understood why they were called the black cells.

The tunnel sloped downward. The two druks were not strong enough to illuminate more than a meter around them. A faint wail of pain echoed off the stone walls just a few steps before a fetid stench slapped her in the face. She covered her nose with the sleeve of her tunic, but it was far too late. The combination of unwashed bodies, urine, and shit had invaded her senses. Her eyes watered and bile pushed up her throat, threatening to gag her.

Rendor leaned close. "Do not look into the cells we pass or you're likely to throw up."

She peered at him. If he was bothered by the terrible smell, he didn't show it. He waited until she nodded. It was easy to keep her gaze firmly on Rendor's broad muscular back, but it was impossible not to hear the frantic pleas for help, for water, for food. The implorations for death stabbed her right in the heart. Those poor souls.

Shyla shivered as the temperature dropped again—almost as cold as the top levels during darkness. Puddles of…muck stained the floor. Out of the corner of her eyes, she noticed bars lined each cell.

Rendor stopped and gestured to the left. Shyla turned and stifled a gasp. Lying on a stone bench in a tiny space, Banqui squinted his swollen black eyes in the weak violet light. Bruises and cuts marked the rest of his face. His clothes were ripped and bloody.

Banqui pushed up to his elbow and blocked the light with his other hand. "Shyla?"

Too horrified to speak, she just stared.

"Shyla!" He scrambled off the bench and grabbed the bars, pressing his forehead against them. "I told you to run and hide! You stubborn girl. Now, you're caught, too."

"No. I'm not..." Unable to meet his concerned gaze, she dropped hers. A disconnected part of her mind noted that Banqui's feet were bare and the source of the stench came from a hole in the floor. Presumably there must be one in every cell.

"What's going on?" Banqui asked. "Why are you here? Did you find The Eyes?"

"I'll wait for you over here," Rendor said, moving back the way they'd come a few meters, giving the illusion of privacy.

"I haven't found them." She quickly explained what had happened. "I need to know who you asked about them."

Banqui ran a hand over his face. "Everyone."

"What about before they were stolen? Did anyone know you were searching for them? One of your colleagues perhaps?"

"No. I didn't even tell my diggers it was Tamburah's temple they'd opened. You and I are the only ones who knew." He lowered his voice. "There is only one explanation. You need to find out more information on that ancient symbol. That will lead you in the right direction."

"I tried. I went to the university's library and found nothing."

Banqui reached through the bars and touched her arm. "You have to keep trying. Please don't give up. That symbol will take you to The Eyes. *Trust me.*"

How could she refuse his desperate plea? "All right."

He wilted with relief. "You'll find them, I know you will."

For his sake, she hoped so. She said goodbye and followed Rendor to the guard room. Distracted, she didn't bother to gawk at the prince's rooms. Her mind whirled, trying to figure out her next move.

When they reached the main entrance, she asked, "Can I take the lift up to level twenty?"

Rendor said, "You wear the prince's sigil, you don't need to ask."

"But you said it doesn't work on you?"

His eyes lit with appreciation. "You were paying attention. The Water Prince has assigned me to keep you safe. If your requests are counter to that command, I can ignore them."

"Does that mean I can order you to move Banqui to a…guest room? Why is he in a cell anyway?"

"He's one of the those people who has angered the prince. And no, you can't override the Water Prince's directives."

No one could. Except… "What if I had a sigil from the King?"

Rendor laughed long and hard. When he caught his breath, he said, "Yes, in that case, you could."

Annoyed, she asked, "Then why did you laugh?"

"Because the more I've gotten to know you, the more I believe you just might pull something like that off. And I'd love to see the Water Prince's face when you do."

* * *

She rode the lift up to level twenty. Then she climbed the seven levels to Banqui's work rooms. The dull ache in her legs was the only reminder of her forced march to see the Heliacal Priestess.

Unlocking the door, Shyla slid it open. Multiple voices shouted as a mass of people rushed toward her.

"Where's Banqui..."

"...have you done?"

"...thief...our boss..."

"...should search her..."

She help up her hands, signaling for quiet so she could speak, but they continued with their barrage. Banqui's diggers had returned from the Shem burial grounds and were demanding answers. Their dusty uniforms fogged the air with the scent of the desert.

Finally a commanding voice cut through the din. "Enough. Let the sun-kissed alone. I will talk with her. Get back to work."

As the grumbling group reluctantly broke up, Shyla spotted the person who had come to her aid. Chofa, the diggers' supervisor.

"Come on," Chofa said, beckoning her to Banqui's office.

Relieved, she followed the short woman. Chofa's black hair fell in ringlets to her shoulders. Banqui had called her tenacious and one of the hardest workers he'd ever met. Chofa expected the diggers to adhere to the same work ethic. Those that didn't were no longer employed by Banqui.

As soon as they entered the relative privacy of the office, Chofa rounded on her. "Start explaining."

Shyla told her everything except about the ancient symbol that might represent a group called the Invisible Sword.

"Try again, Sun-kissed. There's no way that Banqui searches for a priceless artifact without letting me know."

Pointing to Banqui's desk, Shyla said, "There's the map I marked for him. See for yourself."

Chofa unrolled the skin and studied it for a while. "This doesn't prove anything. You could have planted this here after Banqui was arrested."

"For what purpose? If I'd double-crossed Banqui, I'd be long gone by now. Face it, Banqui didn't tell you everything."

The woman scowled, but didn't argue with her.

Pressing her advantage, she said, "Now I've some questions for you. What did Banqui tell you about Tamburah's temple?"

"I'm not helping you." She tossed the map onto the desk and turned to leave.

"Then you'll soon be out of a job."

Chofa paused and glanced over her shoulder. "What are you implying?"

"I'm not implying anything. I'm stating fact. If I don't find The Eyes, then Banqui dies. Do you really think the Water Prince's next archeologist would hire you and your crew? There's a person out there who knew what Banqui was looking for. Odds are in favor of him or her being one of his workers. No one will trust you again."

She curled her fingers into fists and faced Shyla. "Fine. Banqui didn't tell us much—not even the name of the temple. We uncovered the main entrance, dug our escape tunnel, reinforced the structure—there were a few weak areas—shoveled out a ton of sand, and opened up a few air vents. He wouldn't let us explore, said he was worried about booby traps. After we saw those hideous faces carved into the walls, we were glad not to go in too deep."

"Did anyone on your crew seem overly interested in finding treasure?"

"No. My crew knows better. Stealing from Banqui is stealing from the Water Prince. Too dangerous."

Shyla didn't quite believe her. "Was your entire crew at the burial ground dig?"

"Yes, they were all there."

"Did anyone leave or disappear for a few angles?"

"No. He or she would have been gone for most of a sun jump and I would have noticed."

"And everyone is here now?"

"Yes."

Shyla considered. If she could trust Chofa, then none of the crew was involved in the theft. But that didn't mean they were innocent. One of them could have recognized the temple as Tamburah's and put the clues together. It was easy enough to pass the information along to fellow conspirators. Then the digger just needed to wait until everything died down before joining the others.

"Are you finished?" Chofa asked. "I need to update my crew."

"Yes." But Shyla was no closer to an answer. At least she had a possible lead—sort of.

She left Banqui's and asked the first guard she encountered to deliver a message to Rendor for her. The man balked until she flashed the sigil. Then he was more than happy to comply. The warm satisfaction of being treated with respect flowed through her even though she knew it was dangerous to get used to.

The time was close to angle ninety so she climbed to level nine for second meal. After that, she'd have to follow up on her promise to Banqui and do what she'd been dreading—visit the monks and the First Room of Knowledge.

CHAPTER

6

When she finished her meal, Shyla filled her water skin and took a dozen sticks of gamelu jerky just in case the information she sought proved elusive. The monks would allow her to remain in the monastery during the darkness—actually as long as she needed—but they would not provide food or water.

After she gathered supplies, Shyla still had to wait twenty angles for the dangerous surface heat to dissipate. She returned to her room. Even though the temperature was hot, it wasn't too uncomfortable for her. Sorting through the tablets and scrolls of her own collection, she hoped one of them might mention a secret organization. She cleared a spot on her floor and read through them.

A knock on her door startled her. She shot to her feet. No one except Banqui ever visited her. While she debated if she should grab a weapon, the cracked glass slid aside, revealing Rendor.

Sweat streaked his face and darkened his tunic. "Seven hells, Shyla, what are you doing up here?"

"Research."

He grunted. "It's not safe."

"The temperature—"

"Not what I'm talking about." Rendor gestured to her broken door. "Although how can you stand the heat?"

She shrugged. "I'm used to it."

"I'll have someone fix your door. Do you have someplace to stay in the meantime?"

Was that actual concern? No. She had one purpose—to find The Eyes—and Rendor's purpose was to ensure that she fulfilled her goal.

"Yes."

"All right. What do you need?"

Shyla explained about the diggers. "One or more of them could be waiting for the right opportunity to slip away and join up with their collaborators. I want you to assign unobtrusive guards to keep an eye on them. Maybe follow them if they leave."

He crossed his arms and tapped his fingers on his biceps, his gaze growing distant as he considered. "You're thinking they would lead us to the person who stole The Eyes?"

"Possibly. It's worth the effort at least."

"You might be on to something."

"Wow. Tone down your enthusiasm there," she snarked. "I'd suggest you get those guards in place right away. You do have people who can blend in, right?"

He tilted his head. "Not all my staff wear uniforms."

Ah. Good to know.

"Most of the time, once they change into ordinary clothing they're practically invisible."

Shyla almost choked. Did he just say... Was he implying... No. No way he was part of the so-called Invisible Sword.

"Are you all right?" he asked, watching her expression closely.

"I...just...can't imagine you blending in at all."

"Oh? Why is that?"

Sweeping a hand out, she indicated his body. "You're too...muscular." She'd just dug herself in deeper.

A sly smile crossed his face. "Is that a compliment?"

The man was certainly full of himself. "Hardly."

"You're not a very good liar."

Time to deflate his ego. "Do you know what happens to all that muscle when you get old? It turns to fat."

"No need to worry about that, sunbeam. I'm the captain of the Water Prince's guard. We don't grow old."

Shyla grappled with that comment. She ignored *sunbeam*...for now. "Is your job that dangerous?"

He laughed, but it wasn't a happy sound. "What happens if you don't find The Eyes?"

Sensing there was more, she answered the obvious question. "Banqui dies. I'll probably be arrested."

"No probably about it. And I'll be killed," Rendor said in such a matter-of-fact voice that it took her a moment to process his words.

"Why?"

"If they're not found, then I failed. Twice. One too many times for the prince."

"But he can't…" She sighed. The prince *could.* Although she had a hard time picturing him ordering his captain's death. Regardless, she didn't need another person to worry about. One she wanted to hate, or at least strongly dislike. One who was supposed to dislike her in return.

"Now you know why I'm so invested in this investigation," Rendor said.

"Then you should hurry up and assign your agents to watch the diggers." She tried to shoo him out.

He wouldn't budge. "And you're going to remain here and do research?"

"No. I'm going to the Monks of Parzival to ask them about that ancient symbol Banqui mentioned."

Rendor didn't deny knowing about it. Even though she and Banqui had lowered their voices, stone walls and floors tended to reflect and amplify sounds—all part of the charm of living underground.

Alarmed, he asked, "When are you going?"

"As soon as you leave. It should be cool enough by now."

"You need an escort. Wait for me, I'll be back in fifteen angles."

"No, I don't. I've traveled to the monastery on my own plenty of times. I know what dangers to avoid." The monks had taught her how to survive in the desert. Well, everything but living through the killing heat—nothing worked in that case.

"This time there may be others who want to stop you."

"Like who?"

"It is hardly a secret that you are searching for The Eyes. If the thief is still in Zirdai, he or she would wish to prevent you from discovering his or her identity."

His argument had some merit. Plus the person who stole The Eyes had been on the surface, which meant he or she was comfortable topside—many citizens avoided going into the desert, preferring to remain within sight of the city's entrances.

"The monks won't let you pass the public areas and I might be there all darkness and you'll need provisions, dillo boots, and a sun—"

He held out his hand, stopping her. "Got it. I'll be back." With two massive strides, he reached the door.

"If you're not here in twenty angles, I'm leaving without you," she called, already regretting allowing him to accompany her. The monks wouldn't be happy. They didn't like the Water Prince or the Heliacal Priestess or anyone really. Unless you were a fellow monk, then they treated you as family. Until you weren't.

Shyla shook her head as if the motion could dislodge the memories. But which ones would she discard? The ones of being loved and cared for, or the ones of being shunned? She decided the loving recollections should go. After all, the people of Zirdai had all but shunned her. This way, her entire life experiences would match and there would be no longing or loneliness.

Enough wallowing. It'd been her decision to leave and she had to live with the consequences. While waiting for Rendor, she packed her supplies and spread her sun cloak out, smoothing the slightly hairy white fabric. No trace of blood stained the garment and the tear had been expertly repaired. Gauging the time by the temperature, she shouldered her pack and donned the cloak. She'd give Rendor another angle or two before going topside.

Just her luck, the big man arrived soon after. His sun cloak reached his knees. Because of his bulk, he resembled an oversized velbloud. A chuckle escaped before she clamped her mouth shut. He frowned, but it seemed more of an automatic response. The spots of gold in his eyes sparked in amusement.

"Let's go," she said.

He followed her to the exit. It was angle one-forty and still too hot for the sand cleaners, which she was glad of, but then again...

"Did you tell anyone where we're going?" she asked Rendor.

"I sent a message to the Water Prince."

Not a surprise. She wondered if any of the guards sold information to the Heliacal Priestess's deacons. Not that her trip to the monastery was a big secret, but she'd rather the woman didn't know.

Once they exited, they paused for a moment to allow their eyes to adjust to the brightness and the unending reddish-orange desert. The hot air dried her nose and throat with her first inhalation. The scorching sun's rays pressed on her head. Shyla pulled her hood up. When the light no longer caused her pain, she set out. The searing sand crunched under foot, warming her feet to an uncomfortable level even through the dillo leather soles.

She set a brisk pace on the compacted sand. Once they left the path, the soft sand would slow their steps and they had to travel at least six kilometers from the city. The monks enjoyed their isolation and safeguarded the monastery's location. Only the determined few found them. This was also the case for the other Korahaian monasteries. A monastery was located within ten kilometers of each city's main entrance.

They passed a couple velbloud flocks. The animals descended in the cooling air, reeling in their tethers as they drew closer to the sands. Shyla slowed to watch for a moment.

The velbloud was an oval-shaped fuzzy white creature. About a meter high and wide, it was two meters long with four short legs that ended in sharp claws. Males and females looked the same—only a caretaker could tell the difference. The velbloud was one of only three creatures that could survive on the surface of Koraha. During the killing heat, it floated high into the air, its long tether keeping it connected to the sand. Its white pelt reflected the deadly sunlight, keeping it cooler. During darkness, the hot air it collected in its internal air bladders to float kept it warm. The inhabitants of Koraha revered the velbloud. Each animal was lovingly cared for until it died. Once dead, every part of the creature was used to aid in the people's survival.

Concentrating on the task at hand, Shyla scanned the sand along the path, looking for an almost too-perfect smoothness among the dips and swells of the desert—evidence of the monks' passage. They wore a special wide-soled shoe that didn't leave recognizable tracks.

She spotted the sheen of the monks' passing to the left of their trail and stepped off the path. Rendor followed without comment. Sinking into the sand up to their mid-calves, they left clear imprints behind as they trudged. Although she doubted those marks would last long. Either the light wind or the monks would sweep them away.

Sweat soaked the neck of her tunic and collected underneath her breasts. It trickled down her back as they crested a dune. Stopping to catch her breath, she glared at the row of dunes lying along their route. How was it that a small grain of sand could fly on the wind, yet when it gathered with all its friends, the blasted stuff weighed a ton? No doubt it also filled her boots and stained her socks as well.

"Don't tell me you're lost," Rendor said. His face glistened with sweat.

"Just getting my bearings."

He grunted.

Walking side by side, they crossed two more dunes. Halfway down the third one, Shyla grabbed Rendor's arm, halting him.

"What is it?" His hand grasped the hilt of his sword.

She pointed at the spot right in front of him. "Cap sand."

Rendor stepped back. Peering down, he asked, "How can you tell?"

"It's lighter in color."

"All I see is red sand and pink sky."

Shyla grabbed a fistful of sand and tossed it at the center of the meter-wide deposit of cap sand. A whoosh blew sand into the air, exposing a hole in the dune underneath. It spiked down into darkness. Depending on the size of the hole, an unwary traveler might twist an ankle or break a leg by stepping on cap sand—so called because it mounded over and hid the danger. Bigger holes would swallow a person completely, trapping them. If the victim was alone or if it was too deep for a rescue, it wouldn't take long for the sand demons—the second creature able to survive the killing sun—to arrive for an easy meal.

"I thought you've been in the desert before?" Shyla asked.

"On the pathways."

Now it was her turn to grunt. "Stay close, then."

They clambered over two more dunes before she spotted the monastery. Unlike the city's entrance, its surface building matched the desert's color. No tiles decorated its exterior. Plain and practical—the monks' two favorite words.

Before they descended, Rendor leaned toward her and lowered his voice. "I count five…monks. They're wearing red clothing that blends in with the sand. Are they armed?"

"Not armed with weapons, but I doubt you could draw your sword fast enough to do anything useful with it."

"I'm the prince's captain because I'm the best," he snapped.

"I'm sure you are." She placated, which just increased his annoyance. "And, by the way, there are twelve monks hiding in the sands. Eight between us and the monastery and four others who have been following us for the last kilometer."

Rendor stared at her.

"You wanted to come along," she said. "Don't get mad at me because you're out of your element."

"You could have told me about them." He sounded like a sullen child.

Shyla suppressed a grin. "We're in no danger. Well, as long as you don't draw your sword, they have no reason to attack us. Come on."

No one approached them as they finished their journey. All asylum seekers could find safety inside a monastery and the monks rescued a handful of lost travelers every circuit. They might act cold and distant to outsiders, but they'd never refuse aid.

They entered the single surface building. It had rectangular openings that allowed the air inside. Velbloud-hair fabric hung in front of them, blocking most of the sand. During sandstorms, the monks covered them with stone shutters. Inside was one large room and one monk sitting cross-legged on a marble bench—the only piece of furniture. His hands rested on his knees and he wore a red robe with the hood pulled down low enough to keep his face in shadow. Behind him was the stairway down to the monastery.

"Can I help you?" he asked without moving a muscle.

She recognized Karlin's voice and wondered what he'd done to be assigned as the greeter—the most boring job of all. But she was no longer allowed to ask him or joke with him about it. Instead, she said, "I require access to the First Room of Knowledge."

"You have permission, but your *companion* does not," Karlin said.

Companion? Interesting choice of words. "He understands and is willing to wait for me in the receiving room."

"Very well, you may enter."

Memories threatened to overwhelm her as Shyla descended the familiar wide stairway down two levels, where it ended in a circular room with two tunnels branching off. There was no need for druk lanterns at this time of the sun jump. Mirror pipes poked through the ceiling and speared the floor, allowing sunlight to fill the space.

"No wonder you like living so high," Rendor said. He pointed to the pipes. "How deep do they go?"

"Six levels. Although a few go deeper."

"Wow. How big is the monastery?"

"Twelve levels."

"Where are the Rooms of Knowledge?"

She wondered if his questions were due to innocent curiosity or for tactical information-gathering purposes. "I'm not allowed to divulge the location."

"Why not?"

"It's part of my agreement with the monks. If I tell you, I would no longer have access." She swept a hand out, indicating the stone benches and tables scattered about. "You can wait here. No one will bother you. If I'm delayed, they will escort you to a safe level during the killing heat."

"Wait, you didn't say it would take you *that* long."

"I don't expect it to take that long, but just in case it does, you don't need to panic."

He crossed his arms. "I don't panic."

"Fine. Just don't leave this area without an escort."

"And if I do?"

"Then you'll find out just how well trained the monks are."

By his stubborn expression, Shyla doubted he really understood just how capable the monks were in defending themselves. Perhaps it would be fun to spar with Rendor so he'd get a better idea. Where did that thought come from? She quickly dismissed the ridiculous notion.

"Make yourself comfortable. I'll be back." She headed for the tunnel on the right.

"Comfortable? There's no cushions," Rendor grumbled as she left.

That was the point. Visitors weren't encouraged to linger. Besides, the monks believed in an austere lifestyle and limited items of comfort. They also embraced what the desert offered and spent as much time on the surface as they did underground.

Shyla traversed the familiar route to the First Room of Knowledge. During the trip, the hallways and stairwells remained empty. Word had probably spread of her visit and no doubt everyone was avoiding her. While a part of her was glad to avoid the awkward encounters, another part longed to see her family members.

After she passed level six, she grabbed a couple druk lanterns. No mirror pipes reached the Rooms of Knowledge. The sunlight would fade the ink, but the yellow glow from the druk wouldn't.

Easan stood outside the First Room of Knowledge on level nine, guarding the entrance. Her childhood playmate had grown taller and broader in the shoulders since the last time she'd seen him. Dark fuzz along his square jaw might be an attempt to grow a beard. His blue-eyed gaze looked right through her as if she were invisible. He gave no indication that he'd recognized her as he unlocked the trio of complex mechanisms installed in the thick stone door that covered the threshold.

Shyla kept her expression neutral despite the sharp bite of pain in her chest. Once the opening was wide enough, she slipped inside. Calling the space a room was a bit of an oversimplification. The shelves extended into a maze of rooms and spanned high enough to be considered a cavern. Narrow walkways wove through the stacks of tablets, rolls of velbloud skins, and other ancient artifacts. Located in the center of this labyrinth were low tables topped with druk lanterns—the reading area.

When the door thumped closed behind her, Shyla turned to check that the call rope still dangled nearby.

After she finished researching, she'd need to pull it to alert the sentry to let her out. While this was her favorite place in the monastery, she had no desire to be trapped inside.

Instinctively, she followed the familiar twists and turns. Small low tables and cushions lurked in various nooks and corners, illuminated by druks. She reached the main reading area—a large open area with wider and longer tables. It was empty. Not that unusual, but she wondered if the others had cleared out before she arrived. She set up a camp of sorts, removing her cloak, unpacking her supplies and the picture of the ancient symbol. Her next step wasn't as clear. Where to start?

According to Banqui, the Invisible Sword formed during Tamburah's reign—approximately thirteen hundred and ninety circuits ago. That meant she didn't need to read anything older than fourteen hundred circuits. But that still left plenty of resources to review.

A memory of Weira teaching Shyla and three others close to her age rose unbidden. Weira handed each of them a large handful of sand and told them to find the single purple grain in each pile. They'd laughed, thinking she joked, but no, it'd been an exercise in patience. And a lesson in the desert's true colors. Those grains ranged from dark vermillion to bright red to orange to yellow and even tan. They did the same with cap sand, lightning sand, and sluff sand.

Focusing on her current task, Shyla wended through the shelves, pulling any tablet or scroll that might mention Tamburah and his rise to power. When she had a number of stacks on the table, she sat cross-legged on a cushion and read.

Many many angles later, she had found no mention of the Invisible Sword. Returning those items, she collected more. And after those proved unhelpful, she gathered another set. Then another. Hunger and thirst marked the angles. She stretched her sore back and stiff legs between sessions. When fatigue pulled at her muscles and fogged her thoughts, Shyla figured it had to be deep in the time of darkness. To stay awake, she practiced a few Yarin techniques. That, and remembering Banqui's fate should she fail, chased the fog away for a while.

* * *

The echoing thud of the stone door closing woke Shyla from a light doze. She jerked upright in horror. How long had she slept? Glancing at the scrolls spread on the table, she tried to remember where she'd left off. Something about a sword maker…

"You've been in here all darkness," said a man whose voice resonated within her.

His voice banished all her loneliness and problems with its rich timbre. Comfort, safety and, at one point, love rested in those tones. Anger, frustration, and heartache also reverberated inside the familiar sound.

Shyla turned. Hanif stood at the edge of the reading room. He hadn't changed at all. Straight black hair with not a hint of grey despite his age. Like most of the other monks, his deep brown skin matched hers. Wearing a simple red tunic and pants, he might be mistaken for an ordinary monk, but there was no misinterpreting the aura of power that surrounded him. The monks considered him their leader. Shyla had looked to him as a father figure. Not anymore.

"Your companion is worried," Hanif said.

"I warned him it might take me a while."

He stiffened at her casual tone. "Do you know he is in the employ of the Water Prince?"

How in the world did Hanif know that? Perhaps the monks were not as isolated as they liked everyone to believe. "I'm well aware."

"Are you aware of how dangerous that man is?"

She refused to answer.

A snort. "Of course not. Not without evidence. Right, Shyla?"

Anger boiled. He'd lost the right to chastise her. "Are you done? I've work to do."

"How much longer will you be here?" The clipped words a danger sign that he, too, was close to losing his temper.

"Until I find the information I need."

"That man needs to leave now. You can come back—"

"No, I can't. And he's allowed succor within the monastery," she shot back.

Hanif drew in a deep breath, held it, then released it in one long sigh. "Why can't you return?"

"I don't have time."

"Are you in trouble?"

The familiar retort—why do you always assume I'm in trouble?—pressed on her lips. But a more sensible part of her refrained. Plus she was. Instead, she considered her answer. Hanif would know if she lied. "My friend is. I need to help him recover an artifact."

"And if you fail?"

"He dies."

"That explains the watchdog." Hanif's gaze swept the table. "What knowledge do you seek?"

She paused. Technically, the monks were under the King of Koraha's protection. In exchange, they prayed for him and warned him of any possible danger. However, she doubted Hanif would bother to report a girl hunting a myth.

Showing him the symbol, she said, "I'm looking for information on a group called the Invisible Sword."

"You won't find it here." He didn't even hesitate.

"I know they probably don't exist, but—"

"They existed. The historical account that you need is located in the Second Room of Knowledge."

Hope bloomed. "Can you tell me about them?"

"No."

"Can I access the Second Room of Knowledge?"

"No."

And hope wilted. She slumped. This gave new meaning to the term dead end.

"Ask again," he said with a glint of…if she didn't know better, she'd say mischief.

Mulling it over, she suspected getting access wouldn't be that easy. Perhaps she needed to ask in a different way. "Other than becoming a monk, what do I need to do to earn access to the Second Room of Knowledge?"

A slight smile curved his lips. It disappeared when he removed a small glass vial from his pocket. "You need to fill this with water from the black river and bring it back to me."

CHAPTER 7

Confused, Shyla stared at Hanif as he handed her the vial. "Where do I find the black river?" She'd seen grey cloudy water and gritty brown water—both unfortunately in her glass.

"Deep in the bowels of Zirdai," Hanif said.

That didn't help. The city was comprised of ninety-seven…no, ninety-eight levels. "How deep?"

"All the way down."

"The prison level?"

"Deeper."

"But there's nothing there."

Hanif didn't respond.

She sighed. "How do I reach it?"

"You'll have to figure that out on your own. I suggest you leave your watchdog behind. His presence would hinder your search." Hanif turned on his heel and left.

Pondering his words, Shyla rolled the vial between her thumb and fingers. He'd given her a hint. This river wouldn't be known to the majority of people in Zirdai. Or rather, to the law-abiding citizens. But those on the fringes…might have heard of it. And they definitely wouldn't be willing to help one of the prince's guards.

She returned the items she'd collected to their various shelves and bins. Glancing around, she wondered if a map to the black river existed. Probably not here. That would be too easy, and Shyla suspected gaining access to the Second Room of Knowledge was going to be very difficult. She curled her hands into fists. A man's life was at stake, but that wasn't enough for Hanif. He'd rather have her go off on some wild sand devil chase. Yet another delay. Shyla shoved her things into her pack along with the vial. Swinging it over her shoulder, she headed for the exit, hoping this visit wouldn't end up being a huge waste of time.

* * *

Rendor paced the length of the receiving room with long graceful strides as if he were a predator stalking his prey. A monk stood at the mouth of each tunnel, blocking the way. Shyla wondered if Rendor had tried to leave. He didn't appear to be injured and his sword remained sheathed.

When she stepped past the monk, Rendor skidded to a stop and scowled at her. Funny, she'd actually missed it.

"We're leaving," he said, sweeping his small pile off the floor.

The sand clock indicated it was angle twenty—plenty of time to return. Something else must be troubling him. She pulled on her sun cloak. "All right."

He shot her a suspicious look before leading the way up the stairs, past the greeter and out into the desert for a few meters. Then he slowed enough for her to catch up and guide their path.

After a few moments, he asked, "Did you learn anything?"

Shyla decided to stick as close to the truth as possible. "I've a lead."

"What is it?"

Ah, hell. "I need to talk to a professor at the university to confirm it."

"And how does this help us find The Eyes?"

Us? "It will narrow the suspects down."

Rendor grabbed her elbow and spun her to face him. "Damn it, Shyla. I've done enough interrogations to know when someone is dodging the truth. What are you hiding?"

"Nothing. That's what I'm hiding. I found nothing. There was nothing in the First Room of Knowledge." All true.

"Then why did you lie?"

"I didn't want to upset you further."

That made him pause. "Further? What do you mean?"

Gesturing back toward the monastery, she asked, "What happened in there?"

"Nothing."

She cocked an eyebrow.

He huffed. "I don't do well with waiting."

"And the guards?"

"They just showed up and blocked the tunnels as if they thought I'd try to go deeper, which made me worry that something happened to you. I asked them, but they just stood there and stared. Creepy."

"And your guards that just stand around in Zirdai aren't?"

"They don't just stand. They're there for your protection and will answer questions," he grumped.

"They're still creepy," she said.

"And you're trying to change the subject."

Instead of answering, she continued trudging through the cool sand. The early angles were her favorite time of the sun jump. A slightly moist air caressed her cheeks as it warmed in the sunshine to a comfortable temperature. She savored the fresh anise aroma. It wouldn't last long before the heat scorched it into the stronger ginger odor.

A line of sand demon tracks crossed their path. Shyla crouched to inspect them, counting. Large paw prints with equally large claws marked the surface. No insect trails over the top of them.

"Only a couple angles old," she said, straightening. "There's twelve in the pack." She scanned the horizon, searching for the creatures in the distant scrub vegetation.

Rendor clasped the hilt of his sword, but she didn't chide him over how futile the weapon would be. Even though the animal was compact, there was nothing small about the top predator in the desert. It had long curved teeth as sharp as blades, thick muscles capable of great speed in a frighteningly short amount of time, and powerful jaws that chomped through bone. Their spotted auburn fur did a fair job of hiding them among the sand.

"Let's not linger then," he said.

She picked up the pace. While most sand demon packs avoided the entrances to the cities and the velbloud pastures, they weren't averse to an easy meal. Rendor didn't relax until they reached the worn paths. They didn't slow until the surface buildings of Zirdai came into view.

"What's our next move?" Rendor asked, breaking the silence.

"It appears the diggers might be our only recourse."

"Not good enough."

She considered. "I'll visit the university's library again. There's an entire section on symbols that I didn't check." That was somewhat true.

"If it wasn't in the First Room of Knowledge, what's the likelihood of it being there?"

"Stranger things have happened."

"Shyla." He practically growled.

"What? Do you want me to say we're done? It's the end of the tunnel and we might as well give the Water Prince the bad news?"

Now he growled outright. "Not helping." Then a beat later, "How is that symbol supposed to help anyway?"

It surprised her that he'd waited this long to ask. At least this time she had an answer prepared. "I think it's connected to an old organization that's still in existence."

"One that we've never heard of?" Rendor sounded doubtful.

"Yes, and they might be the ones who stole The Eyes."

"Okay, so you find out that symbol is indeed the crest or whatever for this secret organization. How does that help you find them?"

The desire to punch him coursed through her body. Why couldn't the captain of the prince's guard be big and dumb? "I'm hoping the research will reveal their tendencies—how they operate, how they pick a leader, who funded them in the past, where they held their gatherings. Many times this leads to…clues to what they're doing now."

His eyebrows rose, crinkling his forehead. His short black hair almost touched his prominent brow.

"It's how I found the location of the Quarry Men's treasure trove," she said.

"You found that? I thought Banqui discovered it."

"It was a team effort."

No response.

They reached the city's entrance. The cleaning crew stood at attention and saluted Rendor as they entered. The temperature dropped a few degrees. Shyla slowed to allow her eyes to adjust to the decreased light. Rendor followed her to her room. The cracked door had been replaced.

"That was fast," she said in surprise.

"My staff might be creepy, but they're efficient."

Was that a joke? Instead of responding, she pushed on the new door. It slid open easily. The key to the lock had been left on the inside. "Please thank them for being efficient."

A grunt. "I suggest you rest and eat before going to the library. I'll follow up with the guards regarding the diggers."

"All right."

He squinted at her and she kept her expression neutral—nothing to see here. "I'll catch up with you later."

She nodded, entered her room and didn't breathe until she shut the door and locked it. Did he suspect she had no intention of resting? Or going to the library? She hoped not. Because if he suspected she was going on a crazy mission for the monks, he'd either stop her or insist on tagging along. Instead of worrying about Rendor, she restocked her pack with items she need for the deeper levels, exchanged her sun cloak for a warmer wrap, and waited another couple angles in case Rendor remained outside.

Easing the door open, she peered out. No one in sight. Relieved, she secured the door. Once she ensured no one was following her, she stopped by her hidden cubby hole on level four. It was tucked underneath a staircase and not accessible unless you crawled through a tight opening, which she blocked with a piece of velbloud skin painted to match the surrounding stone. In the darkness, it was invisible and no druk light ever reached this area unless it was purposely shone in this direction. But just in case someone grew curious and managed to find her spot, they'd be surprised when they reached into the cubby hole. All those circuits studying ancient ruins taught her not only how to spot a trap, but how to build one as well. A couple of broken fingers would chase most intruders away.

After she neutralized the trap, she sorted through her treasures. It was a pitiful collection. For now. She opened her map of Zirdai and scanned it. Not that she really expected the black river to be marked on it, but she had to make sure. It wasn't. She tucked the map into her pack and reset the trap.

Her next stop was the dining cavern. She'd missed first meal by five angles. Refilling her water skin, she grabbed more jerky then set out at a brisk pace. When she first arrived in Zirdai, no one would talk to her directly, but they had loud conversations nearby. During one such encounter, Shyla had overheard a group of people speculating on how long it would be until that sun-kissed could no longer afford the living fees. They guessed it wouldn't be more than a couple dozen sun jumps until she was forced to join the destitute who illegally lived in the far western reaches of level sixteen. At the time, Shyla wondered if, in some warped way, they believed they were helping her. Now, she hoped their information was still good.

Avoiding the guards and populated areas, she navigated through remote tunnels and dark stairwells. Her plan was to use the prince's coins to buy the location of the black river from the vagrants.

The rank smell was her first clue she neared the settlement. The foul odor matched the one that filled the prison level. No collection stations here. No water or food either. She wondered how they survived. Probably by stealing. So why hadn't the guards arrested them by now?

Before going any closer, she removed her wrap and stuffed it into her pack. They had to have lanterns further in, but keeping the perimeter of their living space dark was sound strategy. She debated if she should take a druk with her or leave her hands free. Too bad she couldn't have both. Then an idea sparked. She used her wrap as a belt to secure the druk to her. It hung from her right hip, balancing her pack, which rested on her left. Perfect.

One problem solved, she continued. The strong smell stung her eyes, causing them to water. Bile rose, pushing at the back of her throat. She swallowed. Repeatedly. Just when she thought she couldn't take any more, the odor eased and soon dissipated. Perhaps that was another protective measure. Only the truly determined would endure the stench.

The slight scuff of a boot sounded behind her. Then another, but it rasped as if dragged. At least two. Her pulse quickened. She kept walking even though a light shuffling noise emanated from the darkness in front of her. Concentrating, she guessed another three or four people. Coming alone might not have been her best idea. She took a few deep breaths to steady her heart and ease the tightness along her shoulders, preparing to defend herself at any moment.

The distant orange-tinted glow of druk lanterns appeared, illuminating three black shapes, but they seemed content to remain a few steps ahead, backing away as she advanced. Perhaps they planned an ambush once she reached the light. Not a comforting thought.

Eventually the tunnel ended into a wide cavern. The three in front allowed her to enter, but they didn't go far. The two behind her slipped to the sides. She scanned the five "guards," assessing them, picking out the strongest and weakest links. All young men, lanky and malnourished. No weapons visible. Their gazes scanned her as well. If they knew how to fight, she'd be in trouble. But they showed no signs of aggression. Yet.

Druks glowing orange hung from the walls of the cavern, ringing an encampment of sorts—small groups of grubby people sitting on cushions or standing in clumps, including children. How could their parents be so irresponsible? Surely they could find a way to pay taxes for their children so they had food and clean water. At least the kids seemed happy. They played, running along the cleared aisles or sitting together. The musty funk of unwashed bodies permeated the air.

It didn't take long for conversation to cease. Even the kids paused to stare at the stranger.

One older man stood and approached her. His stained gray tunic hung on his gaunt frame. Rips in his pants exposed both his bony knees. "Ah, it's the sun-kissed. We wondered when you would show up."

"You've been expecting me?" she asked.

"Since you arrived in Zirdai, but with the recent rumors that you're wanted for theft, we figured we'd see you very soon."

Interesting. Although their information was a couple sun jumps old, they weren't as isolated as she thought.

"You cannot stay here," he continued. "We do not harbor criminals."

"You don't?" She cocked her head, scanning the rag-tag group behind him. Living in Zirdai without paying the fees was a criminal activity.

He stiffened. "Not ones that are currently being sought by the Water Prince's goons. You endanger us all."

Ah. A different degree of illegal. "Then it's a good thing I'm not planning on staying."

"Why are you here?"

"I've come to purchase knowledge."

A shrewd gleam shone in his eyes. "Your fancy monastery and snooty intellectual friends don't have the knowledge you seek?"

This man had an unsettling insight into her life. Except the friends bit. "No. What I need can't be found in a scroll or scratched into a tablet. It comes from living in Zirdai and knowing all its…secrets."

He chuckled. "And it would be hard for you to learn those while living up on level three."

That was just one too many. "How do you know so much about me?"

"You stand out, sun-kissed. The moment you arrived, you caused a stir. Bets were made on how long you'd stay, how long until you joined us, how long before you were chased away or arrested or taken by the deacons—the fates of the three other sun-kissed who came to Zirdai during my lifetime. I must admit, you exceeded everyone's expectations."

"Glad I could provide such extended entertainment," she said.

Not bothered by her sarcasm, he asked, "What secrets do you seek?"

Keeping a close eye on his expression, she said, "The location of the black river." The request caused a rumble of noise from the others, but the old man's countenance didn't change.

"What do you offer in exchange?"

She considered. He didn't say he had it. "As long as the information is accurate, I've coin."

"How much?"

"Oh no, I'm not falling for that. Do you know where the black river is?"

He hesitated.

"It's a yes or no answer," she prompted.

"No, but I can point you in the right direction," he hedged.

Shyla muttered a curse. "Let me guess…the direction is…down."

Tsking, he said, "There's no reason to be nasty. We're being polite despite the fact that we can take your coin and toss your ass out into the desert."

And there it was. The ruffians moved closer to her. Good. Then they'd hear her response. "You believe that you have the upper hand. You don't." Confidence could be an effective way to avoid a fight. Too bad this wasn't one of those times.

The leader flicked his fingers. The ring of young men tightened. Shyla spun, knocking into the skinny guy on the left—the weakest link. Off-balance, the guy stumbled back, and she followed. Hooking an arm around his neck, she trapped his head under her arm then turned to the others, dragging him with her.

His frightened face stared up at her as he tried to wiggle free. But with being bent over backward, he had no leverage. She squeezed his throat to remind him of who was in charge and he stilled. Smart.

"Try anything and your man dies," Shyla said to the others.

They backed off, proving they had no experience with fighting. At this angle she didn't have the strength to break his neck, and they had plenty of time to rush her before he died from strangulation. Killing a person was no easy task. It took both physical effort and mental vigor. Not that she had any experience, but these people didn't need to know that.

Assessing the situation, she glanced around. Everyone in the cavern now stood, but they appeared afraid to move. The guards formed a protective semi-circle in front of their leader, but the old man pushed past them in disgust.

"Let's try this again," she said. "Do you have any useful information for me?"

"A man from another commune mentioned a black river that flows under Zirdai," he said. "I thought he was crazy, but I've heard it a few other times." He gave her a humorless grin.

Basically, the black river was a legend. Wonderful. "Where is this other commune?"

"On level thirty-nine."

"Can you be more specific?"

When the man didn't answer, she pinched her prisoner's ear hard enough to make him cry out with pain.

"Out past the main ventilation shafts." The words tumbled from his mouth in a rush. "There's a maze of abandoned tunnels. They're in there."

"And the name of this man?"

"Vencel."

"Thank you." She released the youth, pushing him toward the others. They caught their friend, but remained in place. Shyla removed three osees—more than enough compensation—and tossed them at the old man. He snatched them from the air despite his surprise.

"Next time, let's skip the…niceties and just stick to business," she said.

"There won't be a next time, Sun-kissed. Don't come back."

That shouldn't be a problem. Just in case they decided to attack her again, Shyla walked backward until the light from the cavern was a pinpoint. When no drumming footsteps chased after her, she faced forward.

Shyla mulled over the information she'd received until the putrid stench of offal hit her. This time she covered her nose and mouth and sprinted through the noxious fumes. After she was well away, she slowed as she considered her next move.

The old man might have given her false information. Or he might send a message to his friend, warning him, which would probably lead to a real ambush. Too many mights and probablys, but it was the only direction she had.

Once she crossed to the east side of level sixteen, she found an isolated tunnel to take a break. Sitting on the floor of an alcove, she gnawed on a stick of jerky as she examined her map of Zirdai. The map lacked even the basic details after level eighty, which made sense. The wealthy wouldn't want the ordinary citizens to know where they ate, slept, and kept their treasures.

The most valuable thing down there was the water. It flowed in underground rivers or pooled in deep aquifers. New cities were dug until they reached water, then that level became the residence of the person in charge. The Water Prince, in this city. And he used his proximity to so much water for decoration and piped it through his rooms. Would one of those pipes hold water from the black river? And was she brave enough to ask the Water Prince? Probably not.

Instead, she plotted a course to the commune on level thirty-nine until her vision blurred. Fatigue spread through her body. Were her arms always this heavy? It'd been over a sun jump since she last slept. She leaned back against the wall. No time to sleep, but…maybe…she could rest…just close her eyes for a moment.

Her thoughts drifted, then snagged on Rendor. Was he having better luck? What if his guards tracked one of Banqui's diggers to The Eyes? And here she was chasing a legend. What if he learned nothing? Then he'd— She straightened, wide awake. He might be searching for her. Probably worried. Or angry. Most likely both. And the longer she was missing, the harder it would be to explain it to him. Best to get this mission over with as quickly as possible.

Folding the map, she returned it to her pack. She stood, wiped the sand from her pants and followed her planned route. Or rather, she tried. Within fifteen angles, it became obvious that the map she'd bought was not as accurate as the seller proclaimed.

By the time she hit her fifth dead end on level thirty-two, her head pounded and weakness trembled in her legs. As much as she hated to admit it, she needed to sleep or she'd be useless. At least the dead end protected her back. And at the bottom of her pack was a roll of dried-out gamelu skin. She spread it on the floor about three meters down the tunnel. Not a pretty decoration, but its beauty lay in its ability to snap very loud when trod on. The noise should wake her in time to defend herself.

Closing the druk lantern blocked the reddish tinted light and plunged her into darkness. She stretched out on the cold hard ground, using her pack as a pillow. The fact that she'd slept on the floor twice in as many sun jumps didn't go unnoticed, but she was too tired to care.

* * *

Nothing disturbed her and she woke feeling…better. Not refreshed and energetic, but she suspected she'd need a full darkness of sleep to achieve that state of energy. She abandoned her planned route and risked traveling through populated areas. Plus she needed to use the collection station. While there, she freshened up, rubbing the quick-drying cleanser over her body and on her scalp. Shyla twisted her hair into a knot—she probably should just cut it short to make it easier to hide. Arranging her wrap, she covered the knot and pulled the material out to keep her face in shadow. Once satisfied, she continued her journey.

The public sand clock read angle one-eight-five, just five angles into the time of darkness. She had about sixty angles before most people went to sleep. It should be plenty.

Soon the tint of the druk light turned from red to green as she descended past level thirty-six. Three levels later, she stood at the edge of a hole. Cold moist air rushed upward, ruffling her tunic. When the old man had said it was past the ventilation shaft, she'd thought he meant a tunnel like the one she found on level twenty-six. Not a vertical hole.

She shone the druk light inside the shaft and peered up. No bridges or ladders or anything crossed the shaft. At least not in the five or six levels that the light reached. Same thing below. Nothing.

The old man sent her to the wrong place and was probably laughing at her right now. But then she looked across the gap. Resting against the wall was a long narrow plank, which meant someone lived on that side.

Scorching hells. Shyla backtracked and sought a similar plank on her side. No luck.

What were her options? Search for a level that crossed the shaft and hope there was a way to return to this level on that side. That required too much time and effort. Find something she could use as a bridge. It wasn't a common object and asking at the merchant tiers would draw unwanted attention. Jump over it? She eyed the distance—three, maybe four meters. No way. That left waiting for someone on the other side to use the plank to cross over.

Although upset about the delay, she had to admit the shaft provided an effective barrier to unwanted visitors. That side might be filled with a small city of people who were safe from the Water Prince's guards.

Assuming the vagrants would not leave until angle zero, Shyla set up camp about six meters from the shaft. Once again she unrolled the gamelu skin on the ground behind her and covered the druk. She hoped the noise of setting the plank would alert her from the front. With nothing else to do, she slept.

A scratching sound dug its way into her dreams, pulling her from the safety of her childhood home. Voices roused her to full alert. Greenish druk light shone across the shaft. Two men wrestled with the plank while another held a rope attached to the front to guide it. As they maneuvered it over the gap, she grabbed her pack, the lantern, and the gamelu skin, and retreated down the tunnel until she reached an intersection.

Shyla peered around the edge to keep track of the men. They set the plank and crossed over. The spoke in low voices, but didn't act overly concerned or wary of being discovered. No one remained behind to guard the bridge. They must be pretty confident that the Water Prince's soldiers were unaware of their existence.

As they drew closer to the intersection, she moved back. If they turned this way, she'd have to hurry to stay beyond their light's reach without alerting them. Difficult to do on hard stone. It was part of her training, but it'd been a while since she'd practiced it.

When they continued straight, she relaxed then eased over to the intersection, glancing in the corridor. Darkness pressed back. She waited. No one else crossed over. Now or never. She opened the lantern, and the green-tinted light spilled out. Once her eyes adjusted, she approached the bridge. About a meter wide, it appeared sturdy. Those three men had crossed without plunging to their deaths. Still... She tapped it with the toe of her boot. Other than a hollow knock, nothing happened. Well, except for her heart's efforts to escape her chest.

Using a calming Yarin technique, she drew strength. All she needed to do was walk forward. Not difficult. So why did her legs refuse to move. She huffed. No time for this nonsense. She pressed her lips together and strode onto the plank.

The thin plank vibrated under the soles of her boots as the air rushed past her, threatening to take her wrap with it. The tang of wet sand mixed with the smells of gamelu meat. She clutched her possessions tight. Everything seemed fragile in the moment, as if she'd already lost her balance, but her mind refused to believe it. Strange.

Those unsettling thoughts and the strong wind stopped once she reached solid ground. She checked that her hair remained covered then set off to find the commune.

The old man had been right about the maze of tunnels. She stopped at each intersection and inspected the ground for footprints, listened for voices, sniffed the air for living smells, and covered her druk, seeking a faint sheen of light in the distance. The popular tunnels were easy to spot, but she marked each turn with chalk just in case.

After a few angles, she picked up the distant echo of voices and the blackness ahead of her lantern thinned. As she drew closer, the signs of the community were evident. But when she didn't alert any guards, she worried. Were they really that confident that an intruder couldn't get this far? If so, they were about to get a nasty surprise. Or were they just that good—able to mask the sounds of their passage? Then she'd be the one on the receiving end of a surprise.

Shyla turned into a tunnel. Up ahead, three people holding a couple druks headed toward her. She froze, unsure what to do at first, but realized this was the perfect opportunity. Setting her lantern on the floor to free her hands, she waited. It didn't take them long to notice her.

"Hey," one man said, hurrying forward. "Who are you?"

"What are you doing here?" the woman asked with a strident, almost fearful tone.

Knives flashed—not smooth manufactured blades, but handmade pieces of sharpened metal with jagged edges.

"How did you get in here?" a young man demanded. He held a weapon in each fist.

Shyla showed him her empty hands. "I'm looking for Vencel."

"Why?" the woman asked.

"That's none of your business," she said.

The young man pointed the tip of one of his knives at her throat. "Want to try that again?"

She resisted the urge to knock it from his grip. "All right. Relax. I just need some information and was told Vencel might have it. That's all. I'm not a threat."

"Yeah right." The tip pricked her skin.

"Who are you?" the first man asked again.

She doubted her name would mean anything to these people. Instead she slowly moved her arms and uncovered her hair. Even in the green druk light the yellow strands were noticeable.

"Seven hells, it's the sun-kissed." The man dragged a large hand over his short black beard.

The young man stepped back, but kept his weapons aimed at her. Now that she wasn't in immediate danger, she studied the three. At first glance, they appeared to be ordinary citizens of Zirdai, but the fearful expressions and slightly hunched postures didn't quite match. However, they smelled better than the others on level sixteen and, even though he was lean like his companions, the young man's muscles strained his tunic.

"Are the guards after you?" the woman asked.

"Did you lead the guards here?" the young man snapped.

"No to both," she said. "I'm just looking for information."

"There's nothing *just* about you," the bearded man said. "I'm sure the damage has been done. This is out of our depth. We need to take her to Orla."

Progress.

"Follow me," the man said, turning around.

The woman shot her a glare and the young man waited until Shyla passed him before falling into step behind her. They traveled through a number of tunnels and backtracked through a few of them. Probably trying to get Shyla lost. And she briefly wondered if they planned to abandon her, hoping she'd die before finding her way out. Not a comforting thought. Although if they left her a druk, she had a good chance of retracing their steps.

Even though they took a longer route, Shyla spotted a bright glow of many lanterns—more than necessary, or so she thought until they reached the sprawling cavern. Unlike the ad hoc encampment on level sixteen, this place had cushions, furniture, and doorways with curtains. Ladders reached upper tiers. And it smelled of incense and cleanser.

Before she could gawk too much, the young man pushed her into one of the curtained rooms. It was bigger than her room on level three. A bench had been carved into three of the walls and a stone table occupied the center.

"Sit down." He stood in the threshold with his knives still in hand.

Shyla sat near the back. If this didn't go well, she could hop on the table and fight her way out. Not long after, an older woman and two men arrived. One was the bearded man from before. They sat across from her with the woman in the center.

The woman studied Shyla. Gray hair streaked her black locks, matching her gray eyes. "I'm Orla, the leader of this establishment." She tipped her head to the bearded man. "This is Adair and he's Vencel."

Ah good. That would save her some time. "I'm Shyla."

"Please explain to me how you found us and why." Orla's request sounded more like an order.

She swallowed her annoyance at the delay and repeated her story. Orla scowled at Vencel when Shyla mentioned his comment to the older man on level sixteen. He ducked his head.

After a moment of silence, Orla said, "I see. So all you want is the location of the black river and you'll be on your merry way?"

Finally. "Yes."

"And how can we trust you not to reveal our settlement to the Water Prince's guards?"

"I understand that you're not part of Zirdai, neither am I. I don't care that you don't pay taxes or attend services. I've no desire to report you to the guards. Hell, I'll probably be in your same situation after all this is over." If she survived, it was doubtful anyone would hire her.

"Why do you want to find the black river?" she asked.

"I don't. But the monks sent me to get a vial of water from it."

Orla perked up. "The monks. Why didn't you say so before?"

"I didn't think it relevant."

Before Orla could respond a woman poked her head into the room. "Come quick, Mori's been beaten and left for dead."

All three stood at once and hustled out along with her guard. Curious, Shyla followed them in time to see two men lower a woman onto a table. Blood stained her torn clothes and her arms and legs twisted in unnatural angles. Bruises covered the woman's face. One large lump stood out on her temple. Shyla understood why she was left for dead. Being unconscious was the only positive thing for the poor woman.

Orla shouted orders and people scrambled for supplies. They straightened her limbs and splinted them, then tended her wounds. But they could do nothing about her head injury or any internal bleeding.

Forgotten, Shyla wandered around the commune. Scattered about in no semblance of order were common areas, private rooms and evidence of work projects. She recognized the velbloud-hair head scarves that sold in the merchants' market on level twenty-six. Did that mean they had the coin for taxes, but didn't pay them? Why would they do that?

Most of the residents hovered near the victim, but others remained. A few stared at her. Would she be welcomed here if she ran out of coin? Probably not. She'd return to the monastery, but knew it would never be the same. Never be home again. Neither would this place or Zirdai. No. Her chance to find a new home in another city was gone along with The Eyes.

Orla found her sitting in one of the common areas, idly fixing a broken puzzle box—a child's toy left behind. Probably when the evil sun-kissed showed up at their home and the adults told all the kids to hide. Yes, she was being dramatic, but no one had come within six meters of her and there wasn't a child in sight.

"How's the woman?" Shyla asked Orla.

"Time will tell." The leader slumped into a cushion.

"Why was she beaten?"

Orla shrugged. "Does it matter?"

"Of course. The guards just don't randomly beat people to death. There are laws."

"Is that so." Orla's cynical tone indicated it wasn't a question. She leaned forward. "You want a reason? Then her crime was simply existing. Like you."

Tired of the back and forth, Shyla stood. "Haven't you heard? I'm not a crime, I'm a curse."

Orla laughed. It was a barking rattle. A few people nearby turned and stared as if they'd never heard their leader laugh before.

Shyla didn't have time for this nonsense. "Are you going to tell me where the black river is or not?"

Sobering, the woman nodded. "Vencel and Adair will take you."

A weight eased off her shoulders. She reached for her coin purse. "How much?"

"Ten."

"Seven," she countered just to test the woman.

"Good luck finding your way out," Orla said.

Nice. She placed ten coins inside the fixed puzzle box, closed it, and handed it to Orla, causing more cackling laughter.

"I'm starting to like you, Sun-kissed," Orla said between gasps for breath. She waved a hand to the left. "The boys are waiting for you."

Shyla grabbed a druk first. Vencel and Adair grunted when she joined them, but otherwise didn't say a word as they navigated the maze of tunnels. Nor did they answer her questions about the exact location of the black river.

Finally, she refused to move until they gave her some idea of where they were going.

"There's a hidden staircase on level seventy-eight that goes right down to it," Vencel said, annoyance coloring his voice.

"That seems too easy," she said.

"There's a few twists and turns after that, but not many. No one really wants to go down there anyway."

"When was it re-discovered?"

"Two or three hundred sun jumps ago. A couple of vagrants searching for free water found it." He shrugged. "They told me the story, said that level might be a good place to squat."

He said nothing more. They soon reached the bridge over the air shaft.

"You should post a guard here," Shyla said.

Adair grunted. "We will *now*."

Vencel walked onto the plank, but Shyla hesitated.

"What are you waiting for?" Adair asked.

Courage. But she didn't say that aloud. Instead, she strode out as if she did it every sun jump. Adair followed.

Vencel, though, stopped midway and turned around. "Do you still want to find the black river?"

Confused, she said, "Yes."

"All right." His arm shot out, aiming for her shoulder.

She dropped the lantern. It shattered as she deflected his strike. Then Adair's hands grabbed her hips. He shoved her to the side as Vencel danced out of reach. Off balance, she tipped into the rushing air current.

CHAPTER 8

A scream lodged in her throat as she clawed the air, seeking purchase. The two men stood dispassionately, watching her fall. Shyla gasped as terror and gravity gripped her. Wind rushed by in the opposite direction. Her clothes flapped. Her stomach flipped. Darkness closed around her. No one would mourn her.

She hit something soft and yielding. And for a half a heartbeat she stopped moving. Then she was flung up into the air. She shrieked and flailed in the current before she plunged down, paused, and rose again. This repeated a few times—each time the motion shortened until, at last, she rested on…she'd no idea. Except it saved her life.

Breathless, she lay there with her arms pressed to her chest. Her heart thumping under her fingertips. The air still flowed past her. Once she calmed, she explored the strange fabric underneath her with her hands—a cross-hatching of thin ropes? She spread her arms wide. How far did it extend? Better yet, did she dare move to find out? Without any light to see, she might roll off and continue her fall. She shuddered.

At least she still had her pack and wrap. A small comfort because, if there wasn't a way to escape, she may have exchanged one death for another. And dying of thirst wasn't high on her list of things to experience.

With that dire thought as motivation, she sat up. The motion caused ripples. She twined her fingers through the holes and held on. Except for a slight bouncing, nothing happened.

Faint voices echoed. "…know I heard…"

"Imagining things again…"

"Oh yeah, wanna bet?"

A blue-tinted light appeared to her right, illuminating a short tunnel half a meter up the wall. Thankful for the cheap plentifulness of the druks, she had just enough light to determine that the four corners of the…net under her were tied securely to the walls of the air shaft. More good news, there was only a small gap between the net and the tunnel.

The light brightened and two men entered the tunnel, heading straight for her. She struggled to stand, but didn't have the proper coordination.

They noticed her and slowed.

"See, I was right," the young man on the left said smugly. "We caught something."

"You were right all right, Mojag. We caught ourselves a sun-kissed," his companion said.

"Will she fetch a good price, Jayden?"

"You can't sell me," she said.

"Why not?" Mojag asked.

"Because I'm a citizen of Zirdai."

"If it wasn't for our net, you'd be a *dead* citizen of Zirdai," Jayden said. "We caught you fair and square. You're ours."

"I am very grateful for your net. But you can't own people."

"Why not? The Water Prince does it all the time. And you don't seriously think all the Heliacal Priestess's deacons are there by choice," Mojag said.

Shyla suppressed a sigh and sized them up. Both men appeared to be close to her age, although Jayden might be a few circuits older and Mojag a couple younger. To call them grubby was a kindness. They reeked and soot covered every inch of their skin. They might or might not have black hair, depending on how much dirt stained their shoulder-length hair that hung in greasy clumps. At least there were no visible weapons.

Taking out her purse, she shook it. The coins inside clinked together. "How about a deal? You can have everything in here in exchange for my freedom." She had more in her pack, but no need to divulge that tidbit.

They shared a sly look.

"I'd bet the deacons will pay more than a few coins for her," Mojag said. "Didn't they just put a bounty on her capture?"

Oh no, she'd been gone too long and the priestess must believe Shyla ran away. "I have more," Shyla said, hurriedly. "Help me out of here and I'll double what's in here."

"All right," Jayden said. He set the lantern down, leaned over and offered her his hands.

She tucked the purse into her pack and covered her bracelet before grasping his hands. He pulled her to her feet and then into the tunnel. Jayden was surprisingly strong and about twelve centimeters taller than her. At this distance his sharp features seemed more natural than due to lack of nutrition. He might even be quite handsome if he bothered to wash. Crinkling her nose, she stepped back. Or tried.

He wouldn't let go of her hands. "Don't forget about our deal."

She yanked them free. "I keep my promises." Dipping into her bag, she removed the purse and tossed it to Jayden.

He caught it with one hand. While he tipped the coins out into his palm, she dug for the rest.

"Four? That's it?"

"Plus four more." She added them to the pile. "There."

"That's not enough," Mojag said. He matched her height, but probably weighed less. "We could get fifty from the Heliacal Priestess."

"We had a deal," she said. "Now if you could just—"

"Show you the way out?" Jayden asked. "Not without a price."

Ah. Smart guy. "How much?"

"Ten coins."

"I could just follow you. Unless you plan to stay here indefinitely?"

He tilted his head. "You could, but we'll just take you back to our friends."

"Four," she countered. "Two now and two more when we get somewhere I recognize."

"You don't trust us?" Jayden pressed a hand to his chest.

"The last people I trusted tossed me into the air shaft. So no trust." Not ever again.

"Can't we just knock her out, take her bag and leave, Jayden?" Mojag asked.

Yet another reason not to trust, but Shyla grinned at the idea of hitting someone right now. "Go ahead. Try."

"Eight," Jayden said.

"Six, and I don't tell the guards about your net." As long as the air shaft wasn't blocked, the guards wouldn't notice the net.

"Hey!" Mojag said. "That's not fair!"

"And wanting to sell me and then rob me is fair?"

"Six, then," Jayden agreed.

She gave him three more coins.

He picked up the lantern, but she gestured for him and Mojag to go first. It'd be a long time before she'd be comfortable with someone behind her.

Mojag chattered the entire trip as if the boy—she realized he was much younger than Jayden—was incapable of keeping quiet. Mostly he complained about being conned out of more coins. She ignored him. Eventually they reached the edge of an area she recognized.

Shyla hugged her arms tight, suppressing a shudder. She'd fallen twelve levels to level fifty-one. At least she was familiar with the area. Banqui's main residence was nearby, in an area built for those who had extra coin to spend on a suite of rooms.

She paid her guides another three coins, relieved to be parted with the noxious duo. Covering her hair with her wrap, she grabbed a druk and sought an isolated spot. Now she had to avoid both deacons and guards until she brought the vial back to Hanif.

Once she found an empty tunnel, she consulted her map. The only piece of information she had was that secret stairway on level seventy-eight. However, considering the source of that nugget, she doubted it was accurate. At least she should rule it out before...she'd no idea of her next step.

The map showed her a few ways to go down to level seventy-eight—most right in the middle of the city. She picked one on the edge and hoped for the best. While folding the map, the crunch-shuffle of many boots pierced the quiet. One thing about living in Zirdai, it was difficult to sneak up on anyone while wearing boots. It sounded like two or three people heading toward her. So much for her isolated spot. Time to go.

Except it sounded like the noise emanated from both directions. The blue glows confirmed it. She set her pack and lantern down and stripped off her wrap just as four deacons appeared—two on each side.

"See, I told you I found the sun-kissed," Mojag said from behind one of the men.

Scorching hells, she was going to strangle that little sand rat. He must have followed her. Although she'd no idea how. She shouldn't have dismissed him so easily.

"You're coming with us," one of the deacons said. His short and stocky build under his robe could be deceptive—it was either fat or muscle.

Four against one—not great odds. Best to settle this peacefully.

Shyla tugged her sleeve down as she held up her hands, revealing the sigil. "I'm working for the Water Prince."

"Hey! Look at that!" Mojag said. "I bet it's worth—"

"Quiet," the deacon ordered. Then he gave her a humorless smile. "That means nothing to us. Now, come along or—"

Not waiting for the threat, she moved. Targeting him, she kicked him in the stomach. All his air rushed out in a whoosh as he doubled over. She shoved him into the deacon standing beside him, squeezed through the gap and spun to face them. Now all four were on one side of her.

Two pushed past their bent colleague as if to give chase, but hesitated when she remained in place. No way she'd be able to navigate the tunnels fast enough. She knelt on one knee and punched them both in the stomach. When they leaned forward, she stood, driving her fists in an uppercut to their chins. Grunts and curses as arms grappled for her. She backpedaled as the others descended.

Then it was a dance of blocking punches, kicks, and holds. She fought hard and dirty, her hair coming loose. But she'd lost track of Mojag. Big mistake; the little rat squeezed through legs and under arms. She almost ignored him until he pulled a knife. Son of a sand demon! She knocked his first thrust wide, but his second bit into her thigh. Pain seared through her leg and she went down. One deacon pounced, pinning her to the ground while another trapped her hands.

Before she had a chance to counter, they flipped her over onto her stomach, yanked her arms behind her, and secured them. One sat on her legs while the others caught their breaths. With her cheek pressed to the ground, she sucked in the cool gritty air. Her thigh sizzled with pain as if the knife remained. Panic simmered in her chest. The sigil didn't work and Rendor didn't know her location.

Only Mojag appeared unaffected. "I get her pack and the bounty of twenty osees," he said in a chirpy tone.

Strangulation was too good for Mojag. Coins jangled and his dirty feet stepped past her. She lifted her head. The rat clutched her pack. He flashed her a bright grin, did a little bow, and was soon out of sight.

Thinking of creative ways to make him suffer kept Shyla distracted as she was hauled to her feet and marched between the deacons. Every limping step reminded her of the wound. Blood soaked her pants and she hoped the cut wasn't deep. She'd worry about infection, but doubted that would be her biggest problem in the near future.

Their route avoided the populated areas. Not that anyone would help a sun-kissed. Plus no one challenged the deacons. Neither had she. She'd always assumed the person in trouble was a heretic.

They arrived at one of the dozens of chapels dedicated to the worship of the Sun Goddess. Rows of kneelers lined the floor and faced the altar. A few people prayed, their heads bent over clasped hands. Trol lanterns burned on chandeliers that hung from the ceiling that was lost in the darkness. Decorative tile mosaics depicted various historical scenes. Many of them showed the Sun Goddess performing miracles. A miracle right about now would be most welcome. Shyla glanced at the statue of the Goddess behind the altar before the deacons led her through a doorway on the left side of the chapel and into a long corridor.

This part lacked the same beauty and soon cries of pain bounced off the stone walls.

The stout deacon noticed her panicked expression. "This is where we rehabilitate our lost brothers and sisters, helping them to confess their sins and regain their faith."

They passed room after room after room. Inside each, a deacon "rehabilitated" one poor soul. Some stood with hands chained over their heads. Others were secured to kneelers, backs exposed to a whip's lash.

Dread and fear churned in her stomach. Shyla averted her gaze, keeping it on the deacon's broad shoulders. They reached an empty room and she was shoved inside. With the ease of many sun jumps' worth of practice, they freed her hands, forced her to kneel on the hard marble pew about a meter wide, and clamped her arms to the ledge with her palms face up. Normally, the bar was used to rest your elbows on while you prayed. Then they tied her ankles to the kneeler's supports. This arrangement effectively kept her in a locked position. Sharp pain throbbed from the cut on her thigh. Blood continued to soak into the fabric of her pants, spreading into a large oval. The deacons ignored it. It appeared they didn't care if she bled to death.

Two deacons left, leaving Stocky and another behind. The taller man strode over to a wall filled with weapons and perused it as if shopping at the market. An uncontrollable tremor raced through her legs. Stocky yanked on the prince's sigil. It wouldn't budge. He dug his fingernails into her skin and tugged harder. Pain shot up her arm.

"How do you get this off?" he asked.

"I don't know."

He backhanded her across the face. She rocked to the side as pain invaded her senses. Blood filled her nose and mouth. Tears dripped from her eyes. Her entire face throbbed as she gasped for breath.

Stocky knew just how long to wait for her to recover to ask, "Where's the latch?"

The same answer would result in the same response, so Shyla quickly said, "Captain Rendor knows. He put it on, told me only he can unlock it." She braced for another blow.

Instead, Stocky ran his fingers over the edges. He grunted. "A sharp pair of metal cutters should work." He tapped it. "If not, we'll cut off her hand."

Every muscle in her body turned to liquid. "No," she whispered.

But they ignored her. The tall deacon handed Stocky a long-handled tool with two short curved blades on the one end. "If it doesn't work, wait until after we've punished her," he said in a soft purr. "We don't want her bleeding too much and passing out. She must be fully aware of the consequences of her sins before we inform the priestess of her capture."

Shyla closed her eyes, passing out sounded like an excellent idea. The cold bite of metal dug into her wrist. Opening her eyes, she watched as the curved blades cut through the sigil with a loud snap.

Stocky put down the tool and yanked the bracelet off her wrist. The action left behind a long gash, which matched the two other bleeding gashes and the weeping half-moon scratches caused by his nails. She stared at the newly exposed skin. The Water Prince was going to be angry. And Rendor…best not to think about him.

"There," said Stocky. "Now she's no longer protected by the prince's guards. And this goes into the donation basket." He pocketed the sigil and patted the lump in a proprietary way. "Make sure you don't kill her, Iskemu. Remember, the priestess wishes her to remain alive so the Sun Goddess can finish her divine work."

Iskemu bowed. "Yes, brother."

Stocky left. Iskemu picked a knife from the wall of horror and returned to her side. Not going to kill me, she chanted in her mind, trying and failing to achieve calm. All those angles meditating didn't seem to be helping her at this moment.

Grabbing her hair, he yanked her head back. He rested the blade on her exposed throat. "Normally, we ask the sinner to confess. If she feels she doesn't have any sins to confess, we remind her of her misdeeds. With you, there's no need to confess. Your very existence is a misdeed." He leaned close—almost nose to nose. "First we're going to shave your head. Your hair offends us."

"And your bad breath offends me," she said.

He struck her in the temple with the knife's hilt. Her vision went white as pain exploded.

His grip tightened on her hair, fire ringed her scalp. "If you don't keep your mouth shut we'll rip it out clump by clump."

She didn't have the breath to speak. Satisfied, he brought the blade up to her forehead. Shyla took some comfort from the fact that it would grow back. Well... provided she lived through this. So much for comfort.

Iskemu chiseled at her hair as blood from her temple dripped into her eyes. The scraping sound was loud in her ears. Long hunks of her hair floated to the ground. It resembled the stuffing that had been ripped from her sleeping cushion. Perhaps the deacons would stuff a pillow with her hair and gift it to the Heliacal Priestess. She focused on that comical scene to block out what was happening. Hard to do when cold air kept kissing the skin on her newly exposed scalp.

After her hair was shorn, Iskemu leaned close to her ear. "Now we will shave the rest off and then we'll pluck each offending eyelash, eyebrow, and pubic hair from your unclean body." He exchanged his knife for a straight razor and returned without water or soap.

A dry shave. Shyla curled her fingers tight—all she could do now—but if she'd get a chance—

"Stop," said an authoritative male voice.

Iskemu scowled, but stepped away. Through vision blurred with blood and tears, she saw four deacons in the doorway. Three men and a woman.

"What's this intrusion?" Iskemu asked. "We're in the middle of a confession."

"The Heliacal Priestess has learned you have the sun-kissed. The Blessed One wishes to speak with her."

The woman was scary, but Shyla would happily take her chances with her to get away from Iskemu. The two men entered and released Shyla. She slumped in place, but they hooked their hands under her arms and pulled her upright.

"Careful," warned Iskemu, still holding the straight razor. "She put up quite the fight and she's not as injured as she pretends."

Tattletale. Their grips tightened. Shyla decided she'd wait until they left the chapel before she tried to break away. Limping between the two deacons, she struggled to match their pace. By the time they left, she panted for breath, but they didn't slow at all. In fact, they increased their speed.

"Hurry, hurry," the woman urged in a whisper.

They entered a tunnel and zigzagged down a number of corridors. Soon no one was around, but there was enough light. As good a place as any.

Shyla dug her heels into the ground, stopping while the two men lurched forward. Dropping her weight to break their hold, she spun, and sprinted. Except a wave of dizziness upset her balance within two strides and she tripped over her own feet, falling hard on the ground. Hands grabbed her shoulders, but she knocked them away and kicked out.

"Stop. We're rescuing you!" cried a familiar voice.

Surprised, she stopped. The deacon…no, Jayden... held his arms wide. He cleaned up in more ways than one.

"Why?" she asked.

"Can we do the question and answer thing later?" the woman asked. "It's not gonna take them long to catch on. And then we'll all be confessing. And I don't know about you guys, but I've a lot of sins."

Jayden reached out for her hand. She ignored it and pushed to her feet.

"Let's go," the woman said.

"Thanks for the help, but you go on. I can find my own way," Shyla said.

"Come back with us, and I'll explain everything," Jayden said.

"Not happening." She braced for…well, she wasn't sure if they'd try to force her or not.

"Look, you're in no condition to be on your own right now," he said. "We have water and food and medical supplies."

"No. I can take care of myself."

"Come on, Jay, leave her," the woman said. And when he didn't respond, she shrugged. "I'm going."

He rounded on her. "Stay put," he growled. "The deacons move in packs of four. This is only going to work if we stick together, Gurice."

Turning back to Shyla, he said, "I have your pack. Please let me help you."

"Do you have Mojag too?"

"Yes, and something better."

She brightened. "A knife I can stab the little sand rat with?"

Gurice laughed. "I like her."

"I know the location of the black river."

She blinked at him, then demanded, "How do you know about that?"

"I'll tell you after we're safe. Just trust me. Please. I won't toss you into an air shaft. Promise."

"Here." Gurice handed Shyla her knife. "Come on, guys."

Jayden didn't hesitate, but the others reluctantly gave her theirs.

"Now you have all our weapons," Gurice said. "You can scream and call the guards to arrest us. If we wanted to hurt you, we wouldn't have rescued you."

Well…when she put it that way. "All right, but I'm keeping the knives." Not that she ever fought with one. The Ways of the Yarin focused on defensive versus offensive fighting.

"Figures," Gurice muttered.

With two in front and two behind her, Shyla tried to keep track of the tunnels, stairwells, and ramps they traversed. They descended a number of levels, finally ending up on level sixty-two. The druks shone purple and made their green robes appear brown.

When they reached a settlement, Shyla no longer cared if they ambushed her. Every muscle ached. The cut on her thigh had stopped bleeding, but dried blood glued the fabric of her pants to her skin, every step a sharp hot poker of pain as it pulled. Her face throbbed and the swelling around her right eye made it difficult to see. And when did the cavern start to spin?

You're safe.

What was that? She didn't have the energy to care nor to knock away the hands that cupped her elbows, guiding her. They entered a room.

You're safe.

Other people lay on cushions. Some were wrapped in bandages, some had splints, and some had both. Shyla was lowered onto something soft. The knives clattered to the floor and the last thing she saw was Jayden's face hovering over her.

She was safe.

* * *

Shyla woke with a cool cloth pressed to her forehead. And for a brief blessed moment, nothing hurt. Then she moved and every cut, bruise, and the stab wound flared to painful life. A groan escaped her lips before she clamped them together.

Pulling the cloth off, she tried to sit up.

"Rest, rest," an older man said, pushing down on her shoulders.

She collapsed back. Either he was super strong or she was super weak. "But..."

He waited. His bushy white eyebrows floated like velblouds above his kind gray eyes.

"I have to—"

"Regain your health, I know. Here." He helped her drink from a cup.

The liquid tasted like green tea, but it had a sharp aftertaste. Alarmed, she sat up. The room spun for a moment, but settled on the man's wrinkled face.

"You drugged me," she accused.

"I'm *healing* you."

A heavy lassitude flowed through her. "I need..."

"To heal, I know. That is what I'm endeavoring to do, dear child."

"But..."

"You are resisting, I know."

Unable to fight the drug, she sank back down. "You're exasperating."

"I know."

* * *

The next time she woke, she was allowed to sit up and eat. Shyla fingered the flesh around her right eye.

While still bruised, it wasn't as swollen and her vision was clearer. A prickly stubble met her fingertips when she touched her hair. Tears threatened as a hard knot formed in her throat. Her hair shouldn't matter to her since she covered her head most of the time anyway, yet it did. The gash on her right leg had been stitched closed. A bandage ringed her left wrist. Other than the deep ache in her muscles and a persistent throbbing in her forehead, she felt fine.

When she finished her meal, Mr. I Know set a tea cup in front of her.

"No thanks," she said, pushing it back.

"You think I drugged your tea again."

"Yes."

"There's no need for that, dear child. I've already drugged your food."

Outraged, she tossed the fur off of her. "But I'm—"

"Still healing, I know." He nudged the cup closer. "Drink up before you fall asleep."

* * *

The third time she woke, she was determined to not eat or drink anything. But this time Mr. I Know wasn't nearby. Instead Jayden appeared once she stirred.

"How are you feeling?" he asked. He'd exchanged the deacon's robe with a plain tunic and pants tucked into leather boots. His clean golden brown hair was brushed back away from his face, revealing amber eyes and his true skin color—a light sienna.

"Better." Surprisingly so.

He cocked his head. "Why don't you sound happy about that?"

She glared at Mr. I Know, who tended another patient.

Jayden followed her gaze. "Ah. Annoying, but effective. Zhek's saved lots of people's lives."

"He drugged me. Twice."

"He believes sleep is the best medicine and that patients are too stupid to take that advice so he ensures they do. If it makes you feel any better, Zhek did it to me when the guards broke my ribs and I even knew about his sneaky methods."

Strangely enough, it did. "How long have I been here?"

"About two sun jumps."

She bit down a groan.

"Are you ready to get out of here?" he asked.

"Oh yes."

When Jayden smiled, his features softened. He appeared circuits younger and he was rather good-looking. Too bad, he knew it. Jayden's grin turned cocky when she continued to study him. As he helped her stand, she wondered how he'd ended up here. Was he born to this life, or had he found himself in dire straits? What about those ribs? And why did she care?

He led her out into the main area. Unlike the other communes, no one stared at her. They bustled about doing…she'd no idea. The few who did make eye contact actually nodded hello to her.

She slowed. Was he leading her into a trap?

"What's wrong?" he asked.

"Just give me my pack and the location of the black river. I've already wasted too much time."

He studied her somewhat panicked expression. "All right. This way."

She didn't quite relax, but at least there weren't any air shafts around here. She hoped. That reminded her. "How did you know I was searching for the black river?" When he hesitated, she said, "You promised to tell me."

"When you were up at Orla's commune, a runner came down. Orla wants me to help you and she's one of our elders." His shoulders tensed.

Something wasn't quite right. "If Orla wants to help me then why did Vencel and Adair toss me into an air shaft?"

He ducked his head. "It's the quickest and easiest way to get to my level." Then he glanced at her. "Some people think it's fun."

Fun? Falling twelve stories was not fun. She glared at him. "They could have warned me."

"Yeah, but they were angry you found their commune so easily."

Good to know they weren't trying to kill her. But still… Shyla and Jayden walked in silence. He led her to a room. Gurice was inside along with—

"Mojag!" Shyla said.

The boy jumped up from where he'd been sitting crossed legged on a cushion. He shuffled over to the corner and picked up her pack. Returning, he handed it to her and scurried back a few meters as if worried she'd strike him. He hung his head. "I'm sorry I sold you to the deacons."

Astounded, she stared at him. "Sorry? You're sorry?"

"Yes."

"They were going to kill me!"

"Do you want my knife?" Gurice asked her.

"Gurice," Jayden warned.

"Why did you do it?" Shyla asked Mojag.

"I was mad. I thought you cheated us. Everyone's always trying to cheat us."

"I gave you almost every coin I had."

"I know." He looked miserable.

"You looked in my pack." She'd reached her limit. Not that she had any valuables in there, but it infuriated her that everyone just...*took* from her. Banqui, the Water Prince, the Heliacal Priestess, and all the people she met while on this crazy hunt for the black water. As if she wasn't a person, but an object to be used.

Anger fueling her steps, Shyla stalked toward the boy. Mojag braced as if expecting a blow.

"Shyla," Jayden said, stopping her.

She glanced at him. "I thought you were supposed to help me?"

"We had to gain your trust first."

"By charging me for a fake rescue? Then selling me to the deacons? Oh, yes, that's an *excellent* plan."

He ignored her sarcasm. "We charged for the rescue in order to get you to trust us. You wouldn't have believed we would help you due to kindness. I was giving you time to reach level seventy-eight and fumble around before offering to lead you to the stairway when Mojag disappeared. I should have told him my plan. I thought he returned to the commune. But he realized he made a terrible mistake. He found me and confessed everything right away. That's why we knew where you were. We rescued you as fast as we could."

It took her a moment to really understand what they had done. "You risked your lives for me?"

"Of course. It was the right thing to do. Anyone would have done the same."

Except they wouldn't. Not for a sun-kissed. She studied him. What scam was he working now? Pretend she wasn't any different to get her to trust him. Unless he really believed she was worth risking his life for? Did it matter why he did it? No. She didn't care about these people and their agendas.

"Just tell me where I can find the black river," she said.

"I'll go one better and show you."

"No. Tell me."

"It's too complicated."

Nice try. "I've a map you can mark." She dug in her pack, checking the contents. Everything was there except the last of her coins. Shyla shot Mojag a sharp glare. He had the decency to look sheepish.

"Mojag, give her back her coins," Jayden ordered, correctly interpreting their silent exchange.

"I already gave them to the collective. Sorry," the boy said to his feet.

"How many?"

"Two."

Jayden dug into his pocket.

"Keep them," Shyla said. They weren't hers anyway. "They should cover Zhek's services." She took out the map and a stick of charcoal, handing both to Jayden.

He spread it out on the floor and studied it. Gurice and Mojag peered over his shoulder. Both had the same oval-shaped face, light green eyes, and chestnut-colored skin. The resemblance between the two was now obvious.

"Brother?" she asked Gurice.

"Yeah," she said, with that combination of exasperation mixed with love.

And for a moment, Shyla stood in the monastery bickering with Karlin and Easan over who deserved that last piece of pie.

"Your map is useless," Jayden said, jerking her from the past.

"Just do your best."

He sighed and sketched a few lines, drew a couple of arrows. "In this area on level seventy-three, I'm not sure of all the turns, but there's this air…conduit that you have to crawl through. It smells like rotten cheese." Then he reached level seventy-eight. "Here's a stairwell that just goes straight down. But be careful, there's steps missing. Then at the bottom…" He drew a curvy line. "And don't make any noise when you're down there. It carries and it won't be long until the entire guard is chasing you." Jayden shot Mojag a pointed glare.

"I had to sneeze," the boy said in his defense.

Jayden marked a thick black line. "The river's not very long or wide, but you should be able to find it." Jayden folded the map and handed it to her.

"Thank you."

He stood and brushed off his pants. "Let me guide you. It'll be safer."

"No. Besides, I don't have the coin to pay you."

"You don't need to pay me."

"Yes, I do. I'm not going to owe anyone a favor."

"Why not?" He moved closer and dropped his voice. "It could be fun."

She huffed in derision.

Gurice covered her mouth, but didn't quite stifle her laughter. Jayden frowned at her, but that just made her shoulders shake harder.

"At least fill your water skin before you leave," he said to Shyla. "We just set up a fresh supply."

A good idea. "All right."

He led her to the communal jug. It was a large glass barrel with a spout and small faucet at the bottom. A young girl with long curly black hair turned the handle and filled her glass. The water was clear—no signs of sand or dirt. Shyla wondered where they procured the water, but wasn't curious enough to ask. Once she filled her skin, Jayden showed her the exit and explained how to get to the first mark on her map.

"Thanks," she said, giving him a short wave goodbye.

"Good luck," he said.

Only when she found that at least his initial directions matched what she encountered did she relax. Whether they actually led to the black river had yet to be determined.

After a few angles, the sound of pounding boots rumbled behind her. Stuck in the middle of a tunnel, she spun to face her attacker. It was Jayden with a panicked expression.

"Don't..." He panted, gasping for breath. "Drink... the water."

Alarmed, she dug her water skin from her pack. "Why not?"

"Poisoned."

"How do—" The image of that little girl filling her glass flashed. "Oh no! Is she all right?"

He hunched his shoulders as pained grief creased his face. Jayden took her water skin. "Come back for a moment, we'll get you a new one. Please."

She'd been about to refuse, but it was the *please* that changed her mind. The scene in the cavern was now one of utter chaos. Jayden disappeared, leaving Shyla alone.

A woman wailed over the little girl in her arms. "Dyani, Dyani, Dyani…my sweet baby girl. Wake up." She rocked the girl, but the body remained stiff and her dull eyes were void of life. Even standing ten meters away, the mother's grief pierced Shyla's heart.

The image burned into Shyla's brain along with the knowledge there was nothing anyone could do or say to change it.

Two men argued over the glass barrel. "…checked!" one yelled.

"I did. It's marked." The other stabbed his finger at a blue circle pattern on the glass. "It's safe…or it was when I brought it in." He ran a hand through his hair.

Both men glanced around as if the poisoner would be standing there smirking at them.

Jayden returned with an empty water skin. "I figured you wouldn't trust our water. Will you be able to find some?"

The fact that he was concerned about her, when one of his people just died, amazed her. "Yes, I'll be fine." She gestured to the barrel. "Who would poison the water?"

He gaped at her a moment, then recovered. "You really don't know?"

"A rival commune?"

"No," he said with such vehemence, she almost stepped back. "It was the Water Prince—or rather one of his guards or spies. His goons try to poison all the water that has been obtained illegally. They miss a fair amount, which is what keeps us alive. And we test all our water, but this..." Jayden's gaze swept the group of people hovering around the dead child. "This means either we have a spy in our midst or one of the Water Prince's agents has discovered how we mark our barrels safe."

That was beyond awful. "How do you test your water?"

"Sand rats. The younger kids catch them and we let them drink from a barrel. If they're still alive after a sun jump, we mark the barrel safe. We feed the animals and some of the kids keep them for pets." Jayden huffed. "One rat actually died of old age. We called him Lucky."

The water they served in the dining cavern might be gritty and cloudy, but she'd never had to worry if it was poisoned—and she wouldn't complain about its quality. Not now. Why would these people rather live like this than pay their taxes?

"Is there a special place for..." A tightness in her throat cut off the rest of the sentence.

"Yes. We have our own burial caves and Zhek will prepare the body. In fact, I'd better go help," Jayden said.

She touched his arm, stopping him. "Thank you for coming after me again."

He flashed her a quick smirk. "Now you owe me one." Then he jogged off.

* * *

By the time she reached the spot Jayden had caught up to her, she couldn't focus. Dyani's dead eyes, the deacon's knife, and the memories of falling through the air kept circling her mind like a sand devil digging its burrow.

She found a dark isolated nook and centered her breathing. Drawing on the meditation techniques of the Yarin, she banished the chaotic emotions and images, instead concentrating on her goal. Unable to save future victims like Dyani or to change the deacon's methods of forcing confessions, Shyla focused on what she *could* do. Save Banqui.

Therefore she would concentrate all her efforts on getting that vial filled with the black water. It was her only chance and, damn it, she'd get to that river if it killed her.

However, she still took precautions and avoided the few guards she caught sight of. And, for a change, she caught a break when she stopped at the dining cavern on level sixty-nine to fill her new water skin—the deacon was fast asleep. At one point, she encountered another chapel. She backpedaled before the deacons guarding the entrance spotted her, then went the long way around.

She caught sight of the time and relaxed. It was angle three-ten—well into the darkness. Not many people were awake. She increased her pace, determined to take advantage of the empty tunnels.

When she reached level seventy-three, she slowed. This was where Jayden's directions faltered. She had to find that conduit so she sniffed the air, scenting for rotten cheese. No luck, but after a couple angles she did discover one thing.

She was being followed.

CHAPTER 9

The fact that she was being followed wasn't as alarming as the long list of possible suspects. And to think, just ten sun jumps ago she had been minding her own business, relatively content.

She considered her options. They followed far enough behind so they could use her light for navigation, but remain unseen to her light-adapted eyes. Shyla could allow them to continue following her, letting them make the first move. Or lose them. Or stage an ambush. Or she could make them believe they'd lost her so she'd get a chance to see who tailed her. All except the first one would take time she didn't have. But that one was too risky. She sighed.

Abandoning her search for the rotten cheese scent, she cut down a few tunnels until she found a short loop.

Throughout Zirdai there were dozens of tunnels that branched out in what appeared to be a different direction, but ended up just looping back to that main corridor.

This time one would work to her advantage. She passed it and wandered around as if looking for another route. Using up precious time, she eventually returned to that loop.

Turning left, she strode two meters then set the druk on the ground. Shyla pulled off her boots and ran, trailing one hand on the wall while the other clutched her boots. She circled around until she reached the original tunnel, except further up. Stopping, she let her eyes adjust to the darkness for a few heartbeats, then peered around the corner.

Two figures crept up the tunnel toward the indigo-tinged glow emanating from the intersection. No robes or swords. The tight knot in her stomach eased. When they neared the light's edge, they stopped. She wondered how long they'd wait before investigating.

A couple angles passed before they started gesticulating at each other in a silent communication. Debating who should peek around the corner, she guessed. The shorter and skinnier of the two crouched low and inched forward. As soon as he reached the light, Shyla suppressed a groan. Mojag.

"She's gone," Mojag whispered to...

Jayden stepped into the light. "Seven hells." He ran a hand through his hair.

"You think she heard us?" Mojag asked.

"No, I think she fell into the black river. Of course she heard us."

"I didn't sneeze!"

But Jayden just shook his head. "She'll never find that conduit on her own."

"Why do you care?" Mojag asked.

Shyla wondered the same thing.

"Because *you* need to make up for selling her to the deacons."

"I said I was sorry," Mojag said sullenly.

"Sometimes sorry isn't enough." Then he raised his voice. "Isn't that right, Shyla?"

Ah hells, caught eavesdropping. Although a part of her would have been disappointed if he hadn't figured it out. Probably making a bad decision, Shyla said, "Yes, but it's a step in the right direction."

She joined them. "Why can't I get rid of you two?"

"I don't handle rejection well," Jayden said with a smile.

"He made me come," Mojag added.

Another childish retort. "How old are you?" she asked Mojag.

"Thirteen circuits."

"He's had a recent growth spurt," Jayden said.

That explained it, but not all of it. “Why do you take him with you when a sneeze might get you killed?”

“He needs to learn how to survive,” he said in a matter-of-fact tone.

And she’d complained about living in Zirdai. “Why doesn’t Gurice teach…” She recalled his sister offering Shyla her knife. “Never mind.” Then she remembered poor Dyani. “How did you find me so fast?”

“Short cuts. And I knew where you were heading.”

“Are you going to let us help you now?” Mojag asked her.

“Do I have a choice?”

“Of course, but we’ll follow you regardless,” Jayden said.

“I guess since you’re already here, you can show me where that conduit is.”

“My that’s very magnanimous of you.”

“Shut up.”

He laughed.

* * *

Rotten cheese. The smell drove all thoughts of food from her mind. She was never eating again. It didn’t help they were crawling through a thin stream of…muck, which was the source of the stench. Jayden hadn’t been kidding when he said it was a tight conduit.

When they reached the end, it was a relief to straighten her back. Her thigh throbbed, but she ignored it.

"That was deeper than the last time I was here. We reek. We need to change," Jayden said.

"I don't have extra clothes, and aren't we close to that stairwell?" Shyla asked. She'd already spent too much time on this quest for the monks. The priestess had already set a bounty on her, no doubt the prince would soon do the same.

"We can't go down there. The guards will smell us. Don't worry, there's a commune nearby. They'll have clothes for you."

"I don't have any coin."

"That's okay, they'll help." Jayden strode away.

Shyla had no choice but to follow him. "Why would they help me? I'm not one of you."

"Why do you think that?"

Frustrated, she grabbed his arm and spun him around to face her. Pointing at her blond stubble, she said, "Because I'm not. I'm not one of anyone. No one in this stinking city would help me unless I pay them or do something for them in return."

"Woah that sucks," Mojag said.

"Maybe you're making friends with the wrong people," Jayden said carefully.

A laugh burst from her, uncontrolled, but no humor touched the harsh sound. He had a point. If she wasn't friends with Banqui, she wouldn't be standing here reeking of rotten cheese with two vagrants and running from both the guards and the deacons.

"There's no maybe about it," she said.

He gave her a funny look, but continued. At one point during the trip they descended to level seventy-five. Jayden moved with confidence as if he traversed this route every sun jump. For all she knew, he did.

Finally, they reached the commune. Jayden stopped in the threshold, his face ashen. Mojag cried out and sprinted inside. Jayden joined Mojag as Shyla entered. The cavern looked like a pack of sand demons had attacked. Slash marks ripped through the cushions. Clothing, toys, and personal items littered the blood-stained floor. Mojag searched the area.

"Who did this?" Shyla asked. "Deacons?"

"No." Jayden crouched by one of the cushions, touching the floor. His fingertips came away coated with blood. "This was done with a sword. Only the Water Prince's guards carry them."

"There's no one here," Mojag said. His voice was rough.

Jayden straightened. "They've been arrested." He kicked a pile of clothes. "They're as good as dead."

She stepped back. "No. Their only crime is vagrancy. Why would the Water Prince kill them?"

"Because he can."

No. She wouldn't believe that. Jayden was still upset over Dyani and jumping to the wrong conclusions.

"Mojag," Jayden said.

"Yes?"

"Go back home, tell the elders there's been a raid."

"All right. What are you going to do?"

"I'm going to take her to the black river as promised."

"No," Shyla said. "Just take me to the stairwell, I can find it from there. You need to help your people."

He paused, clearly conflicted, but then nodded. "I'll meet you back here," he said to Mojag. "Now go."

Mojag bolted.

Shyla headed for the exit as well.

"Wait," Jayden said. He rooted through a pile of strewn clothing.

Horrified, she protested. "I can't—"

"You can. Do you want to join them in the Water Prince's cells?"

"No, but..." Although at this point, she suspected it was just a matter of time.

"Here, these should fit you." He thrust a bundle into her arms then turned his back on her.

She changed quickly. The pant legs were too long so she rolled them up at her waist. And the tunic hung down to her knees and past her hands. She pushed the sleeves up.

"Done," she said.

When Jayden turned around a brief smile flashed.

"What?" she asked.

"You look more like a vagrant now."

"Oh." Was that a compliment? She smoothed out her wrap. Sludge stained the ends. Ugh.

"No, wait." He searched another pile and tossed her a clean shawl. "Now you're ready." He strode from the room.

It didn't take long to reach the stairwell on level seventy-eight. Although she had to admit, she'd probably wouldn't have found it on her own.

"I'm sorry about your people."

"Me, too."

"Thanks for your help."

"Stay safe, Sun-kissed."

She opened her mouth, but he was gone.

* * *

The stairwell twisted around and around and around in tight circles. Just like Shyla's thoughts. Why did Jayden call her sun-kissed after using her name all those times? He'd used it the first time they'd met, maybe he wanted to end with it as well. She doubted she'd see him again.

She passed a couple doors and wondered where they led to—she'd lost track of the levels. A number of times Shyla needed to stop her descent and press her hands to the cool moist walls to control the dizziness that threatened to topple her. Only a meter and a half wide, the stairwell's narrow steps were far apart as they corkscrewed into the blackness below the druk's indigo light.

But after one turn, the blackness didn't recede. Shyla caught her balance just before she stepped into the gap. When her breath steadied, she crouched and shone the light down. It appeared that an entire level's worth of steps were missing. Much more than she'd envisioned when Jayden had mentioned it.

Now what? The stone center post remained intact. Perhaps she could slide down it. Or dangle by her hands and drop down. Would the sound of her hitting the next step alert the guards? Maybe. She inspected the post. Notches and grooves from where the steps had been remained. Enough for her to use to climb down. Yes, something going right for a change. Shyla tied the lantern to her pack's straps and wrapped her shawl around it to protect the druk. Then she lowered it as far as she could before letting go. It hit with a muffled thud.

Her turn. She faced toward the steps then slid the toe of her left boot along the post until it snagged on a groove. Leaning her weight on her leg, she moved her hands from the step to the post, hugging it before finding a hold for her right foot. Then she slowly moved each foot lower while sliding her arms until she reached the bottom. Where she promptly sat down and sucked in the damp air. Her legs shook from the effort and sweat slicked her skin.

When she recovered, she shouldered her pack and continued the journey. There were a few more gaps in the stairwell, but all could be bridged easily. She avoided thinking about the return trip. Best to focus on the present.

At the bottom of the stairwell, the lantern shone with a violet hue. She followed Jayden's instructions. The walls dripped with water and a heavy mineral scent flowed on a strong wind that pushed against her back. This had to be a part of the ventilation system. Puddles of water pooled on the ground. She shone the light closer and scooped up a handful, but the liquid wasn't black. Trying not to make any noise, she slowed, careful to avoid splashing or scuffing her boots on the stone. The air would carry the sound rather far.

After a few angles the darkness ahead lightened. When she reached the next intersection, she glanced to the right. In the distance, bright shafts of yellow trol-lantern light streamed down. Her heart jumped in response. Jayden claimed the black river flowed under those beams. Finally!

As she neared the light, harsh voices echoed. Remembering Jayden's warning, she closed the druk and crept onward. Then a sharp crack and a scream cut right through her. She froze. Was she under the prison level? No, that level was dark and stunk of offal and urine. This must be something else.

It didn't matter. All that mattered was the black water. She kept moving until she reached the end of the tunnel, which stopped at a T-intersection. The air flowed in the opposite direction in the new tunnel and it now carried a rancid metallic odor as if raw meat had spoiled. A couple of beams of trol light sliced the blackness from above, then there was darkness followed by another cluster of beams. This pattern extended along the new tunnel both to the left and right.

But what caught her complete attention was the light reflecting off a black river. Well, at a dozen centimeters wide, it was more of a rivulet. The liquid flowed through the tunnel just like Jayden had said.

With her heart jumping in her chest, she fumbled for the vial. It had fallen to the very bottom of her pack. She twisted the cap off. Her fingers shook as she dipped the glass into the slow current. The thick water oozed into the container. Once filled, she sealed it tight. The black water stuck to her hand. She sniffed it and jerked her fingers away at the repulsive smell. It was the source of that rancid scent. Much stronger because the wind hadn't diluted it. And she'd just shoved it right under her nose. Not the smartest move. She wiped her hand on her pants.

Curious about what was above the tunnel, she crept over to the edge of one of the beams of light. She peered up through a metal grate and wished she hadn't.

A dead woman hung upside down. She was naked and every centimeter of her skin was covered with cuts. Shyla pressed her hand against her mouth. Throwing up would be too noisy. Swallowing the bile, Shyla retreated. But she stopped when voices echoed.

Unable to resist, she continued, tracking the sounds. She passed underneath room after room—all quiet so she didn't dare look up. The tunnel seemed to go on forever. The voices grew louder.

"...I don't...please...I...don't...know..."

"Where is..."

"...not...we didn't..."

"...the sun-kissed...tell me..."

"Not us...I swear...haven't...her..."

Ice shot through her. Her stomach lurched and she dug her fingernails into her skin to keep from heaving. But she forced her feet to continue forward to find the room with the poor man who begged for mercy.

And there he was, also upside down. Blood running down his naked body.

A guard stood in front of him with a long blade in his hand. He pressed it to the man's genitals. "Last time. Tell me where the sun-kissed is. What did your people do to her?"

"Nothing. We did nothing! We haven't seen her! Check with the deacons! We heard rumors the deacons caught her on level fifty-one. Please, I'm telling the truth."

"I believe you," the guard said.

The victim relaxed.

"But the Water Prince is very upset that his sun-kissed is missing." The guard twisted his wrist. Blood splashed.

"Nooo!"

Horrified, Shyla covered her face with both her hands, stifling sobs. Tears flowed down her cheeks and her nose filled with mucus, making it hard to breathe. She gasped, pulling air through her fingers to muffle her panting. They were looking for her. He was torturing that poor man because of her. She had to find Rendor. Had to stop this.

She straightened and backed away a couple steps. Then bright red liquid poured from the grate she had just stood under. It splashed into the black river and a terrible realization seized her. She stumbled over to one of the shafts of light and held the vial up.

The liquid inside was a blackish red. Her fingers numbed and she almost dropped the vial. She staggered away from the river of blood—new mixed with old.

Who could…

That meant…

All her fault…

A weakness flowed through her. Unable to stand, she knelt on the ground as the walls spun around her. Bending forward, she pressed her forehead to the cold stone. More people would be tortured unless she let the prince know she was alive. That was all that mattered at this moment.

By sheer force of will, Shyla steadied her breathing. Then she pushed to her feet and raced to the stairwell. Going up the steps at a fast rate required coordination—something that she lacked due to little sleep and sustenance, which resulted in banging her shins and tripping often, slamming down on her hands. When she reached the large gap, she took a quick break—just long enough to drink a couple gulps of water and eat a stick of jerky. Otherwise, she'd never have the strength to climb the post while carrying the extra weight of her pack and the druk that remained tied to the strap.

Finished eating, she repacked and slung her pack over her neck. She mapped out a route, searching for hand and foot holds on the post. Then she began climbing. Slow didn't even come close to describing her pace. Sand dunes built faster than it took her to reach the top.

By the time she neared the steps, sweat stung her eyes, her arm and leg muscles trembled, and her fingertips bled. As she transferred her weight from the post to safety, her right foot slipped. She dove to the side, clinging to the bottom step with her legs dangling in the gap and her heart slamming in her chest. Worming her way further, she pulled the rest of her body up on the steps. Relieved, Shyla lay there for a moment. A warm wetness spread on her right thigh. She had probably ripped the stitches, but it ranked pretty low on the list of things to worry about. Once she recovered, she continued up the stairwell to level seventy-eight.

Shyla leaned against the tunnel's wall to catch her breath. A boot scuffed on the floor nearby. Turning to deflect an attack, she paused then dropped her arms. Jayden stood just on the edge of her druk's light. His expression was guarded. He knew what she'd seen down under the Water Prince's special rooms.

"Why didn't you tell me?" she demanded.

"I thought you knew."

Shyla rounded on him. "Why would you think that?"

"'Cause you called it the black river."

Did she really need to explain what black and river meant to this man? "So?"

"So, it's a code or a shorthand, however you want to describe it."

"For what?"

"You really don't know?"

"Jayden," she warned.

"All right. Well, as you saw, there's quite a bit of blood and death in our community. And because we're hunted, we keep to the shadows as much as possible. Blood looks black when there's not that much light, so the black river is when someone is bleeding heavily."

Heartbreaking. "Why are you here, Jayden? Your people need you."

"I wanted to know what you saw."

An image of the dead woman flashed in her mind as the man's screams echoed in her ears. Did he wish to learn if his people were suffering? Would it help him to know? No. "I found the river of blood. Why did you think I wanted to see it?"

"Orla said you were on a mission for the monks. We hope you will tell them of the Water Prince's atrocities so they will help us."

Jayden's efforts to aid her despite her resistance now made sense. "They can't help you. They're not allowed to interfere." But she could.

She headed the way they'd come earlier.

He fell into step beside her. "Will you tell them anyway?"

"I—" A sudden realization hit her. The monks already knew about it. Then why send her to the black river? So she'd witness how horrible living in Zirdai was and return to the monastery.

"Shyla?"

"I'll tell them, but it won't matter. I'm sorry."

"Me, too."

They continued on in silence. When they reached the next intersection, she asked, "Do I have to go through that smelly conduit in order to reach the main area of this level?"

"Are you going back to the monastery?"

"Not yet."

"Where are you going?"

"I need to find the guards."

Horrified, he asked, "Why would you do *that*?"

"They're looking for me."

"Which is usually an excellent reason to *avoid* them."

"They think I'm missing and your people are to blame. They're…interrogating them and I need to stop it."

Jayden stepped in front of her. "Wait. Why would the guards care that you're missing?"

Scorching hells. How to explain? "I'm working—"

"You're working for *them*?" His entire demeanor changed from friendly pest to dangerous.

"It's complicated."

"Start explaining," he ordered.

She bristled at his commanding tone. "Your people don't have the time for—"

"They're dead regardless." Stated as fact.

"But they won't be tortured anymore. And the guards are going to make a lot of trouble for you until they find me."

"They make trouble for us regardless. Are you spying for the Water Prince? Is that why they're so keen to find you?"

"No. Not spying. He *hired* me to do a job." She held up her hand to stop him. "It doesn't have *anything* at all to do with your people. I need the...black water to get information from the monks to help me finish *that* job. That's the only reason why he's concerned that I went missing. So once I get word to him I'm fine, his guards will stop harassing your people."

"So you want me to believe the Water Prince hired a sun-kissed to do a job? Do you have any proof?"

Shyla pulled back the sleeve on her left arm, revealing a bandage. Seven hells, she'd forgotten the deacons had stolen it. Jayden waited. Did she have anything else? No.

"I had his sigil, but the deacons cut it off," she tried.

"How convenient."

"Look, I'm trying to help."

"Yeah, help the Water Prince." He moved closer. "I gotta admit your quest to find the black water for the monks was a pretty good ruse in order to locate our communities."

Shyla searched for some way to convince him, but realized it was hopeless. "Believe what you want, but I'm going to find the guards before more of *your* people die."

"You're not going anywhere." The menace in his voice was clear.

"You're acting like you're in charge, but you're not." She gathered the dregs of her strength just in case she needed to flee or fight. Then she stepped away from him.

He lunged.

She ducked and spun, avoiding getting trapped in his arms. But he was quick to recover and she scrambled to block his attacks. Her pack and the druk hindered her movements. Jayden, however was unimpeded, uninjured, and hadn't just climbed up twenty levels.

Still, she held her own. For a while. Unwilling to injure him, she fended him off, but as her energy lagged she knew she'd have to resort to a few dirty tricks. With a surge of speed, she swept his feet out from under him and followed him down with an elbow strike to his temple. Hard enough to disorient him, but not enough to knock him unconscious. It worked. All fight gone, Jayden lay there, pressing a hand to his head.

"Sorry," she said, backing away. By the time he was able to stand, she'd be long gone.

He pushed up to an unsteady elbow. "Mojag, stop her."

Annoyed, she spun to face the boy. Except he wasn't alone.

CHAPTER 10

Mojag stood with four other vagrants. Huh. Jayden brought back-up?

"You're outnumbered," Mojag said.

"I guess I should be flattered you brought so many." She assessed the group. Not as skinny or malnourished as one would think. The men appeared downright healthy and strong. "Why did you bring them?"

"Since *your* prince raided one of our communes and arrested everyone, we've been ordered to travel in packs for our safety. Good thing, too, or a traitor like you might have gotten away."

So Mojag heard their conversation and Shyla hadn't known they were just out of sight. She must be more exhausted than she thought. Too bad it was a horrible time to figure that out.

"Just give up already," Mojag said when the silence lengthened. "We don't want to hurt you."

Mojag was a terrible liar. "Really? Did you bring your knife?"

He squinted at her as his fingers grazed his right pocket. "I always have it."

"Good." She pounced on the boy.

Mojag squawked as she yanked his weapon free, spun him around, and rested the blade on his neck. He stilled in an instant, but it took his companions a few heartbeats to realize the situation.

"Don't come any closer or Mojag gets a pretty red necklace," she said.

They stopped. But the big brute in the center said, "She's bluffing."

"Mojag, do you want to explain or should I?" she asked.

"She's serious guys!" His voice cracked.

"What now, Sun-kissed?" big brute asked.

"Mojag and I are going to take a walk. Once we're in public, I'll—" A force slammed into her from behind. She fell atop Mojag. The knife hit the ground with a clang and skittered out of reach.

Sandwiched between Mojag and the man on top of her, Shyla's range of motion was limited. Since she'd lost her hostage, the others joined the fray. Soon her arms were pinned behind her. She was yanked to her feet and immobilized between two goons. An attempt to break their hold left her winded. Gasping for air, she didn't even have enough energy to panic.

The others stood, brushing sand from their pants. At the bottom of the pile was Mojag and…Jayden. That explained who knocked into her.

"Son of a sand demon, that blow was supposed to keep you off your feet for a while," she said.

He gave her a lopsided grin. "My mother says I've a hard head."

"It's not a compliment." At least the beginnings of a nasty bump marked his temple. Small comfort. "I'm just trying to help."

"Yeah. Help yourself. We know," Jayden said. "Mojag, go keep watch so we're not disturbed."

The boy hurried off. Jayden rubbed his forehead, studying her. "Did you tell the guards the location of Orla's commune?"

An utterly ridiculous question. It deserved an equally silly answer. "Yes. In fact, I had tea with a very nice lieutenant during all that free time I had between being sold to the deacons and finding the black river. I told him everything."

Jayden wasn't amused. "Are you done?"

"You don't want to know how the Water Prince and I schemed to discover all your hideouts? Because sending a sun-kissed to infiltrate your network was a stroke of genius. I blended right in."

"Cute. You—

"Aye-up!" Mojag called from the darkness.

Everyone froze.

Mojag rushed toward them. "Guards coming."

Jayden cursed.

"What do we do with her?" the goon asked. "She'll slow us down."

"Or yell for the guards," goon two added.

Thanks for the idea. Shyla drew a breath but froze when Jayden pulled a knife.

"Sorry." He charged.

Energy suddenly sizzled through her muscles. Shyla wrenched sideways as the blade stabbed forward, slicing the skin just under her breasts. She plopped to the floor as Jayden's forward momentum caused him to trip over her legs. Hells! He'd been aiming for her heart!

The thudding of boots echoed as the violet glow of multiple druks appeared.

"Guards," Mojag said. His voice cracked with panic.

"Go!" Jayden ordered.

And just like that, they split up and disappeared into the darkness. Shocked by the turn of events, Shyla remained frozen in place. The son of a sand demon was going to kill her! As if responding to her thoughts, the wound flared to painful life. She explored the cut with her fingertips seeking its depth and agitating it in the process. The cut was not too deep, but blood coated her hand and saturated the ripped edges of her tunic. Not hers, but a vagrant's. And...*the son of a sand demon was going to kill her!* If she encountered Jayden again, she would...none of the options that formed in her mind seemed a fitting response. At least she'd knock him upside his hard head.

Two guards rushed toward her. She braced for discovery.

The faster of the two held a lantern in one hand and his sword in the other. He slowed as soon as he spotted her. "It's the sun-kissed! Which way did the vagrants go?" he asked her.

She gestured to the three tunnels around her. "All of them."

The man glanced behind him as four more guards caught up along with Rendor.

"Pair up. Pick a tunnel and go!" Rendor ordered.

The six of them did as instructed and took off. Rendor remained behind. He held a small yet bright druk. His fierce countenance didn't bode well for their reunion, but the sudden relief at his arrival surprised her. Huh. She was genuinely glad to see him.

He scanned her from head to toe. She must be a frightful sight with her dirty, ripped, and bloody clothes, her butchered hair, bruised face, and cuts all over her body.

Rendor's gaze snagged on her blood-soaked torso before meeting hers. "What happened?" he demanded.

Speaking required effort, and exhaustion had settled deep into her bones.

"Shyla?" He sheathed his sword and crouched next to her. Concern flashed before he hid it behind his familiar scowl.

"Long story," she finally managed.

"Then you better get started."

She shook her head. "Just…stop torturing those people. Please."

Confused, he asked, "Which ones?"

That question stabbed into her core. How many people—no, not thinking about it. Focus, Shyla. "The vagrants…the ones arrested and questioned…about me." Why was it so hard to form a sentence?

"Why should I?"

"They didn't…"

"Kidnap you? Hurt you?" He pointed to her torso and bloodstained pant leg. "It certainly appears that way."

"Not them. Please."

"Not until you tell me everything."

The scuff of boots announced the return of one of the teams.

"The scorching sand rats disappeared," the guard reported. He tilted his head at Shyla. "Did she say where they're squatting?"

"Not yet," Rendor said.

A shudder rolled through her at his confident tone. The second and third teams arrived soon after, describing the same thing.

"All right, let's go back so I can have a private chat with our sun-kissed," Rendor said.

Did she actually see the sly knowing looks on the guards' faces or did she imagine it? At this point it didn't matter.

"Can you stand?" he asked.

Only one way to find out. She staggered to her feet and wobbled. Rendor reached for her, but she straightened. Her body screamed in protest, but she could walk. Three guards led the way, then Rendor strode beside her and the last three followed behind. Quite the parade.

A numbing weakness climbed her legs as they traveled through the tunnels. Her pace slowed. The ground beckoned. *Sit a spell,* it said. *Just an angle or two. I'm softer than I look.* She couldn't argue with its logic. Sinking down, she—

"Seven hells." Rendor scooped her into his strong arms.

"But…the floor invited me."

"I'll pass along your regrets," he said dryly.

Cradled against his warm muscular chest, Shyla felt safe, which was a sure sign of her utter exhaustion. At least Rendor hadn't tried to kill her. Yet. She lasted about two steps before she fell asleep, rousing briefly when he laid her on a cushion.

"The captain certainly has a way with women," one of the guards teased.

"Shut up," Rendor growled.

* * *

The snap of a lock woke Shyla. Blinking the sleep from her eyes, she peered at her surroundings. She was alone.

A couple violet-hued druks hung from the walls, revealing that she wasn't in one of the Water Prince's lavish chambers. Utilitarian and neat, it was three times the size of her room. Everything was bigger than her room, why did she insist on comparing spaces to it? A desk and a number of low tables occupied the main space—probably an office. Rendor's? Figured he'd have a sleeping cushion. He seemed the type to work late. The sand clock read angle three-forty-eight, only twelve more angles until the sun started its jump.

She sat up. Her entire body ached. A bandage was wrapped tightly around her chest. Underneath it pain burned. She rubbed a purpling bruise on her right shoulder, and remembered Jayden's solid punch. Blood stained her clothes. Both her elbows and knees were scuffed. As she'd suspected, the stitches on her leg had pulled apart. Each new discovery increased her pain, so she stopped her inspection.

Instead, she found her pack lying next to her. Rummaging through its contents, she located the vial. It was intact. One less worry. Water sloshed in the skin so she took a long drink, then chewed on a roll of jerky.

The meal revived her enough to attempt to stand. Her leg muscles protested the motion. Groaning, she clambered to her feet. The floor remained steady underneath her. Progress. After that she confirmed that the door was indeed locked. Whether to protect her or detain her, she'd no clue. Wiped out by even that small effort, Shyla returned to the cushion.

What was she going to tell Rendor? She rubbed her left wrist. Would he even believe her? One thing she did know. She wasn't going to reveal the location of the communes to him. Dyani's lifeless eyes stared at her, reminding her that children lived there. And what about Jayden, the Vagrant Prince? She grunted. That title suited him. She still couldn't believe he was going to kill her! To be fair, it was only after he believed she was spying for the Water Prince. Jayden did rescue her from the deacons. Guess she would call them even and hope to never encounter the man again. And if she did? She wouldn't pull her punches next time.

While waiting for Rendor to return, she considered how much to share with the captain. Sometime… later…metal rattled, rousing her from a light doze. Rendor appeared, carrying a tray of steaming eggs. She sat up. Was that tea? Timin followed Rendor into the room and she bit back a groan. It was angle zero.

"Are you purposely trying to kill yourself, or are you just *that* lucky?" Timin asked with a hefty dose of sarcasm. He carried a leather satchel.

"Nice to see you, too," she shot back.

"I'm sure. Now, lie down and let me take a look."

With a sigh, she reclined on the cushion. As Timin rummaged in his bag, Rendor set the tray on one of the tables. He leaned against the edge and crossed his massive arms. His scowl was fixed firmly in place and his hard gaze promised no mercy. But he brought food. Shyla focused on that as Timin cleaned her wounds—which covered most of her body—and inspected the damage underneath the bandage and on her thigh.

"Someone stitched up this knife wound. An expert job, until you managed to rip them all out," Timin said. He tsked over the slice on her torso and the bruise on her face. Then he rubbed the numbing paste on her torso and thigh, repaired the damage, and covered her new stitches with clean bandages. When he finished, he said, "Try not to get into any more trouble." He stared at her. "At least for a couple sun jumps."

"No promises."

Timin shook his head. "She's all yours, Captain. Try not to upset her, she needs to rest."

"No promises," Rendor said.

She stilled—that didn't bode well for her future.

"I don't know why I bother," Timin said as he left.

Rendor straightened and tilted his head at the tray. "Eat."

Although her appetite had soured, once she tasted the velbloud eggs, she dove in and cleaned the plate. The ginger tea warmed her and she clutched the cup for strength. Rendor remained standing. Almost looming—no, definitely looming in his I'm-big-and-bad-and-you-*will*-tell-me-everything stance.

Before he could start, she asked, "Did you stop torturing those people?"

"That's none of your concern."

"Yes, it is. They were—"

"I'd worry more about yourself right now," he said. "You were missing for four sun jumps. The Water Prince is livid."

Four! That was… Wow. "Banqui?"

"Still alive. For now." The threat was clear. "Start explaining, Shyla."

She told him about the mission for the monks without revealing what she had to fetch or the location of the communes. But she was more than happy to detail the encounter with the deacons. "The chapel's on level fifty-one. A stocky deacon cut off the prince's sigil. If you send—"

"We don't interfere with the deacons, and they don't bother us," he said.

That comment stopped her. "Why not?"

"There are just as many deacons as there are guards. They're equally well armed and trained. Why do you think both the Water Prince and Heliacal Priestess wish to claim The Eyes? They would tip the balance of power."

She didn't have the energy to correct him about The Eyes. "They already have so much power."

"Doesn't matter. They're like children, they want what the other one has."

And all she wanted was to free Banqui and the vagrants. Since she wasn't getting anywhere with the vagrants—for now—she switched her focus to Banqui. "Did any of the diggers act suspiciously?"

"Oh no. You need to finish answering *my* questions first. What did you retrieve for the monks?"

"Does it matter? I have it and all I need—"

"You lied to me about where you were going. I've been searching for you for four sun jumps. Yes. It matters."

"Fine." She dug into her pack and removed the vial.

He peered at it. "What's inside?"

"The black river."

"Ah."

"Ah? That's all you can say? Your men are torturing people down there!"

"And you're surprised? Haven't you heard about the Water Prince's special rooms?"

"The prince mentioned it, but..."

He waited.

"I thought it was one of those empty threats." The horrible image of the dead woman hanging upside down flashed. "How can you be a part of that?"

"It's my job to keep the Water Prince safe."

"But they're not a threat. They're innocent."

"They're stealing water and food from law-abiding citizens and living in Zirdai without paying their taxes. Hardly innocent."

"But hardly a threat to the prince."

"And you're an expert now?"

No. She thought of Jayden trying to stab her in the heart. Of Vencel and Adair pushing her off the plank and into the air shaft. What did she know about them? About anyone? Nothing. She shook her head and drained her cup.

Rendor sat next to her. "Why do the monks want a vial of blood?"

"I don't know. I don't care. It'll get me into the Second Room of Knowledge and that's all that matters."

"And that's going to help you find The Eyes?" He sounded doubtful.

She didn't blame him. At this point, she didn't know what to think anymore. "I hope so."

"Because of that symbol? Are you going to tell me about that now?"

"Yes, it has to do with the symbol. But it's probably just a legend."

"So we're no closer to finding The Eyes?"

"The diggers—"

"No leads."

She cursed. "Then that vial is all we've got."

"And the symbol?"

"According to Banqui, it represents a secret group who claim they have magical abilities. He believes they stole The Eyes."

"I haven't heard of an organization like that."

"Of course not. It's a secret!"

He glared at her.

"Sorry. But they don't have magic. No one does."

"The Heliacal Priestess—"

"Think about it. Have you truly seen her or her deacons do anything magical?"

"The monks—"

"I lived with them for eighteen circuits. No magic."

"The Eyes—"

"Artifacts. Valuable not magical."

"If magic doesn't exist then this group shouldn't exist either," Rendor said.

"I said they *claim* to have magic. I can claim to be the Queen of Koraha, but it doesn't mean it's true. Regardless, I need to follow up."

Rendor fingered the hilt of his sword. "Then we have a problem. I've orders to arrest you."

She tensed. The desire to bolt pumped through her heart, but she'd have to climb over Rendor. Instead she remained sitting. "In that case, he will never get The Eyes."

"But you said they didn't have magic."

"It doesn't matter if they do or not. My deal with the prince was The Eyes in exchange for Banqui."

"You care for him," he said a little too casually.

"He's my only friend. He gave me a chance when none of the others would acknowledge my very existence, so, yeah, I care for him." She stood and glanced down at Rendor. "Are you going to arrest me?"

His shoulders drooped. "This is probably going to get me killed, but no. Not yet."

The wave of relief almost knocked her over. "Then I need to return to the monastery."

"*We* need to. I'm not letting you out of my sight."

She was smart enough not to argue. "Let's go before it gets too hot."

Rendor grabbed his things. They took the lift. Rendor remained quiet the entire trip up to level twenty. But as they traveled to the surface, he asked her, "Why are you protecting those vagrants? They tried to kill you."

"They've probably relocated by now."

"That's not what I asked you."

"Not all of them were involved."

"It doesn't matter. They're breaking the law."

"Well, some of us don't see it quite so black and white," she said, annoyed. "Besides, I don't want their suffering on my shoulders. I just want to recover The Eyes and be done with all of this."

When they reached level three, Shyla stopped in her room to change into fresh clothes and exchange the borrowed wrap for her sun cloak. By the time they reached the surface, it was angle twenty-five—plenty of time to walk to the monastery.

During the early angles of a jump, the sunlight warmed instead of burned as it swept over the dunes, leaving behind cool pockets of shade. At this time, the creatures of darkness returned to their burrows while the animals who thrived in the heat woke.

This trip, Shyla didn't need to search for the monks' trail markings. The route was still fresh in her memory, but she kept a close eye for sand demon tracks—they too took advantage of the early angles.

When they arrived at the first row of dunes, she stopped. Something was…not quite right.

Rendor sensed it as well. He clasped the hilt of his sword, but didn't draw the weapon. "Monks?"

"No." And that was the problem. "There should be one or two."

"Maybe they trust us."

"Not likely." Not ever again. "Come on." Shyla trudged up the dune with Rendor right behind her.

At the top of the rise, she scanned the horizon. Still no monks. Not that they stood out among the rolling red terrain and sparse clusters of vegetation, but she had experience spotting them.

She faced Rendor. "I think we should—"

The sand around them exploded into the air with a whoosh. The mini sand storm obscured everything. Shyla yanked her cloak over her face to block the grains from getting into her eyes and lungs. Rendor pushed her behind him as he pulled his sword, but she turned so they were back to back. They had probably triggered a huge area of cap sand. Still, better to be prepared.

When the air cleared, they discovered it hadn't been cap sand after all. A ring of people surrounded them. Stunned, she gaped at them. They must have been hidden underneath the sand. Except the dune had been undisturbed when they'd climbed it. And even now, the sand appeared…pristine. Impossible.

No. She'd figure it out later. Right now, she needed to concentrate on the problem at hand. They wore form-fitting clothing the same shade as the sand. Turbans covered their heads and faces, leaving only their eyes exposed. Shyla counted twelve.

"Monks?" Rendor asked.

"No."

"How can you tell?"

"They're armed."

CHAPTER

11

"Friends of yours?" Rendor asked. His voice remained steady despite the twelve armed figures surrounding them. Each held a sword in hand.

"I wish."

"How many can you take?"

Was he serious? She glanced over her shoulder, but his attention was fixed on the enemy. "Two."

"That leaves ten for me."

"Can you really—"

"Enough," called a voice. "Take the sun-kissed and leave the prince's dog in the sand."

Before she could figure out what that meant, the ring of ambushers tightened. Then it was all flashing swords. She ducked, dodged, rolled away, kicked, blocked, and threw handfuls of sands at those exposed eyes—all she could do against so many armed opponents. The deep sand didn't help, slowing her down and causing the nicks and slices along her arms to add up. Her stitches tugged painfully with each movement. The clang of swords and grunts meant Rendor fended them off. But for how long?

The answer came a fraction of an angle later when pain laced Rendor's loud curse. Another sharp hiss and the big man crumpled to the sand. Shyla kept fighting and managed to disarm one attacker. A tiny victory savored for the length of a heartbeat before she was pinned. She struggled until the cold prick of a knife at her throat warned her to be still.

Rendor lay on his side, skewered by two swords. One pierced his left shoulder, the other protruded from near his right hip. Although in pain, his expression promised a violent retribution. One of the attackers pushed Rendor onto his back with his foot. The captain groaned. Her stomach clenched as fear for his life surpassed her own fright. The intensity surprised her.

Then the ambusher grabbed the hilt of the sword in Rendor's shoulder and shoved it deep into the sand under him. Rendor's low-pitched scream seized her heart. Despite the tip of the blade digging into her neck, Shyla fought to break away to help him. Another person thrust the sword above Rendor's hip into the dune. The captain's hoarse cry cut through the air and right through her.

"Quit fighting or you'll join your friend," the man holding the knife said to her, pressing the blade a little deeper. A searing sting bit into her neck as blood rolled down her throat.

She stopped. For now. What they had planned for her could be worse and joining Rendor might be the better option.

"Do we need a third *stake* or is two good enough?" a woman asked the person with the knife.

"Two's good. He's not going anywhere. By the time the sun finishes its jump, he'll be cooked and eaten by sand demons," the knife wielder said.

"No! Let him go," Shyla cried. "There's no need to kill him. You have me." She guessed she was the target.

A bark of laughter. "Oh, I think there's every need."

"But the Water Prince—"

"Will promote another as his captain. But getting the best of *this one* will send a message. Prep for departure," he ordered the others.

They sheathed their weapons and tightened their turbans. Then they pressed their arms tight to their sides and closed their eyes. Odd.

"What about the sun-kissed?" the man on the left asked. "She's going to spook."

The knife wielder stepped behind her and pulled her close to him. Unfortunately he kept his grip on the blade. "I've got her. Go!"

Shyla witnessed the scene in front of her, but she had to be hallucinating. Or dreaming…no, she'd never dreamt something like that. Perhaps she was drugged—or the Sun Goddess just altered the very fabric of her world. That had to be it! Because people didn't just sink down into a dune and disappear like a sand devil. Except that a sand devil left spirals, and these people left nothing behind but a cloud of sand grains which rained down, covering all the evidence of the impossible thing that had just happened.

"Our turn," he whispered.

No way. She'd rather die. Grabbing the hand holding the knife, she yanked it away from her throat.

"Thought so," he said.

He clamped his other hand over her nose and mouth, blocking fresh air. She bucked and kicked, but couldn't dislodge it.

"Relax," he said, drawling the word out. Then he repeated it over and over right into her ear.

Soon a strange lassitude wove through her. Sand sprayed like one of the Water Prince's fountains around them, moving in slow motion. A tingling started at her toes. It swept up her legs, erasing them. The pain from the cuts on her arms dissolved along with her arms and her torso. Then she disconnected from the world. Nothing left but a thought.

* * *

She reformed…later. Or rather she hoped she'd regained her senses. Because it didn't seem to matter if her eyes were open or closed, the view remained the same. Either there was no light at all or she was trapped in the blackness of oblivion. A simmering unease bubbled as memories fluttered to life. She chased them, catching up with a sequence of events…black river…blood…a climb…and—Jayden!

He tried to kill her. If it hadn't been for—Rendor!

The image of him impaled in the sand flashed in her mind. She slammed her fist down on the stone floor underneath her, hoping that pain would eclipse the horror and grief warring in her chest. Being cooked alive was a horrible way to die. No one deserved it. Perhaps it wasn't too late to help him. Except she'd no idea where she was or how long she'd been…gone.

First step was to determine her location. Lying on her back, she swept her arms out from her hip to above her head, running her hands over the rough stone ground, encountering nothing. Then she reached overhead, seeking a ceiling—it wouldn't do to bang her head again. It'd been through enough.

Nothing within the length of her arm. She sat up and immediately pressed her cold fingers to her temples as a lightheadedness threatened to send her back down. When her world steadied, she once again used her hands to feel for obstacles. Satisfied she wouldn't bang into anything, she moved to stand and froze as a sound echoed.

To those living underground, there were a number of noises that caused alarm—the unmistakable rumble of a cave-in, the boom from the flame of a trol lantern encountering a trapped pocket of gas, and the harsh scrape of metal on stone. The last had multiple causes, but not many of them good. For example, a knife's blade hitting a wall, or a pick digging a hole to bypass a locked door, or a chain dragging along the ground.

Shyla remained in a crouched position. If she didn't move, then she wouldn't confirm her worst fear. However, the injury on her thigh burned with pain. Sitting down, she reached for the icy band around her lower left leg. Perhaps the temperature was due to having lost her boots, but when her fingers touched the metal circling her ankle, the cold shot right to her heart, freezing it in place. Further exploration confirmed what she'd dreaded. Someone—the knife wielder?—had cuffed her to a thick chain.

Crawling, she followed the links until she reached a metal loop secured to the ground. She panicked and grabbed the chain in both hands. No matter how hard she yanked on it, nothing budged. Then she tried pulling the loop from the ground. It didn't move. And tugging on the cuff did nothing but cause the metal to bite into her skin, making her bleed.

Spent, she curled into a ball. Her palms stung and her dire thoughts whirred. No way to rescue Rendor if she couldn't save herself. Had they left her here to die of thirst? How long could she last without water? A gritty bitter taste coated her already dry mouth. Did she have three or four sun jumps left? Why not kill her outright? Why bother with all this? Did they have other plans? And the most important question, who were they? Not the Water Prince's guards or the Heliacal Priestess's deacons. The Vagrant Prince's minions? Another vagrant group? The treasure hunters? The professors? The monks? How did she manage to get so many enemies in a few sun jumps?

Since no magical answers popped into her head, she'd have to figure it out on her own. Well, as much as she could. At least having a goal helped.

What did she know?

The…room was cool, but not cold. From the little bit of moisture in the air, she guessed she was somewhere between levels twenty and thirty.

She pulled the chain slowly through her hands. It was smooth and not rusted. Fingering each link, she discovered they were welded closed with no broken or weak ones along the entire length, which was about four meters.

She crawled in circles around the loop, starting close and ranging further out with each circuit. At first she encountered nothing, but about a meter away, she found her pack. From what she could tell, it contained all her possessions, including the vial of blood, the remaining gamelu jerky, and her half-filled water skin. The crushing pressure around her ribs eased and she drew in her first real breath since she'd been captured.

Continuing her explorations, she touched a wall on the right side, but the chain prevented her from finding the edges. At least she would have a place to rest her back and to protect it as well. She ran her hands over every centimeter that she could reach, searching for anything on the wall that might help her. Nothing.

Shyla resumed her crawl. When she hit a low table with her arm, she slowed. On the top sat a glass pitcher. Dipping a finger inside, she touched a cool liquid. She sniffed it then tasted it. Water. Rolls of jerky were lined up next to it. She sat back on her heels. So they didn't intend to kill her. At least, not yet. She wasn't about to celebrate because, from the amount of provisions, she worried they'd planned to keep her here for a while, which might be worse. And Rendor would be dead.

The last thing she discovered was a collection station…well, not quite that elaborate, but it had lids and cleanser and would do. And it confirmed her fear over the length of her…stay. So why didn't they leave her a druk as well? To keep her on edge?

She retreated to the wall and sat down to consider her situation. Her only chance to escape was if her captors returned and she jumped one of them. As for weapons, she had four meters of chain and the glass pitcher. Once she refilled her water skin and drank the rest, she'd break the pitcher, hoping to get a decent-sized shard to use as a knife.

While waiting, she'd practice the Ways of the Yarin.

* * *

It was disorienting without any way to tell how much time had passed. Shyla kept track of her meals, scratching lines into the wall with a piece of glass. She counted one sun jump for every four meals since she was eating more because of her increased physical activity. After she marked one sun jump, she grieved for Rendor. The captain probably had many deaths on his soul…well, no probably about it, but he'd treated her decently and saved her a couple times. Hanif's comment replayed in her mind. *Not without evidence. Right, Shyla?* She had her evidence—the black river caused by those dead bodies in the prince's special rooms. Tortures ordered by the Water Prince, but carried out by Rendor's men. Based on that, she should be celebrating his death. Yet, she mourned his laugh—that small part of him she'd imagined was untainted. That part of him she, if she was being honest, liked. Probably more than was healthy.

Being in the darkness alone with her thoughts wore away the small kernel of hope she clutched tight. Instead, she redoubled her physical efforts. The heavy chain hindered her movements at first, but then she started incorporating it into a few of her defensive moves. A plan of action formed. She'd pretend to be weak or asleep when they entered, drawing them closer, and then she'd pounce.

As her incarceration lengthened, Shyla learned a few things about herself. She expected to miss having a cushion to sleep on or food other than dried jerky, but what she longed for the most was the sun. The warmth on her skin as it soaked up the sunlight and darkened. The rays streaming into her room through the mirror pipe and how they changed direction during the sun's jump across the sky. And she'd give anything to argue with Banqui again. He always demanded accuracy and challenged her finds, but, at the end of a job, he always praised her work. She hoped the Water Prince didn't kill him because she had gone missing again.

Even though she rationed as much as possible, her water ran out after two sun jumps. Anxiety churned in her stomach. Would they care that she needed more? Would they come? Would she be able to grab one of them? Would she be able to see after all this time in the darkness? No doubt the lantern light would hurt her eyes. She'd have to fight by feel.

It finally happened on the third sun jump of her captivity. A brightening. The darkness diluted just a fraction. It grew, revealing a tunnel. Eventually, the weak light exposed her surroundings. About what she expected—bare walls, the metal anchor in the floor, the collection bins and the table. Only one exit to the tunnel beyond. Because of the chain there was no need for bars or a door.

The light strengthened until it grew too painful for her to look at the tunnel. She closed her eyes, but it still stabbed through her eyelids. Tears leaked. Sitting with her back against the wall and her legs bent, she arranged the chain just so and palmed the glass shard, keeping it hidden under her forearm. She rested her forehead on her knees and listened.

The faint scuff of footsteps. An echo of voices. Then a deep hum. A rhythmic chanting. Odd. The sound wove through her. It pulled and tugged. It twisted and dipped. She concentrated, trying to determine the direction of the sound, but it surrounded her. No. It was inside her. It filled every space in her body.

And then with a snap, it was gone. So was the light. And her glass shard. In fact, after exploring her prison, she discovered her water skin was now filled. Another full skin sat on top of the table along with more sticks of jerky, and the broken pieces of the pitcher had been removed. The collection station had been cleaned out as well.

* * *

She paced around her small space. The chain rasped and clanked with her agitated movements. What in seven hells just happened? Did she fall asleep? Not during her only chance to escape! She ran her fingers along her scalp. Had she been knocked senseless? No lumps or tender spots anywhere on her head. Her stubble felt longer, but it was hard to tell without a mirror.

Frustration welled and the desire to punch the wall until her knuckles bled grew inside her. The pressure built until she screamed. The shrill sound bounced off the walls. At least the tension eased a bit.

A strange thought occurred to her then—what if help was just a shout away all this time? It was the first thing a person would do when in trouble, but she never considered it. Manic laughter bubbled. All her training and no thought to seek aid. She doubled over, hysterical, tears streaming from her eyes as she imagined a group of people coming to investigate the strange calls. They'd chastise her for not yelling sooner, break the chain, take her in…

Her crazed amusement died. The people who'd captured her had thought all this out in advance and wouldn't make a rookie mistake like that. Plus only two people cared enough to come to her rescue. One was dead. The other was probably hanging upside down bleeding to death in one of the prince's special rooms or was also dead by now. And if Jayden knew of her situation, he'd be the last person to help. No chance of her spilling vagrant secrets when there was no one for her to talk to.

Shyla sat against the wall and rested her head back. What if her captors sat in the tunnel listening? Perhaps waiting for her to voice her questions aloud? Or to beg for her freedom?

Feeling silly, she called, "What do you want from me?"

No answer.

"Why am I here?"

Silence.

"Who are you?"

Nothing.

"Please let me go! I don't care about your agenda. I'll go back to the monks and you'll never see or hear from me again."

No response.

Well, she tried. Shyla thought about her last comment. Would she really return to the monks? Her relationships with them would never be the same as before she'd left. And she'd never get to travel. It'd be just like her current situation, except with sunshine, better food, and no chain…well, not a physical one.

If she lived through this, there'd be no other place to go. No client would hire her, the treasure hunters wouldn't trust her, and the deacons would be after her. She'd tried so hard to do all the right things, pay her taxes, give her tithe to the church, earn an honest living, and it fell apart after one incident that wasn't even her fault. Her attempt to save Banqui had failed. And Rendor died. She never should have left the monastery.

But she did. And she was trapped. At least she could try to figure this out. Thinking back to when the light arrived, she reviewed the sequence of events. That strange deep hum had been similar to the low chanting of the word *relax* that the man with the knife uttered in her ear before she was…well, whatever he'd done to her. Although it was ridiculous that a word or sound could render a person unconscious, she assumed it worked.

Therefore, she needed to plug her ears, blocking the hum the next time the light arrived.

Shyla ripped pieces of her tunic into small strips that she rolled into tubes. It took a few tries to get the rolls just the right thickness to fit into her ear and stay there when she moved. With the tubes dampening all sounds, she practiced the Ways of the Yarin and the moves she'd invented with the chain. Both her sight and hearing would be restricted, so she'd need to depend on touch and smell.

Rolling up her pant legs, she knelt on the ground and settled back on her heels—the best position to quickly launch to her feet. She banged the chain on the floor. A slight vibration brushed her shins and a puff of air grazed her face. Working with other items, she practiced relying on two senses. She only stopped to eat and sleep.

Three sun jumps after the first light appeared, another slow lightening of her prison warned her of her captor's return. This time, she faced the tunnel, kneeling with a length of chain between her hands and her plugs in her ears. As the light turned painful, she closed her eyes and focused.

Shyla inhaled slowly. The scent of roasted velbloud meat filled her nose with its savory mix of spices. Then the funky odor of sweat mixed with the desert's fiery hotness. At least two possible opponents. One had recently been on the surface.

A feeble vibration licked her shins as they neared. She tensed. The tremor under her increased into a steady beat. It throbbed inside her leg bones, pulsed in her hips and then gripped her heart, forcing it to follow its rhythm. To slow down. To be at peace. The rhythm unwound her tight muscles. And it didn't matter how much she struggled to stay…together, she floated like a velbloud on the end of its tether.

With a harsh yank, she plummeted back into the darkness and isolation. Her provisions had been restocked and collection bins once again cleaned. And the useless rolls of fabric remained wedged tight in her ears.

Disappointment, frustration, and anger welled. Grabbing the chain, she hauled on it with all her strength, grunting and cursing until she was exhausted. Shyla slumped to the floor. Perhaps this was the Sun Goddess's sign to her that the Heliacal Priestess was right. Shyla had cheated death and was cursed.

Lying on her side, she curled up into a ball and unleashed the self pity. It surged through her, knocking out hope, smothering motivation, and extinguishing stubborn persistence. Empty, she remained in place until time ceased to have any meaning. Thirst barely registered. And she had no desire to eat. Her thoughts drifted and memories popped up at random.

One set of recollections kept nagging at her like a child tugging on her sleeve. They were all of when she lived at the monastery. Memories of Hanif chiding her for giving up too easily. The hot tears of frustration. The monks asking the impossible. Brute strength no match against intelligence. The games of strategy that had no solution—or so she thought. The righteous conviction that she'd been right only to have it shattered with the truth.

It was a bleak succession of all the times she'd reached a point of despair. A place where she'd been convinced she could go no further. Yet. She had.

Scorching hells.

Her sulk had run its course. At least Hanif wasn't there to gloat. Yet, she'd bet he'd just had the sudden desire to arch an eyebrow and ask in a snide tone, *Are you done feeling sorry for yourself?*

Yes, Hanif I am. And if you have any suggestions on how I can get out of this, now would be a good time to tell me.

No answer. No surprise. He'd let her bang her head against the wall for sun jumps rather than give her the answer.

Shyla clambered over to the table and considered what had happened while she gulped some water and chewed on a jerky roll. Once again she'd been… What? Knocked out? Forced to sleep? Enthralled? Before it'd been a hum and now a vibration. Blocking the sound didn't work and she couldn't levitate off the floor. What else could she do? Her limited options didn't take long to list. If only one of them came close enough for her to—

The answer flashed into her mind, energizing her.

* * *

Approximately nine sun jumps since she'd been caught, the light arrived for the third time. Shyla waited until the sound of boots on the ground reached her. Then she slammed the metal chain on the floor, hard. Sparks flickered along with a loud bang. Shyla kept up the noise, rattling, scraping, banging, and crunching the links on the ground. All to counter their rhythmic humming. Varying the tempo so it was impossible to match, she avoided repeating any patterns.

The light seared her eyes, but it grew brighter than any time before. Progress! She moved around in unpredictable directions, hoping to brush into one of them or catch their scent. Theoretically, their arms would be full with a new supply of provisions. A tactical disadvantage on their part to be exploited by her.

Except this time the persistent humming drilled right into her thoughts. It smoothed her actions until the metal links jingled in an almost musical accompaniment. The weight of the chain grew so heavy, it pulled her down. Turning into a liquid, she poured through the cracks in the floor and dripped into a void.

Jerked up to the surface, Shyla emerged into the blackness, lying on the hard cold ground. Her palms stung and her sweat-damped tunic covered her like a coating of ice. She remained there until thirst drove her to her feet. Bringing the water skin over the wall, she sat against it.

She'd tried to block the hum. Then to drown it out. Nothing worked. Was it time to admit defeat? What would they do if she went on a hunger strike? Put her into a trance and force feed her? Was that even possible? They managed to get that damned hum through her defenses; a roll of jerky shouldn't be a problem.

Wait. She straightened. Perhaps the hum didn't come from outside, but originated within her. Yes, it was an insane thought. One born from nine sun jumps isolated in the dark. Still… She'd been so focused on the physical, she hadn't considered the mental. If she viewed it that way, then perhaps she just needed her will to be stronger than theirs.

The Ways of the Yarin included meditation techniques. They were normally used to calm a person's body and mind. To relieve stress and achieve peace. The state was similar to the hum-induced trance. Except when she meditated, she controlled the journey rather than being forced there and abruptly yanked back.

Without any other ideas or options, she decided to practice her meditation and give it one more try. After that… Shyla preferred not to think of after. Instead, she spent time settling her thoughts and worries into that peaceful state. With each effort, she tried to attain that inner calm faster than the time before. If her captors took control first, there would be nothing she could do. However, Shyla didn't neglect her physical exercises. Balance between the mind and body was very important to the Ways of the Yarin. Huh. She'd forgotten that in her panic over being chained to the floor, which in her opinion was an acceptable excuse.

The return of the light marked sun jump number twelve. Shyla knelt on the floor, resting on her heels. A loop of chain in her hands and the rest arranged around her just so. But this time she kept her back to the tunnel and faced the table and collection bins.

She smoothed her breathing and her heartbeat—which had thumped harder in anticipation at the first glimpse of the lantern—slowing both to a matching rhythm. Instead of floating with the velblouds or sinking through the cracks, she centered herself in the space around her, using the anchor in the ground.

Keeping her eyes closed, she sensed rather than saw the items nearby. The light intensified, turning the insides of her eyelids reddish.

The hum dug into her bubble of calm, attempting to redirect her awareness to another place. It stabbed orders into her mind with brute force. *Go. Leave. Be free.* And it pushed its will with a solid punch. Her control slipped with each blow, as bits of her calm fractured. Through the fissures she knew lurked the darkness that would reclaim her.

With a surge of energy and determination, she nudged the insistent commands off course so the demands landed in a distant part of her mind. Into one of those places where thoughts sounded warnings and gave advice that was acknowledged as viable, but ignored.

Now a bright yellow glow pierced her eyelids. She struggled to keep her expression neutral, hoping they hadn't realized she remained aware of her surroundings. Voices and footsteps sounded behind her.

"What do you think she's trying this time?" a man asked.

"She has her back to us. Maybe she believes that will block our magic," a woman responded with an amused tone.

Magic? Shyla used every ounce of her will not to react to the woman's statement.

"At least she has recognized it. Remember the guy that just didn't get it?" The man chuckled.

Painful white light stabbed through her closed eyes. Tears welled. But she centered all her focus on listening and smelling.

A clank of the lantern set on the floor behind her.
Shuffling feet. The sloshing of a full water skin.
A plop as it's set on the table.
An exhalation of disgust.
The creak of a collection bin.
The acrid odor of excrement.

A whiff of flowery scent nearby.

A brush of fabric on her right sleeve.

Shyla surged to her feet and hooked the chain around a neck. Pulling it taut, she scurried backward, dragging her sweet-smelling victim with her until she hit the wall. The distance from the anchor caused the chain to cinch even tighter, but not enough to kill. The motion distracted her prisoner enough for Shyla to search for a weapon. She found a knife, but really the best part of being in this position was that the woman made an effective shield until Shyla's vision could adjust to the light.

"Don't try anything or she dies," Shyla said.

CHAPTER 12

Shyla hunched behind her prisoner. The bright lantern light still blinded her, but her captive had enough sense to keep still. Otherwise the chain around her neck might strangle her. After twelve sun jumps in captivity, Shyla would have a hard time feeling any remorse if that happened.

"That's a neat trick," the man said from her right—about a meter away.

Shyla shifted, keeping the woman between her and the remaining threat.

"What do you plan to do now?" he asked with amusement.

"Order you to remove the cuff around my ankle," Shyla said.

"Hmmm. And what if I say no?" he asked.

"I'll kill this woman."

"Then you'll have nothing to bargain with."

"True, but I'll have the satisfaction of taking one of you out."

"So you're a cold-blooded killer?"

"Yes."

He chuckled. "I don't think so."

The bastard had called her bluff. Seven hells. The Ways of the Yarin focused on defensive moves, and this one usually worked well, limiting the number of opponents one needed to engage. But this tactic had now failed her twice…well, if it wasn't for Jayden's hard head then taking Mojag hostage would have worked.

"Besides, it takes time to strangle someone. Enough time for me to reach you before my companion even gets dizzy from lack of air."

The son of a sand demon knew what he was doing. But did he know she held a knife? Her vision adjusted enough for her to discern a blackish blob crossing slowly to her left exposed side. Shyla thrust the woman at him. They collided with an oomph. She tackled them both and they all landed in a heap with Shyla on top. She pressed the knife to what she hoped was the man's neck.

"This'll get the job done faster," Shyla said, digging the edge into his skin to make her point.

"Well done," he said. "So you'll kill us both. Then what?"

Not the reaction she expected. "I search you for the key."

"And when you find none?"

"Then I do this again with the people who come searching for you."

"Hmmm. That leaves quite the body count. Not to mention the stink."

"Ximen, will you stop fooling around," the woman said in a hoarse croak.

"You're no fun." Ximen moved, wrenching the knife from Shyla's hand.

They wrestled. She'd like to say they fought for a while, but in fact Ximen pinned Shyla within a few breaths. He sat on her hips and his knees pressed on her shoulders. Not quite painful, but the position left his hands free and her arms trapped. She braced for a blow. Or perhaps for the slice of cold steel into her neck. Fear coiled around her heart.

After a torturous wait, he rocked back onto his heels and stood. Would it be bad if a tiny bit of disappointment touched her core? The thought of remaining alone in the dark… No. She'd find another way to escape.

The clinking of metal drew her attention. Shyla sat up. Using her hand to block the light, Shyla squinted. The man helped his partner to unwrap the chain from around her neck. The woman rubbed her throat and glared at Shyla.

"Go lower the druk, Bazia," Ximen said.

Bazia turned her glower onto him, but he failed to react. Muttering, she strode over to the lantern on the floor and dimmed its glow.

"Better?" Ximen asked.

Shyla jerked when she realized his question was directed at her. She lowered her hand. The light still burned, but her vision cleared a bit. "Yes."

"I must admit you surprised us," he said.

"Not that it mattered." Shyla wiped the blood seeping from around the cuff on her ankle. The metal had torn into her skin. Again.

"Oh it matters very much. Most of our guests take ages to figure out what's going on and some don't at all."

"Being chained to the floor didn't tip them off?" She couldn't resist the sarcasm.

"That's not what's going on and you know it," he chided.

"All I know is that you're keeping me here against my will. And doing some kind of hypnosis to knock me out. Other than that, I got nothing."

"You figured out how to counter our magic."

Oh boy, more evidence these people were delusional. "No. I figured out how to counter your stupid chanting. Why am I here?"

"You're being tested."

"For what?"

"A few things. We learned you're not a cold-blooded killer."

"That can change," she growled.

He laughed. "Also, you're resourceful."

"Not enough, I'm still attached to this fucking chain."

"No need for that kind of language."

"I think there's every need."

"The biggest challenge was our magic and to test if you could block it. Which you did."

Best to humor the crazy man. "Great. Does that mean you'll let me go now?"

"Not quite."

She gauged the distance to him. Perhaps if she was fast enough—

"Don't try it," Bazia said. "He's one of our best."

He beamed at her. "That's sweet."

"Finish this, I've other things to do," she said.

"We'll be back with another and he'll explain everything," Ximen said to Shyla as Bazia completed restocking Shyla's provisions and cleaning out the collection bins.

Panic boiled up her throat at the thought of being left alone in the darkness. Again. "No. Please, take me with you." She hated how desperate she sounded.

"I can't. I don't have the key. Don't worry, we'll leave the druk and it won't be more than a sun jump. I promise," Ximen said.

No way to stop them. She kept the sob locked in her throat as they left. As promised the druk remained on the floor. A cold comfort. Once her eyes stopped tearing due to the light, she lifted the lantern and explored her prison. Numerous old scratch marks scored the wall, hinting at prior desperate occupants. Long-dried stains painted the floor. Evidence of what happened to those Ximen said hadn't figured out their trick? Or just accidents? And who was this other person?

Questions without answers swirled in her mind. Why was she being tested? And what else did they have in mind? More isolation? Torture? What would happen next? Anxiety swelled and dipped like the dunes in the desert. Only the reminder that she still lived helped calm her thoughts. Eventually she dozed.

* * *

The chanting stole into her dreams, darkening the pleasant dreamscape of lying on warm soft sand as the sun's landing streaked the sky with bands of color. It ordered her into the cold hard ground. Now familiar with the compulsion, Shyla dodged the commands with minimal effort and woke.

A muscular man wearing a sun cloak crouched near her. Joy licked her heart. Rendor! But this man's wide scarred face, while sour, didn't even resemble the captain. Besides, Rendor was dead. Grief laced with icy dread coated her insides. She shivered as the man continued to study her. His song drummed inside her head, but she pushed it back.

Ximen and Bazia stood behind him. Red marks shaped like chain links ringed Bazia's neck. Not a bit of remorse touched Shyla.

The strange man changed the pitch of his chant. It deepened and soaked into her bones. An odd flickering impeded her vision almost as if her eyelids slowly fluttered. The three people flashed into and out of existence. Then they disappeared altogether.

She jerked to her feet in surprise, but soon figured it was just another trick. Her captors had not vanished. They remained in place. She was unable to see them.

Concentrating, she followed the low sounds smothering her senses. They clung to her like sand grains to a damp hand. Shyla swept them away with her will, but they returned thicker than before no matter how quickly she moved. Her head ached with frustration. She needed a new tactic. A way to unstick the sounds. If they really acted like grains of sand, then once the surface dried, it would be easily brushed off.

Shyla imagined a wind. But not one that gusted past her. No. This explosion of air burst from inside of her and blew all the sand—sounds—away in one mighty whoosh. The three people popped into view. Ximen smiled with approval, but Bazia crossed her arms.

The other straightened, pulled a short sword and charged her.

Without thought, Shyla side-stepped him. By the time he checked his forward momentum and turned to face her, she'd scooped up the chain—her only weapon. He paused. She kept the eagerness that flowed through her body from showing on her face. Finally, a direct attack. None of that crazy chanting nonsense. Plus she'd been training hard, learning how to use the chain to her advantage.

He lunged, stabbing the blade at her stomach. Shyla blocked with the chain, causing a screechy metallic scrape to echo off the walls. Undaunted, he continued his assault. Her pulse kept up a quick tempo as she countered his thrusts and slashes. Sparks flew as metal scraped along metal.

The links of the chain dulled and nicked his blade with each loud clash. Sweat glistened on his brow as his breath puffed. While not yet fatigued, her palms and wrists stung from the impacts. He executed a quick flurry of strikes, pressing forward. Too late she realized that maneuver wasn't to stab her, but to shorten her strike zone. While she'd countered, a part of the chain snagged on the heavy stone table, limiting her range of motion. A smile broke through his intense expression.

Scorching hells. A thread of fear knotted in her stomach. She only had one option left and the timing had to be perfect. When he sprang with his sword extended, she stepped toward him and twisted her torso to the side. The blade cut along her stomach. Ignoring the burning pain, Shyla wrapped the chain around the hilt. Then yanked. Hard.

The sword flew from his grasp. Before he recovered, she looped the chain around his neck. And tightened it, cutting off his air. His brown eyes bulged as his fingers clawed at the links. She glanced at Ximen and Bazia, bracing for their interference, but they remained in place.

After a few heartbeats, Shyla loosened the chain. "Tell me why I shouldn't kill you?"

"Because I'm…the one," he gasped.

She waited.

"…with the…key."

If he was telling the truth. A big if. Both her hands were occupied. "Show it to me."

He fumbled in his tunic and removed a small silver key.

"Unlock the cuff," she ordered.

Allowing him to bend forward, she watched him insert the key into the small hole. A vibration ringed her ankle and the damn cuff fell to the ground. A combination of sensations swept through her. Relief dominated. Too bad it lasted a mere moment.

Her prisoner surged upward. Elbowing her in the nose, he knocked her to the ground. She lost her grip on the chain on impact.

"You need more practice," he said in a rough voice as he removed the links from his neck.

Just the thought of being cuffed again energized her. She leapt to her feet ready to fight despite the blood running from her throbbing nose.

"Relax," Ximen said to her. "Payatt's just mad you caught him in a choke hold even though we warned him you were pretty good with that chain."

Payatt actually growled at Ximen. Perhaps he was Rendor's brother. They had the same dark coloring and almond-shaped eyes. Reminding herself that these people *killed* the captain, she refused to relax.

"Was that another test?" she asked.

"She catches on quick," Bazia snarked.

"Ximen said you'd explain everything," Shyla said to Payatt. "Start talking."

"We are members of the Invisible Sword," he said as if it explained everything.

It didn't. Except maybe the comments about using magic. A delusion that had apparently lasted five hundred thousand sun jumps. Just her luck. "Did you steal The Eyes?"

"No. They are ours. We simply reclaimed them."

Her pulse quickened. "So you're in possession of them?"

"Yes, but we won't be giving them to the Water Prince or the Heliacal Priestess. They do not belong to either of them."

"Technically they belong to Tamburah. Are you a descendant?"

He snorted with disgust. “It does not matter. We’ve been called. Power is being abused again. Our world is unbalanced.”

It wasn’t the only thing unbalanced. She bit back her sarcastic response. “And you plan to use the magic of The Eyes to restore balance.”

“Exactly.”

Shyla couldn’t resist. “Been called—by who?”

“The people’s suffering.”

All right then. Although Shyla spoke fluent crazy, she’d had enough of the vague answers. “Why did you kidnap me?”

“To test your abilities.”

“For what?”

“To see if you’re worthy to become a member of the Invisible Sword.”

“And?”

He gestured to her ankle. “You are.”

Lovely. “What do you do exactly?”

“We help the helpless. We chip away at the prince’s and priestess’s power structures. Eventually they will collapse. We search for our true leader. The one who is able to use The Eyes to restore balance.”

Now she was confused. “Isn’t that you?”

Payatt shook his head. “Like Ximen and Bazia, I’m just one of many lieutenants.”

“So you have The Eyes, but no one can use their magic?” Nice logic. No wonder their delusion had lasted this long.

"Only one person has the power to wield The Eyes."

Of course.

"Will you join us?" Payatt asked.

She considered. If they truly had The Eyes, she could join and steal them—what the hell was she thinking? Her chance to save Banqui was long gone. The Water Prince would hunt her down for not retrieving The Eyes and for getting his captain killed. And the Heliacal Priestess would force her to confess before sacrificing her to the Sun Goddess. Shyla could no longer live in Zirdai. Die, yes. Live, no.

"No. Besides you don't want me. I may have passed your tests, but I failed at the only thing that was important to me."

"Freeing the archeologist?"

"Yes. He's dead by now."

Payatt exchanged a glance with Ximen and Bazia. Hope warmed the cold emptiness inside her.

"Banqui lives," Ximen said.

Her relief nearly knocked her to her knees. Now if she could—

"We also know why you've been seeking The Eyes," Ximen added.

Which meant they'd never trust her enough for her to steal them back. "I don't suppose you'd give me them so I can free Banqui?"

"No, but we are interested in Banqui. We think he might play an important part in our organization. He found The Eyes after all."

"He can't do anything while he's in the Water Prince's black cells."

"We're aware. We have a plan to rescue him, but we need your help."

"Mine?" The comment swirled around her mind. What could she possibility offer— "You want me to show you how to get underneath the prince's special rooms."

"No. We will share our plan only when you have joined us by pledging your loyalty."

Pledging your loyalty was exactly what the Monks of Parzival had asked her to do. It meant giving up on her dreams. At least then she had a future. Now…not so much.

"What's required of a member of the Invisible Sword?" she asked.

"We have many levels of our organization," Payatt said. "Those at the lowest level are not tested for magic because they do not have the ability. For them, it is a small commitment: passing along vital information, hiding a member for a few jumps, or donating resources. They go about their lives as if nothing has changed. The next level has people with magic. They play a more active part, living in the fringes with the vagrants, and being a part of various…missions, for lack of a better word, when needed. For you…"

His heavy tone suggested this wouldn't be good.

"You would need to be among the truly invisible." Payatt gestured to Ximen and Bazia. "Like us."

"You want me to go around doing that crazy chanting thing so no one can see me?"

Bazia cocked her hip. "If she doesn't believe, then she'll never be able to wield the magic."

"Wow. You're still mad she got the drop on you, Bazia," Ximen said. "Shyla already learned how to tap into the power, the rest is easy."

"How do you know to test someone or not?" she asked.

"We're able to sense magic locked inside a person. However, only the person can unlock it."

Another vague answer. "What exactly does it mean to be truly invisible?" she asked Payatt.

"As far as Zirdai is concerned, you don't exist. You move through the city unseen."

Not much different than her prior existence.

"You don't have a room, or pay taxes, or a tithe. You'll no longer have clients and do research. All your efforts will be to help us restore balance."

"Can you give me an example of that?"

"A few small things that we've done are ensuring the vagrants get clean water and stopping a quartet of deacons from killing a man."

"Is it dangerous?" she asked.

"Of course." He gestured to the chain. "Those at our level need to have special skills. Those you demonstrated by escaping our trap."

No matter how much she wished it otherwise, her old life was over. Again. Shyla thought joining them sounded better than living with the monks, but there were two problems. They believed in magic and they killed Rendor. And then another thought hit her so hard, she almost stepped back.

"What happens if I refuse to join?" she asked.

"I'd think either the Water Prince's guards or the Helical Priestess's deacons would capture you eventually."

"Five coins on the guards getting her first," Ximen said to Bazia.

Bazia ignored him.

Smart girl. Even Shyla would bet on the guards. They were probably upset over their captain's death and blamed her. "And when they torture me for information…"

"You'll have no memory of this encounter," Payatt said.

"But I thought I was resistant to your…magic."

His smile chilled the air as the scars on his cheeks added to his menacing expression. How was that even possible?

"You've experienced a few basic techniques. You've no idea what we can do."

"I need time to think about it."

Payatt glanced at the chain at her feet.

"No. Time free of here. If you want me to trust you then you need to trust me."

"Where will you go?"

"The monastery. I need to deliver something to them."

"You will not be safe there. Once the Water Prince learns of your location, he'll come after you."

"But they serve the King."

"Hasn't stopped the prince before. The monks walk a thin line and have refused succor when protecting a certain person will cause problems too big for them to handle."

She wanted to protest, but she knew very little of what the older monks did with their time. "And you believe word of my presence would get back to the prince?"

"Yes." There was no doubt in his voice.

"The prince has a spy inside?" Hard to believe, they were a close-knit family.

Ximen laughed. "No. But Captain Rendor has been making a giant nuisance of himself as usual."

Did he— "Rendor's alive?"

"Why are you so surprised?" Payatt asked.

"You staked him to the ground with two swords!" Rendor's cries of pain still reverberated in her ears.

"Both in non-vital locations. The monks rescued him after we left, nursed him back to health…well, he has a significant limp and it'll be a long while before he can swing a sword, or fight for that matter, but he refuses to leave the monastery. He's convinced you'll show up there eventually."

Shyla rubbed her forehead. Too much information and too many questions. However, inside her heart thumped its happiness. Its strength scared her more than anything so far. She needed to remember he was the enemy.

"The Invisible Sword doesn't kill unless there is no other choice," Ximen said. "Otherwise, we'd be just like those we're fighting to stop."

"But, it seemed—" The image of him bleeding in the sand had been seared into her mind. Could they be lying to her?

"Our people were perhaps a bit overzealous," Payatt said. "Captain Rendor's been a…very difficult opponent and some feel he deserves to die, but we left that decision up to the Sun Goddess. She chose to save him."

"You seem rather concerned about the captain. Is there something we should know?" Bazia asked.

"Actually, knowing he's alive is a point in your favor," Shyla said.

"Why?" Bazia challenged. "You know his people tortured those vagrants. You should have been glad when you thought he died."

"He's not the problem and you know it." Why was Shyla defending him? This wouldn't go well if she tried an I'm-not-a-threat-and-you-should-let-me-go-with-my-memories-intact defense.

"I suggest we erase her memories now and give her to the Water Prince's dog," Bazia said. "She'll end up betraying us or causing us trouble."

"And you know this how?" Shyla asked. "Does your *magic* allow you to see the future?"

"Enough," Payatt ordered. "We will give Shyla one sun jump to consider our offer." He turned to Ximen. "Take her somewhere familiar but safe."

Ximen nodded. Shyla went to get her bag. She packed a few rolls of jerky. Although if she never ate another one of them again in her lifetime, she'd be just fine with that. Ximen came over and picked up a water skin and the druk.

The four of them left together, but after a few turns Ximen led her in another direction. Shyla breathed easier. Payatt was too intense and Bazia obviously didn't like her, while Ximen appeared to be reasonable. They climbed a few levels. Then they entered a corridor with eyeless faces contorted in pain carved into the walls. Oh, this was familiar all right. The hallway of the dead ended in a circular room ringed with stone benches facing an altar. They were in Tamburah's temple.

Son of a sand rat. Had she been on one of the lower levels of the temple the entire time?

"You can stay here while you consider our offer," Ximen said.

There were six doorways, one of them leading to the surface. And because of her attention to detail, she knew exactly which one.

As if reading her thoughts, he said, "Remember the ambush in the desert."

"I thought you were going to trust me."

"Within reason. If you run away, then your answer is obviously no. We have many lives depending on us. Too many to risk exposure by a selfish sun-kissed."

Selfish? Everything she'd done since Banqui knocked on her door had been to save him. How was that selfish? And now she was supposed to just trust that these crazy people had a plan to rescue him. They told her nothing of substance. Did they even have the resources to execute such an endeavor?

Selfish? That grated more than being called sun-kissed.

Ximen must have sensed her darkening mood. "I'll return for your answer."

A deep bass pulse rolled through her, blinding her. By the time she blocked it, Ximen had disappeared. She cursed. The words echoed in the empty chamber. At least he left the druk. It had enough light to illuminate Tamburah's giant face etched into the wall behind the altar.

"This is all your fault," she said to him.

His smug expression irritated her. She glared back. The blue and purple sand painting his skin probably represented his control of the water sources. Back then, it flowed closer to the surface. Or maybe it meant… Shyla picked up the druk and moved to inspect the pattern. A familiarity resonated within her. Could the lines be a map? Excitement built in her chest. Of Tamburah's temple? No. Zirdai? No. Perhaps somewhere else. It wasn't random.

However, she'd never get a chance to figure it out. Her enthusiasm fizzled. If she agreed to join the Invisible Sword her life would no longer be her own. Was her disappointment selfish? Should she not be sad? Shyla had witnessed the horrors of Zirdai that she never knew existed—or had refused to acknowledge. Had she turned a blind eye, selfishly focusing on her own problems? Was it selfish to want to be independent? The vagrants were independent, yet they were hunted by the guards and deacons. And yet, they aided Shyla in her search for the black water. For a price. And then Jayden...

Shyla rubbed her chest, where the knife wound had healed. But that poor girl who'd been poisoned would never see the sun again. At the time, Shyla couldn't do anything to help, but did this Invisible Sword truly assist the vagrants or did they have their own agenda?

Perhaps it would be better to hide with the vagrants. Would they even allow her to live with them? If she found treasures they could sell, would they protect her? Or would she endanger them all? Hadn't she already endangered them? The image of the vagrants who'd been hung upside down and tortured to death flashed in her mind.

Her head ached. If she refused the Invisible Sword's offer, they'd erase her memories, she'd be caught by the Water Prince and killed. Shyla never had a real choice. But it was nice of them to pretend that she did.

She stared at Tamburah. His eyeless gaze peered back. The red sand lining the empty sockets sparkled with a crimson hue, representing blood. A dramatic touch probably added by the rebels.

The scrape of boots on the stone broke the silence. Shyla set the druk down and moved into a fighting stance, wishing she'd thought to bring the chain along.

Ximen, Bazia, and—Jayden!—burst into the chamber. Scorching hells, she should have known he was involved. Their gazes met—his worried and hers livid—but there were no signs of the cocky Vagrant Prince who tried to kill her. Did they bring him along hoping his presence would convince her to join them? If so, it was the wrong decision.

"There's been an incident," Ximen said. "We need to accelerate the timeline of Banqui's rescue."

"What happened?" she asked.

"The Water Prince's patience has worn out. His guards have captured the entire population of the commune on level sixteen."

"Even the children?" she asked, remembering the rambunctious kids.

"Yes. All twenty-two of them. We need your answer before they're tortured to death."

She'd already decided, but the news gave her another reason. "I pledge my loyalty to the Invisible Sword. What do we need to do?"

"The pledge is a bit more formal than that," Ximen said. "It needs to be a magical vow or else we can't trust you."

"Fine. Whatever."

"It won't work if she doesn't believe," Bazia said.

"It will as long as she's truthful," Jayden said. "Shyla, roll up your left sleeve like this." He demonstrated by pulling his all the way up to his shoulder, revealing a muscular bicep.

"Oh no, no, no." Shyla crossed her arms and turned to Ximen. "He thinks I'm a traitor. He tried to kill me. Why should I trust *him*."

"Jayden."

"I don't believe you're a traitor anymore," Jayden said, "I'm sorry I tried to kill you."

Not good enough. "Why did you change your mind?"

"I wasn't aware of your…arrangement with the Water Prince. All I knew was you were on a quest for the monks and I was tasked with aiding you. But then you were determined to go to the guards, endangering my people. I have all the information *now*." He glared at Bazia, who ignored him.

Not sure if she was ready to forgive him but unwilling to delay any longer, Shyla rolled up her sleeve as instructed.

Ximen pulled a knife and grabbed her upper arm with his free hand. He glanced at Jayden. "Ready?"

"Yes."

Ximen met her gaze. "Relax. Let Jayden's song in and this won't hurt."

Relaxing while a blade touched her just below her shoulder wasn't possible. However, she allowed the strange humming to fill her mind.

"Go," Jayden said.

Ximen drew the Invisible Sword's symbol into her skin with the blade's tip. His motions were smooth and sure and there was no pain. Odd. Blood welled and dripped but nothing hurt.

When he finished, he cut the same symbol into his palm then pressed it to her wound. "Repeat after me. As a member of the Invisible Sword, I swear I will embrace the beliefs and tenets of the organization and fully support its efforts to help those in need."

She recited the words.

"As a member of the Invisible Sword, I swear I will not betray its existence or the identities of its members to anyone and would give my life to keep its secrets."

Panic burned in her stomach, but she echoed Ximen.

"I pledge my loyalty to the Invisible Sword."

Her throat tightened as if sand blocked her windpipe. The monks had wanted her to make a similar pledge. She wouldn't do it for her family, but she had no choice but to do it for a group of strangers. Otherwise twenty-two people would be tortured and killed. Her freedom was worth the price. This was also for Banqui. And for Dyani.

Swallowing the lump, she said, "I pledge my loyalty to the Invisible Sword."

Pain blazed on her arm as an unseen force knocked her and Ximen apart. The symbol burned deep into her like acid eating through stone. Shyla pressed her hand to the injury as the agony intensified. Was it because she was a cursed sun-kissed? Unable to stand, she collapsed to her knees then lay on her right side on the ground, curled into a ball. The torment continued. Did they believe she hadn't told the truth?

Why wouldn't it stop? She muffled her sobs into the crook of her right arm.

"Why is it taking so long?" Jayden's concerned voice seeped through her misery.

"Perhaps she's pledged to another," Ximen said.

"It's because she lied," Bazia said. "Her word is worthless."

Bazia's comment turned Shyla's pain into anger. A hot sun-at-angle-ninety type of fury. She gathered it into a ball of rage and pushed.

The others flew back and slammed into the walls. The burning on her arm eased, then disappeared. She uncurled and lay panting on the floor. Sweat drenched her tunic. The three stumbled to their feet and returned to her side. Shyla didn't have the energy to worry if they planned to retaliate.

"Well, that was different," Jayden said, rubbing the back of his head. He knelt next to her and helped her to a sitting position. "Shyla, can I see your arm?"

Her right hand remained clamped over the injury. Reluctantly, she released her hold. The skin was smooth and unmarked. No cuts, no bruises, and no blood. Not even a scar.

"Does that mean it didn't work?" she asked in confusion.

"No." Ximen held up his palm. It too, lacked any evidence of an injury. "It worked."

"How?"

"You know how," he chided.

But she couldn't accept it. Even thinking the word… magic proved difficult.

"You're now an official member of the Invisible Sword. Your invisible mark," he tapped her arm, "will reveal itself only to another member who has magic."

"Not everyone has magic?"

"No." Jayden gestured to the others. "We all do, but many in our organization do not."

"Okay, but you're right here and I don't see the mark."

Ximen smiled. "But I can."

Jayden once again pulled up his sleeve. The symbol shone on his skin like light reflecting off glass. It hadn't been there before. Ximen rolled up his sleeve as well. Bazia scowled, but she did the same. Both had the same symbol, proving they were all members. Handy.

She'd try to figure out how it worked at another time. As soon as she recovered enough to stand, Shyla asked. "What's your plan to rescue Banqui?"

"Don't you want—"

"No. Banqui and the others first and all this…" She gestured to the three of them "…can be explained later."

"All right," Ximen said. "Our plan is simple. You're going to give a fake set of The Eyes to the Water Prince in exchange for Banqui."

CHAPTER 13

Ximen's words echoed off the hard stone walls of the empty judgment room of Tamburah's temple.

"I'm going to do *what*?" Shyla hoped she had misunderstood him.

"The Invisible Sword has a fake set of Tamburah's precious Eyes," Ximen said as if she'd just hit her head too hard. "We will give them to you to exchange for Banqui. Once he's free, you'll bring him to us."

So many questions and emotions boiled in her chest. For a moment she was too overwhelmed, then she focused on the most concerning aspect. "Why do you want him?"

Ximen hesitated.

She tapped her shoulder where the symbol of her loyalty shone...well, to him anyway.

"He's the one, Shyla. We believe he can use the magic of The Eyes and we'll finally be able to break the Water Prince and Heliacal Priestess's stranglehold."

Back to the magic thing. Great. But that wasn't the biggest problem. "How good are these fakes? The prince isn't a fool."

"They're practically identical. The fakes have all the right gemstones, just none of the power."

Okay. "How do I explain my absence and how I managed to find the stolen artifacts?"

Ximen looked to Jayden. "It's your idea, you tell her."

Oh, this ought to be good. If it involved magic, she was sunk.

Jayden rubbed his hands along his pants as if nervous. "Captain Rendor witnessed your capture. When you're reunited, you'll explain to him that your inquiries about The Eyes made us nervous, so we grabbed you with the intent of getting information from you before we…er…killed you."

"Us, as in the Invisible Sword?"

"Did you tell him our name?" Bazia asked with concern.

"No, I told him the symbol represented a secret organization who claimed they could use magic." And that reminded her of a question that'd been bothering her. "Why did you leave your…our…symbol in the vault for Banqui to find?"

"We wanted him to know we had The Eyes," Ximen said.

"Why not just tell him?" It would have saved her a lot of trouble and pain.

"Too easy. Our members must prove their worth. Banqui suspected we existed and he was close to discovering the truth. And his will is strong—none of our magic worked on him, which is one of the signs of our true leader. We hoped the symbol would allow him to make the connection and find us."

"It did," she said, remembering his reaction and his crazy story. She needed to apologize to him.

"But right after you discovered the symbol, the prince's guards arrested you both," Ximen said. "You had some nice moves. Too bad you were outnumbered."

She rounded on him. "You were there. Why didn't you help?"

"Nothing I could do."

Still.

"Do the vagrants know you're part of the Invisible Sword?" she asked Jayden.

"Only those who are members as well. And no, Mojag is not one of the them. Not yet."

"Did you sing me to sleep after you rescued me from the deacons?" she demanded.

"You were injured and too stubborn to accept help. I—"

Ximen cleared his throat. "Back to the plan, Jay."

"Right. So you're our prisoner for a few sun jumps and then you ingratiated yourself into our organization, helping us with our efforts. It takes a while, but we start to trust you and then…pow!"

"Pow?" Now he sounded more like Mojag.

"You steal The Eyes and make a run for it. We pursue you, but you bolt for the monastery and as soon as you get inside the monks will protect you. We back off and put a bounty on your head."

She sighed. Another bounty. "Do you have to do that?"

"Yes, so everyone believes you stole them from us."

"Us? I though you…we were invisible."

"We are, but treasure hunters are not."

Lots of details and even more questions. "Your…our members pretend to be treasure hunters?"

"No pretending. Many are. How do you think we finance our operations?"

Clearly she had a lot to learn about the extent of this Invisible Sword. "So I've been helping you find treasures?"

"Yes." Ximen beamed at her as if she'd just mastered a new trick.

"But if you put a bounty on me, then I won't make it to the Water Prince." Not alive—an important detail.

"The captain is still at the monastery. He'll escort you back. As soon as you reach the city, he'll have you surrounded with armed guards. Once we hear the news that the Water Prince has The Eyes, we'll drop the bounty," Ximen explained.

"And you can tell Rendor that the secret organization was just a group of treasure hunters who've been laying low until all the ruckus over The Eyes has died before selling them," Jayden added.

She considered. Convincing Rendor about her adventures would be difficult, he'd demand details and he wasn't stupid—far from it. Then what would happen if the prince reneged on their deal? So many things could go wrong.

"Let's say by some miracle everything works as planned. Then what?" she asked.

"You return to your research job. Banqui has already been replaced and won't be trusted, so it makes sense for him to leave for another city, or rather to pretend to. After a number of sun jumps, when it's obvious no one will hire you, you'll return to the monastery. At least, that's what the rumors will say. In fact, you'll join us in our work with Banqui as our new leader."

"And you called this a simple plan," she said. "What if someone comes to the monastery looking for me?"

"That's unlikely," Bazia said.

"Bazia," Ximen warned.

"It's true," she shot back. "Shyla has no friends except Banqui. No one will miss her."

"Bazia, that's enough," Jayden said.

"She's right." Shyla hated defending the woman, but she had to give the lady her due. Bazia must have been the one to collect the information on Shyla. Too bad she didn't inform Jayden about her deal with the prince in time. Unless the bitch purposely kept it from him.

"Look, we're running out of time. Are you going to help us?" Jayden asked.

She tapped her arm. "I thought I didn't have a choice."

"We're not like that."

"Really? May I remind you about being chained against my will for twelve sun jumps?"

"We'll explain how our organization works at another time," Ximen said. "But if you're not committed to the plan, we'll have to find another way or it just won't work."

"I'm determined to help. What's the next step?"

* * *

Shyla ran up the side of the dune. Or rather, she tried. Her boots sank into the sand up to her knees, limiting the speed of her ascent. And the sun... Oh the sun… It seared through the fibers of her sun cloak like tiny hot iron pokers. If she didn't know better, she'd swear flames danced on the garment.

As she struggled to keep ahead of the figures pursuing her, she mentally cursed her big mouth. Ximen and Jayden had wanted to stage this getaway at angle thirty, but no, *she* had to insist that if she'd just stolen a priceless artifact with magical powers, she'd wait until angle sixty-five to take off. The logic being that they wouldn't chase her at such a dangerous time of the sun jump. And if they did, they'd retreat when the sun reached angle seventy in order to get to safety, giving her a greater chance to escape.

A nice bit of logic until she reached the surface. Even through the layers of the scarf wrapped around her eyes, the bright orange light just about blinded her. And the heat... Oh the heat... It sucked every bit of moisture from her nose, mouth, and eyes. Her tongue shriveled to a piece of velbloud leather. Blinking hurt. What she sucked into and blew out of her lungs was no longer air. No, it burned like invisible fire. And it pressed on her like a physical force, cooking her from the outside in. She feared she'd be a pile of ash by the time she reached the monastery.

At first she kept a slow pace, each step an effort of will. Each dune felt taller and steeper than the last. When the first arrow zinged by her and thudded into the sand nearby, that was her cue. Behind her a group of Invisible Sword members fanned out to give chase. An act for the monks who remained on the surface as lookouts until just before the danger zone. They had circuits to develop a tolerance for the harshest angles.

Another arrow whizzed by her ear. She scrambled, her desperation genuine as the sun crept toward the danger zone. Reaching the top, she spotted the monastery. A group of monks stood near the entrance, staring at her as if she was the Sun Goddess arriving for a visit. A third and fourth arrow flew past, motivating her to hustle down the other side. When she staggered to the bottom, she envisioned her pursuers standing in a line on top of the dune, but she didn't have the energy to turn around. And the monks wouldn't help until she crossed the monastery's threshold.

With the last of her energy, she sprinted. But she wasn't fast enough and an arrow nicked her left thigh. The entrance loomed. Only two more—

Son of a sand demon! An arrow pierced the back of her right shoulder. The force knocked her to the ground, and she sprawled forward in the blazing sand, the pain of the arrow a mere annoyance compared to the blisters erupting on her exposed palms and wrists.

Your escape must appear genuine, Ximen had warned her.

Shyla belly-crawled the remaining meter. The monks waiting for her grabbed her under the arms. She cried out as the motion jostled the arrow, but they whisked her deeper underground. The cool air sizzled on her hot skin. A shiver raced through her followed by relief to no longer be frying alive in the sunlight.

When they gently laid her down on her stomach, the cold stone table equaled the finest silk cushion.

"Water first, then we'll remove the arrow," a voice said.

They tipped her on her uninjured side and handed her a water skin. She squeezed it so hard, it sprayed her face. Not caring, she sucked the rest down, making more of a mess. The water doused the heat in her mouth and throat. When she finished, they returned her to her stomach.

Fingers prodded the skin around the arrow's shaft. Shyla bit down on a cry.

"It hit the bone, but it's not deep," a monk with a raspy voice said.

She didn't recognize him.

After a few moments and more poking, he tsked. "The arrow is barbed."

She groaned. Damn thing would hurt more coming out than going in. Thanks *so much* Ximen. The arrows had been his idea.

"Here." The monk handed her a cup of green liquid. "Drink it." When she hesitated, he added, "Unless you'd rather be awake while I cut this arrow out of you?"

She drained it. Someone took the cup from her numb fingers before she dropped it. All sensations fled her limbs. Wow, that was…

* * *

Fast. The word spun in circles around her mind. But nothing else matched. All her dreams featured slow burns and legs mired in deep sand as she struggled to move forward even though her destination remained a tiny spot in the distance.

Even pulling her consciousness from her dreams required a protracted effort. First she acknowledged the dry gritty taste in her mouth. Then the familiar and comforting scent of herbs. Followed by the throb of various injuries along with an overall bone-deep ache. The weight of a fur pressed down on her now cool skin. Softness cradled her. Sounds turned from melodious murmurs to words, which transformed into a conversation.

"…depends," said the raspy-voiced monk.

"That's not an answer," growled Rendor.

Shyla opened her eyes. The captain leaned on a cane, his left arm in a sling and his glower firmly in place. The sight of him eased the tightness around her heart. A part of her had worried the Invisible Sword had lied to her about Rendor. Now she could replace the horrible image of him dead and desiccated that her imagination had conjured during her imprisonment. She smiled even though the effort cracked her dry lips.

"It's been two sun jumps." Rendor loomed over the monk.

Unintimidated, the monk said, "Nice to know the prince teaches his dogs how to count. She'll wake when she's ready." He left the small room.

Rendor's grip tightened on his cane. He stared at the door with an expression that promised pain. The image of the big man limping after the monk to whack him with the cane rose in her mind. She stifled a giggle. Well, she tried.

He turned to her. Their gazes met. She clutched the fur, bracing for his anger, his demands about her whereabouts, his suspicions.

But his expression softened. "We've got to stop meeting like this."

She laughed. It hurt everywhere, but she didn't care. It was the first time in so long, she'd lost count. Nice to be unafraid and not worried. At least for a little while. "But this time you didn't have to carry me here."

"Who says I didn't?" He smirked.

"That cane and sling."

His good humor faded and a scowl creased his face. "They wouldn't let me go out there and get you. Said you had to cross the threshold on your own."

A strange hitch caught in her lungs as if she couldn't draw in enough air. He would have risked his life. For her?

"Took three of them to hold me back." Rendor sounded disgusted, as if it should have been more. "I argued I wasn't a monk. But they said if anyone interfered, the Water Prince could claim you were kidnapped and come *rescue* you."

That wouldn't be good and not according to the plan. She needed to bring— Seven hells. She struggled to get up from the sleeping cushion. Her shoulder blazed with pain.

Rendor limped over. He set his cane down, knelt, and helped her sit up. "What's wrong?"

"My pack! Where is it?"

"Why?" And there was Captain Rendor in all his suspicious glory.

Confiding in him was part of the ruse so Shyla glanced at the door and lowered her voice. "I found them."

He leaned closer. "The Eyes?"

"Yes."

Rendor sat back on his heels. Surprise, disbelief, suspicion, and calculation all rolled through his eyes before he settled on worried. "How?"

"It won't matter if I lost them."

He used his cane to help him stand, then went over to the chest. She was in the standard small room that all the monks had. Furnished with a sleeping cushion, chest, and desk, it embraced one of their tenets—simplicity.

Opening the chest, he removed her pack. She froze as a sudden thought speared her. Would he take The Eyes? Bring them to the prince and claim he recovered them? Instead, he handed the pack to her. She almost collapsed back in relief. Rummaging through, she found the container and removed it. The box was about five centimeters wide, ten centimeters long, and four centimeters high. It had been crafted from marble with a blue, purple, and silver pattern. According to Ximen, it was the original container.

She opened it, showing Rendor the contents. Nestled in silk padding were two small identical "eyes" that stared back at them. Black diamonds for the pupil, a ring of green emeralds for the iris, and white topaz for the rest.

"They're smaller than I thought," Rendor said.

"I think they're life-sized. From a distance they resemble real eyes. It's creepy. And take a look at the back." She held up the box.

Rendor carefully picked one up and turned it over. More white topaz, but also streaks of rubies.

"That's odd isn't it?" she asked.

"It's realistic." He set the gemstone back into the container.

"How do you— Oh." Shyla imagined many people would be very cooperative if you threated to cut their eyes out. She shivered. At least he had the decency to look grim.

She closed the box and returned it to her pack. There was a hole in the leather that hadn't been there before. Sticking a finger through it, she glanced at Rendor.

"Arrow. You were extremely lucky that it's hard to hit a moving target with sweat stinging your eyes." He sat on the floor next to her. If the movement pained him, he didn't show it. "What happened after…" He made a vague gesture.

"After they staked you to the sand?"

A grunt.

"I thought you died," she whispered.

A nod. "It seemed inevitable, but the monks…I've no idea why they saved me. They hate me." He shook his head. "But you were just about to explain what you've been doing for the thirteen sun jumps you were missing."

"I was?"

"Shyla." A dangerous rumble.

At one point that tone would have scared her, but no longer. "All right."

She repeated the story the Invisible Sword had concocted. Her fear and confusion had been real so she allowed them to color her words. "Once I convinced them that I would help, they allowed me to be part of their organization, but they didn't trust me." She continued with her fabricated story of working for the Invisible Sword, giving details of artifacts she found for the treasure hunters—actual ones they had stolen during that time, just in case Rendor followed up.

"They still didn't trust me, but I learned enough about their organization that when the opportunity arose to snatch The Eyes, I did." She touched the bandage on her shoulder. "I didn't think they'd chase me so close to the danger zone."

"Why not?" Rendor asked, but didn't wait for a reply. "You saw how they popped up from the sand when they'd ambushed us. Obviously they have secret tunnels. And they disappeared soon after you were brought inside."

Secret tunnels made more sense than magic. Perhaps the Invisible Sword just used tricks. Shyla rubbed the place she'd been marked. The knife had cut into her flesh. Blood had spilled. And no one healed that fast.

"What are you going to do with The Eyes?" Rendor asked a little too casually.

"Exactly what I said I'd do. Trade them for Banqui."

"He's still alive?" Rendor sounded surprised.

That alarmed her. "You don't know?"

"I've been here healing and hoping. I figured if you were still alive, you'd eventually come here."

"But the Water Prince—"

"Has already replaced me."

"Does he think you're dead?"

"According to the monks, he knows I survived."

"How do they know?"

"They're not as isolated as they want everyone to believe. However, they don't know if the prince decided if it is worth the trouble to come after me."

"What does that mean?" She hoped it wasn't as dire as it sounded.

"When I did not arrest you, I gambled. I believed that you would find The Eyes and the Water Prince would forgive my disobedience. But he's not a patient man and he'd already given me a second chance when you went missing for four sun jumps. When you disappeared again and I failed to protect you—"

"There were a dozen of them!"

"Doesn't matter. They key word is failed. And…" He jiggled his cane. "I'm no longer the best."

"But you were almost killed. And once you get better—"

"Again it doesn't matter. I'm no longer the captain of his guard. And if I return to Zirdai, the guards have orders to kill me on sight."

That stunned her. "You can't go back?"

"No."

When he'd said he gambled, he'd meant more than just his career. Guilt gnawed on her soul. If she'd figured out the Invisible Sword's chanting trick sooner, he'd have his life back.

Rendor leaned closer. "Don't. *I* made the choice. I failed. None of this is your fault."

"Nice try, but this is *all* my fault. Perhaps I could negotiate with the prince and get you reinstated."

"No. The guards would no longer respect me and that's critical to leadership. And I no longer want the position."

"But what about your family and friends? Don't you want to be able to see them?"

He laughed. Not a happy sound at all. "There is no such thing as friendship within the prince's guards. As for my family…they always thought I was worthless and wouldn't amount to much." Rendor shrugged. "Family is a distraction and those that keep close ties never rise very far through the ranks."

"Why did you sign up?"

"I liked to fight and I was good at it. Enough so that I worked hard to become the best in Zirdai."

"You'll recover and can be again."

"True."

Ah, there was his ego, she'd been worried.

"But it won't matter to the prince," he said. "Remember, I warned you."

Shyla held up the box. "But technically you didn't fail."

"I've accepted it. Why are you so concerned about me?"

Good question. She should be glad that he'd no longer be torturing people for the Water Prince. But…there was something about Rendor… "I've already ruined my life, I don't want to be responsible for yours as well."

He studied her a moment. "If you'd never gotten involved in my life, then I would have continued to be the prince's captain for a few more circuits unless I was killed in the line of duty—most likely ambushed by a large group." He paused. No doubt thinking how close he'd come to that scenario. "If I managed to survive, then eventually I would be challenged for the position as captain. I'd win a number of challenges and remain captain for a few more circuits, but it would be only a matter of time until the right person challenged me and I lost."

"Lost, as in…"

"Died, yes. There's no retiring once you reach that level of the prince's service. Everyone who challenges for the captain position knows this going in. As I see it, you've done me a favor as I managed to survive my job—something no one else has accomplished. As long as I don't irk the Water Prince before I'm healed, I can move to another city and start over."

That was a warped way to look at it, but it eased her guilt. And she envied his freedom. "Which city?" There were so many!

"Shouldn't you be worried about yourself?"

All dreams of travel fled. She rubbed her arm, considering. The Invisible Sword's plan to exchange the fake eyes for Banqui had depended on Rendor, which meant they were unaware of the change in captains. Now Rendor couldn't protect her in Zirdai and, with the bounty on her head, it would be rather difficult moving through the city. Regardless, she needed to get to the prince. Would the guards believe her and escort her to him? She asked Rendor.

"Depends on who you find," he said. "A few know what's been going on and will take you down so they gain the prince's favor. A few will think you're crazy and either ignore you or arrest you. But a few will decide to keep The Eyes for themselves and leave to sell them in another city."

"So I have a thirty percent chance of finding the one honest guard?"

He smiled. "Actually it's lower than that. The guards assigned to the upper levels are usually new and not privy to what's going on."

Great. "What can I do to reach the prince?"

"If you still had his sigil it'd be easy. Otherwise the guards won't let you get close to him even if you made it down to his entrance."

More reasons to hate the deacons. Too bad the scars on her left wrist hadn't disappeared like her Invisible Sword mark.

"I don't suppose you have another one?" she asked.

He made a show of patting his pockets. "Sorry, sunbeam, fresh out."

Ah sarcasm. She ignored the sunbeam crack because she knew he wanted to provoke a reaction. Why, she'd no idea. But it did give her another idea. "What's the sigil made of?"

"Gold and silver."

Two precious metals that she didn't own. And even if she did, she would have to risk capture to get to her secret stash. Which made her wonder… She glanced at Rendor.

"What?"

"How are you going to afford moving to another city?" she asked.

"Are you hoping I have some gold and silver to lend you?"

"No. It just occurred to me."

"Captains are paid very well, and because of the inherent danger of our job we tend to splurge and spend all our money. No need to save for the future."

That was sad, no wonder he was always grumpy.

"But on the flip side, we don't have much free time. I've a nice stockpile hidden, but that's down on level ninety-seven. Good thing I also had my last pay with me." He dug into his pocket and drew out a large handful of osees. "I'll give most of these to the monks to pay for their…kindness. The rest will cover the travel fee. Once I'm there, I'll find a job."

He didn't sound concerned at all. So easy for those not sun-kissed.

"If I had the choice, I'd go to Apanji," she said. "They have these pink marble columns that are massive and emit the purest white light in all of Koraha. They also have a river of water that falls nine levels and splashes down in this huge pool. I'd love to see that."

Rendor regarded her with an odd expression. "You don't have to give The Eyes to the prince. You could sell them and have enough coins to travel all over Koraha."

"I could."

"But you won't." He paused. "Your dedication is admirable. Banqui must mean a lot to you."

Was he jealous? "If you had a true friend, then you'd understand."

Rendor didn't respond. Sighing, Shyla pulled her attention back to the problem at hand. Unfortunately, she had no way to contact the Invisible Sword. Except Jayden, but that meant getting down to level sixty-two. From her explorations, she'd learned that her map of Zirdai was useless and she didn't know the city as well as she'd thought. She doubted anyone did. Which meant trying to sneak down to the deeper levels without being seen. Impossible for her. She either needed a guide or a fake sigil or a better map to reach the Water Prince.

Shyla wondered if the monks would help her. Guess she'd have to swallow her pride and ask.

Although he didn't look happy—then again when did he ever appear happy?—Rendor helped her to her feet and followed her out into the hall. She slung her pack over her good shoulder. The floor dipped underneath her and she leaned against the wall to keep upright. Druk lanterns hung every ten meters, which meant they were below the public levels.

She turned to him. "They let you down here?"

He lifted his left elbow, indicating the sling. "I'm hardly a threat and they understand my connection to the prince has been severed and I need to lay low. But I'm limited to only a few locations, and I've been told once I'm recovered I'm no longer welcome."

"Subtle."

"Not surprising. Even though the monks remain out of Zirdai's affairs, that doesn't mean they don't know what's going on. I've plenty of blood on my hands." He stated it as fact. No emotion tainted his voice. If it bothered him, he hid it well.

"And also, the prince might order the monks to hand me over. It would cause them considerable trouble if they refused, even though they do have that right. It's best for all if I leave as soon as I can."

That the prince had that much influence over the monks still surprised her. She glanced around and noted the numbers on the doors—they must be in one of the housing levels of the monastery. Probably an unoccupied one far from the others.

"Where are you staying?" she asked.

He pointed at the door across from hers. "We have the wing to ourselves."

Keeping him isolated was yet another not-so-subtle indication they wanted him gone.

"Stay here," she said. "I need to—"

"Get something to drink and eat?"

"No. I—"

"You've been asleep for two sun jumps. When's the last time you ate?"

She thought back. Had she eaten in Tamburah's judgment room?

"I thought so. Come on." With both hands occupied, he'd no choice but to nudge her forward with his good shoulder.

She didn't have the strength to fight him. They headed toward the dining area. Stopping every few meters, Shyla placed her outstretched hand on the wall to keep from falling down. Rendor limped along beside her at a slow pace, seeming content to pause when she needed. What a pathetic pair.

When they finally arrived, the hall was empty. The sand clock read angle forty-five, right between first and second meals.

"This way," she said, going into the kitchen. The coals in the hearth had been banked. The room smelled of garlic, stirring memories of late night raids with an accomplice or two. One perk to growing up here, she knew where they stored the food and kept the jugs of water.

Not bothering to go out to a table, they sat on stools next to a counter to eat. It wasn't much of a meal—gamelu cheese, thin slices of velbloud meat and a couple hunks of bread, but after all those sun jumps of jerky, it tasted divine. She was careful not to overeat or drink. But what she managed to imbibe revived her.

Rendor stared at her with his eyebrows slightly raised.

"All right. You were right. I feel better," she admitted.

"Progress. There's hope that some time you'll be able to say it without the grumble."

"Don't hold your breath."

He opened his mouth to reply, but two monks burst into the kitchen. One of them was Easan—the monk who'd guarded the First Room of Knowledge when she was here before. She didn't recognize the other.

"Why didn't you alert us that she was awake?" Easan demanded of Rendor.

"No one asked me to," Rendor said simply.

"She'd been shot." Easan swept a hand out. "And you just let her leave?"

"I've no authority to stop her."

Shyla almost laughed. Authority, no. Muscular manhandling, yes. "Is there a problem?" Shyla asked.

"Hanif wishes to speak with you," Easan said.

"Now?"

"He's waiting in your room."

Oh. Not good. No wonder Easan was in such a state. Shyla stood. This time the floor remained firm underneath her feet. Easan set a fast pace. Or rather, he tried. Although steadier after the meal, Shyla still moved with care. Her injuries throbbed with each step. And she didn't want to outpace Rendor. No idea why. Perhaps because he was her only ally and she felt safer with him beside her. She slowed at the unexpected thought. How in seven hells did that happen?

When they reached her room, Easan moved between her and Rendor. "You're not invited."

Rendor met her gaze as if seeking her permission. Easan almost snarled in annoyance.

"Go on," she said, tilting her head to Rendor's room. "I'll talk to you later."

"Call if you need me," he said.

"And just what are you going to do?" Easan demanded, rounding on him. "Whack me with your cane? You can barely stand."

"Stop it," Shyla said. "Hanif is waiting."

Easan strode into her room, muttering. The other monk remained in the hall as if ordered to guard the door. Shyla glanced over her shoulder before following Easan. Rendor stood in the threshold of his room, a sly grin on his face.

Son of a sand demon! She'd bet a hundred coins he'd been faking just how injured he really was.

Inside her room, Hanif sat on the chest with his legs crossed underneath him. His eyes were closed as if he were meditating.

Shyla walked to the cushion and sank into its softness. The trip to the kitchen had worn her out more than she'd expected. Easan leaned a shoulder on the now closed door. His arms were crossed. The tension in the air thickened.

Hanif opened his eyes and his serene gaze surveyed them both. "Easan, please wait outside."

Easan straightened with a surprised jerk, but he left as ordered.

Hanif studied her a moment longer. "Did you know you're the most wanted person in Zirdai?"

"Most wanted? Not bad for an outcast sun-kissed."

"This is serious, Shyla. We can only protect you if you take the oath and become a monk."

That was no longer an option. "I can't stay here." She held up a hand, stopping him. "For many different reasons. Some beyond my control. And I need to leave soon. Would you be able to provide some help?"

"Depends on what you need."

He didn't say no. "I need an accurate map of Zirdai."

"There's no such thing. The city is alive in more ways than one and changes each sun jump."

"How about a guide so I can navigate the city unseen?"

"We don't—"

"Come on, Hanif. The Monks of Parzival are more involved than you'd want the Water Prince and Heliacal Priestess to believe."

"Point to you. Except we don't get *involved*, we simply keep an eye on things so we're not surprised when the prince learns you're here and sends a squadron to retrieve you. Or when the priestess deploys her Arch Deacons to come fetch you."

"Arch Deacons?"

"An elite squad."

She shivered. The regular ones seemed bad enough. "They still wouldn't get close to the monastery."

"No. But there's a chance of fatalities and I'm not willing to risk *my* monks for an outsider."

Even though it was true, it hurt.

"And I've no doubt that, for you, the Water Prince would keep sending more and more guards until we are simply overrun."

"All right, I get it. All the more reason for me to leave. So how about that guide?"

"None of *my* monks have that much knowledge of the city."

She'd curse, but Hanif would scold her out of habit. "I don't suppose you have a replica of the Water Prince's sigil?"

"No."

"And I don't suppose you're willing to let *your* monks provide protection so I can reach the Water Prince."

He cocked his head. "If you want to get to the Water Prince, you just need to wait here. Protocol dictates that he'd send an emissary with that squadron to ask us to hand over the person of interest. Usually he or she is a wanted criminal and we oblige. We can do that with you and they'll take you to the Water Prince."

"No. I can't be *taken* there. I must show up on my own." Or else the prince would never believe that she'd planned to give him The Eyes.

When Hanif's brow creased, she added, "It's complicated." She thought about his comments. "What if the person the prince wants is a sworn monk?"

"We don't oblige," he said with steel in his voice.

"And the prince?"

"Has to decide how badly he wants that person."

"And his response?"

"So far, he's been smart enough to decide that it's not worth the trouble." Hanif unfolded his legs and stood. "I'm sorry Shyla, but I can't ask *my* monks to risk themselves guarding you in Zirdai."

Shyla stared at him. That was the third time he stressed that they were *his* monks. Why would—Scorching hells.

CHAPTER

14

"I'm going with you," Rendor said in that don't-argue-with-me-you-won't-win tone.

"No," Shyla said, for the tenth time. She adjusted the sleeves of her borrowed tunic, and then checked her pack, ensuring it still held the fake Eyes. The container was wrapped in multiple layers of cloth and secured in a safe position.

"I know the guards," Rendor said. "I know the city. I can get you down there with minimal trouble."

"No."

"Why not?" he ground out.

"Because the guards also know *you*."

"But I'll be—"

"Recognized right away." She gestured to him. "Mr. Broad Shoulders and what…about ten centimeters shy of two meters tall? Besides, you're still recovering."

"So are you. It's only been a sun jump since you woke from being shot by an arrow."

She jabbed a finger at his cane. "You won't be able to fight."

He tossed it onto the cushion and moved closer without limping. "I can fight. My sword is in my room."

Ha! She'd been right. "How well? They have orders to *kill* you. Can you defend against more than one guard?"

"It won't come to that."

"Are you insane? I've guards, bounty hunters, vagrants, and deacons after me. It'll be a miracle if we don't have to fight our way down each level." She swung her sun cloak around her shoulders. The poor thing had been cleaned and repaired again, yet the velbloud fibers remained strong. Its hide had saved her hide many times.

A knock interrupted them. Shyla opened the door. Four monks…well, not quite monks…stood outside.

"Ready?" one woman asked.

"Yes," she said.

"No," Rendor said. "She'll meet you on the surface."

The woman looked at Shyla.

She sighed. "Give me a moment. I'll be right up."

"All right." She left with the others.

"Now what?" Shyla snapped at Rendor, but regretted it when she noticed his shoulders had relaxed as if he'd accepted defeat.

"If this all works out and you rescue Banqui, can you do me a favor?"

This softer Rendor scared her more than the gruff-bark-orders Rendor. "If I can."

"Remember that flight of stairs I found you on? The landing where you fell asleep after your visit with the Heliacal Priestess?"

"I remember falling asleep." Stupid holy water. "But aren't there a number of stairs connecting the two levels?"

"Not public ones. The others are only used by the guards and their locations are kept secret."

That made sense. Having one access point was easier to defend. "What about that staircase?"

"Under the lip of the third step up from that landing is a small keyhole at mid-point. If you unlock it, the step lifts up. Inside are my savings. I want you to have it and go travel to Apanji and all the other cities you've been wanting to visit."

He'd shocked her to her very core. That was the nicest thing anyone had done for her. Ever. Everything she'd always wanted within reach and…she couldn't accept. "Oh, Rendor that's…incredibly generous, but it's yours. You earned it. I'll bring it back for you."

He shook his head. "I don't want it. If you can't keep it, then give it to the monks or the vagrants. I'll be gone by the time you return."

Gone. The word reverberated in her mind despite the fact that it was expected. It made sense. There was no reason for him to stay. Yet.

"Where are you going?" she asked.

"Thought I'd head to Apanji, someone told me it's worth seeing." He scratched his stubbly chin. "Can't remember who."

His teasing tone was the only thing that kept her from crying. Which was crazy. He'd killed, tortured, and done unimaginably nasty things to people, all for the Water Prince. Then why the hell did she want to tell him to stay! Why did she want to throw her arms around his neck, pull him close, and kiss him? Besides, it was dangerous for him to stay. He'd be killed.

Rendor stared at her in concern. "Shyla?"

"I think you'll enjoy Apanji," she whispered, avoiding his gaze.

He closed the distance between them, stopping only a few centimeters away. "Once this is over, come join me." A huskiness roughened his voice. "We can visit those other cities together."

The desire to step into his arms pumped through her. The need as vital as the water that nourished her. Instead she widened the gap. "I'm sorry. I can't."

His expression flattened into neutral. "I understand."

"No. You don't. I've made…a promise that I have to keep."

"Once Banqui is free—"

"This goes beyond Banqui." She wished to explain more.

"You promised to become a monk. That's why they're helping you."

Close enough. "Yes."

Rendor's shoulders and arms tightened with anger and probably frustration. Shyla was getting pretty good at reading his body language.

"They took advantage of you," he said.

"No. It's where I belong, Rendor. I'm sun-kissed. None of those cities would ever welcome me. It's best I just disappear."

"How do you know?" he demanded. "Not all the cities in Koraha enforce that barbaric ritual sacrifice. You can live in one of them."

"They might not enforce it, but many parents still sacrifice their sun-kissed babies. I've read about it in the First Room of Knowledge."

"Just because you have access doesn't mean you know everything," he said.

True. She'd learned so much about Zirdai since she'd left the monastery.

"In fact..." He wrapped his arm around her and pulled her close. "Do you know what it's like to be kissed?" Without waiting for an answer, Rendor bent his head and pressed his lips to hers.

Warmth spread from her core. His kiss matched the rest of him, powerful, demanding and so very insistent.

Having no desire to stop him, she deepened it, parting her lips and letting him in. Spikes of heat flashed through her and ignited desire. She craved his touch.

He broke away, leaving her gasping and bereft.

Resting his forehead on hers, he said, "And that's just the beginning. Remember that before you take your vows. You know where I'll be." Then he released her and pulled a thick black cord from around his neck. A small key hung on it. "You'll need this to get into my stash." He looped it around her neck. Without another word, he left the room.

Shyla stared after him, fingering the key hanging from her throat. And for a few racing heartbeats, she considered being selfish, running away with Rendor and discovering what comes after a kiss like that. Then the parade of people depending on her marched through her mind, ending with an entire commune. She tucked the key under her tunic, smoothed her cloak and ascended to the surface building.

The four "monks" waited with obvious impatience. Sweat beaded their brows and they aimed sour looks at her. The sun was higher in the sky than they'd planned, but she hadn't expected to be blindsided by Rendor. Her lips still tingled and his scent clung to her sun cloak.

Hanif had joined them to see the group off. He thanked the two men—Elek and Jaft—and two women—Lian and Rae—who had volunteered to escort and protect Shyla. They were acolytes near the end of their training, but not yet sworn monks. A loophole. Not everyone who joined the monastery had been rescued as abandoned babies. Many came seeking solace or asylum later in life or some arrived when they reached their legal adulthood.

These four were a few circuits older than she was. Since the monks couldn't get involved, the acolytes wore nondescript khaki-colored tunics, pants, and turbans. Semi-sheer material protected their faces from the sun and from recognition. Only their eyes were visible.

Shyla planned to keep a fast pace as they descended to the prince's level to reduce the number of people who would attack them. She also decided that when they entered the city, she would uncover her very short hair. No sense hiding. Besides, this was the last time the citizens of Zirdai would see her. Once this was over, she'd become invisible. For real this time.

* * *

They reached the main entrance of Zirdai at angle fifty. Using it would make a statement—they were on a mission. When they entered the sweepers stared at them, but shrugged and kept working. The air cooled quickly as they descended the first ten levels. Shyla pulled her hood down, but the acolytes kept their veils in place.

She led them down the main hallways and stairways. The familiar smells and sounds of the city resonated within her. It'd been twenty-five sun jumps since this entire mess with Banqui and The Eyes started. She drank in the sights as if she'd never see them again. Silly, and maudlin. Many citizens stopped what they were doing and gawked at the quintet. No doubt they'd run and gossip to their friends and word would spread, eventually reaching the guards, the deacons, and bounty hunters. They'd passed a few guards already, but as Rendor had said, they were new and uncertain of what to do. A couple trailed after them.

The first challenge waited for them on level twenty-three. Six of the Water Prince's guards blocked a main tunnel. Shyla's group approached to within three meters and stopped.

The guard standing in front rested his hand on the hilt of his sword and stepped forward. "What is this about?"

"I've a meeting with the Water Prince," Shyla said.

"I haven't been informed of a meeting," he said.

"Of course not," she said in her most dismissive tone. "You're not ranked high enough."

"Then you won't mind if I verify this meeting?"

Shyla and her companions moved closer. "Actually, I do. We're in a bit of a time crunch."

The four acolytes blurred into motion before the poor guard could draw his sword. The others had more time to react, but swords were useless when fighting inside a tight two-meter wide space. Shyla remained in place. Her shoulder still throbbed, and four people trained in the Ways of the Yarin against six upper-level guards was already overkill. She'd fight when she was needed. Instead, she witnessed the four knock the guards unconscious in a handful of heartbeats. They stepped over the prone forms, continuing their journey.

A dozen levels deeper, they encountered the next set of guards. Smarter than the last unit, this group of eight waited in a wide cavern that traders used to exchange goods. The traders, though, had already abandoned the place, giving the guards plenty of room to fight. Swords in hand, the prince's thugs spread out among the empty tables.

"We have orders to *arrest* you, Shyla Sun-kissed. Not kill," the female lieutenant said in a strong commanding voice. "Your…companions are free to go. No need to fight."

Shyla Sun-kissed? That almost sounded like a title. "Give us a moment, please," she said to the lieutenant.

"You have half an angle."

The acolytes drew closer to her.

"Should we draw this out? Make it appear as if they have a chance?" Lian asked Shyla in a whisper. "Or else they'll send twice as many next time."

"A good idea, but we can't linger," she whispered. "Knock them out fast, so they can't go run for help."

"What about the ones who've been following and watching us from the shadows?" Jaft asked her.

Jaft impressed her by picking up on that. The shadows watchers were either vagrants or hunters. "We can't engage them until they attack. Focus on the octet in front of us. Follow my lead and jump in after I go." Shyla's words may have sounded confident, but a nervous tremble accelerated the beat of her heart. They'd only reached level thirty-five. And even the acolytes had limits to their strength and stamina.

Shyla put her arms up. "All right, I give up." Waving her hands to opposite sides of the cavern, she shooed the acolytes away. "Go before the lieutenant changes her mind."

As if leaving, Elek and Lian moved to the left, while Rae and Jaft moved right. Shyla walked slowly toward the officer with her arms still raised. "I don't know why there's all this fuss over me." She gesticulated wildly and altered her route just a bit to keep a table between her and the woman. "I told the other guards, I've a meeting with the Water Prince."

"Then why did he order you arrested on sight?" she asked.

"A miscommunication." Shyla reached the table and lowered her arms.

"Uh huh. Then why the bodyguards?"

"I've something very valuable to deliver to him. And, no offense, but I don't trust his guards to make the delivery for me." Shyla removed her pack. Careful not to make any sudden movements.

The guards tensed. All their focus trained on her. The lieutenant eyed her with suspicion as she set the pack onto the table. All the woman had to do was thrust her sword forward and stab Shyla in the stomach, which tightened with anxiety.

"How about a deal?" Shyla asked her.

Her eyebrow quirked.

"I've a priceless artifact inside here." Shyla fumbled at the clasp as if in a hurry then "accidently" dropped her pack onto the floor. "Oops. Sorry." She crouched down on her haunches to retrieve it.

Instead of grabbing it, she launched up and jumped onto the table. Taken completely by surprise, the lieutenant gaped at her.

"Sorry," Shyla said right before she kicked the woman in the head, aiming for her temple.

As the woman toppled, her team charged Shyla. Except they'd forgotten about her bodyguards, who had used the distraction to maneuver around behind them. They too used the tables to gain a height advantage.

The fight wasn't pretty. Nor was it fair, but they didn't have time for fair.

When the last guard collapsed to the ground unconscious, Shyla gestured for the acolytes to follow her. She sped through the tunnels and stairwells, leading them to the outskirts of Zirdai. The shadow watchers wouldn't wait much longer, and now they knew she carried something precious.

This strategy gained them another twenty-one levels. She found a secluded spot to rest on level fifty-six. The acolytes needed food and water before the next encounter. No doubt there would be one since Shyla's map showed tunnels that no longer existed. Any more wrong turns and they'd end up being the dead part of a dead end.

Shyla explained her plan. Once rested, they would creep back to the more populated areas until they reached level sixty-two. From there she would lead them toward Jayden's commune and then follow Jayden's directions down to level seventy-three. The commune there should be empty, but she would avoid it regardless. It'd be during the time of darkness, which would limit the number of people in the public tunnels. The acolytes agreed with her reasoning.

Her confidence in the plan lasted until level sixty-one. She expected deacons to come after her. That wasn't the surprise. No. What amazed her was the sheer numbers of deacons roaming the level searching for her.

Now she wished she could do that chanting thingy that turned her invisible. She and her accomplices just managed to avoid a couple quartets before retreating to level sixty.

"What's next?" Jaft asked.

No way they'd get past all those deacons. Shyla searched her memory. When Jayden and his team had rescued her from Iskemu, they'd encountered no one along the route they took. Unfortunately, she'd been a bit traumatized by her encounter so she hadn't paid attention. If only there was some way to skip the level—Scorching hells!

"Shyla, what's wrong?" Lian asked her.

"Did any of you bring along a spider kit?"

* * *

They peered down into the blackness as the air blew into their faces. The acolytes' veils flapped in the wind rushing through the air shaft.

"Smells like sweaty feet," Elek said.

"You said a *net* saved you?" Rae asked. Her tone doubtful.

"That was on level fifty-one. We can't assume there's another one," Shyla said. "We have to spider down to level sixty-two."

"What if there are deacons waiting there as well?" Rae asked.

"In that case, there won't be as many. We can defeat them." Shyla knew doubt was a bigger enemy than the deacons so she explained. "The Heliacal Priestess is following a logical strategy. Instead of assigning teams to different levels and areas, she has put all her deacons on one level, guarding all the tunnels and stairways."

"And the air shafts, too?"

"Not likely. No one knows we can spider."

"How long has it been since *you've* spidered?" Jaft asked Shyla.

It'd been more than two circuits ago. She rolled her right shoulder, stretching the muscles which ignited sparks of pain. "Don't worry about me."

He'd watched her. "Your injury will impede your mobility."

"Do you have a better idea?" she asked him, but her gaze scanned all of them.

No one spoke up.

"I thought so. Let's get started."

Jaft, Lian and Rae tied the end of a long thin velbloud rope around all their waists. Elek wrapped the opposite end around his body, creating a harness. Although he was the heaviest of the group, he was also the strongest. Once ready, he faced them and eased over the lip of the shaft. When he let go of the edge, the other three provided a counterweight, keeping him from plummeting to his death. Dangling near the top, Elek removed a metal anchor and small mallet. He pounded the anchor into the rock wall.

The low whomp of the mallet echoed oddly and Shyla imagined every deacon on level sixty-one rushing to find the source of the sound. The desire to urge him to hurry warred with the need for their safety.

He placed a second anchor about twenty centimeters to the left. Then he clipped on carabiners to both anchors. Threading the rope through them, he signaled Shyla, who waved the others to lower Elek about a meter. When he stopped, Elek repeated his task, adding two more anchors and carabiners. Again he fastened the rope and motioned to be dropped another meter. The rope above him now resembled a square with one side missing. A third set was fixed, then a fourth.

By the time Elek reached level sixty-one, the rope looked like a long snake, but instead of smooth S-shape curves, it had sharp corners, making it appear boxy. It didn't really matter how it looked as long as the series of horizontal ropes that acted like a ladder held their weight.

Once Elek stood on firm ground, the others removed the rope from their waists and tied the end to the first anchor. Now came the hard part. While Elek did all the work, he remained secure. They, on the other hand, just had to climb down, but without anything to keep them safe if they slipped and fell.

"I'll go first," Jaft said. "Make sure the knot will hold."

Elek wound in the extra rope, then provided tension when Jaft descended, or as the monks liked to call it, he spidered. Shyla wasn't sure where the term had come from. Perhaps it'd been due to the way the rope moved and flexed like a web or because a person could only fit one hand or one foot on a "step" at a time.

Jaft arrived safely. One less worry. Lian went next. The limber acolyte moved with a quick fluid grace. Show off. Rae also climbed down as if she weighed nothing.

Remembering her last trip down an air shaft, Shyla summoned her courage before she grasped the first "step" with her left hand and lowered her right foot to the second step. The rough strands of the rope dug into her palm. Grabbing the side rope with her right hand, she stretched her left foot to the next step. For a moment all her weight pulled on her arm. Pain stabbed hard into her shoulder before her foot caught the rope and eased the pressure.

She remained in that position to catch her breath.

"Something wrong?" Jaft said low enough that his voice didn't echo.

"No." At least not for every other step. With no time to linger, Shyla continued down, keeping a quick pace despite the daggers of torture. Imagining Banqui free kept her going until she reached the others.

Shyla gasped for breath as a warm wetness soaked the back of her tunic.

"You ripped your stitches," Rae said. "Will you be able to get down to the next level?"

"I have to," she panted. "There's no other choice."

"That's not an answer."

"Does it matter?" Shyla countered.

Rae considered. "No."

"Jaft, if you set the next level, I can carry Shyla," Elek said.

"No," Shyla said. "I need you to conserve your strength."

"And you need yours, too," he shot back.

"I'm fine. Get moving, I don't want to be on this level any longer than required." Her imagination once again conjured images of deacons converging on their location with knives in hand. She ran a hand over her short hair.

By the time the four acolytes reached level sixty-two, Shyla had recovered. Knowing what to expect helped her deal with the agony during her slow descent. She still required a few moments to recuperate once she touched firm ground.

"Leave the rope in place," Elek said. "We might need it to get out."

The thought of climbing up… Shyla shivered. Jaft looped the extra rope around the last two anchors, hiding it from view. Not that there was much left.

"Now where?" Lian asked.

Shyla consulted her map. The starting point of Jayden's directions was nearby. She led them through a network of short tunnels. Encountering no one, she hoped to get down to level seventy-three well before angle zero. And for once, all went as planned. They rested in a nook of an abandoned tunnel on seventy-three.

"Twenty-four more levels to go," Jaft said, chewing on a roll of jerky. "Frankly, I didn't think we'd make it this far." He'd removed his veil and exposed a pleasant, friendly brown face with rounded cheeks. He had a wide smile and dimples.

"Ye of little faith," Elek teased. He stretched out his long legs. He was not only the strongest of the group, but the tallest. Elek guzzled half a water skin.

"Not all of us have those gigantic feet," Jaft retorted. "I don't know why you don't kick more."

Elek shrugged his wide shoulders. "That seems like cheating."

"Don't forget the deeper we go the more skilled the guards," Lian said. She had taken off her veil and turban to rebraid her long black hair. Twirling the rope of hair around her head, she secured it with slender delicate fingers. Pretty, with a heart-shaped face and pointy chin, she seemed familiar to Shyla.

The youngest and smallest of the quartet, Rae, remained covered and silent, but every time Shyla glanced at her, she caught Rae staring at her. Rae's long dark eyelashes curled up, almost touching her equally dark eyebrows.

"What is it?" Shyla finally asked her.

"Can I ask you something…personal?" the girl asked.

Silence descended and everyone gazed at Shyla. Caught off guard, she tensed. "You can ask, but I'm not going to promise to answer."

"Fair enough," Rae said. "Why didn't you stay at the monastery?"

Ah. That was easy. Or was it? Shyla rooted for an answer. "I grew up there. I wanted to explore the cities."

"And how did that work out for you?" Jaft asked.

"That's not nice," Lian admonished.

"Obviously not well. But for a while…" Shyla's memories floated back to when she'd finally broken through and been hired by legitimate clients. Her excitement over being independent. "For a while I proved it is possible for a sun-kissed to live in Zirdai. I made a friend, earned a living."

"And then the city chewed you up and spat you out," Elek said.

"Pretty much."

"I was glad to leave," Lian said quietly. "Growing up constantly afraid and worried about where we'd get our next meal." She covered her hair with her turban. "No thank you."

"The monks saved me," Rae whispered. "I'd do anything for them."

The others agreed and Shyla sensed they thought her ungrateful. She was very thankful the monks found her and taught her so much. It was just that…they never told her why she needed all these skills. And she wasn't smart enough to figure it out. She guessed she lacked faith that their intentions for her future might be better than her own desires.

Not without proof, right Shyla, Hanif had said as if that was a bad thing. She'd prided herself on not believing rumors and relying on facts to live her life. However it was obvious that she'd refused to acknowledge the horror stories of Zirdai, because in order to live there, she'd turned her back on what she now realized was her home and family. She'd fought hard to not find anything that would suggest she'd made a big mistake.

As far as mistakes went, it was a doozy. At least she could acknowledge it now. Yet. If she'd stayed safe inside the monastery, she wouldn't have met Rendor or Banqui or even that little sand rat Mojag. Well, it was out of her hands now. Deliver The Eyes, save Banqui and the others, and report to duty. Obeying the orders of the Invisible Sword was pretty much the same as obeying the rules at the monastery. Either way, no more independence. No travel. No Rendor.

Rae touched her arm. Shyla glanced at her.

"Sorry, I didn't mean to upset—"

"No. Don't apologize. The four of you are risking your lives for me. The least I can do is answer a few questions."

"I've got one," Jaft said. "How do we get deeper?"

"How do you feel about the smell of rotten cheese?" she asked.

* * *

"Ugh. I'm not feeling good about rotten cheese," Jaft said. "It reeks in there."

He indicated the tight conduit before them. The one Jayden had shown her. On the other side of it was a series of stairwells that would get them down to level seventy-eight. Shyla hoped one of the doorways she spotted as she had spiraled down to the bottom of the city would lead to a way to get to level ninety-seven.

"This is the only way I know," Shyla said. "Elek, do you think you can fit?"

He lifted the druk, aiming the indigo-tinted light inside. "It'll be tight, I'll have to slither on my belly."

And get completely soaked. Poor guy.

"I should go first," Jaft said. "This way if you get stuck, I can pull you while the ladies push you from behind."

Elek stared at Jaft without blinking.

Jaft cleared his throat. "Or…maybe not?"

"Shhh," Lian said. "Do you hear that?"

Elek dimmed the druk as they all listened. A strange humming noise sounded behind them. They turned. It grew louder and Shyla centered her breathing. If it was the Invisible Sword's…magic, she didn't want to be knocked out with the rest of them. But the rumbling filled the tunnel—an external vibration.

A large glass orb rolled from the darkness along the hard stone floor and straight at them. That explained the source of the noise. The orb slowed to a stop and flashed a bright green light.

"What the hell—" Jaft started, putting his hand up to shield his eyes.

Then the green light died, successfully blinding them despite the druk's weak glow.

Boots shuffled and the scent of incense invaded.

"Oof," Elek grunted as the druk crashed to the ground.

Now in complete darkness, Shyla slid into a fighting stance. Soon hands reached for Shyla and she countered, letting her other senses guide her blocks and strikes. To think all those sun jumps training in the dark was actually proving useful. From the distressed curses and grunts, she guessed her acolytes struggled with their attackers.

Another blinding flash of green.

"Don't look," Shyla yelled, closing her eyes, but not before the light revealed about six...maybe eight people dressed in green tunics similar to the ones the acolytes wore. Not guards or deacons. Treasure hunters? Vagrants? Neither would bother to wear matching uniforms.

However, that was the least of her problems as another opponent joined in. She backed away, keeping the wall behind her—she hoped. But this new person ducked under one of her punches and slammed her into the wall. Her shoulders hit hard and pain blazed, disorienting her long enough for them to pin her.

Soon all sounds of the fight stopped.

"We good?" a male voice asked.

Shyla counted the affirmations that sounded around her. Nine total. The acolytes would have had a fighting chance if it hadn't been for that green flash. Despite her growing fear, she had to admit it was an effective strategy.

Someone opened a druk, illuminating the scene. Elek sprawled unconscious on the ground with three figures standing over him. A cut on his forehead bled. Lian was also pinned against the opposite wall. Two held her tight and her hard gaze promised pain if they'd dared to give her a chance. A crumbled heap—Rae—lay on the floor next to Jaft, who was secured in a head lock.

The man holding the druk pointed to Lian and Jaft. "Knock those two out."

"No," Shyla cried, trying to struggle to no avail.

They ignored her. The man squeezed Jaft's neck, cutting off his air until he hung limp, then let him drop. One of Lian's captors slammed the hilt of her knife into her temple. She slumped to the ground. Guilt and regret pulsed. Once again the people close to Shyla were injured and hurt because of her. The title of sun-cursed fit her the best.

"Bring the sun-kissed," the druk man ordered.

The three holding her yanked her forward, flipped her around, and secured her wrists behind her back in one smooth motion. A familiar move… Deacons? Without robes?

"Arch Deacons?" she asked, dreading the answer.

"Yes. Our mistress has been waiting for you."

CHAPTER 15

The Heliacal Priestess had won the race. With so many groups after Shyla, the priestess had managed to capture her. She'd sent her elite squad, but they fought dirty, which Shyla took some comfort from. They hadn't been confident they could beat her and a quartet of bodyguards in a fair fight. And they didn't kill the acolytes, just left them unable to follow. Her guilt eased as they pulled her through the tunnels, leaving her four protectors unconscious on the ground.

But that left her thoughts free to fret about her impending audience with the priestess. The woman would take the fake Eyes and send Shyla topside for the Sun Goddess to claim.

To keep from having a panic attack, Shyla kept track of the tunnels and stairwells the Arch Deacons used.

The route avoided populated areas. It was the beginning of the sun jump and the citizens would be stirring. And since she'd just learned about the existence of the elite deacons, Shyla guessed the priestess wished to keep the populace equally ignorant.

By the time they reached level eighty-four, the injury on her shoulder pulsed with agony and the ropes around her wrists had rubbed her skin raw. Using her meditation techniques, she drew in a deep breath, calming her frantic heart, and lessening the tightness that circled her throat and threatened to choke her. It also reduced her pain, allowing her to think clearly. Being able to achieve that state so quickly was again due to her time spent chained by the Invisible Sword.

An idea sparked. A desperate, nothing-to-lose type of idea. Inside her mind, she concentrated on the ten people around her, then she chanted the same word the Invisible Sword had used on her.

Relax.

She pushed it out in a circle. It was the opposite of what she had done to block Ximen's commands.

Relax.

The effort required a fair amount of energy.

Relax.

The Arch Deacons slowed. One yawned.

Relax.

"Maybe we should take a break," one of the women said.

Relax.

Murmurs of agreement. A few plopped onto the ground as if exhausted.

Relax.

Three more joined them.

Relax.

Now they all lounged, looking sleepy. Shyla would have celebrated, except they still remained awake. And she'd used all her energy. She leaned against the wall as tremors raced through her legs. That didn't work as she'd hoped. Taking small steps away from the group, she slid her shoulder along the wall. Perhaps they'd be too tired to chase after her. But the leader roused when he noticed her widening the gap.

He surged to his feet. "Stop her!"

Shyla managed to gather enough energy to sprint to the next intersection, turn left and stumble right into—

Her acolytes!

The two women grabbed her to keep her on her feet while Jaft…no…it wasn't him. Although dressed in identical clothes, the man didn't have the same build.

Confused, but with no time to figure it out, she blurted, "They're coming."

Not-Jaft stepped forward. Ten against one. This ought to be…a disaster.

As the Arch Deacons rounded the corner, they stopped, also puzzled to be confronted by a single man.

Holding out his hand, Not-Jaft stood there.

The strong desire to sleep brushed by Shyla, but she recognized it as a mental command and fought it off. However all ten of the Heliacal Priestess's elite unit sagged to the ground. Wow. Impressive.

Not-Jaft sank down onto one knee. Propping an elbow on his thigh, he rested his forehead on his palm.

"Are you all right, Jayden?" one of the women—Gurice!—asked.

"Give me a few more moments," he said in a strained voice.

Too tired to be surprised, Shyla turned to Gurice. "You, too?"

"Yup." She pulled out a knife and cut the rope around Shyla's wrists.

A burning pain rushed into her hands and ignited a small fire across her shoulders. "Who else?" Shyla scanned the other two. Only their eyes were visible, but she didn't think the other guy was Mojag. No, it was— "Ximen!" She met the last one's gaze. "And Bazia."

"Give the lady a prize," Bazia said.

"What are you doing here? And why are you dressed as my bodyguards?"

"We've been following you," Gurice said as if that explained everything.

It didn't.

"Why didn't Captain Rendor come with you to the city and protect you?" Ximen asked.

"He's no longer the captain."

"He isn't?" Ximen exchanged a baffled look with Bazia. "I thought you said the information is accurate."

"It was."

Which implied that the information was old and could have changed.

"Then the Water Prince is keeping his new captain's identity a secret or..." Ximen studied Shyla. "Or Captain Rendor is lying."

"Why would he lie?" Shyla asked. Then the answer popped into her head. To steal The Eyes! No, to *romance* them from her. *Come join me...we could travel to those cities together,* he'd said. Yeah, right. Rendor probably hoped she'd keep The Eyes and run away with him. Then he'd ditch her the first chance he got. She was an idiot.

"The captain lies all the time," Bazia said.

"Yes, but Shyla has a point. Why? He wouldn't risk The Eyes getting into the Heliacal Priestess's hands."

"He's injured," Gurice said.

"Doesn't matter. He could have surrounded them ten deep with loyal guards," Ximen said.

Jayden straightened and met Shyla's gaze. "It's obvious. He wants The Eyes for himself. If he told Shyla that he couldn't protect her, she might have remained in the monastery long enough for him to steal them from her."

She kept her expression neutral. They didn't need to know how tempted she'd been to go with him. Stupid Sun-idiot.

"That makes sense," Gurice agreed. "Everyone wants The Eyes." She eyed Shyla. "Except you."

"I want them."

"Yeah, but to exchange them for your friend."

Shyla had enough of this conversation. "Are my acolytes safe?"

"Yes, we found them and exchanged clothes. Our people will take care of them until they are recovered enough to return to the monastery," Ximen said.

"That was super fast. How'd you catch up?" Shyla asked him.

"Jayden knows a short cut. In fact, he knows this city better than anyone. And your attempt to will them to sleep slowed them down." He cocked his head. "It shouldn't have been possible, considering you had no training."

She clenched her hands, digging her nails into her palms. "I learned quite a bit from those twelve sun jumps you had me chained up."

"I bet that was hard to admit," Bazia said.

"You've no idea."

Bazia laughed. "Oh yes I do. They test *everyone* with magic that way."

Nice to know the woman could actually be civil. A bit of Shyla's energy returned. "Do you know how to get down to the Water Prince's level?" she asked Jayden.

"Yes."

She looked at the Arch Deacons sprawled on the ground. At least the Invisible Sword would also protect her—probably better than the acolytes because of the whole chanting thing. "How long will they be out?"

"Long enough," Jayden said. "Come on."

They followed him through abandoned tunnels, down a few unstable ladders, and twisted around a couple corkscrew ramps. According to Jayden, cutting through a number of populated areas was unavoidable. But their fierce gazes kept the curiosity to a minimum.

Unfortunately, their little parade attracted a few guards. Shyla glanced over her shoulder. They followed along at a discreet distance, as if afraid to engage them. Perhaps they had set up an ambush and were waiting for Shyla to reach it. Each time she checked, they seemed to grow in numbers the deeper Shyla's group descended.

"Don't worry," Jayden said after she glanced back for the fifth time. "We're about to lose them. Be ready to run on my mark."

He turned left at the next intersection, then made a sharp right. "Go!"

They raced along the tunnel. At first, she matched their pace, but her exertions caught up to her and she slowed.

Ximen grabbed her elbow, tugging her along. "Just a little bit more."

Jayden made a quick series of turns, zigzagging through abandoned and empty tunnels for what seemed like forever. Then he skidded to a stop over a metal grate. "Help me."

Ximen dropped her arm. He, Jayden, and Gurice stuck their fingers through the holes and heaved. The metal groaned and creaked and finally popped free with a loud squeal. Expecting the noise to bring attackers, Shyla tensed. They moved the grate far enough away to allow them to fit through.

Jayden remained crouched next to it as Bazia dropped down feet first, then Gurice.

"You're next," Jayden said to her.

When Shyla reached it, she hesitated. Cold moist air blew from below, ruffling her hair. "Air shaft?"

"Air conduit. Big difference," Jayden explained. "No need for a net." He winked.

"Not funny." She copied the women, turning so her hips leaned on the edge as she dangling her legs. Then she lowered herself to the ground. It wasn't as deep as she expected. In fact, she had to hunch over to keep from banging her head on the ceiling.

She moved further in so Ximen and Jayden could join them. The two men pulled the grate back into place, creating another horrendous screech.

"Now we need to keep quiet. We're right above level ninety-six," Jayden said, leading the group.

The Heliacal Priestess's level. She rubbed her wrists without thinking. Bad idea as her irritated skin flared to painful life with the motion.

Jayden and Ximen bent forward in the narrow space. Gurice dipped her head like Shyla, but Bazia was fine. Shyla wondered if the reason Bazia was picked for this mission was because she fit into Rae's uniform. Or if Bazia had actually wanted to help protect Shyla. Hard to tell with Bazia.

After a few angles, her right shoulder complained with increasing spikes of agony. The blood-soaked material of her tunic stuck to the open wound. She wondered if they reached the Water Prince if he'd let Timin take care of her injuries. Somehow she doubted he would. At this point, she guessed the prince's reaction to their visit would initially be hostile. Hopefully, they'd be able to reach an accord.

Jayden stopped at another grate—this one also on the floor. "When we get down there, we're going to sprint to a stairwell. At this time, most of the deacons are on the surface with the Heliacal Priestess worshipping the Sun Goddess," he whispered.

"Most? What if some remained behind?" Shyla asked.

"Then we fight. Only one level to go."

Which reminded Shyla. She fingered the key-shaped lump under her tunic. "Is that the only stairs to level ninety-seven?"

"Yes, so it's important we get to them." Jayden knelt to pull the grate up.

Shyla touched his arm. "When we get down to the prince's level, those guards will sacrifice their lives to keep us from him. I don't want anyone to die."

"We'll use magic."

It still sounded crazy even though he said it so matter-of-factly. "What about finding the prince? He owns the entire level."

"Magic again. Don't worry Shyla, we'll get you there. The rest is on you."

Why did it sound as if he had the easier job?

Jayden lifted the grate. It didn't squeal and she suspected it'd been oiled. How many times had he been down here? He peeked past the edge, signaled the all clear and dropped down. They each took a turn. Then Ximen knelt on one leg. Bazia used his other leg to hop up onto Jayden's shoulders. Sitting on him, she was tall enough to pull the grate back into place. She grabbed his hands and dismounted with ease. The entire maneuver had been executed in silence and with such precision that Shyla figured they'd been a team for a while.

They encountered no one as they ran to the stairwell. She didn't breathe easy until they were in the stairwell. Amazing, since she'd never really thought they would get this far. And now she needed to execute a small task of her own—something she hadn't had an opportunity or secure location to do before.

Jayden stopped them on the landing. "This is where it gets interesting. About five meters to the left is the main entrance. There will be guards there. Five or six. We need to save our magic for when we get closer to the Water Prince. Once we're inside we'll interrogate an official to discover the prince's location. Got it?"

Nods and affirmatives.

Shyla glanced up, counting steps.

"Shyla? Are you ready?" Jayden asked.

"Can you give me a moment alone?"

The four of them exchanged looks. Postures stiffened. Muscles tightened. Eyes narrowed.

"Do you really think I'd abandon you now?" Her tone was as hard and cold as ice.

"Why do—"

"It's better you don't know." She put her hands on her hips. "Does this mean you don't trust me? Even after I pledged my word?"

"Not long, Shyla. Time is critical," Jayden said.

They continued down the stairs until they were out of sight. Shyla pulled the key from underneath her tunic. Her heart slammed in her chest. Was Rendor lying? Had his kiss been an act in order to steal The Eyes from her? Sliding her fingers along the lip of the third step, she found a keyhole. Inserting the key, she twisted it and a click sounded. She pushed on the step and it lifted. Inside was a bulging velbloud leather pouch. It jingled when she picked up the heavy bag. Rendor hadn't lied about that, but was that part of his plan? With no time to consider the implications, she stuffed it into her pack then left something else in its place before closing and locking it.

By the time she joined the others, the key was back underneath her tunic. They didn't ask her to explain about the noises as they descended the remaining flight.

Jayden paused before stepping out. "We'll march up to the guards and demand entrance."

"Let me do the talking," Shyla said. "You're here to protect me. From here on out, I'm in charge."

Jayden cocked his head.

"Of the talking and negotiations," she amended. "You can still do all that…" She twirled her hand in circles. "Chanting thingy…magic. …"

"Oh joy, a true believer," Bazia said.

"Me and Gurice will take point, Ximen and Bazia, take the rear," Jayden said. "Walk with confidence."

Striding in the middle of the group, Shyla wiped the dust from her face and straightened her aching shoulders. Druks still lined the hallway, but inside the trol lanterns would expose all her cuts, bruises, dirty smudges, and her ripped and stained clothing. At least her disheveled state would prove her difficulties in reaching the Water Prince.

The guards watched them approach. All gripped their drawn swords and stood in fighting stances. Jayden and Gurice stepped aside, revealing Shyla.

"I've a meeting with the Water Prince," she said.

"We'll be happy to *escort* you to him," the big guard in front of the double doors said. "As long as your… friends remain here."

"They'll be joining me. And no need to *escort* me, I know the way." She shooed him with a hand…or she tried.

He refused to move, so she rushed him, side-stepped his lunge and tackled him into the doors with a loud thump.

"Subtle," Jayden said as he and the others joined in the fight.

The Invisible Sword hadn't learned the Ways of the Yarin, but they had their own…unique fighting style that didn't involve weapons this time, but might have involved magic. Effective, efficient, and intense, it worked and that was all that mattered. Soon all the guards lay unconscious.

"You *were* pulling your punches when we fought," she accused Jayden.

"So were you."

"That's different."

"Are you two done? We've work to do," Gurice reminded them.

The Water Prince's grand entrance was unlocked—a surprise. Or was it part of an ambush? Ready for another fight, they burst into the main foyer and encountered… no one.

Shyla smoothed her tunic. "All right. Let's keep our poise." She walked through the lobby area and various grottos. Water fountains splashed merrily and Bazia had to grab Ximen's arm and pull the awestruck man past them. Most of the servants stayed out of their way. And a few guards unexpectedly changed directions after a brush of Jayden's will.

"Do you know where you're going?" Ximen asked her.

"No. But when we see an official, we'll ask for directions."

"Using our chanting thingy?" Bazia asked.

Shyla ignored her.

When they reached the next grotto, Jayden stopped. "A unit's heading this way. There are too many of them to redirect."

"Can you read their minds?" she asked. That would be terrific.

"No. I have to touch a person for that. And it doesn't always work."

"What about—"

"Questions can be answered later," Gurice said in a low rumble. "I hear footsteps. Everyone ready?"

"This deep in the belly of the beast, we've no choice," Ximen said.

"A simple yes would have sufficed," Gurice grumbled, before a dozen guards marched into view.

Shyla once again claimed she was expected. This time, a burly guard with long black hair pulled into an intricate knot stepped forward. Dark-skinned like Rendor, his shoulders, arms, and torso were corded with thick muscles. He wasn't as tall as Rendor, but he appeared like he could punch a hole in a stone wall without much effort.

"Enough with this nonsense, Sun-kissed," he said. "All you have is a reservation in the prince's favorite special room."

"I guess you're not ranked high enough to be privy to his social engagements." She kept her tone firm and impertinent despite the cold wash of fear that accompanied the image of being hung upside down.

"Nice try, but I'm the Water Prince's new captain. Captain Yates."

So Rendor hadn't been lying about that. Shyla shot Bazia and Jayden a glare.

"Your companions have a choice," Captain Yates said. "Remain here and die, or leave now and live." He stared at them as if they'd already stopped breathing.

Son of a sand demon. Shyla wouldn't blame them if they bolted. Jayden and Gurice exchanged a significant glance.

Jayden grabbed Shyla's wrist and dragged her to the captain. "Here." He thrust her at the man, twisting her around. "She's not worth dying for."

Shyla didn't have to feign surprise. The captain instinctively clamped his huge hands on her shoulders when she hit his chest with her back. As she suspected, it was rock solid and the explosion of pain from her injury about knocked the wind from her lungs.

"Now," Jayden said to her.

She crossed her arms and pinned the captain's hands to her body so he couldn't reach his sword when Jayden attacked.

The other three launched at the guards behind Yates, but Jayden spun around behind him and pressed his palms to the sides of his head. The captain yanked his hands free from Shyla, gripped Jayden's wrists and heaved. His actions almost sent Jayden flying over his head. Jayden wrapped his legs around Yates's waist to keep his position behind the captain.

Shyla stayed close to the big man, punching and distracting him so Jayden could extract the location of the prince.

Even with Jayden's weight hanging on his back, Captain Yates blocked her punches with ease. And those that did pass his defenses hurt her knuckles more than they affected him. Switching to kicks, she stepped back and managed a few nice blows. But it only annoyed him and he drove his fist into her stomach. She flew backward, landing hard on her butt. Pain streaked through her back and the contents of her stomach pushed up her throat as she struggled to breathe.

Yates reached for a knife, but Jayden's efforts finally slowed him down. Instead he wobbled and stumbled to one knee before falling over to his side. When he remained still, Jayden released Yates' head and untangled his limbs.

By the time Jayden reached her, Shyla had regained her ability to fill her lungs without the threat of throwing up all over the floor. The muscles along her middle ached when Jayden hauled her to her feet.

"Thanks for the help," he said.

"Thanks for the warning. Oh, wait, I didn't get one."

"It worked, didn't it?"

"Does that mean you got the prince's location?"

"Yes, but I don't know the layout of this place. Here." He touched her temple with two fingers.

A sharp sizzle burned her and then a picture of the room that she'd awoken in when this entire mess started jumped into her head.

She jerked away from his touch. "Seven hells. Can you give me a little notice next time you zap me?" A shiver gripped her just thinking about *next time*.

"Sorry. It's the quickest way. Did you recognize it?"

"Yes."

Jayden turned to the fight, but most of the guards were already on the ground. Bazia fluttered around one big man who tried to squash her, but was too slow. Ximen held his hand out and the last two went down. Shyla counted. Nine prone forms including Yates.

"Three are missing," she said.

"No time to linger. Lead on," Jayden said.

Shyla glanced around to get oriented, remembering the route Rendor had taken from the prince's office to the cells. She just needed to backtrack, starting…there! She raced down a corridor with the others right behind her. A couple of turns and more than a few startled servants later, they arrived at the prince's location. Four guards confronted them, but Shyla and her crew didn't slow, just plowed into the four men like boulders during a cave-in. The poor guys didn't have a chance.

Unlike the main entrance, this door was locked. Jayden smirked and pulled a set of keys from the pocket of his pants.

"Where—" Gurice started.

"Captain Yates was so kind as to lend them to me." He flipped through the keys.

"Hurry up, reinforcements are coming." Gurice angled her head. "More than ten…maybe twenty."

Jayden held a bright silver key then unlocked the door. They rushed inside and relocked the door.

Gurice leaned on it. "It's not going to stop them for long."

"You're correct," the Water Prince said. He stood in the center of the room, holding a short sword in one hand and a long knife in the other. Behind him lurked four more guards all equally armed. The furniture and sleeping cushion had been pushed to the sides, leaving a big open area. Guess the prince expected a fight.

"You won't be able to assassinate me in time." He looked relaxed in his loose-fitting training uniform. Balancing on the balls of his feet, he was poised to defend himself. And he appeared…bigger. As if he'd been strengthening his muscles.

Shyla held out her hands. "We're not here to kill you."

"What possible other explanation can there be? You fought your way through ninety-six levels, and a number of my personal guard."

She straightened a bit at his impressed tone—that *was* quite the feat—but she explained her reasoning to him. "…would you have believed me if I'd arrived as a prisoner?"

"You wouldn't have arrived here, that's for sure," he said. Then he frowned. "No, I wouldn't have believed that you intended to keep our bargain if you'd been escorted by my guards." The prince glanced at her bodyguards. "I'm very concerned you and only four companions have made it this far. They must be monks. Am I to assume the monks have decided to get involved?"

"They're not monks," she said. "The Monks of Parzival are remaining neutral as always."

A loud thump sounded from the door. Gurice grunted and Ximen joined her to keep it closed.

"If not monks, then who are they?" he asked.

"None of your business," Jayden said.

"This is *my* city. Therefore it is *my* business." He advanced.

Jayden tensed. "It won't be your city for long."

That sentence hit Shyla as hard as Captain Yates' fist. Was this all a ruse to get them down to the prince so they could assassinate him?

Everyone stared at her as if she'd made a strange noise. Perhaps she had. She didn't have enough information and she'd been doing nothing but running around in the dark for so long. At this point, all she had left were her instincts. And they sucked. So she focused on what she'd set out to do—save Banqui and the vagrants. If it all went to hell, then it was out of her hands.

Stepping between Jayden and the prince to keep them from fighting, she said, "They're my friends."

The prince raised an eyebrow. "I thought Banqui was your only friend."

"I picked up a few more. A lot has happened since the last time we talked."

"I can only imagine," he said dryly, eyeing her shorn hair and stained clothing.

"Good, because I'm not going to explain it to you. This is what's going to happen." She dug into her pack and slowly removed the marble case. "I've reclaimed The Eyes for you." Opening the case, she held up one of the Eyes. The jewels glinted in the bright trol lights. "Please tell your guards to stand down and ask the ones outside to stop their efforts to bust through the door."

He hesitated.

"If we were going to kill you, you'd be dead by now," Jayden said. "We fought through a dozen, we could handle you and your goons."

"All right." The prince gestured to one of the four guards behind him. "Go outside. Tell the others to wait for further orders."

"Sire?"

"Do it."

"Yes, sire."

Gurice and the others stepped aside. The guard banged on the door and yelled a nonsense word. The ruckus died down and he unlocked and opened it. A mass of guards had piled into the hallway. He relayed the instructions and remained in the threshold, leaving the door open. The other three inside the room remained behind the prince. Guess she couldn't blame the prince for being cautious.

"Next, you'll bring Banqui here and I will give you The Eyes in exchange for him and for all the vagrants you've captured on level sixteen."

"That wasn't part of the deal," he said.

"Consider it a bonus for all my troubles."

"Who stole The Eyes?" he asked.

"Treasure hunters. They had a spy working on Banqui's crew."

He considered. "All right. Banqui and the vagrants for The Eyes."

"And you'll allow all of us to leave here unharmed."

The Water Prince's expression hardened. "O*nly* if you, Banqui, the vagrants, and your friends leave *my* city by the end of the sun jump. If any of you are found after that, you're mine."

That had been the plan, yet a strange emptiness filled her at the idea of no longer being an official part of the city. "Agreed."

He held out his hand. "The Eyes."

She placed the box into his palm.

His green eyes shone with greed as he opened the lid. Then they darkened. He stared at her in fury. "There's only one."

CHAPTER 16

With the exception of Shyla, the entire room and the guards clustered outside all gasped in shock. Jayden glanced at her in concern.

"What's the meaning of this?" the Water Prince demanded. "There's no deal unless I have *both* of them. Otherwise, you're *all* dead."

"I'm not stupid," Shyla said. "You'll get the other Eye once Banqui and the vagrants are here with us and we're all safe outside your domain."

"You don't trust me?"

"Of course not. I've seen what you do to your enemies and right now I'm not your favorite person."

"The Heliacal Priestess ranks above you right now."

"Now that's just mean," she said.

He stalked toward her, coming within striking distance. "And why should I trust you, Sun-kissed?"

A bit unnerved, she wondered why Jayden didn't try to intercept him. Did he think she'd blown the plan? "Because you know I wouldn't sacrifice all those people. And you can bring along a bunch of guards just in case."

"I could just search you and your companions for the other Eye."

She spread her arms wide. "Go ahead."

Jayden flinched. Son of a sand demon, did he have something hidden to kill the Water Prince with, or did he think she was stupid enough to have the second Eye with her?

The prince moved closer. Sweat slicked his neck and the light gleamed on the edges of the sharp blades of his weapons. Around his face, his black hair clung to his damp skin. He'd acted so calm when they'd first entered and then he had expected to be assassinated. Now he'd no need to be overly worried. So why the sweat?

He met her gaze. Unhappy with the situation, but too power hungry to risk not getting the other Eye, the prince ordered his guards to fetch Banqui and the others.

"Bring them to the blue grotto. We'll meet you there," he ordered. Then he sheathed his weapons. The prince removed the Eye and inspected it near a trol lantern. If he figured out it was fake, they'd wish they were dead. It sparkled in the light, casting flecks of color around the room.

A strange notion occurred to Shyla. What if it was real? What if Jayden was waiting for the Water Prince to have both Eyes in hand before he made his move? She mulled it over. The guards would witness their prince unable to hold on to this powerful magic object.

When the Water Prince returned the Eye to its case, Shyla let out a breath. He strode to the bright yellow and orange mosaic on the wall behind his desk, turning his back to them, he fiddled with something and a large tiled section of the wall swung open. The prince placed the marble case in the hole, which appeared to be constructed from metal, then closed the section.

Sweeping an arm out, the prince pointed to the door. "Shall we?"

The guards in the hallway parted to let them through. As they walked through the corridors to the blue grotto, Jayden stayed next to Shyla. She met his gaze once and saw that anger burned in his amber eyes. Instead she focused on the prince's back. He moved stiffly and she wondered if he was injured. Perhaps training too hard.

The rings of tiles expanding out from around the water fountain were different shades of blue, giving the impression of ripples of water. Standing near the column of water, the Water Prince watched as his guards moved so they lined the walls, effectively surrounding Shyla and the others in the round cavern. More guards arrived and soon they were standing shoulder to shoulder. A sheen of water coated the floor, which would make the footing slippery if they needed to fight. Did the prince plan to double-cross them?

Waiting with an angry prince and dozens of upset guards, Shyla thought that the tension in the room might crack the stone walls. Jayden stood near Gurice and they conversed in low tones. She wondered if they were discussing a new plan to assassinate the prince.

The Invisible Sword wanted to stop the prince and that would certainly do the trick. But Shyla wouldn't let that happen until after Banqui and the others were out of harm's way.

She spent the time observing the prince and Jayden. The other Invisible Sword members paced and glared at her, or so she thought. Difficult to tell when only their eyes were visible.

A ruckus of voices outside the grotto announced the arrival of a number of guards. The stench of unwashed bodies and blood was a good sign that Banqui and the others accompanied them.

The group entered the cavern. Two guards supported the weakened archeologist. Everyone who could took a giant step back. Except Shyla. Pure relief spread through her body and without thought, she waded through the rancid fog and hugged Banqui tight.

"You found them?" he asked her, his voice barely a whisper.

"I did."

"The Water Prince has…"

"Has one, he'll get the other when you're safe."

"You shouldn't…I'm not…worth…the city will… suffer."

"We can argue about it later." She stepped back, but he swayed so she put his arm around her shoulder.

He smiled. "I'm looking…forward to…arguing with you."

"That's enough," the Water Prince said with disgust. "Where's the other Eye?"

"Not until we're all out of your domain," Shyla said.

"Take them out past the main entrance and wait for me there," he ordered the guards that had brought them in.

Jayden gestured for Gurice and Ximen to follow them out. But he stayed behind and eyed the prince. With all the guards watching, this would be an ideal time for an attempt on the prince's life. However Shyla had a bad feeling deep inside. If he failed, they were all dead. She grabbed Jayden's arm as the prince passed them. Jayden tried to shake her off, but she held on.

"Let go," he hissed between gritted teeth.

Only when the prince was far enough away did she let go. Jayden's gaze promised pain, but she ignored him and followed the others.

Once they reached the outer foyer, everyone looked to Shyla. She faced the prince. "Let the vagrants go."

"Release them," the prince said.

They bolted for the stairwell. Jayden sent the other Invisible Swords to go with them. "See to their injuries," he ordered.

Gurice hesitated. "What about you?"

"I'll be along with Shyla and Banqui."

The prince's guards allowed the three of them to leave.

"I've been more than patient, Sun-kissed. Where's the other Eye?"

"This way." She took them to the landing. Because it wasn't that big, only she, the Water Prince, Jayden and a couple guards fit. She went to the third step and opened Rendor's hiding place. Retrieving a small pouch, she opened it and removed the other Eye. Shyla showed it to the prince. "Banqui," she called, "come up here."

The prince's gaze didn't move from the jewel. "Let him up."

Banqui had to use the wall to keep upright, but he managed to join them.

"Go with…my friend," she told Banqui. "I'll be along in a moment."

Jayden paused. He curled his fingers, rubbing his thumb along the pads before making a fist. Was he getting ready to reach for a hidden weapon? She tensed. Would he strike now? He cursed under his breath, but helped the archeologist navigate the steps up to level ninety-six. Shyla relaxed.

The prince held out his hand. Shyla placed the Eye on his palm. He inspected it as he had the other. Shyla hoped that once the Heliacal Priestess learned the Water Prince had The Eyes, she would no longer be a target. Then again, she was still sun-cursed.

"How do I access the magic?" he asked.

"All I know is that a true leader will be able to do so." The truth.

He studied her. She braced in case he decided that she'd lied or that he'd lost enough in this exchange and she shouldn't be allowed to live.

"I can't say it's been a pleasure, but I can admit I have underestimated you." He tugged on the collar of his tunic, pulling it away from his neck as he rolled his shoulders. "Remember you and your friends are no longer welcome in Zirdai. My guards will have orders to kill you and the others on sight starting at the end of the sun's jump."

"Noted."

He turned and descended the steps, taking his guards with him. The immense pressure on her shoulders since she woke in the Water Prince's office twenty-four sun jumps ago lifted. Shyla leaned on the wall to keep upright. It'd worked. It had actually worked. She'd freed her friend and the others. No one died and they had plenty of angles to disappear.

Satisfaction surged through her. Perhaps a bit more confidence as well, but why did the thought of catching up to Jayden make her uneasy?

The threat of the Heliacal Priestess returning with her deacons spurred Shyla to hurry up the steps, quickly passing level ninety-six. But it seemed the others had disappeared. Already? Having no choice, she continued her ascent. Bazia waited for her on level ninety-four. The woman had removed the turban and veil.

"Look at that," Bazia said. "The Water Prince didn't kill you. Too bad, I'd bet two osees he'd stab you after you pulled that stunt on him."

"That stunt worked."

But Bazia just shook her head. "Are you going to have enough energy to climb to level seventy-five?"

And with that one question all of Shyla's injuries woke, clamoring for attention with aches, stings, and throbs, draining her motivation. Why seventy-five? The answer trudged through her memories. "Isn't that the commune that the guards raided?"

"Yes, which is why they probably won't come back. And if they do, we'd just use *that chanting thingy* so they can't see us. We figured if we survived this little adventure, we'd need a temporary location to recuperate."

Ignoring the barb, Shyla noted that the Invisible Sword already had a plan in place. Were they anticipating the successful rescue of a bunch of people, or had they planned all along for Jayden and the others to be there instead of the acolytes when she exchanged The Eyes for Banqui?

"I can make it," Shyla said.

Her determination to keep up with Bazia lasted a few levels, but soon she lagged behind. At least Bazia didn't make another snarky comment.

After another few levels, she asked, "What about having to leave the city by darkness?"

Bazia snorted. "Once everyone's healthy, the vagrants will just disappear back into the various communes and we'll return to our current headquarters." She pressed her lips together in a frown. Probably locking down a nasty comment.

The rest of the trip to the commune blurred into one long march of misery. When they neared the hideout, Shyla noted a few watchers lurking in the shadows. At least they'd have a warning if the guards or the deacons invaded.

Inside the commune, a number of people buzzed about the freed vagrants, providing food and water, tending to their cuts and helping them remove their tattered, stained clothing in order to wash the filth off. All evidence of the raid had been cleaned up.

Zhek fluttered from patient to patient. Shyla searched the large area until she spotted Banqui. He remained with Jayden. They sat at a table. Banqui shoved food into his mouth while Jayden drummed his fingers on the surface as if waiting. His frown at odds with the general jovial mood in the cavern.

Energy shot through her exhaustion and Shyla strode over to the pair, waving Zhek off as he approached. Jayden spotted her and a flash of anger creased his face before he smoothed his expression. Let him pretend, but she would no longer tolerate being in the dark.

Not bothering with pleasantries, she said, "You planned to assassinate the Water Prince."

"Yes. Until you ruined it," Jayden shot back.

"It wasn't part of the plan."

He stood. "Not the one that *you* were privy to."

"Why not?"

"You were too focused on Banqui." He gestured to the archeologist who had stopped chewing to stare at them. "We couldn't care less if he lived or died."

Banqui sputtered in indignation, but Jayden ignored him. "Assassinating the prince was the priority. Gaining power the goal. Then we could have focused on releasing his prisoners."

"So you lied to me? Banqui isn't your true leader?"

Jayden snorted in derision. "Hardly. Would you have agreed to the plan if you knew?"

Would she? No, it was too dangerous, too much could have gone wrong.

Jayden saw the answer in her face. "That's why we lied to you."

"What was your plan? To kill him when he held The Eyes in his office? With what? Your magic?"

Jayden twisted his wrist and a slender blade slid from his sleeve and into the palm of his hand. "I would have sent this straight into his heart." He met her gaze.

The desire to cross her arms over her chest pressed on her skin. "And the guards?"

"Have no love for the prince."

True. "Do you have more knives?"

"I never miss."

"You missed me," she shot back.

"You surprised me. I didn't think you could move."

"What if one of the guards surprised you? What if a guard decided to claim the power from you?"

He gave her a pitying look. "My magic."

"You had energy left to take care of them all?" Shyla challenged.

"I had enough to show what I can do. After that… fear can be a powerful tool."

True again. Seven hells. Had she ruined the Invisible Sword's only chance to gain power and help the people of Zirdai? All she wanted to do was free Banqui. Was that selfish? They had made her believe he was vital to their organization. And they suggested Rendor lied.

"Did you lie to me about Rendor? Did you know the Water Prince had a new captain?" she asked.

"We knew. Rendor is a dangerous man and he's after The Eyes as well. You needed to learn not to trust him and stay far away from him."

"But why did you make me believe he and his guards would help me get to the prince?"

"So you wouldn't decide the plan was too dangerous before you left us."

Would she have backed away?

When she didn't respond, Jayden added, "Think about it. Once you found out that there would be bounty hunters, guards, and deacons after you, you were motivated to convince the monks to help you since you couldn't contact us to abort the plan. It worked."

"Not monks, but acolytes, who could have been killed." The image of them lying on the ground flashed in her mind. Now anger burned in her chest as she made another realization. "You tipped off the Arch Deacons to ambush us so you could take the acolytes' place."

Jayden didn't deny it. Son of a sand demon! Could she trust anything this man said? They glared at each other.

"I'm very grateful the plan was successful," Banqui said. His voice was rough from disuse. "However, the prince has The Eyes." He shuddered.

Jayden shook his head. "Those were fake. We're not idiots." Although the quick glance at Shyla suggested he wasn't including her in that statement.

But she was just as happy as Banqui when Jayden confirmed they were indeed fakes.

The archeologist leaned back and pressed a hand to his chest. "Thank the Sun Goddess!" The motion revealed his thin arms and raw bands of flesh around his wrists. His borrowed clothes hung off his gaunt frame. He'd lost quite a bit of weight as the prince's prisoner. While the prince—

Odd bits that she'd noticed during the exchange joined together. "The prince!" she cried, snapping her fingers.

Banqui and Jayden traded a had-she-finally-lost-her-mind look.

"Okay, I'll bite. What about him?" Jayden asked.

"You only had one knife, correct?"

A sigh. "Yes."

"Then you couldn't have assassinated the prince."

"I—"

"Supposedly never miss, I know. But he was wearing armor under his tunic. That knife wouldn't have killed him."

"How could you possibly know that?"

"His tunic was loose—and the times I saw him, his shirt was form-fitting. He was sweating, he moved stiffly, and, after he'd gotten that second Eye and the danger had passed, he tugged at his collar as if it was too tight, but it wasn't."

"That's crazy," Jayden said.

"That's Shyla," Banqui said. "She notices seemingly insignificant details like that and then puts them all together. It was why I kept hiring her. I wouldn't have been so successful without her." He picked up his glass of water and saluted her. "And now she saved all our lives."

Jayden didn't appear convinced, but her guilt over ruining their plans eased.

"If you have the real Eyes, why don't you use them to overthrow the Water Prince?" Banqui asked. "You said you didn't care about me. Why the subterfuge with Shyla?"

Good question. If they had them all this time, why not use them? Probably because they didn't have any magic, just as Shyla suspected all along.

"It's complicated and I'm not at liberty to discuss that," Jayden said. "When you've finished your meal, one of the Invisible Sword will escort you to your rooms to pack your essential items."

"And then?"

"You can stay at our headquarters until you're fully recovered. Then I'd suggest you leave the city." Jayden strode away.

His comment about leaving reminded Shyla of Rendor. She wondered if he had left the monastery yet. Why did the possibility of never seeing him again hurt? Like Jayden said, he was a dangerous man and she'd no idea of his motives or where his loyalty lay now that the prince had cast him out. His invitation to her was probably only a ruse to get The Eyes. Too tired to think, Shyla sank into the cushion opposite Banqui. The motion hurt and now with the tension gone, her injuries demanded attention. But the effort to find Zhek required too much energy.

"When's the last time you ate?" Banqui asked.

"I've no idea."

Banqui pushed his half-finished plate toward her. And he refilled his cup and handed it over. Her shoulder blazed with pain when she lifted the cup to her lips. After a mere sip of water she set it down.

"Your injuries need—"

"I know."

He huffed. "Stubborn to the last."

"No. Tired."

"I'm sure you have quite the tale to tell. How about you come with me to Nintri? I've friends there that would be happy to pay us to find artifacts. The university there actually displays the treasures for all their citizens to see. Can you imagine?" Banqui's dark brown eyes shone with wonder. "You can fill me in on all the details while we travel. Nintri is—"

"Fifty-one sun jumps away," she said. Her voice warbled with the strain of holding back her tears. No… sobs. Unlike Rendor's, Banqui's offer was genuine. And perfect. So very perfect. "I…can't." Shyla clutched the edge of the table. "I've…made other plans." That last bit came out in a rush.

"Ah, too bad. Are you returning to the monks?" Banqui asked.

"No." She tilted her head at Jayden, who talked to Gurice and Bazia. "I'm part of the Invisible Sword now."

Banqui laughed. "Good one. Really, what's next?"

"No joke. I've joined."

He rubbed his hand along his face. "For me?"

"Not just for you." The image of Dyani flashed in her mind. The people on level sixteen.

"I'm sorry."

"Not your fault. Besides, after this, I'll probably be assigned guard duty or something equally boring and unimportant." She'd done it at the monastery when she was younger and could do it again.

"If they do that, then they're idiots."

"Thanks Banqui."

He reached over and squeezed her hand. "No. Thank you."

* * *

After Banqui finished his meal, Ximen and Zhek arrived.

"Feeling better?" Zhek asked Banqui.

"Surprisingly so."

"You're malnourished so I've put a restorative in your food." He gestured to the vagrants. "It's an essential supplement for our people during the lean times."

The vagrants clustered in sober groups. No doubt not all of them had survived. The seriously injured slept, probably due to Zhek's healing "touch."

"How bad?" Shyla asked the healer.

"They lost five members and one might not live to see the next sun jump. I did what I could."

She'd been too slow.

"You saved seventeen. That's the good," Zhek said. He turned to Banqui. "With regular meals, you should recover your vigor soon. Ximen is here to escort you to your rooms."

"I won't leave Zirdai without saying goodbye," Banqui promised Shyla.

"I'll hold you to that," she said.

He smiled and shuffled away with Ximen. She stared at them until Zhek blocked her view.

"Your turn," he said, cupping her elbow and pulling her to her feet.

No energy to protest, she swayed in place, but he tugged her along to a small room. It contained a long thin table and a counter full of medical supplies.

"Take all your clothes off," he ordered.

"But—"

"I don't trust you to inform me of the extent of your injuries. I need to examine you. Don't worry, no one will bother us in here."

"Then you're going to have to help me." She doubted she could lift her arms to remove her pack.

Shyla expected to be embarrassed—no one had seen her naked since she learned how to dress herself—but Zhek remained professional as he assisted in removing all her stained and bloody clothing which went into a heap by the door. She kept her pack nearby. That pouch full of Rendor's coins would be too tempting for almost anyone. And she hadn't decided what to do with it yet.

Zhek helped her onto the table and examined her front and back. He tsked over the mess she'd made of her right shoulder. Then he cleaned her cuts, numbed them and closed the ones that required stitches. He left with a promise to return shortly and although she was naked and cold, she lacked any energy to protest or even care. Except the dull throb of bruised muscles, nothing really hurt for the first time…in forever. She rolled to her left side and drifted to sleep.

"…my care until *I* say so." The harsh words woke her from a light doze and must have come from outside the room. It sounded like Zhek. Not that he'd ever spoken to her in that tone.

"Off you go," Zhek ordered. He strode into the room carrying a set of clothing and a cup.

And right behind him stormed in Jayden. He spotted her on the table and stopped so fast it appeared as if he'd slammed into an invisible door. His shocked expression matched. If he wasn't staring at her body with his mouth open, she would laugh.

Zhek stepped between them. "Leave."

"Ah…okay." Jayden turned on his heels and fled.

"My apologies, dear child." Zhek handed her the clothing. "Do you need assistance?"

Not as much. The tunic, pants and undergarments were plain and a bit oversized. But they smelled clean and were no doubt donated from one of the ladies. She'd have to thank her later. After she was dressed, she grabbed her pack. Zhek led her to another room. This one had a sleeping cushion and a fur. He handed her the cup. Inside sloshed a light brown liquid.

"Your special healing tea?" she asked.

"Yes."

"I'm already tired. Do you really think I need this?"

"Yes."

"You're the boss." Shyla downed it in a couple gulps.

"Ah, progress. Now if only we can keep you healthy for more than a few sun jumps at a time." He took the cup from her.

Shyla shoved her pack under the cushion, then eased down and stretched out. Zhek covered her with the fur, tucking her in. He turned to leave.

"Zhek," she murmured.

"Yes?"

"Thank you."

"You're welcome."

Comfortable, safe—for now—and warm, she embraced oblivion.

* * *

Opening her eyes, Shyla spotted Mojag sitting cross-legged in the threshold of her room.

He met her gaze, scrambled to his feet, and bolted. "She's awake," he shouted loud enough for the entire city of Zirdai to hear.

She grunted, rolled over, and groaned. The numbing paste had worn off. Her shoulder pulsed with pain and the rest of her battered body ached as if she'd been pummeled by boulders. Thinking of the sturdy Captain Yates, she thought it was an apt comparison.

She snuggled deeper into the cushion and pulled the fur over her head. If she tried really hard, she might be able to pretend that she slept in her own room on level three and everything that'd happened was all a vivid nightmare.

"It's about time," Jayden said, intruding on her efforts of delusion. "She shouldn't have slept this long."

Zhek harrumphed. "Her body decides that. Not some young sand rat. Now shoo and let me tend to my patient."

Despite her woes, she smiled at the healer's bossy tone.

"He's gone. You can come out now," Zhek said.

She poked her head out. Zhek stood nearby with a tray of food and a glass. Eyeing his offerings with suspicion, she sat up. The smoky aroma of gamelu meat reached her and her stomach growled in ravenous response.

"Eat and drink it all, it will make you feel better." Zhek set it on her lap.

She debated. The thought of annoying Jayden by falling back to sleep propelled her to do as requested and Shyla finished every last bite. However, instead of growing drowsy, a bit of energy pushed away some of her discomfort. How…

"The restorative?" she asked.

"Yes. We need to leave this place. It's no longer safe."

That was all the motivation she needed. Shyla clambered to her feet then waited a moment for the room to stop moving. Then she retrieved her pack and followed

Zhek to the main cavern. The vagrants were gone. Only Jayden, Mojag and three druk lanterns remained.

Surprised, she asked Zhek how long she'd slept.

"Not long enough," he said.

They reached the others. Jayden had changed into a clean tunic and pants, appearing like a normal citizen of Zirdai. But Mojag wore his tattered, stained vagrant clothes.

"Do you need anything from your room?" Jayden asked. "Mojag can fetch it for you. It's well past the prince's deadline so you shouldn't be seen."

Well past? By the scowl on Jayden's face it would be best not to ask. She considered. Everything in her room had been destroyed. And her meager valuables should be safe inside her cache. "No."

Jayden pressed a hand to his chest and mocked, "That was too easy. Zhek, have you discovered an antidote for a difficult sun-kissed?"

"Watch it," Zhek said. "I can inflict pain as well as heal it."

Her opinion of Zhek rose considerably.

Duly subdued, some of Jayden's huffy posture deflated. "Are you able to climb?" he asked her.

"How far?"

"About forty levels?"

"I'll try."

"Don't overdo it, Jayden. There are plenty of places to hide and rest."

He nodded.

"Come on, scamp," Zhek said to Mojag. "Let's go check on my other patients."

The two of them each grabbed a druk and headed deeper into the cavern.

"The back exit," Jayden explained. "We need to wait until they're gone before we leave. Too many people appearing from one location draws attention."

Ah. They stood in awkward silence for a while. Shyla perched on the edge of a low wall to save her energy for the climb. She ran her fingers through her hair. The stubble wasn't as stiff, but she was glad there wasn't a mirror in sight. She caught Jayden staring at her. He glanced away with a frown.

She guessed she'd need to cover her hair. "What happened to my sun cloak?"

"It's beyond repair. We'll purchase you another one."

A strong wave of sadness flowed through her. Odd that all her possessions being destroyed hadn't affected her like this. But that cloak… It had been with her through some tough times. How pathetic. She dug into her pack and removed her wrap. Arranging it to cover her head, she tucked in the ends to keep it from slipping.

"Why don't you dye your hair?" Jayden asked.

Memories of her fight with Hanif before she left the monastery rose. Stubborn, he called her. But she was going to change everyone's minds about sun-kisseds.

Show them how wrong they'd been. Except after getting nothing but stony silence, outright derision, and angry insults, she retreated, hiding from most of the city.

"Pride," she said. "I had something to prove."

"Did you?"

"No." Instead, she proved Hanif right. "Is the Invisible Sword going to require me to dye my hair?" It didn't look natural and she'd have to do her eyebrows and eyelashes.

"No. You're too recognizable. Actually…" He fiddled with a loose thread on the end of his sleeve. "You're not part of our future plans. The commanders think it'd be best if you return to the monks."

A strange mix of emotions knotted inside her stomach. She'd no idea what they even were, but they seared her body as she thought through his comment. The commanders? As in Jayden, Ximen, Bazia and Payatt? Or were there others?

"And my pledge to help?" Proud that her voice remained cool and distant, she tried to catch Jayden's gaze.

He avoided it. "That's what you can do to help."

"I see." It made sense.

Yet.

"No, you don't see," Jayden said, finally meeting her gaze. "Even though the pledge worked, it took much longer than for anyone else. You're clearly conflicted and not committed."

Not committed? The pain stabbing her shoulder disagreed. And those seventeen freed people would also side with her on this. But to argue would be the same as trying to change everyone's minds about sun-kisseds, doomed to fail. Why waste energy when nothing she had done so far influenced the Invisible Sword's opinion of her? Only Banqui had been open minded enough to accept her as she was. If the Invisible Sword wanted her out of the way, then she'd go with Banqui. Perfect.

Yet.

"It's been long enough, we can go," Jayden said. He swiped the last druk.

She followed him. They traveled in silence. His knowledge of the city was impressive and they avoided almost everyone. The sand clock read angle fifty-six. As for what sun jump it was, she had no idea.

Her leg muscles hurt after ten levels and her energy lagged. Jayden noticed and stopped to let her rest. He could wield powerful magic, but was afraid of Zhek. It'd be funny if she wasn't so…conflicted. But not about joining the Invisible Sword. No conflict there. No it was this new…wrinkle. They were giving her an out. But her thoughts keep circling back to why they'd gone to all the effort to test her, only to toss her aside. Plus she'd learned how to use…magic. Well, a little bit. Then she remembered their threat.

"Are you going to erase my memories?" she asked.

Again he couldn't meet her gaze. "Just about the Invisible Sword. It's for the best."

That mass of emotions inside her wound tighter. They continued the journey, once again they traveled in silence. She replayed what'd been said and done since she blocked the Invisible Sword's magic in that dark prison.

Another rest stop—she lasted twelve levels this time. She drank from her water skin and chewed jerky. Her thoughts snagged on little clues. Little gestures. Little lies.

"Where are we going?" she asked.

"Headquarters, until Zhek thinks you're healthy."

When they reached level twenty-two, Jayden made a bunch of confusing turns and backtracked a number of times. Shyla didn't bother to pay attention as she was preoccupied.

"Making sure no one followed us," he explained.

Then he opened a…not-quite-a-door, as it was pretty hard to see, and they slipped inside. Jayden secured the not-door and held the druk up. It shone on a long straight tunnel.

Just then, everything connected. She knew.

The turmoil inside her snapped. Shyla touched Jayden's arm, although she wanted to slam her fist into his guts. He glanced at her.

"It was *all* part of the plan," she said.

"What are you talking about?" Wary, he shifted his weight, balancing on the balls of his feet.

"From the very beginning. The Invisible Sword purposely allowed Banqui to find The Eyes, then they "stole" them back, getting me involved. All of it, just to get close enough to the Water Prince to assassinate him."

Jayden didn't deny it.

CHAPTER 17

Son of a sand demon! They manipulated and ruined her life for their own needs. Jayden looked braced for an attack. But Shyla just stood there unable to absorb the magnitude of their planning and deceit. The more she thought about it— Shyla gasped.

"Banqui?"

"Not part of our organization or plans," Jayden rushed to assure her.

The storm inside her eased slightly. At least their friendship was genuine.

Still. "So that entire time you were helping me find the black river was all an act?"

"No." He frowned. "I was told to help you. I *believed* you might intercede for us with the monks. It was only after they took you for testing that I learned of their plans."

"Their? Aren't you a member of the Invisible Sword?"

"I am, but I'm also a leader of my people."

Huh? "Then who is in charge of the Invisible Sword?"

"I'm not allowed to divulge that information."

"How convenient."

Yet.

"I'm a member, too, why can't you tell me? I swore an oath. Or was that all a ruse as well?" Shyla demanded, her anger flaring again. Jayden stepped back. "No, that was legit. But the commanders feel it's best for you to go back to the monastery." When she didn't respond, he said, "If you'd been more…attuned to the city's plight, we would have approached you directly to become a true member and help assassinate the prince."

Attuned. Nice word. They'd assumed they needed to trick her instead of just talking to her. Maybe befriending her. No. Instead they ignored her like everyone else in Zirdai until they needed her. Then they ruined her life. Shyla liked to think she would have agreed to help on her own. However, it was a moot point. One thing she did know, she was done with him and his organization's manipulations.

"Shyla, are you all—"

She tapped her temple. "Do it now so I can leave."

"Do what?"

"Erase the Invisible Sword."

"Not my specialty. Payatt will do that once you're stronger."

"Fine."

She refused to say more. Jayden guided her to their headquarters—a series of small rooms over three levels with larger areas designated as gathering places. Shyla had a room to herself on the bottom level—twenty-four. Following Zhek's instructions she ate, slept, and rested, preferring to sit in the dark corners during meals. She spotted Ximen a few times in the common area on her level, but not Jayden, Bazia or Payatt. The other Invisible Swords chatted, but the voices bounced off her. She'd turned to stone.

Shyla visited Banqui a couple of times, but Zhek wouldn't let her stay long. Banqui still had a long way to go until he was fully recovered.

After two…three—she'd lost track—sun jumps, Shyla regained her strength and considered leaving. She lay on the small cushion in her semi-dark room, staring at the ceiling. The Invisible Sword had been ignoring her and, if she figured out how to open the not-door, she had a decent shot at making it to the monastery before they realized she'd left. Not like she had anyone to divulge the information about them to. The monks didn't care. Hanif would accept that she'd changed her mind about taking the oath.

Then what? Spend all her free time in the Rooms of Knowledge? For what purpose? Or she could finally do what she'd been longing for. Leave Zirdai. She had Rendor's coins. Enough for the trip, a decent set of rooms, and to purchase plenty of hair dye.

Yet.

The thought no longer held any appeal. It rankled, actually. At least at the monastery she knew people. Perhaps Lian, Elek, Jaft, and Rae would welcome her company. They had protected her without knowing why. Or did they? The Monks of Parzival could have easily been a part of the scheme to assassinate the Water Prince. Hanif had sent her to the black river. Shyla no longer trusted anyone. It'd be best to find a new city and start over.

Decision made, she planned a way to sneak out. Except soon after, shouts and cries of pain interrupted her scheming. She looped the strap of her pack around her neck and raced toward the common area on her level. The press of magic slowed her steps. She countered the unwanted commands, pushing them aside. The harsh clangs of weapons echoed off the walls. Shadows danced in rhythm with the scuff of many boots.

A flash of a green tunic crossed the mouth of Shyla's tunnel. Fear shot through her. She crept to the end, peeking into the cavern. Arch Deacons fought with Invisible Swords. Magic thickened the air and many of the prone forms wore green. But an equal number of the Invisible Swords lay injured and the Arch Deacons kept streaming into the space.

Unable to stand there doing nothing, Shyla stepped forward. A hand grabbed the crook of her arm and yanked her back into the tunnel. She spun to attack. Jayden deflected the blow.

"Come on," he said. Blood streaked his face from a cut across his forehead. Dark wet stains marked his clothes. He clutched a bloody short sword in one hand.

"What—"

He gripped her wrist and pulled her with him. "Betrayed. You need to get out of here."

A thousand questions spun like a dust storm in her mind. "Your people—"

"Vastly outnumbered. I'll return, but first you need to go."

"Go where?"

He didn't answer. Just increased his pace, towing her along at a run. They ducked through tunnels and raced up a couple sets of stairs. Jayden skidded to a stop in front of one of those not-doors. He sheathed his sword and opened it. Taking a druk off the wall, he shoved it at her. She clasped it automatically.

"Go. Get to safety." Jayden pushed her through the opening.

"Wh—"

"We're in Tamburah's temple. Go up. Fast."

"The others?" They should be escaping as well.

He shook his head. Grief shone in his eyes.

"Banqui?"

"Gone." Now anger blazed.

She sucked in a breath. "Dead?"

"No." He swung the door.

Shyla put out her arm, stopping it. "Why are you helping me?"

"I've caused you enough pain." Jayden pushed her back and closed it.

Shyla stood in the small space. What did he mean Banqui was gone? Had he been captured by the Arch Deacons? Dimming the druk, she allowed her eyes to adjust. Instead of wasting time making sense of what had just happened, she concentrated on escaping. She was in Tamburah's temple and at the bottom of a stairwell. The temple was obviously deeper than twelve levels. How long had it housed the Invisible Sword's headquarters?

Stop it. Focus on the facts.

He'd said to go up. She ascended. After ten levels, she recognized a few features that marked this level as the one where Banqui had found The Eyes. The diggers' escape tunnel to the surface was on level three.

The air warmed as she climbed. Sweat rolled down her back by the time she reached Tamburah's judgment chamber, which was six levels underground. Heat baked the curved walls. Of the chamber's six hallways of the dead, one of those led to the surface. Tamburah's sand mural faced the correct one.

Except if it was this hot in here, then going to the surface would be suicide. She needed to find a hiding spot a couple levels deeper. Turning to retreat, she froze. Four Arch Deacons blocked her path. Had they found the not-door and come up from below? Did it matter?

Then just to complicate matters, four more Arch Deacons stepped from the hallways surrounding the area. It was a perfect place for an ambush after all. She'd proved it. Twice. She'd also proved she was an idiot. Twice.

They formed a semi-circle around her. Nowhere to run except the tunnel behind her, which they all knew led to death.

"The Heliacal Priestess wishes to speak with you, Sun-kissed," the bulky man in the middle said. "You have two choices."

"Yippee for me."

He ignored her sarcasm. "Allow us to escort you to the Blessed One, or we'll knock you senseless and carry you there."

"I don't have The Eyes. I don't know where they are," Shyla said.

"Do you really think we'd believe you?"

"Worth a try." Going with them meant being tortured and then being staked to the sand to be sacrificed to the Sun Goddess. Not happening. "How about a deal?"

"No."

"You haven't even heard it yet."

"You're just delaying the inevitable."

True. But it would be on *her terms*. Not anyone else's. Not anymore. Shyla settled her panicked thoughts.

Pushing outward to the eight minds around her, she projected an image of The Eyes to the Arch Deacons.

The Eyes.

"How about I'll tell you where The Eyes are and you let me go?"

The Eyes.

"No."

The Eyes.

"But if you tell us where they are, then it will save you a great deal of pain," he said.

The Eyes.

"There's a third choice?" she asked. "You should have told me that before."

The Eyes.

Shyla pointed to Tamburah's giant face behind them. "King Tamburah has regained his sight."

They turned and she increased her will, projecting a vision of The Eyes inside his empty eye sockets to them. He stared at the Arch Deacons with malice.

"She's telling the truth," one man said in surprise.

"Quick, get a bench over here." Another gestured.

"Anyone have a small knife? If we nick them, the Blessed One will kill us."

A number of them dragged a stone bench closer to the mural. As they worked to reach The Eyes, Shyla backed up. She kept pushing that image. Reaching the tunnel to the exit, she spun and jogged through the thickening heat, hoping her illusion would last an angle or two more.

After slogging through the oppressive air, she found the escape tunnel. It rose, slanting up to the hatch. It gaped open. Sunlight stabbed almost straight to the ground—not a good sign. Waves of heat rolled through the narrow tunnel, stopping her. She guessed the sun neared angle seventy-five. That meant five angles to find shelter. Impossible.

Voices echoed, but faded as they realized to remain in the upper levels meant death. No doubt they'd wait at the access point to level six for her to return, but she wouldn't give the Heliacal Priestess the satisfaction.

Two choices. She could die here or die outside. The Sun Goddess beckoned. She had marked Shyla. It was time.

Shyla wished for her sun cloak as she summoned the strength to climb through the hatch and onto the burning sand. Blisters erupted on her palms and forearms. The sun pierced her with a thousand tiny red-hot needles. She staggered to her feet even though she doubted her dillo boots would last. Hot air seared her nose, mouth, throat, and lungs. Blocking the sun over her eyes, she scanned the undulating sand around her—an illusion due to the super-heated air rising. No shelter. Nothing except a flock of velbloud slowly lifting into the air.

The caretakers! Those that tended the creatures had something… Her thoughts evaporated as fast as the sweat on her skin. She trudged toward the flock with boots melting under her feet.

Emergency! They had a shelter for emergencies. Where?

Weaving through the tethers, she searched. Needed to find it before her blood boiled. She needed…

To end her misery.

To die.

No.

To be a velbloud.

To fly.

To…

To be so desperate she'd try anything.

Seven hells.

Dredging the last bit of her stubborn determination, she grabbed a velbloud's tether and yanked the creature back to the surface. It squealed in distress—a high-pitched warble. Too bad. When it hovered right over her head, its shadow gave her a moment's reprieve from the killing sun. It shrieked again. Louder. And clawed at the top of her head with its sharp talons.

She let it rise enough so it couldn't reach her. Wrapping the tether around her chest like the harness Elek had used to spider, she then looped it around her right wrist. Shyla grabbed it and towed the velbloud to its neighbor and started to reel in another creature. It wailed as well. Shyla wrapped its tether the same way except she wound it over her left wrist. How many would she need to fly?

And then something amazing happened.

Either that or the sun had fried her brain.

Other velblouds descended to their stricken brethren and latched onto them. More and more until they all rose into the air, taking Shyla with them.

She hung below them, keeping her elbows tucked close to her ribs as the tethers squeezed her chest. Holding on with her blistered hands, she ignored the pain. They shielded her from the sun's deadly rays and they floated above the killing heat.

Shyla's feet dangled as she gazed at the world below her in utter amazement. Various shades of red sand spread out in all directions, appearing like a rumpled fur. Precise shapes poked through the rolling terrain, signaling buildings. She recognized Tamburah's temple and the monastery. Flashes of color indicated the surface level of Zirdai.

As she ascended, remote travel shelters popped into view. Herds of gamelus—the third creature to be able to survive the fatal heat—stained the sand yellow as they hunkered down. Nothing moved on the surface. The other desert inhabitants had gone to ground. Except her and the velblouds. Distant fuzzy dots of other flocks spotted the pink sky all around her.

Even at this height, the heat baked her, stealing all the moisture from her body. The danger was far from over, but the view… Oh, the view. Worth dying for.

She scanned the horizon and caught sight of the colorful surface level of Catronia and over to the left was… The fiery air seared her thoughts. The map of Koraha that she'd memorized floated out of reach. Its edges curling as it burned. The world spun…or was that her?

Dizzy and weak, she clutched the tethers and wondered what the caretakers would think when they found her dried-out husk tangled in velbloud tethers. She giggled. Well, it sounded more like a cat hacking up a hairball. That thought sent her into new spasms, triggering a terrible headache. It hammered her skull as fast as her heartbeat.

Shyla clung to consciousness as hard as she grasped the tethers. The view expanded as they continued to rise and she didn't want to miss one angle of it. Eventually, though, the effort to breathe proved too difficult despite the slightest cooling of the air. A breeze?

No. The exhalation of the Sun Goddess.

The goddess had finally arrived to guide Shyla home. Beautiful, with bright yellow and gold hair flowing down to her feet and as tall as the sky, she smiled at her. Shyla welcomed her, allowing the goddess to fold her into her embrace. A cool peace flowed through her.

Does this mean I'm not cursed? she asked the goddess.

You're a blessing, Shyla Sun-kissed.

Guilt ached in her chest. *Then I belonged to the monks, I should have stayed.*

You belong to no one.

A deep sadness soaked into her body. *I'm alone.*

Far from it. The monks are your family. And you are mine, *dear child. I do not enjoy seeing my people suffer. Make it stop.*

Confused or probably just brain dead by this time, Shyla peered at the goddess. *You have the power to stop it.*

So do you. Being sun-kissed is a gift.

I wish you would let the rest of the world and especially the Heliacal Priestess know that. Shyla grumped, but then panicked. She'd just yelled at a goddess! Now she'd be cast down into the seven hells.

The goddess's amusement flowed through Shyla like a healing balm. *That is your job, Shyla Sun-Kissed.*

I tried.

Try harder.

I can't. I'm dead.

Who says?

Are you going to perform a miracle? For me? Hard to believe. Shyla hadn't been the most devout. Or devout at all.

You've performed your own miracle by being resourceful. It will serve you well in the future.

Future? Shyla would rather stay in this soothing state. The future meant betrayals, lies, and pain.

It also includes love, happiness, and family.

Are you sure I'm not dead?

Wake up Shyla Sun-Kissed, someone is waiting for you.

* * *

Cold. So very cold. Ice coated every centimeter of her body. It numbed her limbs, slowed her heart and dulled her senses. She floated. But not hanging under a velbloud float. Nothing solid surrounded her. No hard surfaces pressed on her body.

No…wait, something cupped her nose and mouth. She inhaled and then exhaled. Not dead then. And not sure if she was happy or sad about that fact. She'd figure it out later.

Unable to open her eyes, she flailed. Her arms and legs moved through a viscous substance. Water? No. Water would move with ease…flow like air. Not stick to her skin and resist her motion. A brief image of being inside a velbloud's stomach rose unbidden. Had the creatures eaten her for disturbing them? A ridiculous thought, but it helped ease her panic.

Just as she had when she'd woken up in the darkness, Shyla explored her immediate surroundings. She spread her arms to the side and encountered smooth…walls. Same with over her head. She was prone. Touching the cup on her face gently, she confirmed it kept the goo from seeping into her nose and mouth. Then she found a tube trailing from her chin. She followed it with her fingertips as it curved and rose.

Her hand broke through the substance and someone grabbed it. Heat soaked into her cold skin. Then a gentle squeeze and she calmed. Until the hand released her.

"No," she said. But her raspy voice sounded inside her head—between her ears. Odd. She reached with both hands. Nothing.

Then an arm scooped around her shoulders and another under her knees. She was lifted, cradled against a warm body—a man's, he wasn't wearing a shirt—and carried. When he laid her down on a hard cold surface, she mewled in protest. But her hand was once again grasped.

The cup was lifted off her face.

"What—why can't I see?" Had her eyes been cooked? And again with the strange echo in her head. "And what's wrong with my hearing? Who's there?"

A wet cloth rubbed gently over her eyes, cheeks, forehead, and ears, removing the goo.

"Open your eyes," Zhek said.

She met his gentle gaze.

"Better?" he asked.

"Yes. What—"

"Not yet. Let's get you cleaned up, dressed, and fed before you pester us with questions." He rinsed the cloth in a bucket and continued to wipe off her skin.

Us? She glanced pass Zhek's shoulder and spotted Hanif. He smiled at her. She'd made it to the monastery without any memory of how she'd arrived. Then she turned to see who held her hand.

"We have to stop meeting like this," she joked.

"I couldn't agree more." Unlike her, he wasn't joking. Rendor's expression remained neutral, but emotions swirled in his gaze. Worry, relief, and uncertainty. His arms and muscular chest glistened with the viscous gel.

Ah. He released his hold, but before he pulled away, she gripped it tight despite the slimy residue that coated both their hands. He stilled. Later she'd figure out if she could trust him and why he was still here. Right now, she needed his strength.

"Are you sure?" he asked in a low voice, tilting his head to her body.

"Yes." She wore nothing but a thick coating of goo, but she didn't care. Instead of red, angry blisters and blackened, scarred flesh, her brown skin was healthy and smooth. Another miracle or just Zhek's healing expertise? Did Zhek have magic? And was that considered a gift? Thinking of miracles and gifts, she wondered if her conversation with the Sun Goddess had been real or just a delusion brought on by extreme heat exposure.

Zhek moved with quick efficiency and soon Shyla wore a comfortable soft tunic and pants—an acolyte's uniform. Hanif took her to the narrow room she'd awoken in after being shot with the arrow. Zhek followed a few moments later with a small portion of velbloud eggs to eat and plenty of water. He shot Rendor a pointed look—the big man took up quite a bit of space, but Rendor refused to leave her side.

When Zhek handed her a cup of his special tea, she said, "I'm clean, dressed, and fed. Time for me to pester you with questions." She set the cup down.

"As long as you answer ours as well," Hanif said.

"Deal. How did I get here?"

"The monks on patrol found you," Hanif said. "The velblouds seemed overly distressed so they investigated. You were close to death and they carried you back here as fast as possible." Hanif nodded to Zhek. "Good thing he was here. Or you would have died."

"His magic goo saved me?"

"Goo!" His fluffy eyebrows spiked up in outrage. "It's a healing gel. And it cured your burnt hide."

"Thank you."

Not willing to be mollified, he grumbled, "Don't know why I bother, you're determined to get yourself killed."

"About that," Hanif said. "What in seven hells were you doing outside?"

Hanif had cursed. He never cursed. Never showed the monks or acolytes any strong emotions. She hunched down, trying to be small like she'd done when she was a child and in trouble. Not that it helped.

Then she realized they all waited for her answer. "It was either the sun or the Arch Deacons. I chose the sun."

Rendor clenched his hands and stiffened. Zhek and Hanif exchanged a glance.

“How did you survive the sun?” Hanif asked.

She explained about her desperate measures, but neglected to mention her conversation with the Sun Goddess because she still wasn’t convinced it had happened. Extreme heat caused hallucinations. And that was a doozy of one.

Zhek appeared impressed and Rendor scowled, but, for him, that could mean anything.

“Flying with the velbloud…that’s…quite the tale.” Hanif peered at her with his I-think-you’re-lying-but-I-can’t-prove-it look.

She didn’t blame him. The monks didn’t go out on patrol until after the danger zone—around angle one-ten, which meant she’d been outside for roughly thirty-five angles. Far too long to survive.

Yet.

Remembering Hanif’s comment about Zhek, she asked him, “Why are you here?”

Sorrow pulled at the healer’s face. “I brought the survivors here.”

Shyla perked up at this bit of good news. “Invisible Sword survivors?”

Both men frowned. Hanif tilted his head at Rendor.

“Oh, please,” Rendor said. “Give us some credit. We’ve known about the organization for some time. We figured they’d stolen The Eyes and that Shyla would eventually find them for us.” He rubbed his bad shoulder. “If all had gone according to plan, the prince’s guards, not the priestess's deacons, would have raided the Invisible Sword's headquarters."

She'd known he lied and kept things from her, but to hear him admit it tore through her, ripping the last bit of her heart from her chest.

"How many survived?" she asked, focusing on the positive. She could wallow in self-pity later.

"Not enough. Many were captured. Some have disappeared. Others killed. Only ten escaped."

"Jayden?"

"Captured. Payatt and Bazia are among the dead."

The heavy weight of grief settled on her shoulders. Bazia and Payatt had chained her to the floor, but they tried to help others in need. They deserved to live more than she did.

"Gurice?"

"Complaining about my ministrations every chance she gets."

Sounded about right. "Her brother?"

"Mojag's with her, driving her crazy."

Shyla smiled. Fair punishment for betraying her. "Ximen?"

"Unconscious, but he should wake."

And last. "Banqui?"

"Disappeared. We're not sure where he is," Hanif said.

Jayden had said they were betrayed and that Banqui was gone. Could Banqui have double-crossed them?

Perhaps he'd stolen The Eyes during the raid and slipped away. Or he'd been working with the Heliacal Priestess all along. At this point, she'd no idea and she was reluctant to seek the full truth. It might drive her back into the sunlight.

Such pain and suffering all due to Tamburah's Eyes. She shot Rendor a nasty look. "Why are you still here? Is this part of *your* plan? I don't have The Eyes. No need to romance them from me."

"I never lied to you," he said.

"Oh yeah? What about when you said you never heard of a secret group that claimed to use magic?"

"I hadn't heard of a group like that. You never mentioned the Invisible Sword by name."

She huffed, not buying it. He was smart enough to figure it out.

"I never lied to you. Can you say the same thing to me?" Rendor asked.

No. She couldn't. But she also refused to believe him. When she didn't answer, he nodded to the two men and left the room.

After a tense silence, Hanif said, "When you've regained your strength, I would like a full report."

"What else is there to know?" she snapped.

"Give yourself some time to heal then reflect on what happened. There are some…gaps."

"What about the Water Prince and the Heliacal Priestess? Are they going to demand that you hand me over to them?" she asked Hanif.

"No."

"Why not? Before you said—"

"Everyone except the monks, Zhek, and Rendor think you're dead. And we don't plan on correcting their assumptions."

Good news. She wouldn't have to worry about them coming after her. The monks and Zhek would keep her secret, but why would they trust Rendor? She asked Hanif.

"I have my reasons."

Typical.

His eyes glinted. "If you wish to know all about the Monks of Parzival, you need only to take the oath."

"You still want me?" she asked in surprise.

"You're welcome to return at *any time*."

Now what was *that* supposed to mean? "What about The Eyes? Do you know what happened to them?"

"The Water Prince is aware he'd been given fakes. The Heliacal Priestess is still seeking them."

In other words, no. A chill rolled up her back. Between the two of them, they'd tear the city apart. "Then it's probably best for me to stay dead. Relocating to another city seems like the smartest course of action." She waited for Hanif to make a comment about her running away, but he kept his lips pressed together.

"Zhek, do you have any mag—medicine to change the color of my hair?" she asked.

Zhek picked up the cup of his tea and handed it to her. "No. And that's enough questions for now. Your skin is healed, but there's still quite a bit of damage to the inside of your body. Drink this, dear child."

The Sun Goddess had called her the same thing so perhaps that proved her "conversation" had been nothing but a delusion. She saluted Zhek with the cup and downed the drink in a few gulps.

* * *

When she woke, one word kept repeating in her mind—gaps. What did Hanif mean by that? She was alone for the first time in sun jumps. Usually Zhek hovered nearby to ensure she ate and drank, after which she promptly fell back to sleep—an ideal existence, as she avoided painful memories. She also hadn't seen Hanif or Rendor since she'd been taken out of the goo. Bonus!

However, with her mind clear, her traitorous thoughts returned to the series of events that had been triggered when Banqui first burst into her room, announcing The Eyes had been stolen and the Water Prince believed she was the thief. Despite the sad ache of losing her friend and the sharp barbs digging into the empty place where her heart used to be, she sought those gaps. Just so she could inform Hanif he'd been wrong.

She started with the facts. The Invisible Sword plotted to assassinate the Water Prince. Using The Eyes as bait, they had known the prince would hunt Banqui and Shyla down and that Shyla's naivete would convince him she was innocent—which she was! The prince would then turn on the charm and get her to agree to seek The Eyes for Banqui's release—not that she had a choice really, since the threat to Banqui's life had been real. Maybe Banqui betrayed the Invisible Sword due to revenge? They had ruined his reputation. Plus he'd suffered the most while the Water Prince's guest.

Meanwhile, the Water Prince had his own agenda. He suspected the Invisible Sword had The Eyes and figured her resourcefulness and attention to detail—not to mention her desire to save her friend—would lead Shyla to the Invisible Sword's headquarters where Rendor would report back. The HQ would be raided by the guards and he would not only have The Eyes, but eliminate an adversary. No gaps.

Rendor had confirmed this when he'd said, "if all had gone as planned."

The plan was ruined by the Invisible Sword. They'd realized the Water Prince was after them and ambushed Rendor—almost killing him. And to think she had grieved for him. Stupid. And still no gaps.

Then the Invisible Sword imprisoned her. Why? They had claimed to test her for magic. She hadn't mentioned magic to Hanif. A gap? It could have been a form of hypnotism. Except…she'd seen Jayden and the others use it. And she'd used it as well. Hanif probably already knew about magic. Maybe the monks had the talent as well. But the fact that she didn't tell him or Rendor about her magic made it a gap. A small one.

The Invisible Sword had gone to quite a bit of trouble to convince her of their intentions to help those in need and that they needed Banqui to use the power of The Eyes. And once she'd vowed to be a part of their organization, they had a ready plan to free Banqui, which really was a way to get close enough to the prince to assassinate him. No gaps there.

But why would the Invisible Sword "wake" her magic? If all they wanted was for her to bring them to the prince, then why bother? Had they thought she'd need to use that magic in order to reach level ninety-seven? Unless they hoped once the prince was dead, she'd join them for real? But then her pledge took longer than anyone else and Jayden had said, "You're clearly conflicted and not committed." And he'd also said, "If you'd been more…attuned to the city's plight, we would have approached you directly." Obviously he and the Invisible Sword didn't trust her despite her actions. Then why did Jayden try to save her when the Arch Deacons attacked? Since she was unable to ask Jayden, that was another gap.

Rendor had then tried to romance The Eyes from her. She'd been tempted, which she hadn't mentioned. But that was personal—no need for Hanif to know how close she came to falling for that betrayal. And the pouch of Rendor's coins in her pack…he hadn't lied about that, but it had been a last-ditch effort to get her to run away with him. Then why stay at the monastery? Argh! Another gap. Scorching hells.

Back to the assassination attempt. That plan was inadvertently ruined by Shyla. Keeping one eye hidden until Banqui had been released had been a smart thing to do. If they'd trusted her and told her the plan, she'd…

Hmmm. Would she have supported it? The Ways of the Yarin were all about defense. The Water Prince was abusing his power and the people were suffering. But to kill him? There had to be a better way. No. She wouldn't have supported that plan. What would she have done instead? Shyla laughed. It was a harsh sound as her throat still burned. She would have done exactly what she had done! And their plan had been doomed to failure. The man wasn't a fool and had worn armor. No gaps.

After Banqui's rescue they returned to the Invisible Sword's headquarters and, according to Jayden, had been betrayed. By who? Banqui was the most obvious suspect, but it could have been any of the Invisible Swords. Gap.

And Shyla's conversation with the Sun Goddess? Real or imagined? Gigantic gap.

Great. Just great. Once again, Hanif managed to be right. Did it matter? Did Shyla have the desire to fill in those gaps? The old Shyla wouldn't have been happy until she uncovered all the facts. Now, she learned that pain accompanies knowledge. Lots of it. Could she leave Zirdai? Leave Jayden's fate in the hands of the priestess?

Never find out if Banqui betrayed the Invisible Sword? What about Rendor?

She hadn't been conflicted when all she cared about was saving Banqui. Now, opposing thoughts, emotions, and desires whirled through her without stopping.

Time to visit the only person she could trust and who might be able to help her…or confuse her even more.

* * *

When Shyla poked her head into Hanif's rooms, he appeared to be meditating. But then again he always seemed to be in a state of extreme calm—except when she riled him, which was quite often. Hanif's door was also always open.

"Come in, Shyla," he said before opening his eyes.

She entered the austere main area. The set-up was similar to an office—he had a desk and a work area—yet he preferred to do his business on the cushions arranged in an oval on the right side with everyone holding a cup of tea. Hanif's only vice.

He gestured to the cushions. "Sit. Are you here to fill in those gaps for me?"

She chose the blue and silver one—her favorite. The design reminded her of the patterns a small dust devil leaves in the sand as it swirls through the desert.

"You already know I can't fill in all those gaps," she said.

Settling into a big brown and gold cushion, he crossed his legs. "Are you sure?"

"Quite sure."

"Then you haven't spent enough time in reflection."

"You believe if I sit around and think about it long enough, I'll find answers to how and why the Invisible Sword can use magic? Why I can? Why Jayden saved me even though I'm not member of his organization? Who betrayed them, and the reason Rendor's still here?"

"Yes." He beamed as if proud.

A familiar frustration built inside her chest. Eventually, she'd storm out of his office about to burst from the pressure of it.

This time, she centered her emotions and released them in one long exhale.

"Any chance you can help me out?" she asked.

"Yes. You can ask Rendor about his motives. No need to waste time contemplating that," Hanif said.

After a few moments grappling with the desire to shake him, Shyla drew in another calming breath. "One last thing." She described her "conversation" with the Sun Goddess. "Was it a delusion or real?"

"Does it matter? Delusions are manifestations of your inner thoughts and feelings. Or the Sun Goddess has truly spoken to you. Either way the message is the same. You need to have faith."

"In the Sun Goddess?"

"No. In yourself."

CHAPTER 18

Faith? In herself? What a laugh. She trusted all the wrong people. Vagrants had died because of her. Why would the Sun Goddess ask *her* to make the suffering stop? Shyla had even caused some of it. Why not Jayden? He obviously cared deeply for the welfare of Zirdai's citizens and had dedicated his life to helping them. Except now the Heliacal Priestess had him. A couple doses of holy water and he'd spill all the Invisible Sword's secrets. Or would his magic protect him? Shyla ran her fingers through the stubble on her head. She doubted his magic could counter the pain of torture.

A strange idea struck her. Could Jayden be rescued? Gurice and Mojag might know where he was being held. If enough members of the Invisible Sword survived…

Stop it.

She left Hanif's office and swung by the dining area. Only a few angles were left for second meal so not many people occupied the tables. A hard-to-miss figure sat at a table near the back, but he wasn't alone. Jaft, Elek, and Lian chatted with Rendor. Shyla quickly ducked out of sight. She snagged a bowl of velbloud stew and carried it back to her room to eat.

However, after she ate, the food settled like a heavy mass in her stomach. In an effort to ignore the discomfort, she picked up her pack. It had endured her adventures in the desert and been brought to her room. Opening it, she found Rendor's pouch still full of coins. The idea of using it to relocate to another city had been tempting. But deep down, she knew she'd never keep the osees. Time to return the pouch to its owner.

Shyla left the door to her room ajar and waited for the sounds of footsteps. Apprehension burned up her throat and she wondered if she'd have to bolt to the collection station to expel her meal. Curious that she'd faced deacons with more aplomb. Finally boots drummed on the stone floor. They paused outside. Did Rendor spot the gap in her door? No. The creak of hinges sounded followed by a click.

Now or never. Shyla grabbed the pouch, gathered her courage—which took longer than it probably should—and knocked on Rendor's door.

"Come in," he called.

She hesitated a moment, but then entered his room only to stop after a few steps. He lounged on his sleeping cushion without a shirt. At least he wore pants and it appeared as if he was studying a tablet. A bright purple scar marked his left shoulder and another one curved up from his hip. She jerked her gaze to his eyes. He studied her with a cautious expression.

"You're right," she said. "I lied to you about the treasure hunters, Invisible Sword, and the fake eyes. I thought I was protecting them and I didn't trust you." When he didn't say anything, she set the pouch next to the cushion. "This is yours." She turned to go.

"You were smart not to trust me," he said.

Shyla faced him. "What would have happened to me and Banqui if all had gone according to plan?"

"Banqui would have been killed," Rendor said bluntly. "You may have survived. The Water Prince was intrigued by your skills in finding lost artifacts. He may have *assigned* you to work with his new archeologist."

A nice way to say she would have been indentured for the rest of her life. "And when I disappeared that first time?"

"I told the truth, the prince changed the plan. You were taking too long and we were getting close to discovering the Invisible Sword's hideout on our own. He ordered you arrested."

"So when you disobeyed…"

"A calculated risk."

"You still wanted The Eyes and the Invisible Sword at that time."

"Yes. I hoped the prince would be happy about a successful mission and I could convince him to allow Banqui to live and for you return to your old life."

"Why would you do that?"

He stared at her. "You know why."

She almost growled at him. Why couldn't anyone give her a straight answer? Ignoring his comment, she continued, "And then we were ambushed."

"We got too close. I'd hoped we'd reach the monastery before the Invisible Sword had time to organize an offensive." He rolled his shoulder as if it pained him. "That mistake should have killed me."

And despite everything, she was glad that it didn't. "Why are you still here? Before I left, you acted like you planned on going to Apanji."

Rendor set the tablet down. "When I was lying in the desert waiting for death, I considered my life. Nothing to be proud of. No one to grieve for me. Rather the opposite. I fully expected the sand to open up underneath me and suck my soul down into the seven caverns of hell. Then…" His gaze grew distant. "I was given a second chance."

Rendor stood. The big man moved with a fluid grace. Most people struggled to disentangle from a sleeping cushion. Standing, he was intimidating and she resisted the urge to step back when he drew closer to her.

"I meant what I said before you left on that mission—I would have been overjoyed if you'd agreed to travel with me. But I don't deserve such happiness. And when you refused to allow me to accompany you, I knew you wouldn't make it back alive." He paused, letting the fact that she almost didn't live through the experience remain unspoken. "Leaving the monastery without you held no appeal, so I stayed here. I need to atone and do some good for a change."

His words sounded truthful, but believing him was difficult. "The monks are isolated, they don't do—"

"Hanif said you've refused to see what's really going on here. Is it because you planned to leave once you were old enough?"

"Hanif talks in riddles and won't reveal anything until I take the oath." Her tone was sharp with annoyance. She had grown up here and Rendor had only been here a couple dozen sun jumps.

"And you won't take the oath until he tells you what is expected."

"That's not too much to ask."

"You pledged your loyalty to the Invisible Sword without knowing anything."

That stung even though it was true. "How did—" She sighed. Monks and acolytes were such gossips. "That was different. Banqui's life was at stake."

"So you trusted them."

"And look what happened! It almost killed me."

Rendor said in a quiet voice, "You've been given a second chance as well." He reached for her, but paused then let his hand drop.

Disappointment swept through her. She craved his touch. But she didn't trust herself to make the right choice. Instead she nodded and left before desire overruled logic.

Unable to stay still lest she be ambushed by her swirling thoughts and the image of Rendor's bare chest, Shyla spent the next couple of sun jumps wandering through the monastery. What had she missed as a child? Hanif had already admitted that the monks were aware of the political machinations in Zirdai, including the suffering, but they remained neutral. Which explained her memories of certain monks disappearing for many sun jumps.

They didn't directly help, but at least the monastery was an asylum for those who sought it. As she recalled more and more of her past, certain things stood out. They were protected by the King. Why? It couldn't be due to sentiment or religious reasons. She almost groaned out loud. Of course. The monks spied for him. But how was that doing good? The King must know about Zirdai's suffering, yet he had chosen not to interfere.

* * *

Each sun jump, Shyla thought of Jayden. Was he still alive? Gurice and Mojag had returned to Zirdai.

Ximen had woken, but he had no memories of the fight and who had betrayed them.

Needing exercise, Shyla joined in the angle zero training session. Surprised to see Rendor sparring with a monk, she almost left. Instead, she watched the match from across the cavern. So used to being on the offensive, Rendor struggled with the concept of defense only. The teacher attacked and Rendor deflected the punches and kicks, but couldn't stop countering with a blow or an ankle sweep or a flip.

When he sent the guy flying, Shyla chuckled. He had years of training and it was a waste of everyone's time to try to change his techniques. His opponent had some skills, but Rendor needed a more qualified sparring partner. Someone faster. She wondered if she was up to the challenge. Those thoughts led to dangerous places. Finding another acolyte, Shyla worked out. She'd missed using the Ways of the Yarin.

After the session, she returned to her room, feeling more centered. Sweaty and sore, she cleaned up, and tried to ignore the scars on her body. Too bad Zhek's goo didn't erase them as well as the burns and blisters. Changing into yet another borrowed tunic and pants, she smoothed the short strands of her hair down. It was time to make a decision. Shyla had avoided it long enough.

Zhek had instructed her to remain out of the sun for a few sun jumps, and she'd listened. But her favorite thinking place beckoned. She needed the sun's warmth on her body and to breathe in the crisp cool scent of the early angle air. Already hearing Zhek's admonishment in her head, Shyla would bring her wrap along just in case her skin was still sensitive.

Shyla dug into her pack and found the wrap Jayden had given her. It'd belonged to a vagrant that might have died in one of the prince's special rooms or might have been one of the people she'd helped save. She fingered the cloth, remembering the horrible image of that woman hanging upside down.

Under the material were four rolls of gamelu jerky that had been blasted by the excessive heat when she'd been out during the danger zone. They turned to crumbs the instant she touched them, coating her water skin. It was empty—no surprise. Scratches marked the thick leather. And at the very bottom of her pack…

The vial of black water!

Son of a sand demon. After all this time, it'd survived intact.

* * *

Shyla handed Hanif the glass vial filled with the black water. "I'd like access to the Second Room of Knowledge."

Hanif inspected the vial. "I'm surprised you completed the mission."

"Because it was a sham?" she asked. When he gave her an appraising look, she added, "You wanted me to see the *real* city of Zirdai. To meet the vagrants and see the horrors of the prince's special rooms. I'm guessing it was to show me that I was better off becoming a monk."

"It wasn't a sham, you needed to experience the true heart of Zirdai. You tend to see only what you want and ignore the rest. After keeping to the upper levels of the city for two circuits, it was time for you to open your eyes. I wasn't trying to get to you to return. The reason I'm surprised is because I figured you would have caught on to my intentions and stubbornly refused to continue." He set the glass on his desk. "A deal's a deal. When do you wish to go?"

"Now."

He led her deeper into the monastery. The First Room of Knowledge was on level nine and the Second Room was located on level eleven on the opposite side of the monastery. Each Room was in a different section to minimize damage to the precious tablets and scrolls of information in case of a collapse.

Two monks guarded the entrance, but didn't so much as move when Hanif and Shyla approached.

Hanif stood before the double stained glass doors. "What knowledge do you seek?"

"My original request—more information about the Invisible Sword."

As he swung open the doors, Hanif kept his expression neutral, but Shyla spotted a spark of…surprise? Amusement? Or was that pride?

"Search for their symbol, it marks the alcove where that information can be found. There's plenty of druks inside. The rules for the First Room apply to this Room as well. Good luck." He swept his hand out, inviting her inside.

After she entered, the doors closed and locked behind her. Disappointed that, at first glance, the stacks of scrolls, tablets and various artifacts resembled the First Room. She'd expected something more...exotic. Although the warren of caverns and walkways didn't follow the same pattern. She retreated to the entrance before getting hopelessly lost. Picking up a piece of chalk from a container nearby, she marked her route like a rookie acolyte. Except acolytes were not allowed in here, only in the First Room. A bit of pride puffed in her chest—another accomplishment. She needed to remember those when her many doubts crept in.

As the angles passed without success, Shyla considered returning later with enough food and water. She hesitated because Hanif hadn't said she would have *unlimited* access to the Second Room of Knowledge and he might not allow her back inside. So she ignored her stomach's growling and her dry lips.

When she found the Invisible Sword's symbol carved over the arched opening of a deep recess, all her physical needs vanished. Grabbing a second druk, she entered. And stopped. No stacks of tablets or mounds of scrolls littered the alcove. The bare walls surrounded a single high table. On the top rested a beautiful rectangular marble box and a single tablet.

Shyla moved closer. The box's size matched the one that she'd given to the Water Prince. The one that held the fake eyes. Shyla set both druks on the table, the yellowish light shining on the smooth surface, revealing the intricate pattern. Flecks of silver and gold dotted the rich browns, creams and maroon that swirled through the marble. A very rare type of granite found only at the deepest points of Koraha.

Her hands shook as she lifted the lid. Inside nestled two round shapes covered with precious jewels.

Tamburah's Eyes or fakes? These had blue sapphires instead of emeralds for his irises, but the rest remained the same. She searched her memories. When she'd researched Tamburah, no one had reported what color his eyes had been.

Unable to resist, she picked them up. The alcove spun around her. Her vision blurred and dimmed then brightened as if a trol lantern was suddenly uncovered. She really should have eaten. A strange vibrating heat traveled from her palms and over her wrists, then crawled up her forearms. Terrified, she returned The Eyes to the container and closed the lid.

The odd symptoms ceased. She inspected her hands and arms for burns, but nothing marked her skin. Absolutely nothing. The scars on her left wrist were gone. Did that mean The Eyes erased the scars?

No. No way the monks had the real Eyes. Right?

Shyla picked up the tablet and held it next to a druk. The ancient language matched Tamburah's time. Translating took longer than it would have if she'd been well rested and not recovering from…well, everything.

Eventually, the lessons from her childhood crawled from the depths of her mind and the text became easier to read. It was a set of directions on how to—

Wake the power of The Eyes!

Shyla scanned the instructions. Just holding them wasn't enough, but if The Eyes heated when touched, then the wielder might have the power to use the magic. It didn't guarantee success, just implied it was possible. Her excitement died once she finished the translation. It explained why no one had attempted to wake The Eyes.

A huge sacrifice was required, along with a daunting leap of faith.

CHAPTER 19

"I see you found it," Hanif said.

Shyla jumped about a meter. He'd made no sounds of approach. Or had she just been too shocked over her discovery? Hanif carried a cup of water and a plate of food.

"You'd been in here so long, I'd thought you might be hungry," he said, setting them down on the table.

"You knew they were here." She poked her finger at the container. "Why…don't you…" The words fled as she grappled with the implications.

"It's not our duty. We protect and observe. We encourage and train. But we don't get directly involved."

"So the Invisible Sword…"

"Is an organization we've encouraged."

"Do they know?"

"Their commanders are aware that we have The Eyes."

"Why not give them to the Invisible Sword?"

"They are safer here and have been here since Tamburah's defeat."

"But don't they want to wake the power?"

"Except one, none of the Invisible Swords has… stirred the power."

"One?"

"Many circuits ago, but once he read the tablet…"

She didn't blame him. "So the part about them seeking their true leader wasn't a lie?"

"Yes. They need a person willing to…" Even Hanif couldn't say it aloud.

Shyla shuddered at the thought.

Hanif gazed at the marble box. "Did you open it?"

"Yes."

"Did you touch them?"

"Yes."

"And?"

Shyla knew exactly what he wished to know. Had she stirred the power of The Eyes. Instead of answering, she said, "They're pretty. I didn't know Tamburah had blue eyes." The truth.

Hanif almost glared. She considered that a victory. And she was tired of providing information and getting nothing in return.

"What do you want to know?" he asked.

"Are the monks spies for the King?"

"I dislike the word spy. But yes, we provide information to the King."

"Then why hasn't he sent troops to help Zirdai's people?"

"Because he does not think anything is wrong with the way the Water Prince rules or the Heliacal Priestess's decrees for worshipping the Sun Goddess. As long as they send the proper payments, the King is content."

"Then what do you tell him?"

"If we hear plans for an assassination attempt on his life. If the black-market trade is getting out of hand. If the water is being withheld from legal citizens. If the prince or the priestess are amassing too much power. For example, if the prince had the real Eyes, that would concern the King enough to act."

Ah. "Does he know you guide and encourage?"

Hanif gave her a tight smile. "He does not. Which is why we don't share this information with anyone who hasn't taken the oath."

Except now. Smart enough not to preen, Shyla considered his disclosures. More of her childhood memories bubbled to the surface and a few other oddities no longer seemed as strange.

She gathered clues. Comments. Remembered restricted areas. And then one of the Sun Goddess's comments—or her subconscious—connected a few inconsistencies.

The revelation struck her with the force of a sunbeam at angle ninety. She gripped the edge of the table to remain on her feet. The Sun Goddess claimed the monks were family. It hadn't been figurative, but literal.

"Shyla?"

"I wasn't abandoned and rescued. I was born in the monastery." She met his gaze.

Hanif didn't flinch, but he didn't protest either.

"Why didn't you tell me?"

"For the same reason, to keep our full activities secret. Sun-kisseds—although few—are still left in the desert to die and the monks rescue as many as we can. However, despite the rumors, the monks do not take an oath of celibacy. We raise our children as a collective rather than in individual family units. Some of our children are born sun-kissed."

Her legs trembled and she sank to the floor. "But the children…"

"Are not told until they become a monk. Some, like you, decide to leave and explore the cities of Koraha. Unlike you, they have an easier time blending in and a number do return when they're ready to become a monk."

So much to take in. Shyla rested her head in her hands. "Who are my—"

"I've told you more than I should and have risked our way of life."

"Who am I going to tell? Rendor is becoming a monk, Banqui is missing, and Jayden is probably dead."

"Jayden lives. His magic has protected him, but it won't last."

She glanced at Hanif as hope bloomed in her chest. "Does he know about the monks?"

"Not everything. But he isn't stupid."

No he wasn't. And while taking the oath to become a monk was the safest, smartest thing she could do with her life... she just couldn't. Spying, training, and encouraging held no appeal. Besides, she'd already pledged her loyalty to another organization.

At that very moment, all she wanted to do was to rescue Jayden, despite the risk. The only way to do that would be to gather the remaining members of the Invisible Sword. And the only way to be successful… The room rocked underneath her as terror sank its claws deep into her.

"Shyla, are you well?" Hanif crouched next to her. "Perhaps you should eat."

"The Eyes." Her voice cracked.

"Yes?"

"They stirred in my hands." She showed him her left wrist. "They healed the scars on my wrist."

"Are you sure it wasn't from Zhek's healing balm?"

"Yes. If it was his goo, then *all* my scars would be gone. Check my back."

Hanif pulled the collar of her tunic down, exposing her right shoulder blade. "It's still there." He traced the scar with a fingertip. "Shyla, do you know what that means?"

"I've potential. No guarantees. Plus there's the danger that I'd abuse the power and turn into a female Tamburah and go on a killing rampage."

"And you'd..." Hanif still couldn't say it aloud.

Instead, he gathered her into his lap, cradling her like he'd done when she was a child and been upset. She relished the comfort. Growing up, he'd been extra hard on her, always pushing her to do better, think faster, train harder. So those sweet times had—son of a sand demon!

Hanif was her father.

And that was one revelation too many. Overwhelmed, she couldn't stop an explosion of giggles.

"Shyla?" His shocked tone only increased her mirth.

Her shoulders shook and she gasped for air, but soon her laughter turned to weeping. Deep, painful soul-crushing sobs. For... For...everything.

Poor Hanif held her tight as the storm inside her raged. All he could do really.

Eventually she exhausted her energy. Her emotions had been wrung dry and in their place...calm.

"You need to eat." Hanif set her down and retrieved the water, dried nuts, and the slices of gamelu meat that had grown cold.

Leaning against the wall, she ate every bit and downed the water. A portion of her energy returned. Enough to stand.

"What are you going to do?" Hanif asked.

She stared at the marble container. "I'm going to try to wake The Eyes."

"And if you succeed?"

No need to ask if she failed. Both were well aware of the consequences. "I'll round up the remaining Invisible Swords." She studied her father. "And I'm going to need to recruit from your acolytes if we're going to rescue Jayden." She waited for him to protest.

Instead, he nodded. "I know a few who would join you. But I suggest you gather your…troops first and allow them to witness your attempt to wake The Eyes."

"But if I fail…"

"You'll inspire them."

Terrify them was more likely, but she considered his recommendation.

"And make sure you take Rendor with you. He'll never be happy being a monk."

She didn't think the man was ever happy, but she'd already planned on asking him.

* * *

"No. Absolutely not. I won't be a part of it," Zhek sputtered in anger.

"But you have the skills. I need you, Zhek. I'm begging you," Shyla said.

"No. No. No." He stormed from the room.

She rubbed her wrist, thinking. Ximen and the other surviving Invisible Swords had agreed to regroup without hesitation.

Ximen didn't know if any of the commanders of the organization had survived the attack. "Their identities have always been a closely guarded secret. Only a few of us know their names," he said. "Since I've heard nothing from them, I suspect they're dead."

Gurice brought in a few other volunteers, including Mojag. A number of acolytes, including Lian, Elek, Jaft, and even Rae accepted her invitation.

Shyla hadn't asked Rendor yet. Not sure why she saved him for last, but deep down she suspected Zhek might balk and Rendor… Well, she'd no idea about his reaction. Best to get it over with as soon as possible. Jayden couldn't hold out much longer.

* * *

"Come in," Rendor said.

This time Shyla didn't hesitate. She strode into his room. He sat at his desk, writing on a scroll, but he set the stylus down when he saw her.

"You've been busy," he said in a neutral tone. "I wondered if you were going to visit me."

Meaning the gossip network worked faster than she did. Leaving no time for niceties, she asked, "Would you like to join the Invisible Sword instead of becoming a monk?"

No surprised reaction, just contemplation. "I thought they were routed and only a handful survived."

"I'm rebuilding and recruiting."

"Are you also going to lead?"

"Yes."

"It's dangerous."

An understatement. "Yes, it is. That's why I need you."

"Is that the only reason?" he asked.

This was a part of why she waited to talk to him last. "Rendor…" She summoned her courage. "I'm…confused about you. My heart longs to forgive and forget and jump into your arms. Yet I can't follow my heart because my brain is sending out bright red warning signals. Your desire to atone is wonderful, but it all could be an act. I'm obviously a horrible judge of character because so many people managed to fool me." She laced her hands together to keep her emotions from derailing the conversation. "However, despite my track record, I decided to take a number of risks. And these choices I've made are with no doubts, all in, go for it, one hundred percent. I'm not going to angst over bad choices. I'll either succeed or fail."

"Do or die?"

"Yes."

"If I join the Invisible Sword, you still won't trust me."

"I'll trust you with my life and the lives of the other members, but I won't risk my heart."

"Ah. Then I need to prove to your heart my genuine determination to make amends."

"Yes."

"And then will you jump into my arms?"

Figured he remembered that bit. "Yes."

He grinned. "I'm all in. One hundred percent."

"Before you agree, I need to explain a few things to you about the Invisible Sword." She told him about the magic.

"I thought you said that magic wasn't real. Have they tricked you?" he asked.

"At first I thought it was a form of hypnotism, but it's not and I don't have any factual information to describe how or why it works…it just does."

He rubbed his injured shoulder. "When I was staked to the sand, I watched them vanish with you like burrowing sand devils. Was that magic?"

"Yes. And do you remember those thirteen sun jumps I disappeared?"

His grumpy scowl creased his face. "Hard to forget."

"During that time, I was being tested for magic."

"And?"

"I passed."

"Do I need to remind you that you've been fooled before?"

"Oh no, that lesson's been burned into me."

Rendor flinched. "I'm sorry. That was uncalled for. It's just…" He swept a hand out. "You've been so practical."

While he didn't say it, Shyla knew he wanted to add *up to now*. "Fair enough. How about a demonstration?"

He tensed.

"Nothing terrible, Rendor." She concentrated, collecting her will into one place. Then she pushed it toward him. "I'll just vanish."

Gone.

"You're…" Rendor stood up and reached a hand out in amazement. "I can see through you."

She increased her effort.

Gone.

"Shyla?" He stepped toward her.

She added another command.

Silent.

"Seven hells."

She ducked to the side as he swung his hands through the place where she'd just been standing.

"Are you still here?" Rendor demanded.

Gone.

Silent.

Shyla moved to stand behind him.

"Shyla this isn't funny," he growled.

She ceased her efforts.

"Where are you?"

"Right here," she said.

He spun, grabbing for his sword. Except he no longer wore one. "That's a hell of a demonstration. Did you turn invisible? Is that why they're called the Invisible Sword?"

She hadn't thought about it like that, but it made sense. Perhaps Ximen would know. "Technically, I didn't go anywhere, I just convinced you that I was gone. You need to believe this works because when you're on a mission with the others, you'll have to trust them that the magic is working because you probably won't see it."

"Can I do it?"

Good question. "I've no idea. Perhaps you can be tested after."

"After what?"

"Our first mission." She explained the plan to rescue Jayden.

"You'll risk everyone's lives for one man?"

"We need him. He's powerful and knows the city better than anyone. And it's not up for negotiation. *I'm* in charge."

"And the Invisible Sword is okay with you just taking over?"

"They will be." Might as well be positive that it would work.

"What does that mean?"

"If I wake the power of The Eyes, I'm their true leader."

"You have the real Eyes?"

"Yes."

"And how do you wake the power?"

"That's where you come in."

"Me?"

And now for the difficult part. "You have a certain expertise that is required."

He leaned against the edge of the desk. "Why do I have a feeling I'm not going to like this?"

"You won't. You'll probably refuse and then I'll have to find another person." Ximen said he would if she was desperate.

"What would I need to do?" he asked.

"In order to wake The Eyes, I must sacrifice my own eyes."

CHAPTER
20

Rendor straightened. "Your eyes? Are you in—"

Shyla held up her hand, stopping him. "I'm serious. Once my eyes are removed, Tamburah's Eyes will be set into my empty eye sockets. If I'm worthy, that will wake the power and I'll be able to see again."

"And if you're not worthy?"

"I'll be blind."

"Aside from the insanity of this…sacrifice, what are the chances it'll work?"

"It doesn't matter. I'm taking a leap of faith." In herself.

"You and faith don't exactly mix."

"We do now. Well…I doubt the Heliacal Priestess and I will ever see eye to eye." She laughed at the unintended joke.

Rendor grabbed her shoulders. "Shyla, this is serious!"

"I know."

"Why can't someone else do it?"

She showed him her wrist and explained. "I've potential. Plus there isn't anyone else and Jayden's not going to last long."

"Did I say it's insane?"

"At least once."

"Well, it is."

She agreed.

He continued to stare at her in shock, but soon a realization turned it into horror. Rendor dropped his arms, releasing her. "You want *me* to do it?"

"Yes."

"No. Absolutely not."

Same thing Zhek had said when she'd asked him.

Then his anger flared. "How could you even *ask* me? You know how I feel about you. You know what I'm trying to do here."

"That's *why* I asked you. A sharp knife, a steady hand, and quick reflexes are needed. I know the prince's guards torture his prisoners. What threat is one of the most effective in getting people to divulge secrets?"

"For men it's—"

"Rendor."

"Point made. What about Zhek?"

"He refused."

"Shyla." His voice was rough with emotion. "I can't hurt you."

One last try. "I'm going to do this regardless. Ximen agreed, but he doesn't know how deep to cut. And no one is certain how precise the sacrifice needs to be."

"No. You don't need to do this. We can rescue Jayden without this insanity."

She waited.

"Then I won't let you leave this room." He strode to the door, turned to face her, and crossed his muscular arms.

The stubborn line of his jaw enhanced his looks, but she doubted he'd want to know how hot he was when he was being overprotective.

"Rendor, I can use magic to make you fall asleep."

Alarmed, he tensed. "Can you use magic to force me to..." Unable to say it, he pointed to his eyes instead.

"No. Even if I could, I'd never do that to you." She met his gaze. "I understand your decision. I'd like you to be there if you can."

"You want me to watch?" he asked incredulously. "As soon as Ximen approaches you with a knife, I'll send him into the wall. You know that."

"Not if you're holding my hand."

A slight softening in his stance, but his gaze remained hard.

"Hanif agreed to hold my other hand. I'll need to stay very still."

"Why can't the Invisible Sword magic you to sleep? Or how about Zhek's numbing paste?"

It was the first indication that he might be resigned to the idea. "It's a sacrifice. It's supposed to hurt."

* * *

Later that sun jump as she "prepared" for the…ceremony, she kept repeating *it's a sacrifice, it's a sacrifice* in her mind every time doubt or panic threatened. She loved examining old maps and reading historical tablets, so it was a true sacrifice—a point in her favor. Except she didn't believe The Eyes worked that way. Had Tamburah made the same sacrifice? Remembering his hallways of the dead and those eyeless faces, he'd seemed to be obsessed with eyes. And he had also been insane. Had The Eyes taken his sanity? Or did one need to be unbalanced to wake the power of The Eyes?

Shyla paced circles around her narrow room—there really wasn't anything to do but wait for everyone to gather. Waiting was difficult. The time allowed her thoughts to go to dark places. It was an effort to focus on the positive.

A leap of faith. She'd decided to do this. The Invisible Sword needed a leader, needed to continue their efforts to help to make changes. There would be lots of work, lots of problems, failures and successes. Besides, the Sun Goddess told her to make the suffering stop. Who was she to argue with a goddess? She was Shyla Sun Kissed, damn it.

Hanif finally arrived to escort her to the chapel. It was big enough to hold the entire population of the monastery and had an altar. A bit dramatic, but if one was to make a sacrifice, one might as well do it on an altar.

All the Invisible Swords and those that planned to join had already gathered. The buzz of conversation died the moment Shyla stepped into the room. A familiar occurrence when she'd lived in Zirdai so it didn't bother her. They were here as witnesses, but didn't have to actually watch Ximen cut her eyes out.

Gurice slapped her on the back when Shyla passed by. Mojag pressed against his sister, his face pale. Zhek shot her a nasty look and muttered about the state of her mental health, but he'd reluctantly consented to be on hand in case it didn't work. The four acolytes who had protected her when she rescued Banqui gave her encouraging smiles and Elek pumped a fist in a you-can-do-this manner.

Rendor hadn't agreed to attend, but he hadn't refused either. If he didn't show, Gurice said she'd be honored to hold Shyla's hand. However once she reached the altar, Shyla spotted Rendor on the opposite side. Since he wore his fiercest glower and was puffed up with menace, there was a gap around him. She'd never been so happy to see anyone in her life.

Ximen waited nearby, well away from Rendor. He held a small sharp blade. Zhek had lent it to him, claiming it worked best for delicate operations.

Hanif helped her up on the altar. A cushion was already in position. It was one of Zhek's. He used it to keep a patient's head and neck immobile. When she lay upon the hard stone, and stared up at the chapel's ceiling, ice-cold reality set in.

She reached out in panic and Rendor grasped her left hand while Hanif held her right. Their presence steadied her.

"Ready?" Ximen asked in a strained voice.

No. She swallowed. "Yes."

He gave her what appeared to be a solid leather roll to bite down on—another donation from Zhek—then covered her face and upper chest with a dark red linen cloth—to soak up her blood. A long oval hole had already been cut in the material to expose her eyes. Ximen set The Eyes within easy reach on her chest. Warmth emanated from them, easing the terror. Hanif would use his free hand to place them in her empty socket after...

"All right, let's proceed." Ximen leaned over her. He spread her right eyelids wide open with his thumb and finger. They smelled of cleanser.

A glint of light shone in her eye as the knife came into view. Shyla's grip tightened, squeezing Rendor and Hanif. Hard. Her teeth dug into the leather as her heart protested the entire mad endeavor with violent pounding.

"Stop," Rendor ordered.

Ximen jerked back.

"Your hand is shaking," Rendor said.

"It's not like I do this every sun jump," Ximen snapped.

Rendor released her hand. "Give me the knife. I'll do it."

Ximen's relief was palpable. They switched places. And Shyla…relaxed.

Resting his hand on her forehead, Rendor leaned close to her. "This is my sacrifice," he whispered. "Don't ever ask me to hurt you again. Understand?"

She nodded.

He straightened. "To reduce the pain, this has to go fast," he said to Hanif. "Be ready with those blasted eyes."

"All right." Hanif squeezed her hand.

Rendor drew in a deep breath and let it out slowly. Spreading her right eyelids, he met her gaze. "Go."

Excruciating pain sliced deep as her vision filled with red. She clenched her teeth and tightened her hold, crushing fingers and not caring.

Stay still.

Stay still.

Then a searing inferno ignited inside her eye socket. Before she had time to process, a second sharp agony dug into her left eye. This time she couldn't stop a harsh scream from escaping. Another blazing fire erupted in her left eye socket. Her world turned black.

But the burn. Oh, the burn. No longer able to hold still, she thrashed as the pain intensified, only dimly aware of hands holding her down. Her eyelids scraped over a hard gritty mass like a ball of solid sand. Voices shouted and argued.

"Take those damn things out," Zhek ordered at one point.

She spit the leather roll out. "No," she gasped. It was supposed to hurt. Right?

Another blast of sizzling heat engulfed her. So hot she thought she stood on the surface with the sun directly overhead and not a velbloud in sight. Maybe it wasn't supposed to hurt this bad.

"It's not working," Hanif said.

"No," she screamed. "Let…" Panting for breath, she tried again. "Give…it…time."

A bright yellow light pierced her vision and another intense burn spread. Yet this time the grit and rough edges underneath her eyelids smoothed. She bucked as a second blast of light and pain rolled through. Then a third. And a fourth. Each time the uncomfortable scrape eased. After a final explosion of light, the pain disappeared.

She sagged against the person holding her—Rendor. Energy spent, all she wanted to do was curl up in his arms and stay there. She kept her eyes closed, afraid any movement would bring pain.

"What just happened?" Zhek asked. "Is her heart still beating?"

A rumbled reply.

"Let me examine her, you big brute," Zhek ordered.

She almost smiled. Rendor laid her on the altar, but then took her hand in his.

Zhek's cold fingers pressed on her neck. "She's alive. Shyla, are you awake?"

Her throat hurt too much to speak, so she nodded.

"Well?" Hanif asked. "Did it work?"

"Open your eyes, dear child."

"Too bright," she rasped.

"Lower the druks," Hanif ordered.

The yellow glow on the other side of her eyelids dimmed. She squeezed Rendor's hand and opened her eyes. Blurry figures surrounded her. Smears of faces staring down. Lots of faces. She blinked. Everything sharpened just a bit. Another couple of blinks and the blobs turned into recognizable people. They gazed at her with a variety of concerned, horrified, and anxious expressions. No one breathed. They were waiting for her.

"So nice to *see* you all," she said.

Cheers erupted. Smiles bloomed. Mojag danced around and high-fived Gurice. Hanif beamed.

And Zhek pulled on her lower eyelids to examine her eyes. "There's no evidence of trauma. They appear normal—except for the change in eye color. I hope you like sapphire blue. If you need anything for the pain—"

"I'm not in pain." And it was true. The relief left her lightheaded. And she rather liked blue eyes.

He harrumphed. "I'm sure it won't be long until you'll need my services."

Zhek acted annoyed and upset, but he was glad and thankful that the foolishness worked. Huh? How did she know that?

She turned to Rendor. He still held her hand. Her blood stained his tunic.

"You had us all worried," he said.

If he'd blinded her, he never would have forgiven himself. Again Shyla wondered where those foreign thoughts were coming from. Not thoughts, exactly. She just…knew.

"Thank you for taking over," she said.

"I couldn't let Ximen make a mess of it. You were right, I had the expertise."

A harsh dagger of guilt stabbed him as he remembered following orders, torturing people without any emotions because he had shut them off. Enduring until he moved up through the ranks and proved his loyalty and worth to the Water Prince. His family thought him worthless. But not the Water Prince. And not Shyla.

"Stop it," Shyla said.

He released her hand. Was he hurting her again?

"No. You're not hurting me. Stop…thinking… feeling."

"Thinking?" He was confused.

So was she!

"It's The Eyes," Hanif said. "It's part of the power. You can see into another's soul. The power allows you to know their intentions, thoughts, and feelings."

She perked up. "Does that mean people can't lie to me anymore?"

"Yes I believe so. Although the closer you are to someone, the stronger it is. You're going to have to learn how to…block it if it gets too overwhelming." He worried that he wouldn't have time to teach her all she needed to know about the power and he fretted that her sudden abilities would unbalance his daughter.

Ha! She knew it even before she had the power.

"You're also going to have to figure out what you can and can't do and at what cost," Hanif continued. "According to the historical records, it's different for each person."

"After we rescue Jayden." She ignored Rendor's spike of jealousy and pushed up to a sitting position. Raising her voice over the buzz of excited conversation, she said, "We need to plan. I want ideas and suggestions for Jayden's rescue by angle zero. We'll meet back here then."

The group hurried off. Shyla tried to stand, but her legs gave out.

Hanif helped her to her feet, keeping an arm around her shoulders. "You need—"

"Rest and food before I go running off on this crazy mission," she finished for him.

"This is certainly going to be…interesting. Are you going to uncover all my secrets?"

"I hope not. Right now it seems like I'm getting things that are immediate, that you're worried about at this time. I did figure something out about you, but it was before all this. It was when we were in the Second Room of Knowledge."

"Oh? What was it?"

"I now understand why you pushed me so hard."

"Oh." Comprehension bloomed followed by anxiety. He wasn't supposed to show favoritism. All the children were to be treated equally despite parentage.

"Don't worry, I won't tell anyone." She hugged him, though. Something she'd wanted to do her entire life.

He squeezed her tight. "Can you make it to your room? I should do more research on The Eyes." And he needed some distance before he revealed everything to her, like who her mother was.

"I'll go with her," Rendor said, looking forward to spending some time alone with Shyla.

"Thank you," Hanif said. Then he hurried out. He'd need to make an effort to change his opinion of this man, but after all he'd learned, it might be impossible.

Shyla leaned against the altar and covered her ears and closed her eyes. Perhaps that would block the chatter. But Rendor's concern came through loud and clear.

"Are you all right?" he asked.

She dropped her hands. "I will be. It's just going to take…time to get used to all…this." Fingering the skin around her eyes, she sought wounds or a scar, but encountered nothing but smooth skin. "How do I look?"

"Beautiful." And he meant it with every fiber of his being. After all the ugliness of his life, he'd found a beautiful soul and he'd do anything to deserve her and to keep that beauty in his life.

Rendor had just proven himself to her heart. He didn't even know it. And he wouldn't. Not for a while. He needed to show this commitment to be a better person to the others, especially if they were to successfully rescue Jayden.

"You should get some sleep. Do you need help?" He wanted to carry her, but he doubted she'd let him. Rendor offered his arm instead.

She clasped it and leaned on him as they returned to her room. The first thing Shyla planned to figure out was how to block Rendor's emotions. She'd learned what she needed from him. He could tell her the rest in his own time.

After getting her settled on the sleeping cushion, he fetched a tray of food. Then he stood "guard," ensuring she finished eating.

When she was done, Rendor said, "Do you want me to cover the druk before I go?"

"No." She shuddered. She'd no desire to be in the dark ever again. "Thank you, though."

A smile and a slight bow, then he was gone.

It was a relief when he left. And she was glad they were in an isolated part of the monastery. Distance certainly helped—she was finally alone with her own thoughts and feelings—although, if she concentrated... she could reconnect with Rendor.

Closing her eyes...were they really hers? If someone removed them, would they turn back into precious jewels? Obviously, she had a lot to learn about them and the extent of her powers.

For now, exhaustion pulled her into a deep dreamless sleep.

* * *

Hanif woke her a dozen angles before the sun started its jump. He held an open scroll. Excitement pulsed through him despite his fatigue. She almost groaned as his racing thoughts invaded her mind.

"I found a guide for The Eyes," he said. Hanif's search through the Third Room of Knowledge had taken him all darkness. "It's a bit cryptic."

Of course it was. Shyla sighed. Why can't anything be easy?

"Don't make that face," he admonished. An image of a much younger Shyla flashed in his mind. Her forehead creased as if in pain. "I think I figured out a few basics that will help you get through the next couple of sun jumps."

She sat up. Good news. "Please go on."

"You can block unwanted thoughts and emotions by envisioning a…shield around you. But you don't want to think of something…permanent, like something made of stone. You'll want to be able to lift it or move it aside so you can…" He glanced at the scroll. "Read a soul."

Interesting. "Will I need to be constantly maintaining this shield?"

Turning the scroll sideways, he squinted at it. "It doesn't say. Hmmm…when you close your eyes does it block my thoughts?"

"No. But I think I only read the people who I made eye contact with. You, Rendor, and Zhek."

"Well, you can't go around avoiding eye contact."

As a sun-kissed she had done exactly that all the time. But not as Shyla Sun Kissed, Leader of the Invisible Sword. A scary prospect despite her new magical powers.

"You'll just have to try it and see what happens," Hanif said.

Shyla considered. What would be strong enough to block thoughts and emotions, but light enough to sweep aside? A sun cloak! A laugh burst from her. Hanif cocked his head, curious as to what she found funny, but she waved him off. Instead, she closed her eyes and imagined pulling on a long voluminous cloak made from velbloud fibers. It covered her from her neck down to her fingers and toes. Then she drew a large hood of the material over her head and face. Shyla pictured the material blocking unwanted thoughts just like it prevented the sun from damaging her skin.

Hanif's curiosity ceased. Opening her eyes, she met his gray-eyed gaze. His thoughts were hidden from her. The tightness around her chest eased.

"Did it work?" he asked.

"Yes. Let me try to reverse it." She mentally pushed back the hood. Hanif wondered what she'd envisioned to block him. "I created an imaginary sun cloak to protect me."

He approved. "Apt."

Then she reached. Rendor stood in the corridor, debating if he should check on Shyla. Was she strong enough to go to first meal or should he bring it to her? Would he be welcome? Considering what she had endured at his hands, he probably shouldn't bother her at all.

Amused, she stood and opened the door. "Come on in."

He quickly masked his surprise. Relief flowed through him as he studied her face. Her coloring was much better, although it was going to be hard getting used to her new eye color. "How are you feeling?"

"A little overwhelmed. Give me a moment." Once again, she pictured covering her head with the hood. Rendor and Hanif's emotions ceased to bombard her. She smiled. "It worked."

"What worked?" Rendor asked.

"I can shield your thoughts and emotions."

"Thank the goddess," Hanif said.

Shyla didn't need her new powers to know both men were relieved. She didn't have the heart to remind them she could unblock them at any time.

"What else did you learn about The Eyes?" she asked Hanif.

"Perhaps that's enough for now, you haven't eaten."

"Rendor could you—"

"On it." Rendor strode from the room.

"Next?"

Hanif pressed his lips together, but he studied the scroll. "It mentions being able to influence what a person sees. I think that might be similar to what the Invisible Swords do, but I'm not sure."

She hadn't thought about her own powers. Did she lose them when she gained The Eyes? "Let me try something."

Gathering her will, she aimed it at Hanif.

Gone.

A strong…force resisted her efforts. It took her a moment to remember the shield. She lowered it and tried again.

Gone.

"Shyla?" Hanif straightened in surprise. "Where did you go?"

No flickering?

Sit.

Hanif plopped onto the sleeping cushion. "Shyla, that was uncalled for. You—"

Sleep.

He toppled over, sound asleep.

She waited for the wave of fatigue and/or a headache. Nothing. It'd been easy. Ridiculously easy. Jayden had put ten deacons to sleep but he needed to recover afterwards. Shyla wondered how many she could influence at one time. It'd probably be best to figure that out before the attempt to rescue Jayden.

Gazing at Hanif, she marveled. The man—her *father*—appeared unguarded and vulnerable. A side of him he'd never shown to the monks, let alone to her. She enjoyed the quiet moment because she knew when she woke him, he wouldn't be happy.

Wake.

Hanif's eyes snapped open then he glared at her. "I think that's enough experimentation for now." He stood, smoothed his tunic, grabbed the scroll, and stormed from the room.

* * *

Shyla studied her "army." Ximen, Gurice, the remaining eight members of the Invisible Sword, Zhek, Mojag, Rendor, and a dozen Parzival acolytes—twenty-six total if she included herself. They all gathered in the monastery's receiving room, sitting in semi-circular rings around her. She made eye contact with each one. Sunlight filled the area, warming her skin.

"While you've been recovering from your…ah… adventures, we've been gathering information," Ximen said to her. He'd assumed a temporary leadership of the Invisible Sword, but appeared happy to let her take command. "We determined the Heliacal Priestess has Jayden incarcerated in her private holding cells on the ninety-sixth level."

"Are you sure he's still alive?" Mojag asked. "It's been fourteen sun jumps since the attack."

The boy hunched in his chair, and even with her mental shield around her, Shyla knew he was miserable.

Ximen's expression softened. "As of three sun jumps ago he was, but I'm not too worried. The priestess needs him."

"For what? Torture?" Mojag shot back.

"No," Shyla said. "To exchange for The Eyes."

"Right," Ximen said. "Her deacons have been searching Zirdai for the rest of us and they've put out the word that she's willing to negotiate."

"What about the other Invisible Swords that were captured?" Shyla asked.

Ximen frowned. "Once she extracted all the information from them, she gave them to the Water Prince."

"Why?"

"She doesn't have enough accommodations to keep them long term," Rendor said. "They're criminals and the Water Prince has plenty of cells."

Everyone glared at him. He kept his expression neutral.

"What do the Heliacal Priestess and Water Prince know?" Shyla asked Ximen.

"The priestess knows the location of our headquarters and the Water Prince knows where a number of our other squats are. They know that we only had fake Eyes, but the real Eyes do exist. And they will soon figure out that the survivors are not in the city and correctly assume we've sought asylum with the monks."

Not good for the monks. They needed to find a new headquarters as fast as possible.

"What about Banqui? Has anyone seen him?" she asked.

"No sign of him," Ximen said.

She considered the problems. "Can the Invisible Swords in the cells escape using their magic?"

"No." He gestured to others gathered around. "Except for Jayden, those that can use magic are here. The people who were caught act in a different capacity in our organization."

"Freeing them will be difficult," Rendor said.

An understatement. "All right, we'll focus on Jayden first, then the others."

Mojag perked up. "How?"

"Ximen, can you arrange a meeting with the priestess?"

"Uh…I think so. What—"

"Tell her you will exchange The Eyes for Jayden. See if she's willing to do it on the surface—can you teach me how to hide and move through the sands?"

"Not in time. It's a difficult skill that takes much practice."

"All right. If she doesn't agree to the surface, counter with a public place."

"And if that doesn't work?"

"Then one of her chapels. One high up."

"Wouldn't that be suicide?" Gurice asked.

"She'll have her Arch Deacons there regardless of the place," Shyla said.

"But when she sees that we don't have The Eyes, we'll be outnumbered and in trouble." Gurice glanced at Mojag, probably worried about her brother.

"Outnumbered, yes, but I'll be there." Shyla's statement was met with less enthusiasm than she'd hoped. Only Rendor failed to look queasy at the idea. Time for a demonstration. She removed the mental shield, hoping twenty-five people wasn't too many for her.

"Ah, no offense, Shyla," Gurice said. "But you just got those new eyeballs. And you just learned how to use magic. Do you really think—"

Shyla pushed her will out in a wave.

Gone.

Gasps echoed. Mostly from the acolytes who hadn't witnessed magic in use before. They glanced at each other, confirming what they'd just seen.

"Does anyone see her?" Ximen asked, scanning faces.

No one. Conversation erupted.

Another push.

Silence.

They all stopped talking at once. Alarmed, many of them gestured and a few turned bright red as they tried to speak. Rendor grinned. Shyla stood. Her legs trembled with strain. She'd overdone it. Moving with care, she looped around behind them. And as pain bloomed in her head, she released everyone.

Noise erupted until they spotted her. Then it died as a stunned silence filled the room.

"Yes, Gurice," she said. "I do think I will make a difference."

Gurice stared at her. "You ain't kidding."

CHAPTER 21

By the time she arrived at level fifty-one, Shyla's legs trembled with fatigue. She really should have rested more. But Ximen had delivered the news that the Heliacal Priestess set the exchange time for angle two-twenty. They only had sixty angles to plan. At least no one bothered her or even looked twice at her as she descended to this level.

Pausing at the end of one of the tunnels that led to the chapel, Shyla removed her mental shield. A few people milled about the chapel. She reached and found Mojag hidden in a shadow as he kept watch on the entrance. Before the mission, she'd read Mojag's jumbled soul so she would be able to connect with him. Mojag's emotions swung from boredom to worry about Jayden to fear and back again.

Shyla needed to get into the chapel without anyone seeing her. Even with her limited experience with The Eyes, she suspected using "gone" wouldn't work as they'd have to see her first. She considered a couple different commands, but decided to use "look away."

Nervous energy buzzed in her veins as she stepped from the tunnel. Gathering her energy, she projected her will and chanted.

Look away.

Look away.

Look away.

She pushed it out in a wide circle around her as she walked toward the chapel's entrance. A part of her tuned into Mojag's thoughts. If he spotted her, then she'd know her magic wasn't working.

Her pulse skittered and drawing a breath became difficult, but no one glanced in her direction. Mojag yawned. The two deacons guarding the entrance failed to raise the alarm. She passed them without incident, which gave her the confidence to cross to the hallway that led to the back rooms. A shudder rippled through her as memories welled. The unmistakable sound of a whip cracked the heavy air that smelled of blood and urine. Sobbing and rhythmic cries of anguish tumbled from the confession rooms.

Sick to her stomach, Shyla added freeing these poor souls to her list of wrongs she needed to fix. Too bad she was unable to help them now. Instead, she stole a deacon robe and put it on. It was too big for her. The material sagged on the ground. She checked the others and they all were oversized. Nothing she could do except tuck some of the material into her pants. Shyla returned to the main sanctuary.

Ten rows of kneelers faced the altar, which spanned most of the front of the room opposite the entrance. Behind the altar was another doorway to the back rooms, or so she guessed—having never been through it, she'd no idea where it led. Each row of kneelers held a dozen. Five people knelt in prayer—three citizens and two deacons, scattered in the first four rows. Shyla selected a kneeler at the end of the ninth row where, hopefully, no one would witness her sudden appearance.

When she settled with the robe's hood pulled low over her face, Shyla stopped chanting. She braced for an outcry, but no one noticed the addition of one deacon. Resting her forehead on her forearms, she drew in deep breaths. The effort to remain invisible had drained her energy. According to the sand clock, she had twenty angles to recover. As long as she didn't give in to the temptation to check on the status of her people, it should be enough time. Should was the key word. Shyla really had no idea—not the most comforting thought.

Pulling her mental shield back in place, Shyla calmed her heart and allowed the familiar peace of meditation to flow through her body. Except a memory kept replaying in her mind, stirring her soul.

Right before she had left the monastery on this mission, Rendor had caught up to her on the top level. The sun had hovered ten angles above the horizon as the sands cooled. She'd borrowed a sun cloak from the monks.

"You owe me a favor," he'd said.

She waited.

"I'd like to use it." He held up his hand, stopping her. "This is a rather simple request. Come back alive. Not cooked by the sun or shot by an arrow or stabbed or drugged with holy water."

"Is that all?" she teased, but Rendor was not in a teasing mood. "I'll try."

"Not good enough."

"I'll try really hard."

"Shyla."

"What do you want me to say? I don't want to be injured or killed. But I can't promise something like that."

"All right, then I'd like something else instead."

That seemed too easy. "What else?"

"A kiss."

Her heart reacted immediately, thumping its approval. She didn't need magic to read his emotions or to know his thoughts. They spun in his dark umber eyes, sparking on the flecks of gold—desire, uncertainty, frustration, fear, and a soft yearning.

Shyla closed the distance between them and tipped her head back. He was at least twenty centimeters taller than her. He cupped her face with his hands. A shiver raced along her skin, lifting the fine hairs on the nape of her neck. Dipping his head, Rendor kissed her.

This time his kiss was tender and laced with longing. Shyla snaked her arms around him and tugged until his body pressed against hers. Then she slid her hands underneath his tunic, seeking skin. He sucked in a gasp as her cold fingers brushed the small of his back. Heat poured from him and he deepened the kiss.

Aware of the limited time, she broke away. Taking a moment to recover, Shyla rested her head against his chest, listening to his wild heartbeat. *I did that.* She grinned, then pulled from his grasp.

"I *will* see you later," Render had said before releasing her. It had sounded like a promise.

"Not if I see you first."

His deep laugh had followed her into the desert and it was now nestled deep in her heart.

* * *

The murmur of voices interrupted her memories. The citizens were gone and it was angle two-fifteen. A hand touched her shoulder and she clamped down on a cry of alarm.

"I'm sorry, sister, but we could use your assistance," a man said.

"Of course," she said, standing.

Without looking at her, the deacon gestured to six others grouped at the back of the chapel. "We have…

er...special visitors coming soon and there might be trouble."

"Why kind of trouble?"

"We're hoping everything goes smoothly, but if it doesn't, then protect the Blessed One from harm."

"I will." Not.

She helped the deacons move all the kneelers to the sides of the room, creating an open space so they had room to fight if necessary. The chapel was about five meters wide by twelve meters long. Shyla hovered at the back of the group.

It wasn't long before the Heliacal Priestess entered. She came through the doorway behind the altar, following her came another six deacons—no, six Arch Deacons. Two of them escorted Jayden. Scorching hells.

The waiting deacons all bowed. Shyla copied them, but she gazed at Jayden. His hands were tied behind him. Cuts and large bruises marked his face. Blood matted his hair and stained his torn clothes. He staggered and it appeared the only thing keeping him upright was the Arch Deacons holding his arms. Although exhausted and beaten, Jayden glared at everyone with pure hatred. Atta boy.

"Put him in one of the back rooms," the priestess ordered two of the bowing deacons. "I'll send for you when it's time. The rest of you, spread out."

The two deacons dragged Jayden down the hallway and out of sight. The Heliacal Priestess faced the door. Behind her was a wall of Arch Deacons and behind them the rest of the deacons formed a wide arc with Shyla on the end. Behind her was the altar. Not counting the priestess or herself, there were eleven deacons. Plus two with Jayden. After a moment of panic, Shyla realized that most of the deacons in the back row wouldn't be able to see the inside of the marble box. She relaxed a fraction.

At angle two-twenty, the door opened and Ximen entered with his posse—Gurice, and three Invisible Swords. Except for Ximen, they wore sun cloaks that covered their faces. Smart. He scanned the array of deacons then eyed the priestess with disdain. Shyla wished she had a view of the woman's expression.

"Did you bring The Eyes?" the priestess asked Ximen.

"Yes, did you bring Jayden?"

"He's here. Let me see them," she ordered.

"Bring Jayden out first."

She snapped her fingers. A deacon disappeared down the hallway. After a dozen tense moments, Jayden appeared with his two guards. They brought him up to the line of Arch Deacons. Ximen blanched when he spotted his friend.

"Don't give her them," Jayden said. His voice was rough with pain. "I'm not worth it."

"Of course you are," Ximen said. He slowly reached into his satchel and withdrew the marble box. Now was the time for magic. Shyla removed her shield and endured the sudden surge of emotions from Ximen and the four Invisible Swords. Excitement and fear dominated. But she also sensed strong magic emanating from them as well. Ximen focused his magic on the priestess while three Invisible Swords targeted two Arch Deacons each, and Gurice focused on two of the deacons in the back row. Shyla concentrated on the rest of the deacons just in case they tried to take a peek at what was in the box.

"Open the box," the priestess demanded.

The Eyes.

Ximen did as requested, lifting the lid with a flourish.

The Eyes.

"You want to try that again?" the Heliacal Priestess asked.

The Eyes.

"What do you mean?" Ximen acted confused, but his fear turned sharp.

"I mean the box is *empty*. Where are The Eyes of Tamburah?"

A barrage of emotions from her team slammed into Shyla. She rocked back on her heels under the assault of confusion and fear.

"I…they are there. Don't you see them?" Ximen asked.

He was a terrible liar. The other Invisible Swords increased their efforts, and a few sent the image to the priestess.

"No," she said. "The Sun Goddess protects me from your so-called magic. Where are The Eyes?"

Ximen's gaze jerked to Shyla before returning to the priestess. Shyla cursed under her breath. Why hadn't anyone told her Ximen couldn't bluff to save his life? And all of theirs, too.

The priestess turned around to see who he glanced at. "Remove your hoods," she ordered the deacons in the back row.

All but Shyla complied. Hello there.

Another swell of fear rolled through the chapel. The magic from the Invisible Sword members faded. They took a step back. Time for plan B. Shyla drew in her energy and pushed. Hard.

Sleep.

Three deacons went down.

Sleep.

Two more. And to think Jayden had felled ten at once.

Sleep.

The two holding Jayden dropped.

"Ximen, grab Jayden and go," Shyla ordered. "All of you go!"

The words pierced Ximen's horror. He surged forward while the others sprinted from the chapel.

"Blessed One?" an Arch Deacon asked. "Should we give chase?"

Sleep.

Nothing. The Heliacal Priestess remained standing with all six of her Arch Deacons. Why hadn't her magic worked on them? Shyla must not have enough strength.

"No. They are unimportant. The Water Prince's guards can have them. Bring *her* to me."

Son of a sand demon. They rushed Shyla. She fought them off, but it was a pathetic attempt since she'd exhausted all her energy. It took mere moments for them to subdue her. They grabbed her arms and dragged her to the woman. This wasn't going to end well.

The priestess pulled off Shyla's hood. Even though they made eye contact, the woman's thoughts remained hidden from Shyla.

The Heliacal Priestess's calm composure cracked. "The sun-kissed?" She rounded on her men. "You said she was dead."

"She...should be. I…we saw…she went out into the desert…there was no way for her to reach shelter in time."

"The Sun Goddess protected me." Shyla couldn't resist.

She backhanded her. Shyla rocked back as pain exploded along her cheek and jaw. If it wasn't for the Arch Deacons, she would have spun to the floor. Tears spilled from her eyes. Blood filled her mouth.

"You will pay for that heresy." The priestess stepped close. "You will beg me to sacrifice you to—" She gasped and slapped her hands on Shyla's cheeks, yanking her face so they were almost nose to nose. "Your eyes…they've…changed color." A dangerous fury ignited the priestess's gaze. "You woke The Eyes? But… you are cursed! There is no way the Sun Goddess would have shown you such favor."

Unable to stop the words, Shyla said, "She kissed me. That means she loves me."

The Heliacal Priestess roared. A sound worthy of Rendor, who Shyla would never see again. No, don't go there.

"Lay her on the altar," she ordered. "I will cut The Eyes out of her now."

Seven hells. The Arch Deacons carried her to the stone slab at the front of the chapel. Panicked, Shyla thrashed, trying to get free. But they easily held her still as the priestess withdrew a long dagger from her robes. Shyla caught a glint of the platinum torque around the woman's neck. At this distance, she could see symbols had been etched into the metal. They looked familiar. She stared at them until the sharp edge of the blade moved closer and captured her full attention. The priestess wouldn't be as quick and efficient as Rendor. No, the woman planned to make this as painful as possible.

"The Eyes won't wake for you," Shyla said in desperation.

"Don't be ridiculous."

"Are you willing to sacrifice your own eyes?"

She hesitated.

"Right there! That is why you'll fail." Shyla laughed despite her terror. "We'll be blind together."

"You are wrong." She spread Shyla's right eyelid apart.

Tears blurred her vision—a blessing, considering. The knife dipped.

A crash erupted behind the priestess. She spun around and Shyla caught a glimpse of Elek's broad shoulders. So much for the plan of her four acolyte friends escorting Jayden to safety. However her annoyance over them not following orders was eclipsed by joy as more acolytes poured into the chapel.

The Heliacal Priestess jabbed her knife at the invaders. "Take care of them."

All but one of the Arch Deacons pulled two knives and jumped into the fray. The other kept a tight grip on Shyla—not that she had the energy to escape. Yet.

Instead, she watched as Elek—no, Rendor!—grinned at the Arch Deacons. The big idiot. No mistaking him despite his "disguise." He wore a nondescript tunic and pants. At least he had his sword, which he wielded with expert precision despite his injuries.

The Arch Deacons were skilled, but between Rendor and the acolytes, they didn't have a chance. Halfway through the fight, it was obvious that the Arch Deacons would eventually lose. The priestess ordered the man to bring Shyla.

"We're leaving," she said, heading for the doorway near the altar.

The Arch Deacon hauled her to her feet behind the altar. Shyla summoned the last of her strength and broke free.

Facing her, he brandished a knife. "The Blessed One doesn't care what condition you arrive in."

"I'll make sure to pass along your regrets," Shyla said, sliding her feet into a fighting stance.

"You can barely stand." He lunged.

She twisted away. The blade ripped into the fabric of her robe. Scorching hells, she'd forgotten about the cumbersome garment. He shuffled close and punched. Moving too slow, she stumbled as his knuckles connected with her shoulder. Fire raced down her arm. In a blink, he was past her guard. Without thought, she grabbed his wrist, stopping the blade from sinking into her stomach. They struggled and there was nothing she could do but hang onto his knife hand, keeping the weapon from finding flesh while his fist pounded her ribs.

Her muscles were fatigued and there wasn't much space behind the altar. When her heel bumped the wall, they both knew she was done. He slammed her into the hard stone. Pain exploded in her head.

In the moment it took for her vision to clear, he'd spun her around and pinned her to his chest. Cold metal pricked her neck, warning her to be still as he backed them out the door the priestess used. She scanned the fighters. Sometime during her skirmish, the Water Prince's guards had joined in. He must have learned about the exchange. The guards' swords countered the Arch Deacons' knives.

But no acolytes fought.

And Rendor was…gone!

They'd all left her.

CHAPTER 22

A blast of shock rolled through her. Then logic caught up with her emotions. Her plan had failed and put her people in danger. Hopefully the Invisible Swords, acolytes, Jayden, and Rendor had all escaped to safety. She'd be heartsick with grief if one of them died. At least this way, there would only be one casualty.

Shyla and the Arch Deacon reached a hallway. He turned, pushing her forward instead of dragging her back. Confession rooms flanked them—her guess had been right. Small comfort. There had to be another way out. Sure enough, a tunnel branched off to the right. Soon they left the chapel's back area and entered a semi-dark tunnel somewhere on level fifty-one. Druk lanterns were few and far between in this section of Zirdai.

This was it. Last chance to escape. Shyla dredged up every little bit of energy in her body. Focusing it on one command, she projected.

Stop.

The man kept up his fast pace and she wilted. He stopped in a T-intersection long enough to secure her wrists behind her back. She didn't have any strength left to fight him. But breathing was easier without the blade pressed on her throat. However he kept it in his right hand while he grasped the back of her neck and propelled her deeper. Numb with disbelief, she stared at nothing. She didn't have the energy to pay attention to the twists and turns, ups and downs.

They reached another intersection and turned toward a brighter area. Shyla guessed they'd descended two or three levels. No one walked in the wide corridor as most everyone in Zirdai was asleep by this time. Not that they'd help her. No, she'd was on her own.

A roar suddenly broke the quiet. "Shyla, get down!"

Without thought, she dropped to the ground. A thud sounded. The Arch Deacon grunted and toppled on top of her. His weight pressed on her, making it difficult to breathe. Then the man flew—no, he was tossed. And there stood—

"Rendor," she whispered.

He knelt next to her. "Are you injured?"

"Nothing serious. How did you find—"

"I'll explain later. Can you walk?"

Ah, good question. "Help me up."

Rendor plucked her from the ground and set her on her feet with ease. He untied her hands. She drew in a few breaths.

"We need to go. It's still not safe," he said.

His comment gave her a boost of energy. She glanced at the prone form of the Arch Deacon. Shyla leaned closer, ensuring he was still alive. His chest rose and fell. Good. Then she spotted a platinum torque peeking from his collar. Identical to the priestess's. Something about it… Instinctively she yanked it off and stuffed it into her pack, which, by some miracle, remained looped around her under the robe.

Rendor took her hand and led her…she'd no idea. All that mattered was they were together. He snagged a druk and they ascended a couple…dozen levels, keeping to the edges of Zirdai and away from the populated areas. The trip turned into a test of her willpower.

"Shyla, let me carry you," Rendor said when she'd tripped over her own feet for the third…fifth time.

"No. You need your hands free. We might be ambushed."

"I can put you down."

"No. Not until we're safe."

He huffed, but didn't push the issue. When he finally stopped, she bumped into him. Shyla blinked in the semi-darkness. They stood in an alcove at a dead end.

"Where—"

"We need to wait and let things cool down." Rendor rubbed his shoulder. "Too many people leaving Zirdai will attract attention. And the guards are on high alert."

"I wonder why," she said, giving Rendor a pointed look. "What are you doing here? I thought you agreed with me that you would draw too much attention."

"I changed my mind. I've lived and worked in Zirdai for twenty-eight circuits, I do know how to move through the city unseen."

She hadn't thought of that when she had ordered him to remain at the monastery. "Why didn't you tell me?"

"You wouldn't have believed me."

Opening her mouth to deny it, she reconsidered. It was still hard to imagine the big man going unseen. "You never planned on staying behind, did you?"

"Nope." Another smirk then he sobered. "Your plan had a flaw."

"I'd say." Her bruised ribs and swollen cheek ached in agreement.

"Not that—no one could have guessed the Heliacal Priestess would be immune to your magic. You forgot to account for the Water Prince. He has a network of informants that keep him updated on what's going on in Zirdai. The guards showed up soon after Ximen arrived. There was no way the Invisible Sword would have gotten Jayden through them."

Another good point. "What happened?"

"As soon as Jayden appeared so did I. Surprised to see me, they hesitated. I told them the deacons have The Eyes. They could either go after Jayden or recover The Eyes for the Water Prince. They chose to wait for my signal and go after the prize. "

"Did Jayden escape?"

"Yes."

Strong relief drained her remaining energy. She sank to the ground and leaned against the wall.

Rendor was immediately beside her. "Are you—"

"Fine."

"Zhek warned me you would downplay your injuries and that I should ignore you and do a visual exam." His intense gaze burned.

Two conflicting responses warred in Shyla's body at the thought of Rendor examining her. One desired to strip off her clothing, while the logical one warned her they were still in danger of being discovered. Stupid logic.

When she could trust her voice, she recited her injuries—head, cheek, shoulder, ribs.

Rendor's expression darkened. "I should have killed him. Do you need something for the pain? Zhek—"

"Seems to enjoy meddling in my business," she grumped. "When did you have time to talk to him?"

"While we waited for the exchange." He sat down next to her.

"How did you find me after I was taken from the chapel?"

"Once I determined I couldn't reach you without getting you killed, I retreated. That little sand rat Mojag told me about the back tunnel and where it exited. We figured they were headed to level ninety-six and Mojag knew a good place to stage an ambush. He said something about it making it even. Do you know what he was talking about?"

The little rat, indeed. "Yeah, he owed me one." And she owed Rendor. "Thank you for rescuing me."

"Now we're even," he said.

She glanced at him in surprise. "Not by my count."

"You rescued me from an early death—my fate had I continued to work for the Water Prince."

"That's a stretch."

He shrugged. "It's the truth."

Too tired to argue, she pulled her knees up and rested her head on them.

"Do you have a sun cloak?" Rendor asked.

"In my pack. Why?"

Instead of answering, he pulled her to her feet. She groaned in protest as he yanked off the deacon robe and removed her pack.

Rummaging inside, he handed her the water skin and a roll of jerky. "Drink. Eat."

It required more energy than she had, but he would nag her until she did. She gulped the warm liquid.

While she chewed the tough meat, Rendor arranged the robe and cloak into a sleeping area. He scowled when he saw the rip in the fabric from the knife.

"No blood," Shyla said before he insisted on inspecting her torso.

A grunt, then he finished. "Sleep."

"You do know I'm the one in charge, right?"

This time he pointed. "Sleep. I'll stand guard."

He looked as tired as she felt. "No need." Shyla withdrew the dried gamelu skin and laid it on the tunnel's floor about three meters away.

"I'd rather not depend on that."

"Suit yourself." She stretched out and it was wonderful to be horizontal.

Rendor covered her with an extra flap of the robe. He smoothed her hair and stroked her uninjured cheek. She fell asleep instantly.

* * *

Shyla woke. A solid warmth pressed on her back. Blinking in the dim orange-tinged druk light, she sorted through her memories. The Invisible Sword...Jayden...rescue...Rendor! Where—

His arm was tucked around her waist. His even breathing sounded behind her. They needed to return to the monastery or risk being captured by either the deacons or the guards. Yet she was reluctant to wake him. Lying in his arms, she was safe. An odd sensation, considering the danger. Even stranger, the thought of waking up next to him every sun jump heated her soul.

But that would only happen if they escaped the city. She considered their meager options and it didn't look good. Getting to the surface would be difficult. Maybe if she had a few osees with her, they could bribe the cleaners, but all she had was her sun cloak and— A plan sparked.

As much as she'd like to remain in his arms, Shyla rolled over to face Rendor. Pain flared in her ribs.

His eyes snapped open and he jerked away. "Sorry."

"For what?"

Rendor sat up. "For sleeping on duty."

"You can make it up to me later." She leered, then laughed at his shocked expression.

"I take it you're feeling better," he grumbled.

"Yes and I figured out a way for us to leave the city without any problems."

"Do tell."

She disentangled from the robe, stood up, and handed the garment to him. "This should cover you. And I'll bet that no one in his or her right mind would challenge a big brute of a deacon as he escorts his prisoner to the surface."

"Big brute?" He stood and put the robe on, settling it on his shoulders. It reached just past his knees.

"I call it like I see it."

"You haven't seen anything yet, sunbeam." He stalked toward her, backing her up until she was pressed against the wall. Rendor leaned in. "But I guarantee the word big wouldn't do it justice."

Heat spread across her face at the insinuation.

He chuckled, a deep masculine sound. "You're blushing."

She punched him in the stomach. It was like striking a marble statue. He laughed again, but moved away so she could don her sun cloak. Once they were ready, Rendor's humor fled when he had to tie her hands behind her back to match their cover.

"I made it loose enough so you can free yourself if we run into trouble," Rendor said and squeezed her uninjured shoulder.

"Don't worry, this'll work."

And it did. Everyone cleared a wide path around the oversized deacon and his prisoner as they climbed. When they reached level three, Shyla stopped and gazed down a dimly lit tunnel. A dull ache pulsed in her chest.

"Ambush?" Rendor asked.

"No." Her room wasn't far. No doubt it was still a mess, but…it represented the life that she'd dreamed of when she lived in the monastery. A life she could no longer have.

"Then what's wrong?"

"Nothing. It's just…my room is nearby."

"Do you need something?"

Did she? It held nothing of value. It was just a room. But it was *hers*. She sighed. "No. Let's go."

No one questioned them and soon they reached the surface. The sun hovered around angle one-fifty. She'd slept an alarmingly long time, no wonder Rendor fell asleep.

At least they had plenty of time to reach the monastery before darkness. The monks on duty alerted the rest of her team and, when they entered the receiving room, most of them were assembled. Relieved, happy faces greeted them followed by a barrage of questions.

"Why did you order us to leave?" Ximen demanded, clearly upset. "I thought you were right behind us."

"You needed to get Jayden out of there," she said.

"But you're too important to lose, Shyla." His tone softened. "You can't risk yourself like that anymore."

"Especially since our magic didn't work on the Blessed Bitch," Gurice said.

That reminded her. She pulled the platinum torque from her pack. It was about two centimeters thick at the base and slimmed down to a half a centimeter where it hooked around the neck. She handed it to Ximen. "I think this might be the reason."

He inspected it with growing alarm. "Where did you get this?"

"From around the neck of an Arch Deacon."

"Son of a sand demon! These are ours. They were created to protect us from The Eyes, but they were lost—or so we thought—thousands of sun jumps ago. We searched for circuits." A pause. "They must have been stolen."

"It appears so. Unless the Heliacal Priestess found a way to make them."

"No. This is almost pure platinum. It's a rare metal and very expensive."

"And it protects the wearer from all magic, not just The Eyes," Shyla said. "Guess we'll just have to get them back."

Ximen laughed without humor. "A tall order."

"But not impossible. After all, we have one. I counted seven when we rescued Jayden. How many are there?"

"A dozen, but it might not be accurate. Since the information has been passed down from generation to generation the details tend to not be as precise as something that's been written on a tablet."

"You need to teach me *everything* about the Invisible Sword. We've much to do."

"I'd say."

Shyla answered a few more questions, then asked them a couple of her own. "How many people did we… lose?"

The good mood vanished.

"Three," Gurice said. "Two acolytes and one Invisible Sword. Six others were injured, but will be fine."

"I'm sorry." Guilt wrapped around her like a velbloud tether squeezed tight. Her plan had worked in the end, but people died—too high a price to pay. She asked for their names and her grief deepened because she didn't get a chance to know them. And would never be able to thank them for giving their lives for Jayden. "We will create a memorial for them when we have a new headquarters."

They liked the idea and they discussed what type of memorial they should build.

But Shyla wasn't done with her questions. "How's Jayden?" she asked Gurice.

"He's been tortured, but he'll recover."

"Where is Zhek?" Rendor asked Gurice.

"With Jayden."

"Come on," Rendor said, tugging Shyla deeper into the monastery.

They found Zhek and Jayden in the same wing as their rooms. Jayden was sleeping—probably due to Zhek's "medicine." She spotted an empty tea cup on the table. Zhek sat on the floor next to him. She thought Rendor wanted to learn more about Jayden's condition, but no, he ratted her out, telling Zhek all about her injuries.

Zhek followed them to her room and ordered Rendor to leave. Served him right. She tried to delay the inevitable by asking after Jayden.

"He'll be fine, dear child. It's you I'm concerned about." He fingered the tender lump on the back of her head. "Head injuries can be serious. Are you dizzy?"

"No." She endured his questions and his examination. It wasn't until he'd wrapped her ribs that he was satisfied.

"When will Jayden be awake?" she asked, dressing in a soft pair of sleeping pants and shirt. "I'd like to talk to him."

"I will summon you when he's strong enough." He peered at her. "Are you uncomfortable? Do you want a cup of my tea?"

He actually asked. Progress! "No, thank you."

Zhek pressed his lips together. They twitched as if he was debating his next move. "All right. You rest. Come get me if you're in pain."

"I will."

Another hesitation, then he left. Shyla relaxed. Big mistake. All her muscles decided to ache at that moment. And the dull throb in her head turned sharp. She wondered if Zhek used healing magic on her that disappeared when he did. Next time Zhek tended her wounds, she would lower her shield and see if he used magic. She laughed at the direction of her thoughts. Not *if* she was injured again, but rather *when*.

She tried to sleep. But despite the bone-deep exhaustion that still clung to her, a restlessness hummed in her blood. The lumps in the cushion pressed on her sore ribs. No matter which way she lay she couldn't find a comfortable position. And she was cold despite the heavy fur.

Giving up, she sat up and debated. Her stomach was unsettled, perhaps she needed to eat. She didn't bother putting on her boots over her velbloud socks. In the hallway, the druks had been turned low. Shyla hesitated outside Rendor's door. He might be hungry, too. Or he might be asleep. He needed to rest as well. They could rest together… She sighed. These feelings swirling inside her were unknown territory. And she doubted she'd find a map to show her the way. Scorching hells, girl, just make up your mind.

She tapped lightly on the glass and waited for a heartbeat. Just as she suspected, he was asleep. Turning—

"Come in."

Shyla poked her head inside. Rendor sat up on the cushion. The fur slid down, revealing his bare chest. He seemed surprised to see her. That made two of them.

"Zhek told me you were resting, and *not* to bother you," he said.

"I couldn't sleep."

He waited.

"I was cold."

Understanding smoothed his features and a tenderness shone in his gaze. Rendor reclined back and lifted the edge of the fur. Shyla closed the door and slipped underneath. Only mildly disappointed he wore pajama pants. Warmth enveloped her. All her aches dulled. Rendor pulled her close and she rested her head on his uninjured shoulder. At peace at last, she fell asleep in his arms.

* * *

Someone loudly clearing his throat woke her. She lay on her side with Rendor behind her. His hand rested on her hip. After a second, also loud, throat-clearing, Rendor jerked away.

Hanif stood in the open doorway of Rendor's room, scowling his disapproval. "Shyla. We have much to discuss. Get dressed, I'll meet you in your room."

Ah, that explained his fierce expression. "I'm already dressed." She slipped from the fur and stood. Her bruised ribs protested the motion and fatigue still dragged on her limbs. She wondered how long would it take for her to fully recover. One problem at a time. "What do you wish to discuss?"

Taken aback, Hanif sputtered for a moment. "In your room. Alone." That was directed to Rendor before he left.

She hesitated. "I'll fill you in later."

"Are you in trouble?" Rendor asked.

"No. I'm not a monk and I'm an adult." Besides, all they did was sleep.

"But you're his daughter."

Surprised, she asked, "How did you know?"

"I was there when you talked to him about pushing you so hard. And I can see the resemblance. I may be a *big* brute, but I'm not an idiot."

"I know. Sorry." A pause. "There's a resemblance?" She never noticed.

"Go before he returns." He shooed.

Shyla joined Hanif in her room. He'd regained his composure, but his stiff posture and the tight grip on the scroll he held said he was far from relaxed. It was angle forty-five.

"It won't be long before the Heliacal Priestess and Water Prince figure out you're hiding here and demand I hand you over," he said.

She'd been thinking the same thing. "How long?"

"Four or five sun jumps at most. You and your… people need to leave or I'll have no choice. I can't risk my monks."

"All right, I have a place in mind." If she could remember where it was located. "Can we borrow some digging supplies?"

"You can. Do I want to know where you're going?"

"No. It's best you don't know."

His shoulders loosened as he chuckled. "Now you're keeping things from *me*."

"Annoying, isn't it?"

"Yes."

"Well maybe now you'll be more forthcoming."

He tilted his head. "About what?"

"Like who my mother is." She hadn't forgotten his worried thought.

"Ah."

Hanif moved his arms awkwardly as if not knowing what to do with them. Then he fidgeted like a little kid caught stealing a sweet. It was highly entertaining, and Shyla struggled to keep a straight face.

"Are you reading my mind?" he asked.

"No. That would be a breach of your privacy. Besides, that's something that should be given freely."

"A very mature way to look at it." He squinted at her in suspicion.

Shyla laughed. "Must be due to my upbringing."

"Smooth. As for the identity of your mother, that is up to her to tell you. Like I told you before, we raise the children of the monks together."

She sobered. "I know. But I spent most of my life hating my parents for abandoning me, for trying to kill me because of the color of my hair. I left the monastery and everyone I knew and loved to prove to them that I was worth saving." The truth of that statement slammed into Shyla. She rocked back, stunned.

Hanif set the scroll down, pulled her close, and hugged her. "I'm so sorry. I'd no idea you thought that way."

She didn't either. Not until this moment.

"You are worth saving. You've always been worth saving. You are loved. You've always been loved."

She closed her eyes and rested her head on his shoulder. "I know. It's just…nice to hear it."

"You will always be loved, Shyla."

"Thank you."

A light tapping on her door sounded. Hanif released Shyla and stepped back. She wiped her eyes before opening the door.

Zhek stood on the other side. "Jayden is awake and asking for you."

"That's good news. I'll be right there."

Zhek eyed her and then Hanif before striding away.

"That's my cue to leave," Hanif said. "But first, here's the guide for The Eyes. You should have it." He handed her the scroll. "But you know if you need help, we're… I'm here."

Shyla decided to see how far she could push him. "Along with unlimited access to the four Rooms of Knowledge?"

He straightened. "To *two* Rooms of Knowledge. You have to earn entrance to the others."

And there was the old Hanif. "How do I do that?"

"We'll have to figure it out as we go."

"Typical vague reply."

He gave her a smug smile and left.

Shyla went to Jayden's room and knocked on the door.

Zhek opened it. He whispered to her, "Not too long. I'll be back with nourishment."

Shyla nodded and entered. Shirtless, Jayden was propped up on a bunch of cushions. Zhek had cleaned his cuts and the bruises didn't stand out as much since some of his color had returned. His golden brown hair had been washed and combed. Shyla was struck by how different he was from Rendor. Jayden's thin build with his long lean muscles was the complete opposite of Rendor's, his sienna coloring much lighter than Rendor's dark mahogany. Yet they also had many similarities. Both had strong handsome features and that spark of intelligence in their eyes. Both were natural leaders.

"You're looking better," she said.

He stared at her with such a hard expression she wondered what she'd done wrong.

"It is true," he finally said with a rough voice.

"What—oh. Did you think Zhek lied to you?"

"I thought…" He rubbed a hand over his face. "Truthfully, I didn't believe it. That *you* would wake The Eyes."

"Because I'm conflicted and not committed?" She threw his words back at him. "Because I'm a selfish sun-kissed?"

"Because you wanted to forget."

"At that time, yes, I very much wanted to forget the fact that the Invisible Sword used me and ruined my life."

"What changed your mind?"

She paused. How to explain? Would she tell him about the Sun Goddess, or about Dyani and how all the people she'd met since all this began influenced her, or about Rendor's comments about getting a second chance? "When The Eyes woke in my hands, I knew what I had to do. For the first time in my life, I had a purpose."

"And that is?"

"To lead the Invisible Sword in helping the citizens of Zirdai by stopping the Water Prince and the Heliacal Priestess."

"Do you think you can?"

"I wouldn't have sacrificed my eyes if I thought I'd fail." And the truth of that statement hit her. Hard. Jayden's rescue was not perfect. Not at all. But he was here.

"There's not many of us left," Jayden said. Grief's shadows darkened his gaze.

"We'll recruit more."

"We?"

She huffed. "Of course. We. I need you and Ximen as my seconds."

"What about Rendor?"

"He's committed to our cause."

"Can we trust him?"

"Yes. I read his soul."

"Oh."

"Why are you surprised? You know what The Eyes can do."

He smoothed out the fur over his lap. "Are you… have you…read me?"

Ah. "No. I've created a mental shield so I'm not overwhelmed. I can remove it. Would you like me to read you?"

"No."

Shyla suppressed a smile over his quickness and vehemence. But then she remembered him trying to kill her and being part of the Invisible Sword's deception. Her humor died. "Then don't lie to me again or I will."

He met her gaze. "I won't."

"Good. Speaking of lying, do you know if Banqui betrayed the Invisible Sword?"

"No. I don't."

Too bad. Shyla hoped the priestess might have gloated to Jayden over it.

Jayden sagged back. "I couldn't read…anyone. And then I didn't have the strength."

She told him about the platinum torque. His reaction mirrored Ximen's, including the cursing. "At least, we know why. Now we have to figure out how to get them back."

"And you can do your scheming at another time," Zhek said, bringing in a tray of food for Jayden. He turned to her. "When's the last time you've eaten?"

"Uh…"

"I suspected as much. Go. Eat." He jabbed a finger at the door.

Sheesh. Everyone was always ordering her to eat and sleep. She managed to survive on her own for a couple circuits. But, instead of pointing this fact out, she hurried to obey before he threatened to give her a cup of his tea.

"Shyla," Jayden called.

Glancing back, she paused at the door.

"Thank you for rescuing me."

"You're welcome."

* * *

"Shouldn't you be resting?" Rendor asked for the third time.

Of course she should be resting. Jayden's rescue had sapped most of her energy—not that she'd let anyone know. But she had to find a new location for the Invisible Sword.

"It's here, I just need…to find the…right…" She scanned yet another dusty shelf near the back wall.

"I can help. Just tell me what you're searching for." Rendor had insisted on accompanying her to the First Room of Knowledge. The fact that Hanif allowed him to enter was a miracle.

"It's a map of a small temple that was raided three thousand sun jumps ago. All the treasures and artifacts were taken, the booby traps disabled, and then it was abandoned and forgotten." She hoped.

"You think it would make a good HQ?" He rubbed his shoulder as if it pained him. When he'd helped with the rescue, Rendor had taken off the sling and hadn't used it since, much to Zhek's displeasure.

"Yes. It's close to Zirdai and deep. I saw it…somewhere here." Crouching down, she sorted through a pile of scrolls.

"How long ago?"

She straightened. Dizziness rolled through her and she grabbed the edge of a table to keep from falling.

Rendor steadied her, cupping her elbow. "Deep breaths."

Sucking in a few lung-filling breaths, she was suddenly very aware of his body right behind hers. Nothing soft about it—all hard muscles and…why was she thinking about his kisses? He'd been right before, she had no experience with physical intimacy. But… damn those kisses made an impression. And he'd said that was only the beginning.

The warmth from his presence heated her from the inside out. The temptation to remove the shield and read his emotions pulsed, but she focused on the task at hand. She didn't have time.

"Thanks." She stepped away or rather, she tried.

Rendor anchored her in place.

Shyla glanced over her shoulder and met his intense gaze. "I'm fine."

"You are not. Tell me the name of the temple and I will find it while you return to your room to rest."

She huffed. "I don't remember the name."

"Then how do you—"

"I'll know it when I see it. Just..." She waved a hand at a pile of scrolls. "Pull out all the maps and I'll check them."

Now it was his turn to huff. "Fine, but if you pass out, I'm in charge."

He wouldn't let go until she agreed. Stubborn man. Muttering under her breath, she searched through another stack of dusty tablets. No luck. Perhaps...she turned in a slow circle, trying to sharpen her memories. She'd been ten circuits old and playing hide and seek. Her hiding spot had been perfect. A dark corner deep inside. She'd squirmed under a table and...

Grabbing the druk, she crouched, peering underneath the marble top. Sure enough there was a half-moon opening in the wall just big enough for her to squeeze through. She pushed the lantern in first.

"Shyla, what are you doing?" Rendor asked.

"Reliving my childhood, give me a few moments."

The opening led to a large octagonal room with a high domed ceiling. Colored tiles reflected the weak druk light. Shelves filled with scrolls lined seven of the eight walls—thousands of them. Memories sprang to life and she cleared sand off a part of the tile floor, revealing a large map of Koraha. She'd discovered the map room. Supposedly the only way to access it was through the beautiful and locked stained glass door. This short cut hadn't seemed important to her younger self. However, her older self tucked the information away.

Back then, she'd grown bored when no one found her. To pass the time, she'd studied a few of the scrolls. One of which was the one she sought. Letting her recollections guide her, she trailed her hand along the end knobs, seeing into the past.

Her fingers tingled and she stopped. Sitting on top of a pyramid was one messy roll of velbloud skin. Good thing Hanif didn't know or else she would have been in trouble for not handling the scroll with the utmost care. After confirming it was the map she needed, Shyla sat on the floor and studied it. The map wasn't as old as most of the others, but the ink had still faded. Sunlight would be best, but she didn't want to remove the map. Didn't want anyone except the Invisible Sword to know the location of their new headquarters.

The small temple had been built by a group of Sun Goddess worshippers. They named it the Temple of Arinna—probably after a priestess. Back then there wasn't a dictatorial Helical Priestess ruling over the entire city, but rather multiple groups. They all prayed to the Sun Goddess, but each had its own rules and rituals.

According to the map's diagrams, they had carved a hole in each level so when the sun shone directly above the temple, a beam of light shot through the structure.

Once she memorized the location, Shyla rolled up the map the correct way. Then she carefully slid it in the middle of a pile so it wouldn't stand out if anyone came in there.

"Did you find it?" Rendor asked, scaring her. He'd poked his head through the opening—all he could fit.

She covered her mouth to keep from laughing. "Yes."

He squinted at her. "Good, I'm hungry." He backed out.

His comment caused her own stomach to growl, but it also triggered worry. How would she feed her followers? Where would they get water and supplies? Plus it was going to take some time to clear the sand from the building. She needed to ask Ximen how they had managed to live in Tamburah's temple.

They brushed sand off their clothes before heading toward the dining area.

"We missed second meal," Rendor said, glancing at a sand clock that read angle one-forty-five.

"It's probably best I keep a low profile."

"I thought we could trust the monks."

"We can. It's just…" She struggled to find the right words.

Rendor waited.

"I've always stood out. Growing up, I was the only sun-kissed child at the time. And now…"

"You have these new eyes and everyone is wondering what you can do with them."

"Exactly."

"Some people would bask in the attention."

She suppressed a shudder. "Not me."

"I suspect that is why The Eyes chose you."

"Really? I thought it was because I was stupid enough to actually sacrifice my vision." She half-joked. Then sobered. Tamburah took that leap of faith and look how that ended—horribly.

As if sensing her change in mood, Rendor laced his fingers in hers. "What you did was the bravest thing I've ever seen."

And he'd helped, but it'd cost him. Shyla squeezed his hand. "Would you do me another favor?"

Rendor slowed and asked in an I-know-I'm-not-going-to-like-this tone, "What do you need?"

"If I turn into a monster like Tamburah, I need you to remove these eyes."

"Shyla, you're not—"

"You can't know that. The Eyes' magic might cause insanity. There's no record of why Tamburah turned into a tyrannical maniac. Promise me, please."

He stopped and swung her around so she faced him. "In the very unlikely event that you turn into a monster, I will remove The Eyes of Shyla."

She opened her mouth but her throat closed tight, trapping the words. It hadn't been suffering through the pain or using magic or reading people's souls or worrying about turning into a despot that caused her to realize the enormity of the situation. No. It was Rendor changing the title of The Eyes. And an appalling thought popped into her mind. Would people generations from now kill each other in order to own The Eyes of Shyla?

"What's wrong? You're pale and shaking." Not waiting for an answer, Rendor swept her off her feet. Holding her close, he carried her to the kitchen, set her down on a stool, and rummaged for food. "Eat," he ordered.

Still stunned, she hugged her arms tight to her chest.

"Do I need to feed you?" Rendor all but growled. "You know I will."

She plucked a slice of melon from the plate and shoved it into her mouth. Only when she'd eaten enough to satisfy Rendor did he turn his attention to his own meal.

The meal helped, but her thoughts still whirled as fast as a sand devil. They returned to her room. She stopped in the hallway and stared at her door without really seeing it. Instead, she mentally listed everything she needed to do: move to a new location, learn the extent of her powers, free the rest of the Invisible Swords, free those suffering from the Heliacal Priestess and Water Prince's tortures, and then knock them both from power. Quite the list.

Pressure built on her shoulders as once again the enormity of everything threatened to crush her. Overwhelmed, she struggled to fill her lungs. A tight band of fear wrapped around her heart. What happened to her confidence? What happened to that strong conviction she displayed in Jayden's room?

Rendor turned to her, sensing something was wrong. The Eyes might be in her head, but he was very attuned to her thoughts and emotions. He laced his fingers in hers and squeezed gently. When she met his gaze, he smiled. And just as fast as the panic attack hit, it disappeared.

She wasn't alone.

She wouldn't be alone ever again.

Don't miss the next exciting instalment in the Archives of the Invisible Sword series

THE CITY OF ZIRDAI

Coming July 2020

Acknowledgments

To my editorial dream team, Rachael Donovan, Julia Knapman, and Laurie Ormond: You cartwheeled, somersaulted, backflipped, and stuck the landing! Gold medals all around. Thanks so much for making this story shine.

To my supporters, Bob Mecoy and Natalie Bejin: It was a long, tiring race. Time was short and the pressure intense, but you exceeded your personal bests! Exclusive endorsement contracts for you both. I'm grateful for all your help and hard work on my behalf.

To my promoters, Johanna Baker, Sarana Behan, Michelle Haring, and Jeff Young: The ice was slick and the curves dangerous, but you steered through it all without crashing! Induction into the Hall of Fame for all. And my eternal thanks for helping to spread the word about my books.

To my cover artist, Micaela Alcaino: Before you was nothing but a white expanse, but you traversed the course and hit the bullseye! A Best in Show ribbon for you. Thanks so much for creating the perfect cover.

To my family and friends: You all grabbed an oar and rowed, working together to slice through the waves, and ride out all the ups and downs of having an author in your lives. A golden trophy for everyone. Thank you for all your love and support and patience as I perform my disappearing act to write.

To my daughter, Jenna: You entered the race late, but passed them all in the end! Another plaque for your Wall of Fame. Thanks for catching all the *other* errors.

To my husband, Rodney: You started this marathon twenty-seven years ago and you're still going strong. You get my heart and my gratitude for everything!

CHAPTER 1

2471:333

“The answer is no, Lyra.” My mother utters her favorite—I swear—phrase.

“But—”

“End of discussion.”

Arguing is usually futile. But I’m not about to give up. Not this time.

We are having dinner in our housing unit. I’m picking at my reconstituted mashed potatoes, wilted broccoli and mystery protein…er…meat…while my dad scans his list of packing supplies on his portable, only half-listening to my mother’s efforts to convince me that traveling to the new planet will be a grand adventure.

“Besides,” Mom says, almost breathless. “We’ll be the *first* archaeologists to assess the discovery. This new site on Planet Yulin has the potential to explain *who* transported the Terracotta Warriors to twenty-two different planets. We're getting close to an answer."

I gotta admit, my parents are the experts with a capital E on the life-sized Warriors. It's why they've been asked to relocate to the new planet. As for finding an answer to one of the Galaxy's great mysteries, I'm not as confident.

"Think about it, Lyra," Mom continues. "Over two million Warriors were custom-made on Earth by ancient Chinese craftsmen and transported by an unknown alien race to other worlds. We're bound to find evidence of who they were—or are—and why they used Earth's clay and people to create the Warriors. Why not make their own?"

Dad looks up. "The clay's from Earth, but there's no evidence they were made *on* Earth."

"The Chinese calligraphy on them is all the evidence you need," Mom retorts and they launch into an all-too-familiar debate.

I tune them out. Too bad the archaeologists don't know why the aliens needed all those Warriors throughout the Galaxy. Since we've yet to discover any other alien artifacts or sentient beings, we don't have anyone to ask.

And this recent discovery is all the way out on the edge of Explored Space. Yeah, you gotta say it with those capital letters since it's such a big deal that we've traveled so far from Earth. But what really boggles the mind is we're still in the Milky Way Galaxy. Space is big. Really big.

When my parents finish, it's my turn. I ensure they are both paying attention by clearing my throat. Loudly.

In a reasonable tone, I say, "It's exciting that you have a new site to research. You'll have all the top scientists eager to explore with you so you don't need me. I can remain here while you travel to Yulin. After all, I'm seventeen Actual years old—only a mere A-year until I'm of legal age."

Mom bangs her fork on the table. "I said end—"

I keep right on going. "Staying on planet Xinji, I'll be closer to the university—onsite learning is much more effective than distance. Dr. Wendland's research on learning strategies has proven it. And Lan's parents have already agreed to let me stay with them."

Mom and Dad exchange a look, which means they are doing that silent communication thing that parents do. I study them while I wait, sitting on the edge of my seat and resisting the urge to jiggle my leg with nervous energy.

My dad runs a big hand through his short sandy-brown hair, making it stick up at various angles. He normally appears younger than his forty-six A-years, but a sadness pulls on his face, aging him. "We're going to lose her in a couple A-years anyway, maybe we should consider her—"

"Absolutely not." Mom's brown-eyed gaze focuses on my father with such intensity, I'm surprised he doesn't burst into flames. Even though she is younger than my father by two A-years, my mother is in charge of our family. "I can't…not so soon after…Phoenix."

Before you ask, yes, my parents named me and my brother after constellations. Kinda funny considering we can't see either of those constellations unless we're on Earth, which, by the way, neither of us was born on. My parents have some really strange ideas at times.

The mention of Phoenix effectively kills any support I might have gotten from my father. He ducks his head and I wilt.

"Don't ask again," Mom says in the I've-decided-and-nothing-will-change-my-mind tone.

It's not fair, but arguing is pointless and will result in me cataloging thousands of broken Warrior shards as punishment. Appetite ruined, I push my now cold food away and head to my bedroom.

"Li—" my father calls after me.

I keep going. Our unit is small and narrow with a kitchen, common room, two bedrooms and the washroom. Not much space is allocated for housing in the base. The majority of the place is occupied by the scientists' labs, which is where most of the people living here spend all of their time anyway. We aren't a colony, but a research facility charged with assessing the entire planet. The base is filled with chemists, biologists, geologists, physicists, astrophysicists, meteorologists... Pick any "ologist" you can think of and they're probably here, including archaeologists like my parents.

And those ologists have been drooling happy since the announcement of the New Discovery. As for me? Not so much. While they've been talking in excited, high-pitched voices and making plans for the trip, I've been dreading launch day. Don't get me wrong, I'm glad for my parents. They've dedicated their lives to puzzling out this great Warrior mystery and I've no doubt that they'll eventually solve it.

Well...maybe a little doubt.

However, I'm tired of leaving my friends behind and I need to find my own passion. Not sure what that is yet, but I'm pretty sure it doesn't include researching ancient artifacts.

* * *

My room consists of a narrow bed, a few drawers, a desk, a chair, a screen and a terminal to access the Quantum net...well, a fraction of it—it's like being confined to the shallow end of the pool—very frustrating.

When the Quantum net—Q-net—was invented back in 2066, it changed everything. Earth's technology advanced at a sizzling pace, and inventions like the Crinkler engine, which allows us to travel through space super fast, were designed using the Q-net. Now it's used to keep track of...well, everything, but it's most important for knowing the precise location (and time) of all the space ships. Oh, and all the information collected from all the planets is stored within its amazing vastness.

But admittance to this scientific wonder is limited. Since I'm underage, I'm allowed to access the school programs, game programs, entertainment, and communications. At least the Q-net is able to send text-based communications between planets in Actual time. Can you imagine waiting decades for a reply?

I flop onto my bed and stare at the images of my friends from the other planets my parents dragged me to before Xinji. They fill the screen. The reality of space travel—the dreaded time dilation—stares back at me. Many of my friends have died of old age by now, and my two friends from our last assignment on Planet Wu'an are now in their fifties. Thanks, Einstein.

A musical ping sounds. The images fade into the background as the screen displays an incoming communication from a Miss Lan Maddrey.

"Accept," I say.

The words disappear and my best friend's face appears.

"What did they say?" Lan asks, but she notices my morose expression. "Oh, sorry, Li-Li!"

Only my father and closest of close friends call me that. I used to love pandas, okay? My father thought it was cute and that's how I got the nickname.

Her eyebrows smash together and furrow her brow. "Did you tell them about Dr. Wendland's research? I can send them the Q-cluster location to the paper. And my parents—"

"Won't matter," I say.

"Did your mother utter the three dreaded words?" she asks.

"Yes."

We share a moment of silence. Lan's blue eyes shine more than normal as she nibbles on the blond hair at the end of her French braid. She's fifteen, but soon to be sixteen—a little over a year younger than me, but we bonded over our mutual love of Diamond Rockler—the greatest singer in the Galaxy. Our only disagreement was over who he was going to marry, me or Lan, and that was three A-years ago. I wouldn't have gotten so close to her except my parents assured me that this was their last assignment. Sigh.

"My brother works for the port," Lan says. "You can sneak off the shuttle and he'll hide you until it takes off. By the time they discover you're missing, they can't return."

An interesting idea. My heart races with the possibilities. I could start my own life. I hope to attend Brighton University on Planet Rho, a mere four Earth-years away. We measure distance between planets by how much E-time passes while you're traveling, not by how many

Actual years pass. Which means if I stay here, I'll be fifty A-years older when my parents arrive at Yulin, but they'll only be ninety days older. Crazy right?

Regardless, I'd never see my parents again, which is why they won't leave me behind. Not yet anyway. They're still grieving over Phoenix and hoping I'll catch the science bug and stay with them, but I am tired of hanging around ancient things that have been buried for thousands of E-years. My excitement over running away fades.

"Thanks, Lan, but I can't do that to my parents."

She nods and gives me a watery smile. "I understand." She heaves a sigh, then lowers her voice. "When should we plan your..." Lan hesitates. "You-know-what."

I glance at my door. It's closed, but I sit at my desk and insert the entanglers into my ears—they resemble little round plugs, but they allow me to link directly to the Q-net through the terminal. Then I engage the privacy mode. If my parents walk into my room, they'd see a blank screen, but I can still see and hear Lan—another super cool invention courtesy of the Q-net.

How about at my last required soch-time? Do you think Jarren can fool the snoops? I think.

Of course. Who do you think created the dead zone in the back corner of the supply bay?

I laugh. *You mean the kissing zone? I heard Jarren took Belle there for a smooch fest.*

He did not! Lan's cheeks turn pink.

Oh? Do you have better intel?

Shut up.

A knock at my door prevents me from replying. Lan says good-bye and I disconnect and return to my flopped position on the bed. I might be resigned to leaving, but that doesn't mean I'll let my parents off easy. "Display wall art," I say to the screen. Only when it once again shows images of my old friends, do I say, "Come in."

Dad pokes his head inside as if expecting to be ambushed. "Is it safe?"

I huff. My temper isn't that bad. Well…not since I was seven A-years. "Only if you brought something sweet."

He holds his hand out, revealing a plate of chocolate chip cookies. A warm sugary scent wafts off them—fresh baked! My empty stomach groans in appreciation.

"Then it's safe." I'm not above bribery.

He enters and sets the plate down on my desk. He has a box tucked under his right arm. "You okay?"

"I'm gonna have to be. Right? Unless you're here to tell me you changed your mind?" I sit up at the thought.

"Sorry, Li-Li. We're not ready to lose you." My father hunches over slightly as grief flares in his brown eyes.

My older brother decided to leave for Earth two years ago when he turned eighteen A-years. Earth is about ninety-five E-years away. So by the time Phoenix arrives on Earth, we will all be dead and Phoenix will still be eighteen.

Guilt over my earlier snit burns in my stomach.

"You just have to go on one more assignment with us, then you can decide what you want to do," Dad says.

"It's all right." I gesture to the box. "What's in there?"

He sets it down on my desk. "A puzzle."

I've fallen for that before. "Are you sure it isn't a bunch of random rubble?"

"No. We think we have all the pieces, but my assistant swears no one can possibly put it back together." He raises a slender eyebrow.

Appealing to my ego, he knows me so well. "Let's see."

Dad opens the box and pours out what appears to be shards of pottery—all terracotta, ranging in sizes from a thumbnail to six centimeters. I scan the pieces. They'd once formed a specific shape, and I can already see it has edges. Could be a piece of armor. Or a shield. Intrigued, I sort through the fragments, flipping them over and matching colors.

My father hands me the adhesive. "I'll let you prove Gavin wrong." He pulls my straight black hair back behind my shoulders and plants a kiss on my temple. "Thanks, Li-Li."

"Uh huh." The air pulses as he leaves. I arrange the pieces—about a thousand or so. There are markings on most of them. Odd. I group the ones that appear similar together. Reconstructing artifacts is actually fun. Not I-want-to-do-this-for-the-rest-of-my-life fun, but challenging and satisfying to make something whole again.

No one was more surprised than I. Trust me. I was roped into helping my parents a few years ago when they noticed that, after attending my required socialization time, or rather soch-time, and doing my school lessons, I had plenty of free time. I argued there was a reason it was called "free." It went over as well as my bid to stay on Xinji.

I was assigned all the chores no one else wanted to do, like sweeping and running the 3D digitizers—each of the thousands of Warriors has to be scanned and cataloged. But one night I found a half-finished reconstruction of a face and, well, I finished it in a couple hours. My parents made a big deal about it and now when there's a jumble of fragments that is declared "impossible" by the team, it comes to me. Not that I'm that great. There have been plenty of boxes filled with bits that I couldn't get to go together. A 3D digitizer could do it in minutes, but we only have four so using them for repairing broken pottery is not the priority.

This piece is tricky. Usually once I connect the edges, the rest is easier to match. But the shape is...octangular? Strange. Lan messages me while I'm working.

"It's all set," she says. "All our friends have been informed." Her voice is heavy with dismay.

I glance at her. "Thanks."

There's an awkward silence.

"What's that?" she asks.

"At this point, I've no idea."

"No. The markings on it."

I peer at the symbols etched into it. Silver lines the grooves so they stand out from the reddish orange clay. Lan should recognize them. Her parents are the base's language experts and cryptologists. While life-sized and made of terracotta, the extraterrestrial Warriors have quite a few differences from those discovered in China. One is they are covered with alien symbols that no one has been able to translate.

"Uh…it's Chinese calligraphy. Probably the name of the craftsman who built it."

"That's not Chinese."

"Are you sure?"

"Lyra." Her flat tone indicates she's insulted.

"Okay, okay. So it's one of those other alien symbols."

She shrugs. "I haven't seen markings like those before."

"Well consider two million Warriors with what… sixty some markings per Warrior, makes that…" Ugh, I suck at math.

"The symbols are not all unique. And they still haven't cataloged them all."

"Don't give my mother any ideas," I say, pressing my hand to my chest in mock horror. But the reality is that with limited funds, personnel and equipment, the Warrior Project is a slow-moving beast.

Lan laughs. I'm gonna miss that light trill.

"Seriously, Li-Li. It's different. It might be important."

"Important enough to keep my parents on Xinji?" Hope bubbles up my throat.

Lan straightens with enthusiasm. "Maybe. When you finish it, bring it to my mom."

"Will do."

It takes me the rest of the night to complete the piece. I'm not exaggerating. The faint smell of coffee wafts under my door as my parents get ready for their day. I stare at the…shield—for lack of a better word—because it's a meter wide and a meter long, three centimeters thick and octagonal (of course—the aliens have a serious addiction to the shape…maybe they are sentient octagons? Hmmm).

The shield has a spiderweb of fine cracks and a few fragments missing here and there—standard for reconstructed objects, but the eight rows of markings are clear. Each row has eight different symbols, but they appear to be similar—like they're siblings, with similar swoops or curls. Then another row also has eight unique glyphs that complement each other—sorry, it's hard to explain. But one row looks like Chinese calligraphy, but I'm not sure.

What I'm certain of is, I've been living on Warrior planets all my life, but I've never seen anything like this before. Excited, I rush out to get my dad. He's sitting at the table, sipping coffee and reading from his portable. My mother is at the counter.

Dad spots me. "You're up early."

"Come on." I tug on his hand. "You have to see this!"

He follows me to my room.

Mom trails after us. "Lyra, did you stay up all night?"

Her tone is disapproving so I don't answer her. Instead, I sweep my hands toward the octagon with a flourish. "Ta da!"

Both my parents gape at it in stunned silence for a solid minute. My father reaches toward it, but I stop him.

"It's not dry."

He snatches his arm back as if he's been burned. When my parents still don't say anything, I say, "This is important. Right? Something different?"

The silence stretches. Now it's getting weird.

"Yes," my mother says finally. "Different."

"Lan said her mom, Dr. Maddrey, would want to see it."

"Oh, yes," my dad says. His voice is rough. "I expect there will be *lots* of people who would want to see this."

* * *

There is a great deal of excitement from the scientists in our base over the strange object with the rows of markings. Theories about them fly faster than a Crinkler engine through space. The one that generates the most gossip is the possibility that the octagon is an alien Rosetta Stone even though it's made of the same baked clay as the Warriors. Lan's parents are put in charge of figuring out the mystery.

"I hardly see them," Lan complains one night.

She's lying on her bed and I'm sitting on her chair as we listen to Diamond Rockler. His voice is like honey—smooth with a thick sweetness. Rockler's heart-melting lyrics fill the small room as a video of him plays on her screen. He's talented and gorgeous and intelligent—that's just not fair. Some people don't even get one of those qualities.

"If anyone's going to figure out what it means, it's them," I say. Frankly, I wouldn't mind seeing less of my parents. They've been asking me to join the crews of people searching through the million fragment piles in hope of finding more octagons. *More data, more data*, my mom's always saying. They're drowning in data, but no one's made any connections. I think they have too much data, but that's me.

"Messages were sent to the other active Warrior planets," Lan says. "The other language experts might have some ideas on how to translate it and they're all looking for their own Rosetta Octagon."

"As long as it keeps everyone busy," I say, smiling.

Lan sits up. "Lyra Daniels, you're not thinking—"

"I am." I insert my tangs into my ears and access the Q-net via the two sensors that were implanted in my brain when I turned ten A-years old. Staying entangled in the Q-net for long periods of time is flirting with insanity. So everyone must be able to completely disentangle. It's the reason terminals are needed to interact with the Q-net. It's funny, to me anyway, that the terminal is a bland plate built into the desk. It's some type of rare metal, but otherwise it's boring in appearance.

Lan's terminal has the same limits as mine, but I've learned how to mask my identity and bypass a few security barriers.

"You're going to get into trouble,' Lan says. But it doesn't stop her from inserting her own tangs to trail me.

"Don't you want to find out who Belle's been hanging out with?" I don't listen to her answer. Instead I concentrate. I view the Q-net as a sphere with a zillion layers, like a universe-sized ball of yarn. And, while I'm blocked from most of the layers, I can find...holes...in the security, almost by feel—it's a strange sensation—and wriggle into an area that I'm not "technically" supposed to be able to access. We call it *worming*.

Video feeds from the cameras around the base pop up.

"Oh my stars, Lyra! You're going to end up in detention if security discovers you."

"Big if. Look, Mom, no ripples."

"How did you…" She sighs. "Jarren, right? He taught you? You're getting better at worming."

I scan the images. People bustle through the hallways. Some stop to talk. The labs techs are busy doing whatever they do. No sound. That would be too creepy. And no cameras in private units. That's an invasion of privacy.

"Found Belle." I hone in on the camera in the canteen. "She's flirting with that chemistry tech—what's-his-name."

"Trevor, but he's too old for her. He's like twenty-three A-years," Lan says. "How do you know she's flirting?"

"She's flipping her hair and eyeing him as if she wants to eat him for dessert."

"For dessert? Really? That's gross."

"Ah youth. So innocent."

She smacks me on the arm with her pillow. "And you shouldn't be spying on your friends."

"Oh? Should I spy on someone else?"

"No." She pulls out her tangs. "We should be planning Jarren's surprise sixteenth birthday party."

I groan. "That's not for another hundred and eighty days."

"Planning," she says with authority, "will be the key to success."

I disentangle from the Q-net and we brainstorm a few ideas. "I think we should have it in a spot he'd never suspect," I say. "Like the middle of a hallway. Or outside the base!"

Just then, Dr. Maddrey pokes her head into Lan's room. "Have you finished your school work?" she presumably asks Lan, but she gives me a pointed look when Lan shakes her head no. Dr. Maddrey leaves the door ajar when she retreats.

My cue to leave. "Better get going, I've a physics test tomorrow that I need to ace now that I'm applying to Brighton University."

"It's two years until the next Interstellar Class ship, what are you going to do for that extra year?" Lan asks.

"I think I'll intern in a bunch of the labs and see if anything catches my interest. Chemistry and biology might be fun. Dr. Nese says he always needs help with keeping the weather instruments clean." And any chance to go outside is always taken. "I'm sure I'll find plenty to do." Even if I have to spend the year reconstructing damaged Warriors. It'll be worth it. And once I get my degree, I could be assigned to a colony planet and interact with normal people.

Lan bounces on her bed. "And my parents already agreed that we can attend the university together even though I won't be eighteen yet!"

The best part. We share a grin. Then I wave a goodbye to the Maddreys and return to my housing unit. The place is empty. Not a surprise, my parents have been busy with the new find.

I settle next to the terminal and access the physics lectures. After two hours, I'm doing head bobs and my stomach growls. However, my parents are still not back. I check their work schedules—yes, they've given me permission—to see if I should wait to have dinner with them or just go to the canteen. Scientists tend to get engrossed in their work so the base has a cafeteria for those too busy to cook a meal. I've seen techs carrying trays back to labs for their bosses.

They both have late meetings and a few "evening" appointments. It doesn't matter that Xinji's sun is still high in the sky, every single colony planet and Warrior planet, as well as the people traveling in space ships, all follow Earth's clock. Days have twenty-four hours. Years have three hundred and sixty-five days (yes, we do the leap years as well). The base's lights and window shutters are programmed to keep Earth time. However, we stopped using the names of the months and days—that would be silly. Instead, we track the year and day. Today is the three hundredth and fortieth day of the year 2471, otherwise referred to as 2471:340.

I was born on 2337:314, and I'm seventeen Actual years old, which means I've lived seventeen of Earth's years. But since I've traveled to two different planets and made two time jumps, one hundred and thirty-four E-years have passed during those seventeen years I've been alive. Boggles the mind, doesn't it?

I scan my parents' agendas idly, noting it'll be a couple days before we have another family meal. Odd that they should be *that* busy. And why are they meeting with Dr. Gage and Dr. Jeffries tomorrow, they don't normally interact. I straighten as my heart sinks. My guts churn as I study their itineraries, trying to dismiss my suspicions. When I reach 2471:360, I'm on my feet. I yank my tangs out and sprint from my room.

LET'S TALK ABOUT BOOKS!

JOIN THE CONVERSATION

HQYAAUS

@HQYAAUS

@HARLEQUINAUS